ABOUT THE AUTHOR

GILLIAN HAWSER is an internationally renowned casting director who has worked for over thirty years across film, television and theatre in the UK, Europe and the US. From Bill Kenwright to Warner Bros, Sony, HBO and Universal, she has developed close working relationships with leading producers on both sides of the Atlantic to deliver casts of exceptional talent, imagination and diversity. For more than the past decade Gillian has been a prominent presence at the heart of BAFTA, sitting on the BAFTA film committee, as well as being instrumental in obtaining the first ever BAFTA award for casting in both television and film.

THE
ARRANGED
MARRIAGE

GILLIAN HAWSER

Matador
9 Priory Business Park,
Wistow Road, Kibworth Beauchamp,
Leicestershire. LE8 0RX
Tel: 0116 279 2299
Email: books@troubador.co.uk
Web: www.troubador.co.uk/matador
Twitter: @matadorbooks

ISBN 978 1800463 011

British Library Cataloguing in Publication Data.
A catalogue record for this book is available from the British Library.

Printed and bound in Great Britain by 4edge Limited
Typeset in 11pt Minion Pro by Troubador Publishing Ltd, Leicester, UK

Matador is an imprint of Troubador Publishing Ltd

This book is dedicated to my children;
Peregrine, Elliot and Clemency
and to my grandchildren;
Elodie, Carys, Jagger, Hunter, Noah, Tom and Joe.
They bring unmitigated joy into my life.

CHAPTER ONE

Wakeham Park, as befitted a great mansion and the principal seat of the Dukes of Staplefield, had had a long and illustrious history. There had been a house on the site as early as 1178, although nothing now remained of this original building. In the sixteenth century, Sir Hampden Mordaunt, in celebration of his creation as a baronet, replaced the medieval hall house erected by his maternal great-grandfather with a beamed and panelled residence. He named it Wakeham Hall. During the following 150 years the family grew in stature, becoming the recipients of many honours and titles, so that by the beginning of the eighteenth century it was clear that the Tudor house, even with its additions, was completely inadequate for the needs of a ducal family.

In 1722, however, an event occurred that was to change the face of Wakeham for ever. The fourth duke, who at forty and enjoying excellent health had been expected to last for many years to come, died most suddenly. His death was a blow in a family renowned for its longevity. In addition, at the start of 1721, realising that time was marching on and he had no son, His Grace had married. Lamentably, at the time of her husband's untimely death his young and beautiful duchess had not yet presented her lord with any pledges of her affection. Thus all his titles and estates passed from this branch of the family to his second cousin, Gideon Mordaunt.

The new duke was only twenty-four when, most unexpectedly, he came into his fortune. He was a man who, unlike his forebears, was not an inveterate sportsman, rather his interests lay in the field of artistic endeavour; he was conspicuous for his interest in every aspect of painting, sculpture, music, theatre, literature, but, more importantly for Wakeham, he also possessed an abounding and as yet unfulfilled passion for architecture.

Gideon Mordaunt was a man of enormous energy, vision and a particular flair for detail. He made the restoration of Wakeham, and its transformation into a residence suited to one of England's premier dukes, his life's work. He was not familiar with the estates, indeed he had not stayed in the house above half a dozen times and never for more than a few days. As he had not been expected to inherit, it had not been thought necessary for him to do more than be included when the entire family assembled under the Wakeham roof. The immediate Mordaunt relatives numbered 200, so when he had visited the house he had not been accorded any special privileges.

His first deed, however, on coming into his inheritance, was to learn all that he could about his estates. In this he was aided by an astute brain and an ability to listen carefully, surmise accurately and take appropriate decisions. He was also blessed with a shrewd capacity for appointing the correct people for a particular task. Looking discerningly at his house and grounds he immediately summoned the Palladian architect Leoni and the garden designer Capability Brown. To Leoni he gave the responsibility of extensively rebuilding the house on classical lines and to the tender care of Capability Brown he gave his beloved gardens. These two fine craftsmen were inspired choices, who took their commissions very seriously, and the house and gardens that rose from their designs were generally credited with being some of the finest that the eighteenth century produced.

The house was approached by a long drive that meandered through undulating woods and lawns carefully executed by Capability to appear as if they had been extant for centuries. On turning a corner out of the woods the visitor had his first breathtaking view of the house. It was built around a central porticoed front which was flanked by two colonnaded wings. At the rear of the house Leoni's 400-feet facade faced Capability Brown's park; this juxtaposition of house, parks and terraces was regarded as one of their most successful schemes. There were those protagonists, although not many, it must be admitted, who were heard to put forward a preference for the parks at Stourhead House. But it was generally agreed that the gardens at Wakeham were superior.

The fifth duke's obsession with his house had not ended with the outside, for he had been equally concerned to make the interior as beautiful as his gardens. To this end he toured Europe; he brought back paintings from Holland and Italy, porcelain and tapestries from France. The saloon, an imposing room ninety feet in length, was decorated using designs copied from Inigo Jones. In spite of its size, its embellishment had been accomplished with a quiet delicacy. Studded bosses and spiral pendants surrounded ceiling rondels, painted by Rose and Zucchi. These designs were echoed in the patterns on the specially woven Axminster carpet which covered the entire poplar floor. On the days when the duke saw fit to open Wakeham to visitors, guests were seen to gasp at the intricacy of the complementary designs on ceiling and floor.

However, it was commonly accepted that the real glory of Wakeham lay in its library. This unique room was all that now remained of Sir Hampden's sixteenth-century house and had been specially kept by Leoni and the duke. The original fifteenth-century panelling remained untouched, although the duke, who in addition to his other proclivities was particularly partial to wood carving, had brought in Grinling Gibbons, requesting him to extensively decorate the shelves with designs of his own choice. Wooden music, fruit and images representing the four seasons blossomed from the master's dexterous hands. The library ran the entire length of the west front of the house. Its windows overlooked the home park, enabling glimpses of panoramic vistas of gardens stretching down as far as a small Chinese bridge which enticingly spanned the ornamental water and had been positioned thus by Capability, precisely to enhance the aspects of this celebrated room.

On a particularly fine November afternoon, wintry sunshine filtered through those same windows, shedding its pale light on Gibbons' art, giving his angels trumpets of gold and making his sheaves of corn invitingly ripe. The bookshelves which had been enhanced by these carvings covered the three remaining sides of the room; they housed the immense collection of classical literature amassed by the sixth duke. He was of an entirely different temperament from his father, although perhaps equally obsessive, a scholarly individual who loved old books and ancient objects more than anything; he spent half of his life collecting and the other half lovingly cataloguing his cherished archive. His mind being of an orderly disposition, he hated to be short of any particular volume, thus he spent much time and energy tracking down various missing specimens. The resulting collection was now accepted as one of the most comprehensive ever assembled in private hands.

The library contained only one occupant, who sat idly leafing through a volume of Horace, his long legs stretched out in front of the tiny fire which burnt in the grate. He was a tall man, dressed somewhat casually for riding in buckskins and top boots, his well-cut coat showing to advantage his broad shoulders and strong arms. He was still strikingly handsome, and only the black hair slightly tinged with grey and the harsh lines on his face showed that he was approaching fifty. His eyes were surprising; under heavy dark brows they were a remarkable deep blue, the colour changing from almost black when he was in a rage, to a bright blue when something amused him.

The eighth Duke of Staplefield was not renowned for either his patience or his even temperedness, and as he awaited his eldest daughter his displeasure was beginning to show. Throwing down Horace, he stretched, stood up and began to pace the room irritably. The afternoon sunshine was quickly fading into an early evening gloom. He crossed the room to ring for candles, but before he could do so there was a gentle knock at the door and the Lady Perpetua Mordaunt crept in, followed by Croft. "I have brought candles, Your Grace. No good sitting in the dark getting gloomy and crosspatchy," the butler reprimanded.

Croft had been with the Mordaunt family for forty years. This, he had decided many years ago, gave him the right to talk to the duke as he had when he had first joined the household as personal footman to the young marquis, then aged eight years. A gleam of amusement flitted across the duke's eyes. "Wise, as usual, Croft. Thank you."

The Lady Perpetua waited apprehensively. A summons from her father was a rare and not very welcome occurrence, too sensitive not to be aware that she exasperated him. She was, however, unable to respond to his particular sardonic humour with any kind of equanimity. His ironical questions made her completely tongue-tied and her subsequent incoherent answers merely served to infuriate him. Her numerous brothers and sisters accounted her a mouse. They all relished the spirited arguments that prevailed in the Mordaunt family, whereas Petty, as everyone called her, Perpetua seeming all too stately for such a small, insipid creature, dreaded them; quarrelling and raised voices made her legs turn to jelly and her small body tremble. Her father's tempers were the worst; his flashes of fury inevitably reduced her to a quake, rendering her quite speechless and perfectly unable to think clearly. Often afterwards, she would chastise herself for her want of courage, determined to do better next time, but when the next time came she was generally unable to effect an improvement.

Now she watched him as he laughed with the butler, her stomach churning slightly. He dismissed Croft and turned to her, looking her over critically, his dark blue eyes inscrutable. Under this piercing scrutiny Petty wriggled despairingly; wretchedly she tried to pat her unruly brown curls into place and smooth down the crumpled brown dress.

"It is a pity," he inwardly reflected, *"that Perpetua has to be so undistinguished, would that she had half the beauty of her mother."* He shook his head slightly. *"She has nothing of the others in her either, looks; character; all deficient, the only exception, perhaps,"* he considered, *"her eyes."* In this, he was right, for these orbs were the singular deep blue of the rest of the family, and in her case fringed with long dark lashes. They currently held a look of trepidation, but when she was not scared they were extraordinarily expressive and when something amused her, which was often, they laughed in quite as attractive a way as was found in the rest of the Mordaunts.

"Sit down, Petty," he demanded.

She sat, straight-backed, on the edge of the small chair near the tiny fire, wondering what this unprecedented request foretold. "I have some excellent news for you."

He walked to the window where he watched the black fragile branches of the trees against the red and pale blue of the setting sun. Her curiosity grew more intense. Her father turned back to her; he was dark against the pink winter light. He smiled. "I am pleased to be able to tell you that I have arranged a most advantageous marriage for you."

Petty felt herself grow icy with the shock. It was so completely unexpected. "P... P... Papa," she ventured. Stunned.

"I know you will be surprised. I am myself. For you have had two seasons, at great expense, and, as far as I can ascertain, not the smallest interest was accorded you. I am sure that I do not have to remind you, Perpetua, that your mama was beginning to despair of you establishing yourself creditably. However, you have finally achieved a most credible offer for your hand, from a man whose birth is maybe not quite what one would wish, but whose fortune is everything that is desirable."

He glanced at his daughter. Privately he was astonished that she had managed such an advantageous alliance, but his relief at this solution to their problems led him not to question any aspect of it. He continued.

"I suppose it must be admitted that his wealth is, in the main part, derived from trade, but we should not allow ourselves to be dissuaded from the benefits which will accrue to the Mordaunts, by any feeling of distaste for such an accumulation of fortune. I do not have to tell you, Petty, how the excesses of my father, your grandfather, have depleted our family fortunes. It must be common knowledge that we are all to pieces. Since your grandfather's death I have been worrying night and day, trying to contrive a plan by which the means may be found to bring the family about, and suddenly, as if by a miracle, here is my answer. The settlements when you marry, I understand, will be generous to a point."

Petty's grandfather, the seventh duke had been removed from this world, many months previously, by a fortuitous accident. The news had been brought to her Great-Aunt Hortense while this excellent lady was partaking of a substantial breakfast, and on hearing the report she had bluntly summed up the feelings of the entire family: "Well, I must rejoice in it. I know he was my own brother but I cannot be anything but glad that Gideon's gone. It must be seen as a blessing and that is the truth. I can only be thankful that he did not last longer."

On discovering the sordid details of the accident she was heard to pronounce: "Shot, eh, in Trevor's well, I am sure I am amazed that no one did it before. Gone, and not before time; I am sure I speak for the whole family when I say it must be a time for rejoicing. I am sure I never liked the Melvilles, Lady Melville such an encroaching creature, but I do think we all have cause to be grateful to them now. I look on Sir Stanley as something of a saviour."

"Not before time," repeated Uncle Wilbraham, Great-Aunt Hortense's devoted spouse. "A few more months of Gideon's drawing the bustle and Staplefield would be quite gutted, left without a feather to fly with."

"It is the most excellent news," His Grace continued, smiling at his daughter. "Wakeham is saved, I think we might even be able to keep Staplefield House. I need not tell you how pleased your mama is that your sisters' come-outs will be in Berkeley Square after all."

As he mused pleasantly on, Petty sat frozen. In her mind she went over the men she had encountered in London. There was Lord Mannock. Oh no, surely not! It could not be! He was so pompous, so utterly puffed up in his own conceit. He never stopped telling her in his self-important way exactly how she should go on; being married to him would mean being corrected every time she opened her mouth; would mean being told that he always knew best and that she would do well to follow him in every particular. Horror overcame her, and then relief. Lord Mannock's maternal grandfather had been the Earl of Parham, no sniff of trade there. Her mouth twitched at the idea of Lady Mannock having a father in trade. It was, anyway, a well-known fact that that formidable dowager meant to marry her son well, very well, to a great, but only well-born, heiress. Then there was Sir James Makepeace. Surely not him; no trade but also no fortune, and most definitely at sixty a confirmed bachelor. He had been so kind to Petty, and she had always felt at ease with him, but rather in the way of a grandfather. She could not think of anyone else, except a couple of halflings who had clearly felt comfortable talking to her but not in the way of marriage.

Swallowing hard, her heart beating rapidly, Petty pulled herself together. P... Please, Papa, please, please... who... who is it?"

The duke smiled, a smile of great charm, that Petty was certainly hardly ever privileged to receive.

"My dear girl," he apologised, "your husband is to be Lord Milton."

"Lord who?" Petty was astonished, and somewhat confused.

"Lord Milton – Edward, Lord Milton," the duke repeated patiently.

"But I do not know Lord Milton."

"Doesn't move in the best circles, yet," His Grace replied. "But he wants to, that is why he is offering for you. The Mordaunts are one of the oldest families in the land," he stated with simple pride. "Mordaunts at Wakeham since the thirteenth century. Told you, my dear, Lord Milton is not of the haut ton; if he had been he would hardly have chosen you."

Petty's head was in a whirl. It appeared that she was to be married to the highest bidder to save the house. Her father and mother were quite prepared to marry her to a man she did not know, nay to a man she had never even met, simply to save the family fortunes. Petty knew that girls of her class were frequently subjected to arranged marriages, but these usually took place between the offspring of families who had known each other all their lives, not total strangers. This was now the nineteenth century, not the Middle Ages, and girls in many families were being allowed to have some say in what happened to them. Petty loved Wakeham too, but she did not quite understand why only she should be sacrificed. Her father looked so relieved and pleased.

"It is so wonderful, Perpetua. It would have broken my heart, and your mama's too, to have had to sell Wakeham, and now it seems we will not have to resort to so disastrous a solution. My dear, I had thought it had come to a point where not only Wakeham and Staplefield House would have to go but where my hunters, and those of Anthony and Gideon, would have had to be sold. It was inconceivable to sell my horses; I need not tell you, my dear girl, it was the worst thought. I was in flat despair." He smiled again.

Petty bit her lip. It seemed that the horses were more important than her happiness. She took a deep breath, swallowed hard and, encouraged by the unusually benign expression on her father's face, she screwed up her courage.

"But, Papa... I... l... do not want to marry Lord Milton."

"What! What did I hear you say?" Her father's voice was deceptively quiet.

"l do not want to marry Lord Milton," Petty repeated desperately. "I am not going to."

Her voice trailed off miserably.

"You will do as I say," His Grace thundered. "How dare you! How can you be so ungrateful... ungrateful and uncaring. Lord Milton has been kind enough to offer for you. You will accept him. It suits him to marry into our family, and it suits our family that you should make such an advantageous match."

Quick tears sprang into Petty's eyes. She looked down at the carpet, trying to stop the hot warm drops from trickling down her face. Her father hated crying girls. She knew there was nothing she could do. She realised that she was lost.

Her father looked at her. He said in an altogether different, suddenly gentler, tone: "I must save Wakeham, you do understand, Petty?"

And she did understand. All her life had been at Wakeham; she had roamed the gardens, scampered over the lawns. She and her sisters and brothers had played hide and seek in the spinneys, and on wet days they had explored the endless corridors, hiding in unused attic rooms. It was a beautiful house.

It was unthinkable that they should not live here. She felt alone; a small sob escaped her.

"You accept?" he demanded. She nodded through the unwanted tears, which she seemed unable to control. "Come, Petty, a marriage of convenience may not be such a bad thing; in some respects it may even indeed be more comfortable than a love match."

Petty peeped at her father's face. There was a slightly guarded look in his deep eyes. She wondered slightly. She knew her father had been deeply in love with her mother when he married her.

In his day he had been the biggest catch on what was vulgarly termed 'the marriage mart', but he had lost his heart to one Julia Turcot, the only daughter of an elderly widower, who had so doted on his beautiful child, indulging her every wish and giving her so much her own way that she had finished up hopelessly spoilt. She thought much of herself and ruled the family with a tyranny that included much sulking and temper tantrums if crossed in any way. She knew the way to make everyone feel uncomfortable, if she considered that she had been, in any degree, slighted. Petty thought the duke still adored her, but sometimes she caught a sadness in his eyes, as Her Grace flounced off, her whims not instantly gratified.

"Lord Milton will not interfere with you," His Grace continued. "And you will, of course, leave him to follow his own pursuits. He will expect good breeding in his wife, which I am pleased to own you do have; although you are, I am afraid, rather deficient in the other accomplishments one would expect in a young lady bred as you have been. However, we will hope that when, or if, he discovers these imperfections he will look kindly upon them. You need have no worries, Petty, he will not expect love from you, and you need not expect any in return. You will be free to do as you wish…" Here His Grace seemed to run out of words. "But remember, Petty… you must always be discreet."

His voice became bitter and Petty assumed he was remembering the indecorous exploits of his own father, whose gambling and propensity for loose living had given him a notoriety which must be deemed undesirable in any family.

The seventh duke had been an enthusiastic member of the Duchess of Devonshire's set, losing huge fortunes overnight. He had flaunted a series of unacceptable mistresses all over town, choosing women who were unable to keep a quiet tongue in their heads, and whose importunate demands for houses, horses and jewels he satisfied without thought. The Devonshire set were renowned for their dissipation. Its members consistently threw the helve after the hatchet, but they were nevertheless of the haut ton. Notorious gamesters they may have been, but they were from the three hundred. They paid their gaming debts as of an honour, fortunes changing place in a few hours, but they were gentlemen. The seventh duke, not satisfied with them, had fallen prey to every unsavoury Captain Sharp to hit London; he had squandered his considerable inheritance, amassed by the fifth duke and husbanded carefully by the sixth. In addition he had brought the Mordaunt name into disrepute, until the family were quite sunk with despair.

"Yes," the eighth duke continued, "you must be discreet. Now, Petty, do not cry. Lord Milton will be here to dine tonight. Go try to make yourself look respectable, child. Ask your mama, she has the most exquisite taste, surely she can help you in this case."

Petty curtsied to her father and left the library. Drawing her shawl around her she crossed the icy hall. Automatically she made her way towards the schoolroom; in times of trouble it had always been her sanctuary. Her mind in turmoil, she tried, somewhat unsuccessfully, to make sense of the news her father had told her. Too agitated to collect her thoughts into any order she merely found herself confused and wobbly as she attempted, desperately, to understand the enormity of what she had accepted to do.

As she walked she looked around her. Now that she knew she was about to leave, it was as if she was seeing her home for the first time. She noted how many signs of neglect Wakeham bore which were directly attributable to a shortage of funds. Many of the paintings which had delighted her as a child had had to be sold, and as she made her way down the long gallery the empty spaces on the walls were a constant reminder to her of how it would be if a solution to their financial embarrassment was not soon to be found.

Petty knew this, and yet as she traversed the huge empty rooms her heart rebelled. It appeared that everything would be satisfactory for everyone but her. What the duke had proposed seemed soulless to her. A marriage of convenience; convenient for whom? Her sisters, now to have glittering come-outs; her brothers, whose futures were now assured? It was not that Petty did not love these personages, she did very much, but it did not seem as if anyone cared for her, or how she felt. She knew she was not very good at explaining her feelings, but it was as if no one had even considered how she might greet this news. She gave another small sob, then shook herself angrily.

"No self pity," she told herself firmly.

She stopped by the wall that had held her favourite Rembrandt; the dusty marks showed where the painting had been. She remembered how she and Anthony, her brother, had spent such happy hours telling stories about these pictures.

Anthony. He would help her, he always had. Whenever she had got into some scrape Anthony had always been there.

She shivered. It was getting late and it would soon be time to dress for dinner, soon be time to beard Mama in her dressing room, to ask her for help with her toilette. She shuddered. Casting her mind quickly over her evening dresses she concluded that she had no apparel suitable for such an occasion; nothing she possessed could in any way be described as elegant, and her small frame certainly did not "pay for dressing" as Miss Holtby, her mama's dresser, was forever pointing out.

She pulled her shawl closer around her, and hurried on to the schoolroom; this was a shabby, but cosy apartment, brimming with books. They lined every wall and overflowed onto every surface available. An old globe which showed signs of being much consulted stood in the corner. The ancient dolls' house, Petty's pride and joy when she was a child, bore witness to her industry; many hours had been spent in the manufacture of tiny pieces of furniture, all of which had been painstakingly upholstered and painted. As Petty entered she saw with relief that her younger brother was indeed there.

Lord Anthony Mordaunt was, as the rest of the family, extraordinarily good-looking. The deep blue eyes, which constantly laughed, were set in a wide evenly proportioned face. He had a straight nose, graceful mouth and an abundance of bright blond curls; this gave him a somewhat angelic appearance, a fact that was belied by the broad strong shoulders and the obvious build of an athlete. He stood six foot in his stockings, and towered over his sister. He was in his last year at Oxford, reading Greats, in which it was universally assumed he would obtain a first class degree. He too was dressed for riding, and indeed had been out earlier in the day with His Grace.

His head deep in a book, he looked up as Petty came in. "What does 'Est brevitate opus, ut currat sententia' mean?"

"Let brevity dispatch the rapid thought," Petty replied absentmindedly, her knowledge of the classics as fluent as her brother's.

"Of course, how stupid." He stopped as he saw her face. "What is it, Petty? What's the matter?"

The unwelcome tears started again; Petty brushed them aside brusquely. "It's… It's…" She gave a sob, took a deep breath and said in a small flat voice, "Papa has arranged a marriage for me."

"What… you… you mean someone has offered for you?" He sounded incredulous.

"Well, thanks for your faith, you do not have to sound so surprised," she choked between laughing and crying.

"Oh, Petty, no… no… I did not mean that. You are a top girl, but I cannot quite see you getting married!"

"Nor can I," Petty commented. "I do not want to. Oh! Anthony, what shall I do?"

"Who is it? Do I know him?" Her brother sounded perplexed as he tried to work out who Petty's suitor might be.

"No, you do not, and nor do I, that's what makes it so desperate. He is called Lord Milton and his grandfather made a fortune in trade and he would be quite ineligible, if Grandpapa had not left us without sixpence to scratch with and I were not so plain!"

Anthony burst out laughing.

"It is not a matter for mirth," Petty admonished, half giggling. "It is terrible. I cannot marry a man I do not know, do not love and who is, no doubt, as common as marigolds."

"Well, tell Papa," Anthony suggested.

"I tried," Petty replied. "But it did not work… you know how he reduces me to a quake. I… I just could not make him understand."

Her brother did. "Silly mouse," he said affectionately. "So what are you going to do? Try Mama?"

"Try Mama! "Petty looked utterly surprised. "She would hardly be on my side. She is delighted with the settlements; now Charlotte and Marina will have wonderful balls at Staplefield House for their come-outs. Mama will be able to dress with the greatest finery, and you know that is all she really cares about. She does not think of anyone but herself."

Anthony knew the efficacy of these words, and he also knew that Petty would not be able to take on Her Grace.

"Nothing for it, you will just have to marry this Lord Milton," he pronounced. "And endure the common mama-in-law. It will not be so bad. You will be able to have your own establishment, and do whatsoever you want."

"You know I do not care for any of that. Oh, I cannot, I will not marry him."

"No way out. It seems very settled."

Petty paced up and down the shabby room, while her brother swung his long legs over the side of the deep chair with its frayed edges, and watched her.

"I have it!" she exclaimed. "I will run away."

Anthony hooted with laughter. "What an enlightened idea. Of course, do run away. A young green girl who has never travelled farther than London, and that in her mama's coach, who has not a feather to fly with of her own, will do very well running away alone, penniless and not a notion of how to get about. Now, do not be a goose, Petty, where would you go?"

"To Aunt Amelia in Yorkshire, she would have me," she replied defiantly.

"They would find you out in a moment if you went there, besides, you will have no reputation left if you go haring all over the countryside alone."

"I do not care for that."

"Well, you ought to, my girl. It would not answer, as an unmarried girl. It would be most improper, totally lacking in any propriety, besides, think what Great-Aunt Elizabeth would say."

This made them both dissolve into laughter. Great-Aunt Elizabeth was their grandfather's sister. A most proper lady, she had spent the last forty years bemoaning the excesses of her brother and railing against the impropriety of modern manners. Now that she no longer had him to complain about, her main preoccupation at present was a disgust at the waltz, which, even though it was danced at Almack's, she considered the height of decadence.

"I suppose if I were married it would be acceptable?" Petty remonstrated.

"No, it would not," Anthony replied firmly. "There is nothing for it, you will have to marry this Lord Milton, and make the best of it."

"Never," Petty remarked resolutely. "Oh, please will you help me?"

Her voice choked, but at that moment the door opened, admitting Miss Chalmont, the redoubtable lady who presided over the schoolroom, accompanied by some of her younger charges. The Lady Charlotte, at fifteen, was bidding fair to challenge her mama with her beauty; the Lady Marina, though only twelve, could be seen to have the family looks. Following her was a small boy of eight, who was complaining vociferously at not being allowed to ride that afternoon with his father and brothers, and the imminent prospect of being handed over to Nurse.

Miss Chalfont was a small woman. All her charges, except Petty, towered over her. What she lacked in size she made up for in resolution. She was a strict, but loving disciplinarian, who, highly educated herself, had coped easily with the formidable intelligence shown by most of the Mordaunt children, a level of intellect that would have certainly defeated most governesses; however, she bore it with a good-humoured patience that endeared her to everyone, even on occasions the duchess, a not inconsiderable achievement.

A swift look at Petty's face told her that something was amiss. "It is late, you had better go and change, my dear," she said in her quiet voice. "I will be along in a minute to help you dress."

"Oh, Fonty, I cannot," Petty replied despairingly. "I have to go to Mama to get her to make me look respectable."

"Fine chance of that!" Anthony hooted.

"Be quiet, Lord Anthony!" Miss Chalfont said sharply. "Now, what is it, Lady Perpetua?"

"She is to be married. Her husband-to-be comes to dine. Papa desires that Miss Holtby and Mama make her look the conformable bride."

A quick glance at Petty's stricken face told Miss Chalfont that the bald facts put so bluntly before her by Lord Anthony were obviously true. She was deeply shocked herself. Much in Petty's confidence she knew that that fragile girl had formed no attachment to any young man of her acquaintance.

"How absolutely thrilling," Lady Charlotte, flushed pink with excitement, pronounced. "Now the coast is clear for me, I will be able to come out without the indignity of having an older sister on the shelf."

Her ingenuous words brought Miss Chalfont back to a sense of her duties.

"Lady Charlotte! If I hear one more word from you, you may be sure that you will be dining in the nursery tonight!"

These dread words silenced Lottie, who was much excited by her recent promotion to dine with her parents.

"Lady Charlotte, you will go straight to your room. Marcus and Marina, go directly to Nurse." Her firm tones brooked no argument, and these personages rapidly left the schoolroom. Miss Chalfont turned her attention to an ashen Petty.

"Come, Petty," her gentle voice made Petty choke, "try to bear it." She knew all too well how Petty was treated in the family, and privately thought it no bad thing if she were to be wed, and mistress of her own establishment. "You had best go to Miss Holtby, she will make you look splendid."

She quelled Lord Anthony's unseemly mirth with a firm eye, and propelled Petty gently out of the schoolroom door.

Chapter Two

L eaving the schoolroom, Petty made her way to her mama's chamber. The duchess occupied a suite of rooms on the south side of the main part of the house. They were decorated sumptuously and exhibited none of the financial stringency that was so conspicuous throughout the rest of the mansion. Generous fires always burned in Her Grace's grate! Jonquil walls, pale yellow and cream draperies set off the fragile beauty of Her Grace to perfection. As she entered her mama's rooms, Petty was always sensible of the impression of sunlight and warmth. In addition, the rooms were redolent with the perfume of the exotic blooms especially grown for the duchess in the newly erected rest houses.

This evening, as she greeted her mother Petty was more than ever aware of her own shortcomings. Her Grace had dressed even more carefully than was her wont. She was quite exquisite in an overdress of pale grey silk, embroidered with the most fragile of tiny flowers. Miss Holtby was arranging her hair in the latest style, the reddish-gold locks piled high, with a few carefully arranged fronds escaping to curl over the slim, delicate neck.

The duchess turned as Petty came in, her pale blue eyes shining with excitement. "My love, such excellent news. I am in transports of delight to think that you, my sweetest of daughters, should contract such a propitious and illustrious alliance."

"Illustrious!" Petty was moved to extrapolate, but her mama ignored her.

"The settlements, my dear, the glorious settlements. I was just saying to Holtby that, when we come out of black gloves, I shall have to quite refurbish my wardrobe. I have decided to go to London next week to visit Madame Françoise, you know, my love, she dresses the dear Countess of Bressley, the Marchioness of Carnham, who is quite the most elegant of creatures, oh and so many... She is quite the thing. I must replenish everything. I have nothing that will suffice. Perhaps Paris for hats? What do you think, Holtby? I hear from Lady Hamel that there is a new modiste in the Rue Rivoli who is all the rage."

Petty regarded her mama with a feeling that bordered on dislike. The duchess's wardrobe was so comprehensive that it certainly needed no additions, and when Petty contrasted it with the paucity of apparel that was to be found in her own cupboards, she was overcome with an impotent feeling of despair. Her Grace continued.

"My dear, Lord Milton comes tonight. I feel moved to help you, so I am prepared to sacrifice myself, and lend you Holtby to dress you." She smiled triumphantly at Petty. "She will dress your hair and see if there is anything that can be done to improve your appearance."

With this gesture of magnanimity she dismissed her eldest daughter and her dresser and returned to admiring herself in the mirror.

Holtby sniffed and stared dourly at Petty. She followed her down the endless freezing corridors until they reached Petty's bedchamber. The duchess did not permit fires to be lit in any rooms except hers and the duke's, and during the winter, icicles frequently formed on the inside of the windows. Petty spent as little time there as possible. Now she opened her cupboards and brought out the only two evening dresses that she possessed which could possibly be considered as suitable wear for a family still in black gloves for the demise of a close relative. Holtby looked them over disparagingly, and selected a jonquil and white overdress with grey satin underskirt. These tended to highlight Petty's sallow complexion and drew attention to the thinness of her figure. Miss Holtby commanded that she put them on; ruefully Petty obeyed, knowing that to object would only occasion a severe setdown on the lines of "daughters who were privileged enough to be given the honour of being dressed by their mama's dressers should know better than to complain".

Miss Holtby then turned her attention to Petty's unruly locks; more sniffing and sighing occurred as she attempted to bring order to the curls. Under her breath Miss Holtby complained about "the awfulness of dull mouse colour as compared to corn blonde, the arbitrariness of the badly behaved curls". She pulled and tugged at Petty's hair, interlacing the curls with knots of small flowers. The style, when completed, was one that would have looked enchanting on the ravishing Lady Charlotte, but made Petty look like an over coiffured pet dog. Petty hated it, but knew that to protest would produce a series of grunts and groans from the alarming Holtby and complaints of ingratitude to the duchess.

As Holtby finished her handiwork there was a knock on the door. Holtby, who considered her position as one far superior to this nonentity of a daughter, answered for Petty with a curt, "Come in."

Petty, the horror of the evening growing closer, hardly noticed this extra piece of impertinence. The under-footman, John, entered. He was a good-looking, highly ambitious young man.

"My lady, His Grace requires that you attend Lord Milton in the saloon."

His message delivered, he looked shrewdly at Petty, observing the ridiculous hair, her ashen face, the unsuitable dress which did nothing to enhance her slight figure and the look of dismay in her blue eyes. She returned his look with one of abject terror. In truth he liked Petty and had a certain sympathy for her. He knew that she was much put upon and could, frequently, be heard championing her cause in the servants' hall. He smiled reassuringly at her.

"This way, my lady."

Petty followed him silently down the freezing corridors to the saloon. In her panic she had forgotten her shawl, and her bare shoulders and arms were covered with goose bumps and mottled an unattractive purple. John opened the double doors for her and Petty crept in.

The saloon was bright with candles. In their light Petty was, as usual, struck by the splendidness of the room. No shabbiness, no frayed draperies could disguise its dignified proportions, its delicate ceilings, the perfection of every object set in its requisite place. The room's glory took her breath away and made her dismal spirits rise, as beauty always did. A large fire burnt in the grate in honour of the respected guest, who, unaware of the singular honour which had been bestowed on him, stood with his back to the flames minutely examining Grinling Gibbons's handiwork.

Petty was aware of a tall dark man, whose very real interest in the carving showed in the responsive features of his face. He turned and a flash of extreme boredom replaced the alive look so instantly, that Petty was unsure whether it had ever been there. His eyes under heavy lids were dark and hard as he regarded her dispassionately. She shook, shrinking instinctively from that supercilious glance.

"Well?" His granite tones echoed across the room. Petty quailed, her mouth dried up, no words came. She looked at the floor and dropped a desperate curtsey.

"Well?" he demanded, clearly exasperated by this timorous approach. This exasperation was familiar to Petty, she seemed to inspire it in all kinds of people; her eyes stung with tears.

"I… I… am Petty," she managed.

"I see." He looked slightly shocked by this but sounded less irritated.

They stood. In the uncomfortable quiet that followed Petty remembered the manners that had been so endlessly drummed into her by her mama and Miss Chalfont.

"Please, won't you sit down?" she ventured, crossing the room to perch primly on the edge of the chaise. The silence continued; it seemed interminable. Petty searched hopelessly for something to say, but no words came to her. Her whole body felt icy and her mind, too, seemed to have frozen. This inanimation deprived her of her capacity to produce any intelligible remarks and she felt herself going red with embarrassment. Lord Milton watched her. It seemed to Petty that he was enjoying her discomfort. He sighed, eventually obviously realising that if conversation were to take place he was going to have to instigate it. A non-committal remark about the weather, which was steadily growing colder, made Petty relax a little, feeling on safer ground.

"The frost is so hard, I am afraid there will be no possibility of hunting tomorrow," she returned. She had been peeping at His Lordship through her downcast eyes and had deduced from his splendid physique that he was, in all probability, a notable sportsman. Having been surrounded by them all her life, it was easy for her to identify the natural grace of the complete athlete.

"How disappointing." His Lordship's bored drawl continued, "I had been promised some excellent runs. His Grace assures me that the hunting around here is second to none…"

"What! Better than Leicestershire?" Petty's surprise made her usually musical voice almost squeaky. "1 cannot imagine why Papa should say that, it's quite untrue."

"You are obviously a great huntswoman?" returned His Lordship.

"I… I…" Petty was horrified with where her gauche

comments were leading. Namely to a rapid discovery of her manifold shortcomings.

Suddenly, while trying to wriggle truthfully out of the hole into which she seemed, inadvertently, to have pitched herself, a tiny wicked thought came to her; maybe it would be no bad thing? She took a deep breath.

"Oh no!" she replied. "I do not hunt. I... I... well... I hate horses. Nasty things. They blow at one. I hope sincerely that I never have to deal with them again. For they scare me. Oh! I do not ride or drive."

Lord Milton was clearly surprised, but he made no comment and the silence returned. He was conscious of a feeling of intense ennui, and a hope that someone would arrive to interrupt them. He regarded this unprepossessing girl for whom he had offered, and as he looked at her he found it necessary to remind himself of his reasons for contracting to marry her. As he watched her he reiterated to himself, "*It is expedient that I now form an alliance, and I must remember how well her qualifications suit my present needs.*"

He was now five and thirty and he had long despaired of finding a woman with whom he could form the kind of loving relationship that he had observed in his parents' marriage.

His father, The Hon. George Milton, when hardly out of Cambridge had formed a lasting attachment to a girl of whom his family could not approve. Lord Milton had cut him off, and sworn that if George married Kate Philipson he would have nothing more to do with him. George married Kate, and his father never saw him again. His father's attitude saddened George, but had not seemed to affect other members of his family who happily went along with His Lordship's edict and did not associate with George and Kate and their two children, Edward and Aurelia, either.

For family, they made do with Kate's father, Cuthbert Philipson, who owned vast acres of thriving industry in the Midlands and Yorkshire. Cuthbert was an instinctive businessman. He loved his daughter, he was pleased with his son-in-law, who made his daughter so happy, and he was determined that her children would be brought up as befitted the grandchildren of an illustrious aristocrat.

Edward was taught by the best tutors, he was sent to Harrow; no expense was regarded as too great, if it contributed towards his education in the noble arts, consequently he rode superbly, drove to an inch, sparred with Gentleman Jackson. He flirted with accredited beauties, gambled a little and was in every particular a gentleman, except for the one fact: his mother's background meant that he was not accepted as a member of the haut ton. This inner core of society eluded him. Personally, he was not quite sure whether it was so desirable, but his grandfather felt deeply his daughter's rejection and was determined to avenge her image. Her son would become part of this inner sanctum.

This became, in his grandfather's eyes, even more necessary when, a few years earlier, Edward's life changed dramatically. Lord Milton's eldest son, Edward's Uncle Henry, was unexpectedly killed in a hunting accident. Henry's wife, Honoria, had, unfortunately, so far only produced a bevy of daughters; although it had been much hoped that her next pregnancy would produce the longed-for heir, this would now never be. Henry's untimely accident was swiftly followed by his father's death from a broken heart when he realised that his younger son, 'the Black Sheep', must now inherit. Unbeknownst to his family, however, this same 'Black Sheep', George, had died some years previously, so this left his son Edward, unexpectedly, in possession of the title, and as Cuthbert's heir also in possession of a considerable fortune.

His grandfather pressed and pressed on him the necessity of marrying and setting up his nurseries. Edward, somewhat reluctantly, realised that he was right. He went to London determined on wedlock. He spent three fruitless seasons on the edge of society searching for the right girl, but apart from a few dalliances, never serious, he had met nobody who appealed to his sense of humour, who appreciated his love of beauty and who was intelligent enough not to bore him stiff in a few weeks. He knew he must marry. He needed an unexceptional wife who came from the highest echelons of society. Then Cuthbert learnt of Lady Perpetua and the straitened circumstances of the Mordaunts, which would unequivocally make his grandson's suit favourable. He was all enthusiasm. His grandson would at last occupy his rightful place. After all, the eldest daughter of the Duke of Staplefield must be considered acceptable in every way!

As Edward looked at Petty he was beginning to have doubts as to the efficacy of what he had done, but the die was cast, he was no jilt. He had offered for her hand, her father had accepted; all that remained was a formal proposal to the lady herself and his fate was sealed! He gave a tiny sigh, small but not lost on the perceptive girl who sat so straight on the sofa in front of him.

"Lady Perpetua," he commenced, "I know your father has explained my reason for coming here. I know that he has discussed my proposal with you and that it is acceptable to you."

Petty looked up suddenly; her eyes widened. "Papa said that?" she questioned.

Edward ignored her comment. He ploughed on. "So all that remains is for me to ask you if you will do me the honour of becoming my wife."

There was a long pause. Edward felt his irritation returning. Really, did this appalling girl have no manners at all?

Eventually she replied, "Why do you want to marry me?"

"I imagined that your father had explained," he said slowly, as if talking to an idiot. "I need a wife. Your papa needs to marry his daughters well. I am prepared to settle a great deal of money on your family in exchange for marrying a daughter of the Duke of Staplefield."

"But why me?" Petty implored. "If you must marry a Mordaunt why not one of my sisters? They are far more beautiful than I am and much more conformable."

"I can hardly marry a child still in the nursery," His Lordship, slightly amused, pointed out.

"Can you not wait for them? Lottie is nearly sixteen; it will only be a couple of years. Even Marina is twelve; in six years I am sure she will make a most excellent wife."

"I am a little old to wait for a chit not yet out, do you not think?" he answered impatiently. "I do not desire to postpone matrimony any longer. I assure you that it suits my purpose very well to marry you." He stopped, clearly feeling that these words were a little harsh, for his tone softened appreciably. "I am sure we will deal very well together, my dear. I shall not interfere with you. You will be able to do as you wish. I am sure that as a young lady of quality you have many interests to pursue."

"Oh no, I have no interests and absolutely no accomplishments," Petty responded despairingly. "And... And I am... bookish... You will not want to marry someone who is bookish, I am sure it will not be comfortable to have a blue-stocking for a wife."

The corner of Lord Milton's mouth twitched; he looked at her with an awakening interest, but merely remarked with a straight face, "No accomplishments? Do you not paint?"

"Oh no... no... I cannot paint or draw or sketch... I cannot sew a stitch, embroidery is an art that is lost on me... I have no conversation... no graces... I do not visit the poor with pots of preserves, conserves or compassion. I cannot deal with servants, I do not know how to run a house... I do not dance... I cannot... I cannot..."

"Play the piano," Lord Milton supplied helpfully.

"No, I can play the piano," Petty, incorrigibly honest, admitted. "But not the pieces you would desire to hear. I have no voice, and I will not sing silly songs about lads and lasses for the assembled company," she finished triumphantly.

Lord Milton laughed. "What do you play?"

"Mozart, Beethoven sonatas. You do not want a wife like

me," she pleaded. "You want a genteel well-bred girl who knows how to organise a house, and how to talk to housekeepers, how to entertain ambassadors or… or foreign royalty. My family will tell you I am quite hopeless at all that."

His Lordship, used to having lures thrown at him by young damsels in search of rich husbands and by their matchmaking mamas, found himself suddenly intrigued by this strange, undistinguished girl who made not the slightest push to fasten his interest. She was gauche, she was plain, she was trying, with all the ability she possessed to put him off, and he found himself amused as he had not been for ages. Petty, her face flushed, looked up at him defiantly as she made this speech. He was suddenly aware of the singular beauty of her deep blue eyes. The impression was gone in a second as the sound of the duchess's voice was heard through the huge double doors which were flung open by Croft.

"Come, dearest Lottie, give me your arm. How singularly beautiful you look, my dear."

Petty glanced at Lord Milton as Her Grace swept into the room, assisted by her second daughter and followed by the duke. She had not been a reigning belle for nothing. She paused in the doorway until she was sure that every eye was upon her, then she entered, superb in the soft grey silk, her hair dressed in gentle curls which set off her heart-shaped face to perfection. Her light blue eyes sparkled, her peachy complexion glowed. She was, indubitably, a paragon of beauty. She waited again, conscious of the effect that she had created, so very assiduously. She knew what was her due and she was not disappointed. Lord Milton looked like a man stunned by the vision of beauty before him, but his look, Petty observed, was fleeting, replaced by one of amused disdain.

"My dear Lord Milton," Her Grace murmured ingratiatingly. "How delightful that you are here with us, such an auspicious occasion." She held out her hand to His Lordship.

"Your servant, Your Grace." He bowed over the delicate hand.

"Come, sit beside me," she commanded. "We must become better acquainted."

"As Your Grace wishes." His Lordship obediently followed the duchess across the room to the sofa. Sitting beside her he watched her face, too used to admiration and too self-centred to see anything in his polite gaze except the adoration she regarded as her right. She placed a slender bejewelled hand upon his arm.

"My dear sir, I have no words to describe the joy that I feel in being able to welcome you into our family. I am convinced you too must feel that this is the most important moment of your life. Joining the Mordaunts is to be privileged beyond what is possible for most people. I imagine this must be a time of great rejoicing for you, as you become a member of one of the best and greatest families in the land."

Lord Milton inclined his head slightly; Petty thought she caught a contemptuous smile in his dark eyes, but it was so transitory that she was not quite sure that she had not been mistaken.

He does not like her, thought Petty, somewhat surprised. She was so accustomed to the worshipful attention that her mother occasioned in men, that it was somewhat hard to realise that here was a man who was quite indifferent to the graceful manners, the sweet smile, the limpid eyes.

"The marriage will, of course, take place immediately. It will have to be a private affair as we are still in black gloves and I am, anyway, convinced that Lady Perpetua would not desire any fuss or pomp or unnecessary expense. A very quiet wedding will suit her perfectly." She directed a quelling glance at Petty, and smiled bewitchingly at His Lordship.

"Your Grace's wishes are mine to command," Lord Milton replied politely; the sarcastic undertone lost on Her Grace was not on Petty.

A feeling of despair crept over her. Her fate, it seemed, was sealed. She was going to have to spend the rest of her life with this intimidating stranger, with his hard eyes and cynical manner. She could not imagine talking to him as a friend. He frankly scared her. She did not want a marriage of convenience; she wanted to be with a man who made her feel comfortable, not fearful.

"Then it is all gloriously settled," Her Grace pronounced. She turned to her husband with a ravishing smile. "Shall we go in to dinner?"

CHAPTER THREE

The wedding was to take place after the Christmas and New Year festivities. It was, as the duchess had decreed, to be a small private affair. With her usual affability she took Petty to Tewkesbury and bought her some bride clothes; not many, as she pronounced that Petty really did not need an extensive wardrobe. A few plain dresses in drab colours would suffice. Her new husband must be responsible for dressing her further if anything else was needed. Not that she anticipated that Petty would need any more clothes; small dab girls, in her opinion and Miss Holtby's, did not really have any need of a lavish wardrobe. Petty was docile, her mind made up. She had no further conversation with Lord Milton alone. Her mama considered it unnecessary and for once Petty was grateful to her. He, in any case, went back to London for Christmas and only returned a couple of days before the wedding, bringing with him his best man, a Captain Braybrooke.

Petty was in the morning room, when Lord Milton and the captain were announced. She was sketching with her sisters, the Ladies Charlotte and Marina. Miss Chalfont, herself an able painter, was assisting them. Petty and Lottie were laughing over the latter's attempt to draw a flock of sheep.

"They look like cotton balls," chuckled Petty, "or puff mushrooms with legs."

"Well, yours are hardly better," Lottie pointed out.

It was at this moment that Croft opened the door to announce, "Lord Milton and Captain Braybrooke, my lady."

His Lordship and the captain walked in to a scene of merriment. The captain was aware of a small thin girl with beautiful laughing eyes; she was giggling with the most ravishing girl he had ever seen. He noticed how, upon their arrival, the thin girl, whom he assumed to be the Lady Perpetua, seemed to freeze and close up.

"Lady Perpetua, may I present Captain William Braybrooke," introduced Lord Milton in his cold detached voice.

Petty stood up and curtsied stiffly, muttering a few inaudible civilities under her breath.

She looked, the captain decided, like a scared mouse shrinking from a rather large cat.

Lord Milton crossed the room to present his compliments to Miss Chalfont and her younger charges, leaving the captain to talk to his betrothed. William watched for a moment as Petty stood, her eyes downcast. He made a slight sound and her troubled eyes flew to his face. The captain smiled reassuringly at her. He was a slight, fair young man with warm humorous eyes and a gentle voice. Petty found herself responding to his friendly manner, and the obvious interest in his face.

"Are these yours?" he enquired, picking up her sketches. "How good they are."

"Oh no… no, I cannot draw at all," Petty answered quickly.

"Please let me be the judge of that," he responded firmly. "Where is this? It appears a most picturesque area. Such excellent hills, such well-fashioned sheep!"

Petty chuckled, her confidence returning under the undemanding gaze of this pleasant stranger. "I am inordinately proud of my sheep. They bear the most remarkable resemblance to snowballs! I think if I continue my studies I could become the foremost sheep painter in England."

The captain laughed. "Stubbs had better look to his laurels. I can see that he is about to have competition in the world of animal painting: Lady Perpetua Mordaunt, 'Sheep portraiture undertaken. Commissions on demand.'"

Petty giggled again. "Perhaps sheep are not the wisest animals, maybe I should do dogs?"

"Certainly not wise. Particularly stupid, sheep. If I may point out, not many people painting sheep, lots of demand. I am afeared rather a lot of portraits of dogs being undertaken."

She met his eyes and found them laughing at her. She responded, chuckling, "Then it is quite clear, sheep it must be!"

"Apart from the sheep in this sketch, I am much taken with the scenery. Is this drawn from local views?"

"Indeed, yes," she replied. "We are fortunate in that we have some most excellent vistas to paint around here, but how does this scenery compare to that in your part of England?"

"I come from Yorkshire..." he started.

"Oh, then you are blessed with the most beautiful scenes. I love Yorkshire above everywhere. My favourite aunt comes from there, and my happiest days have been spent in Ripley..."

"Does your aunt live in Ripley? I live near Tollerton, a small estate I inherited from my uncle. I have this year sold out and I am about to take up residence. To be truthful, I do not yet know what must be done to put the estate in order. I believe it has been much neglected. My uncle was infirm, able to do very little in the last few years of his life, but I am much excited at the prospect of running it. I have only faint recollection of the house, but I gather from the bailiff that I have good tenants, and I am hopeful that it will quickly be improved. You and Edward must be my first visitors. I look forward to welcoming you after your marriage..." He stopped.

Petty had stiffened; her small face seemed to close like a book. Watching her carefully, he was perturbed by her reaction; the change when he had mentioned Edward and her marriage had been extraordinary.

He discovered that he liked her, her enthusiasm appealed to him; she was unaffected, obviously intelligent and possessed of a quirky humour. Why then was she clearly so unhappy about being married to Edward, whom he regarded as everything that was admirable? He determined to try to get to the bottom of what was worrying her.

She turned from him and steadily regarded Lord Milton and her sister, with mounting embarrassment. The Lady Charlotte, although not yet quite sixteen, appeared, Petty was loath to admit, to be becoming an accomplished flirt, possessed of the Mordaunt deep blue eyes, her mother's exquisite heart-shaped face, a tiny delicate nose, the softest of complexions, with no hint of a blemish, and a rosebud mouth. This beautiful face was framed by thick golden curls gathered becomingly into a knot on top of her head. She was one of those lucky people who are naturally graceful and with a figure that will always look elegant without effort. She was not blessed with the superior intelligence that characterised the rest of the Mordaunt family, but this was regarded by her mama as something of an advantage. The duchess was as much looking forward to bringing out her second daughter as she had been indifferent to the come-out of her unprepossessing eldest. She knew Lottie would become the rage. The Lady Charlotte also possessed the sporting prowess so sadly lacking in her sister; an excellent seat on a horse, combined with a fearlessness that made her throw her heart over any obstacle, meant that she would be much in demand at the hunting parties so much dreaded by Petty.

Well aware of the sublime picture she made on horseback, she turned her luminous eyes onto Lord Milton. "I know, my lord, that you are a considerable horseman, please, will you ride with me?" she asked archly, accompanying her request with a breathtaking smile. Although Lottie believed that she was up to every trick, she had, up to now, only encountered local besotted halflings. Men of Lord Milton's address and experience were as yet unknown to her. He, on the other hand, well used to the wiles of ravishing young girls, replied in a tantalisingly detached way, "Perhaps."

Turning from her, he wandered across to Miss Chalfont to admire her painting. Petty watched with horror as the Lady Charlotte, used to unquestioning adoration from men, raised her perfect chin and made to follow him to reinforce her request. Blushing for her sister's unbecoming want of conduct, she shot a pleading look across the room to Miss Chalfont. This redoubtable lady, who rarely missed the machinations of her capricious charge, had, in fact, observed the ingenuous invitation.

"Now, Lady Charlotte, time for a walk before the light goes and it is too cold." Lottie opened her mouth to protest.

"An excellent idea, I could do with some fresh air, and I have not had a chance to explore the gardens yet," His Lordship vouchsafed quickly, so the scheme was generally agreed to.

For Petty a walk around the gardens was not an unmitigated pleasure. Apart from Lottie's exceedingly forward behaviour, she hated to see the effects of the enforced neglect, but worse, far worse, was the realisation that in two days she would no longer live at Wakeham. She would be leaving behind her childhood, assuredly not a particularly happy one, but all that she had known since she could remember, all that was familiar and beloved, the house, the estate, the walks; she was travelling into the unknown, with an unknown husband whom she did not know, did not like and who, frankly, scared her.

The captain, watching her expressive face as they walked through Capability's well-laid-out walks, understood something of what she was feeling. He felt at that moment incapable of helping her, but was hopeful that once the marriage was over he could get her to discuss with him her apprehensions, but that was for the future. In the meantime all he could do was to show her his warmth and empathy.

The wedding took place two days later. It was a quiet affair, just the family and Captain Braybrooke. There was to be small celebration later when the family were finally out of black gloves. Petty went through the ceremony in a desolate trance, and as soon as it was over begged to go to her room to rest as she had a raging headache.

"She does look fagged and so pale," remarked a concerned captain to her mama.

"Oh, she is always weak, useless. No strength there," she replied dismissively. "So different from her sisters. Lady Charlotte, now, a delight, so popular, she will, I am convinced, make a marriage of the first consequence, unlike Perpetua, whose husband's mama was not what one would wish."

The captain found the back of his neck prickling with dislike. He, however, maintained his own counsel and said nothing in defence of his friend, for he had quickly realised that to do so with the duchess would be useless.

He had also rapidly concluded that, upset though Petty would be leaving Wakeham, the childhood home that obviously meant a great deal to her, she was actually going to be a great deal better off with Edward.

The forlorn and unhappy demeanour which had so worried the captain had not been lost on Miss Chalfont either. Deeply concerned by the desolate blank look in Petty's eyes, she had offered to accompany her to her room to bathe her aching head with vinegar water. The refusal of this kind offer was made with such fierceness that Fonty recoiled, never having heard such a sharp tone from the normally gentle Petty before. Her hurt face made Petty add guiltily, "Please… Please, Fonty… you see I must have some time alone."

Miss Chalfont, who appreciated how despondent the thought of the impending removal from Wakeham must be for Petty, quickly forgave her, but this interchange had not ameliorated her anxiety but, rather, had increased it.

Lord Milton had decided to effect the removal to London without delay. During his return to the metropolis, before the wedding, he had arranged to purchase a house in Grafton Street and wanted to install his new wife in it as soon as possible. He was also, as he admitted to William, keen to be away from Wakeham and its inhabitants as fast as he could.

"What about the Lady Perpetua?" enquired the captain. "Do you imagine that she wishes to leave in such haste?"

"From what I have observed, they do not treat her with any degree of care or kindness here. I think that in time she will be far happier in an establishment of her own, away from here."

The captain felt that, whereas this was indubitably true, it was also a somewhat simplistic assessment of the situation, but wisely kept his thoughts to himself.

Lord Milton had decided to drive himself and his bride in his phaeton. Their baggage and Petty's belongings were to follow in his chaise, attended by his elderly groom, the devoted Hardwick. He was not, perhaps, as unaware of Petty's anxieties as the captain feared, but he believed that her frozen timidity was occasioned by the indifference and disparagement meted out to her by her family. He hoped that during the drive to London he would have a chance to draw her out a little, and that alone with him on the journey, away from the relatives who so obviously intimidated her, he would find the means to reassure her somewhat, in a way that he realised would be impossible at Wakeham.

When Petty reached her room she took off the white silk dress, hanging it carefully in her wardrobe. It was one of the duchess's, kindly lent to her for the occasion. Her mama considered that to purchase a new dress for Petty's quiet wedding would be a quite unwarranted waste of funds, and as she was so personally attached to the dress, to alter it would be to make it quite useless in the future. The result had been to make Petty look like a rag doll, mistakenly dressed in a huge frilly tablecloth.

Standing in the middle of the room were the corded trunks, containing her few possessions, which had been carefully packed by the under-housemaid. The duchess considered an abigail an unnecessary luxury for her daughter, however inconvenient that may have been at times. It was to Petty's advantage at the moment, as Kate, the under-housemaid, had done just as she was bid. Obeying without question, she had packed an extra small portmanteau with what, Petty had explained, she would need on her journey to London.

Petty opened this, adding various carefully chosen items, then she went to her wardrobe and pulled out a dark serge dress which she had chosen as appropriate to her new career. As she brushed her hair back into as severe a style as she could, she caught sight of the new gold ring on her finger, twisting it around to remove it. She suddenly remembered Anthony's words regarding the lack of desirability for unmarried females to be running around the countryside unaccompanied. Perhaps I had better be a widow, she thought ruefully, and decided to keep it on.

She looked quickly around the room to make sure that she had left nothing behind, then hesitatingly took a final look out of the window. The evening sun was setting, its pink light flooding the gardens; the gaunt winter trees stood up, proud and black against this flamingo sky; the frosty lawns stretched down to the lake, with its Chinese bridge and flowing waterfalls. Tears stung the back of her eyes.

l cannot bear to leave you, she agonised. But I have to. I cannot stay here. I cannot go with a man I do not know. I cannot go to a house I have never seen, to servants who will despise me, to London where I have no one, anything is better than that.

She brushed away the tears, pulled her thickest cloak around her, picked up her portmanteau and her reticule, checking that the hundred pounds she had so carefully removed from Papa's study the night before was in place. She had not enjoyed taking money from him, but she knew she must have funds for her needs, and she comforted herself with the thought that her settlements would more than compensate for his loss.

She peeped out of her door; everything was silent. She slipped out along the draughty corridors, down the back stairs, and through the larder passage, calculating that this part of the house would be deserted at this hour. She made her way past the still room and laundries, and out through the door which led directly to the stable yard. Petty may have told Lord Milton that she hated horses but this was less than the truth. She had never enjoyed riding much, but she was an accomplished whip, and loved to drive.

She had no current ambition to take the phaeton, or even the curricle, her plan was to borrow the old gig with Jumper to pull it; this inappropriately named animal had been given to her as a child and christened by the ten-year-old Petty. He was a small, round, shaggy animal, possessed of a docile temperament, somewhat ponderous as he approached old age, but had been the most excellent horse on which to practice early driving skills, and Petty loved him deeply.

She crossed the empty yard, rounding the corner to where Jumper was stabled. She opened his stable door; he raised his old grizzled head and looked at Petty with a wise and welcoming face; as she put out her hand he nuzzled it gently.

"Hello, old fellow," she whispered. Slipping his bridle over his head, she buried her face in his shaggy neck. "Oh, Jumper, Jumper, it is all so awful." The unwanted but ready tears came again. "What shall I do?" The old horse seemed to return her embrace. Petty shook herself, opened the door and started to lead him across the yard to where the ancient gig was stabled. As she came around the corner she came face to face with John. Petty stared at him in horror.

"Can I help you, my lady?" he asked. "Where are you going?"

More tears coursed down her cheeks. She put down her

portmanteau and regarded him in total despair. She was discovered. Lost.

"I said, can I help you?" he repeated deliberately. He felt very sorry for Petty, and if she wanted to bolt that was her business, he was certainly not going to split on her. Through the unwelcome tears, she glanced at him, reading sympathy in his eyes.

"It is not for me to judge you, my lady," he continued, "I am just offering you my help, wherever you are going. Were you going to harness him to the gig?"

"Yes…" Still Petty was not quite sure. He took Jumper's bridle and led him into the coach house. He quickly harnessed the horse to the gig and led it out to Petty, waiting nervously at the stable arch. He handed Petty into it and jumped up himself.

"Happen it's better I come with you, my lady." The panic in her face amused him. "Just to bring the gig back, my lady, you can't leave it just anywhere."

The validity of his words struck her. She certainly could not just leave Jumper in the middle of Tewkesbury. Why had she not thought of that?

"No! I suppose not." Her voice sounded unconvinced. "But… John… I…"

"I will not be telling on you, my lady, you can trust me."

"I can… thank you. " Privately she felt he should not be implicated in her escapade, but the gratitude she felt at his presence overcame her scruples.

There was little conversation between them on the journey to Tewkesbury. Petty stared ahead, absorbed in her own thoughts. As they reached the outskirts of the town he asked, "I said that I would not interfere, my lady, but I must know that you are safe. Where are you making for?"

Petty looked at his face. Better he did not know the truth. "To my aunt in Yorkshire," she lied.

He seemed satisfied, at least he said nothing until they

reached the yard of the Old Oak; when the gig stopped he felt moved to protest.

"You won't be going on the stage, my lady!"

"Well, I cannot afford to travel post, and I do not believe it would be suitable." She spoke with a firmness she did not feel.

"Very well, my lady," John replied doubtfully. He handed Petty down, showing no inclination to depart until he had seen Petty bestowed. Resigned, she went and bought herself a ticket to York. It was a waste of her precious funds but she knew John would not leave her if he knew the truth of her intentions.

The first stage was to Cheltenham. It rounded the corner and swept into the Old Oak yard. Petty mounted it gratefully. She was aware of a growing lack of ease in John, and she felt that if they had waited much longer he would have bundled her into the gig and returned her to Wakeham. As the stage departed, Petty's feelings of relief that she had finally managed to throw off her bodyguard gave way to a sense of vexation. To one accustomed to the comfort of a post-chaise and four, and whose only experiences of travel had been completing a journey in the easy stages that the duchess considered essential, surrounded by people whose whole function was to accommodate the vagaries of Her Grace, the privations of the stage coach came as something of a shock.

Petty found herself wedged between a fat malodorous woman accompanied by a small urchin with a dirty face and a nose that seemed to pour forth a stream of unpleasant liquid which he proceeded to wipe on the sleeve of a filthy coat, and a thin man who dug her in the ribs constantly with his pointed elbows, and complained about her under his breath the whole time. The difference between a well-sprung, luxurious carriage and this jolting, bumping vehicle was, Petty discovered, considerable. As she lay back on the lumpy squabs and tried to rest, her only thoughts were that this disagreeable journey was for nothing. She was going to have to retrace her steps to get back to Bath!

CHAPTER FOUR

In the late afternoon, Miss Chalfont, now perturbed that Petty had not reappeared, made her way through the endless cold corridors to Petty's bedchamber. She scratched gently at the door. On receiving no answer, she opened it a crack. All was in darkness. Petty's corded trunks stood in the middle of the floor untouched; a cursory glance showed her that the room was uninhabited. Miss Chalfont closed the door. Several unpalatable thoughts crowded into her mind, which she firmly dismissed. Then, pausing a moment to decide the best course to follow, she retraced her steps and hurried down the draughty corridors. As she crossed the vestibule which led to her domain the sound of merriment greeted her ears. Pushing open the door she found the Marquis of Slaughan and Lord Anthony playing chess, laughing heartily like a couple of schoolboys.

She was struck by the picture they presented. The marquis was as dark as Lord Anthony was fair, resembling the duke in every aspect: the dark blue eyes, the sardonic lift to the black eyebrows, the twisted smile, the face, that although exceedingly handsome, could in repose look harsh, the quickness of mind and temper. The broad shoulders and well-proportioned frame of the sportsman.

He was, as his father before him, a notable catch and many a matchmaking mama had set her cap at him. Unlike his papa, however, he was a seasoned flirt, raising hopes in the bosoms of those same mamas and their daughters, which were then dashed as quickly as they had been raised.

It was generally accepted that he was hanging out for a rich wife, and he had made several of the most fashionable and beautiful heiresses the object of his affections, but so far all these entanglements had come to naught. He was of course received everywhere, sensible mamas slipping a word of warning to their ravishing daughters not to lose their hearts to the blue eyes and charming smile. He seemed invincible.

The brothers were well matched intellectually and the chess game appeared as though it might continue for quite some time. They both looked up as Miss Chalfont came in, asking in a worried voice, "Have either of you seen the Lady Perpetua?"

"You mean Lady Milton," the marquis laughed. "Now, Fonty," the nickname he had given her when she first joined the family some twenty years earlier had stuck, "do not get in a pother, she is probably changing." He stood up, towering over her, and gave her a quick hug. "Light of my life, my dearest heart," he teased and she, to whom this first born could do no wrong, in spite of her concern, returned his infectious smile. "What has made this dear face so unhappy?"

"Gideon, I quite see why you leave a string of broken hearts behind you, you are a most appalling star-weaver. No young lady with an ounce of sense should believe a word of your flattery," she reproved gently. "But I am concerned, Petty is not in her room and it is dark and quiet."

"Probably gone for a last walk around the gardens," Lord Anthony pointed out.

"What, in this weather and at this hour?"

"Well, maybe she is with Mama receiving some well-turned advice on how to be an admirable wife and mother." Both young men collapsed in giggles.

"Now, Lord Slaughan and Lord Anthony, will you please stop it," admonished Miss Chalfont. "Not that I do not agree that it is unlikely that she is with Her Grace. Will you be good boys and go and see if you can find her for me?"

"l am five and twenty and Anthony is two and twenty, Fonty, you cannot continue to talk to us as if we are still in the nursery."

Miss Chalfont dropped a mock curtsey. "My apologies, my lord. Would you be so good as to go to search for your sister for me?"

The Lord Slaughan picked her up and whirled her around, depositing a slightly dishevelled governess back onto her feet. He raised his hand to her lips and kissed it. "Your wish is my command. Come, Anthony, you take the west wing and the library. I will search the gardens and the stables. Do not worry, Fonty, we will find her and dispatch her to you as soon as we do."

Miss Chalfont sat down in front of the fire. She was more concerned than she had reason, and she chastised herself for her feelings of disquiet. But her apprehensions would not go away. Petty had been so docile; she had tried to discuss her marriage with her, but all that she had obtained from that usually forthcoming damsel was that she did not want to be married and that she felt she was being sacrificed for the rest of the family. Fonty sat musing by the fire for some time. Petty did not come and neither Lord Anthony nor Lord Slaughan returned. Eventually she glanced at the schoolroom clock and realised with some degree of shock that it was already time to dress for dinner. Giving herself a severe rake-down for her imaginings, she hurried upstairs to supervise her charges, who, as a concession to Petty's wedding, were to be allowed downstairs to dine with the older members of the family.

She walked quickly, intending simply to set her foolish fears at rest, to put her head around Petty's door, and make sure that everything was tolerable, and that Petty was safe. However, before she could do this she was waylaid by an imperious Lady

Charlotte who, meeting her in the passage, ordered instant attention at her side. Encountering an amazed look from the little governess, she amended her demands to, "Please, dearest Fonty, come dress my hair. I need you now. Or I will not be ready. You must... must... must come now!"

The beauty's voice rose steadily. Lady Charlotte's resemblance to her mother did not end with her looks. She had also absorbed some of the less attractive ploys used by the duchess in order to obtain her own way, and her ability to create an unpleasant scene if her wishes were not granted was well known by the family. Recognising that the Lady Charlotte was bordering on a tirade of tears, Miss Chalfont, who was usually not so compliant where the spoilt beauty was concerned, had wisely decided that to attend to her, in this instant, was a priority.

She had been trying, somewhat unsuccessfully it must be admitted, to persuade Lottie to mitigate her behaviour. She was due to come out the next year and such tantrums must be unacceptable to the ton whom Lottie so much wanted to impress. This had been an uphill task, as the example she had seen before her since early childhood had made it hard for her to believe that hysterical storms were not an efficacious way to get what she wanted.

Miss Chalfont decided that if she helped Lottie quickly she would still have time to check on Petty. This, however, was not to be; by the time she had dressed Lottie's hair, then redressed it, there was only enough time to scramble into an evening dress herself and make her way hurriedly to join the celebrations.

The family was all gathered in the saloon by the time Miss Chalfont entered. Lord Milton had been summoned to sit next to Her Grace and was conversing amicably with her. Captain Braybrooke was looking slightly startled as he received the full attentions of the Lady Charlotte. Lord Anthony, who was watching the captain's struggles, his eyes alight with laughter, was trying to stifle his giggles into a rather large handkerchief.

While his elder brother discussed with his father the prospects of hunting the next day, the two younger members, on strict instruction to mind their manners, were sitting, slightly overawed by the importance of the occasion, on a sofa at the far end of the room. Petty was nowhere to be seen.

"Miss Chalfont, at last," His Grace remarked impatiently.

"I beg Your Grace to forgive my tardiness," the governess, flustered, apologised. "But please, has Lady Perpetua joined you?"

"Surely you can see that she is not here?" His Grace replied irritably.

"Naturally, we assumed that she was with you," Her Grace opined. "It is quite typical of her to keep us all waiting in this selfish way."

"No! She is not with me. I have not seen her since she went to her room to rest. Lord Slaughan and Lord Anthony were good enough to search for her for me, but it would appear that they were unsuccessful in their hunt?" She looked enquiringly at the two brothers.

From across the room Gideon, next to His Grace, met Anthony's eye. In accord they both shook their heads, admitting that they had not been able to find Perpetua anywhere.

The room suddenly seemed to go quiet. It was the duke, glancing around, who broke the silence.

"Croft?"

The old butler stopped in the act of pouring a drink for the captain. "Yes, Your Grace?"

"Have you seen the Lady Perpetua?" The butler shook his head. "Please send John to her bedchamber to summon her down to join us for dinner, she is very late." His voice echoed with the irritation that Perpetua always seemed to arise in him.

The footman was quickly dispatched, and the assembled company lapsed into an uneasy silence, until Her Grace, impatient with the seeming interest in her daughter, turned to

Lord Milton and pronounced, "I am afraid that you will find that Perpetua has no consideration for anyone's comfort but her own. I have tried to bring her to a sense of what is due to her mama, but I am afraid it has been hopeless. As you can see she really has no thought for anyone but herself."

Lord Milton's eyes under their heavy lids were bright with indignation, but his voice as he replied to this egotistical speech was deceptively smooth.

"I very much regret to say that I must disagree with you, Your Grace. I have observed no such self-centred behaviour in my wife."

The duchess's eyes opened in astonishment. The other occupants in the room, nervously awaiting the inevitable storm, glanced at each other resignedly. She drew herself up, the spots of red colour in her cheeks a well-known danger sign. What she might have said or done was diverted by the return of John, who went quickly to the butler and under his breath made his report.

"Well, Croft?" His Grace's voice was edgy with exasperation.

"It would appear, Your Grace," Croft replied calmly, "that Lady Perpetua, I apologise Lady Milton, is not in her bedchamber. John took the liberty of consulting with Kate, the underhousemaid, who packed for Her Ladyship, and it would seem that a small overnight bag is missing together with other items of clothing..."

"What!" His Grace's angry tones cut through this speech. "Let her be sent for, the housemaid."

Kate, her eyes wide with awe at this unexpected summons, was quickly brought in. She stood in the middle of the floor, seemingly unable to move a muscle. She stared at the duke transfixed.

"Where," he demanded, "is my daughter?"

The under-housemaid looked terrified; she trembled, opening her mouth, trying to speak but no words came out.

"Come along, my girl." He swung around on her and commanded irascibly, "I do not want to ask you again. Where is my daughter?"

Kate's eyes grew larger and more scared. "Uh."

"Speak, girl. If you wish to remain in my employ, tell me now, where is my daughter?"

"Your G… G… Grace… all… l…"

Lord Milton trod swiftly to Kate's side. "Do not be afraid. No one is going to hurt you. Whatever has happened is not your fault, but please tell us what you know."

She shot him a grateful glance but before she could utter a word the duke thundered, "Lord Milton, you will oblige me by not interfering in these matters. Lady Perpetua is my daughter."

His Lordship's eyes glittered dangerously. "I beg to remind you, Your Grace, that Lady Milton is my wife, and, as such, is my responsibility, not yours."

The duke, nearly bereft of words, spluttered, his face growing purple with ire, "This is my house and my housemaid and my daughter. I will handle this. For the last time, my girl, tell me, where is Lady Perpetua?" He faced Kate, his blue eyes black with fury.

The housemaid started to sob convulsively. She tried to speak but whatever words she might have uttered were lost in a welter of tears. Lord Milton again saw fit to intervene, handing the distraught girl his handkerchief.

"Come, Kate, dry your eyes and tell us what you know."

Only the swift intervention of Gideon stopped the duke from re-entering the fray. Placing a restraining hand on his arm, the marquis said under his breath, "Papa, he is correct, Petty is his wife and the girl is a mere child, raging at her will not obtain the information we seek."

His Grace, somewhat shamefaced and only too aware of his deplorable temper, took hold of himself, saying in an altogether different tone, "Well, Kate, do you know anything about where Lady Milton might be?"

The housemaid sniffed noisily. "No… no, Your Grace. I ain't seen her since, begging your pardon, since I helped her dress for her wedding." Here she sniffed again. "Her dress is all hung up, neat like, and the little case what I packed for her is gone, and she took her brushes and her nightgown and her thick brown cloak and…"

Lord Milton brought this litany of objects to a close by interrupting to ask if she had any idea where Lady Milton might have gone. By this time Kate was beginning to enjoy herself, as she confided later to the housekeeper.

"They was all listening to me like… like I knew something real important and all watching me. That Lord Milton is a proper gentleman, gave me his handkerchief, best hemmed linen too, so polite he was… but I couldn't tell them nothing."

This innocent confidence brought down a severe scold from the housekeeper and an injunction to mind her place.

Lord Anthony, who had appeared not to be paying much attention to the questioning of Kate, suddenly expostulated, "Oh no! Oh my goodness. Papa, Edward… Aunt Amelia…"

"Aunt Amelia? Have you lost your head, my boy? Your aunt is not here, mercifully."

"No, Papa, I can see that Aunt Amelia is not here… but the case is… is… that Petty… Oh dear…" He tailed off.

"Anthony, if you have any information that is pertinent to your sister's disappearance please tell us immediately."

"Yes, Papa," Anthony said miserably. He looked around for deliverance, but none came. "Well… you… understand… Petty… well, is…"

"Yes?" His Grace's impatience was beginning to mount again.

"Petty… Petty… you see, Petty did not want to be married! Sh… she tried to tell you but you would… did not seem to hear.

She told me that she wanted to run away. Of course, I told her not to be silly. I suggested that she spoke to Edward but she feared him, you know what a mouse she is. She told me that you said she had no choice… she was scared of you and Mama. She knew she had to obey you, for the settlements! You made it clear, she said, Wakeham was more important than anything."

Lord Milton stood motionless, his face rigid with disgust. He said nothing. The captain moved quietly across the room and stood next to his friend.

Anthony continued uneasily, "She wanted to run away to Aunt Amelia before the wedding… I told her not to be a goose, that you would quickly find her there. I never thought she would be… brave enough… Do you think that is what she has done… run away?"

Lord Milton had gone white, his face harsh and the expression in his eyes under their heavy lids inscrutable. "It would appear so. Apparently I have a reluctant wife, who finds marriage to me so distasteful that anything is preferable, even exposing herself to God knows what dangers chasing across the countryside to… Incidentally, where does this Aunt Amelia live?"

"My sister, Lady Edgerton, lives in Yorkshire," the duke returned stiffly.

"I see. It would appear, Your Grace, that I have been told less than the truth. You assured me that Lady Perpetua was perfectly happy with our arrangement. That she was, indeed, looking forward to becoming my wife. Whilst pointing out that she was shy, you nevertheless reassured me to the effect that she had been well brought up and had been trained in the art of being an excellent wife."

"Of course she will be an excellent wife," Her Grace interposed. "All my daughters are gently bred and carefully tutored and will make the most admirable homemakers to those men lucky enough to wed them. Is that not so, Miss Chalfont?"

This good lady, her worst fears realised, felt unable to comment.

No such qualms assailed Lord Milton, who turned on the duchess. "With respect, Your Grace, your words must be seen to be idiotic. Your daughter has run away precisely to escape the duties of a good and amiable wife. She may also at this moment be in some danger, a fact which seems to concern you not at all. I am appalled. It appears to matter not a wit to you to marry your daughter to a man she clearly dislikes." A bitter note crept into his voice. "You force your child into an alliance that is distasteful to her, your only wish being to relieve your financial embarrassments. You obviously have no compunction regarding Petty's inner feelings, or the invidious, and I may add, humiliating position in which I find myself."

A hush fell on the room as he stopped speaking. Miss Chalfont, deeply appreciative of sentiments that she had oft felt herself but had never been in a position to say, watched as the duchess drew herself up, her face aghast, her eyes blazing with anger.

"How dare you! How dare you, Lord Milton! How dare you utter such words to me. No one has ever spoken to me in that way before in my life."

"Then it is about time that someone did, Your Grace. Your daughter, my wife, may be in dire danger and it appears to me that not one of you cares at all. If you will forgive me I will start for Yorkshire immediately and see if I can find my wife." His voice shook with fury.

"A moment, Edward." The moderate tones of Captain Braybrooke broke in on his ire. "I think we should wait until the morning before embarking on such a journey. It's very late now, and I am convinced there is nothing to be gained by driving through the night. I think we should ascertain how Lady Milton travelled. If it was post she will have needed to change horses; maybe we can find a trace of her? Perhaps with you driving we can overtake her?"

Lord Milton smiled wryly. "Are you intending to come with me? You are a good chap."

"Of course I am coming."

In the face of the duke's continuing silence the marquis stepped in. "I think, Edward, that I should be the one to accompany you. Petty is my sister. I can see why it appears to you that we show little feeling for her, but I assure you that Anthony and I care very much about her." His voice tailed off lamely. "And whereas I know that the journey to Yorkshire is very familiar to you, I do know Aunt Amelia."

Lord Milton grasped his arm. "Gideon, I exonerate you and Anthony from my strictures and grateful as I am to William, I do think you should be the one to accompany me." He nodded to the captain who, opening his mouth to protest, received a speaking look from those dark eyes.

The duchess, meantime, feeling herself thoroughly neglected, had started a fit of mild hysterics, which were rapidly developing into a major fit of the vapours; her increasing crescendo of wails brought the duke out of his reverie.

"Be quiet, Julia!" he reprimanded firmly.

His wife, so shocked at being addressed in this way twice in so many minutes, stopped her histrionics in amazement.

"Lord Milton is correct. We none of us paid the slightest attention to Petty's wishes. My relief that she had managed a marriage of such consequence overcame any scruples I may have had; my overwhelming and perhaps uncontainable desire to save the estate blinded me to any consideration except to make sure that the marriage took place..."

"And you succeeded with God only knows what disastrous consequences for your daughter and myself."

"I was wrong," the duke admitted stiffly.

"Wrong! How could you be wrong! Augustus! Petty is wrong. How could she do this to me?" Her Grace's voice cracked and started to rise alarmingly. "She is an unnatural child, with no consideration for the sensibility of her mama, no, no feeling at all. She is selfish, thoughtless... Oh, will someone not help me..."

She seemed to stagger. Miss Chalfont, well inured to her ways, crossed quickly to her, assisting her to the chaise, saying in her soothing voice, "Come, Your Grace... Please sit."

Collapsing onto the sofa, sobbing with frustration, she waited. "Holtby... send me Holtby... at least she cares for my wellbeing... at least..."

"Be quiet! " the duke snapped. "Stop it, Julia."

This command had no effect on his wife whose sobs increased dramatically. Lord Milton shot a look at the good captain, who trod quickly to Her Grace's side and said quietly to Miss Chalfont, "Perhaps I can assist you to convey Her Grace to her bedchamber?"

Miss Chalfont grinned at him in relief. "Oh, thank you, sir, I would be most grateful." Together they lifted the duchess and propelled her across the room and into the arms of the indomitable Holtby, fortuitously entering at that precise moment. Miss Chalfont turned with a sigh of relief, and suddenly caught sight of her two younger charges, their eyes wide with fascination. She hurried them out of the room and off to the nursery, much to their dismay.

"Now that she has gone," continued the duke, "we can decide how best to find Perpetua."

The marquis and Lord Anthony stared at each other in frank amazement. They could never before remember an instance where the duke had not placated his wife's tantrums. A worried frown crossed their father's face.

"Edward is right. She is so young, so totally inexperienced. I hope she has reached Amelia without mishap. It is such a long way. I agree, though, there is nothing to be gained by departing tonight. If you are, indeed, sure that you want to go, Edward, please take Gideon with you. He is very familiar with the route.

You may both drive. Now, I think if you are to leave first thing we had better dine." He crossed and rang the bell, and the plan was agreed to, as John, his face inscrutable, arrived to announce dinner.

Chapter Five

P etty arrived in Bath in the late afternoon of the next day. She was icy cold, ravenously hungry, totally downhearted and overwhelmed by anxiety. She had spent a very uncomfortable night in the inn in Cheltenham. Fatigued by the events of the day she had gone to bed expectant of her usual repose, only to find that she tossed and turned all night. The unaccustomed noises of the post house kept her awake. Her heart beat like a drum inside her chest; unnerved by what she had done it seemed impossible to rest.

She rose as soon as it was light and proceeded to the tap room half expecting to find her irate father there preparing to drag her back to Wakeham in disgrace, but the only incumbent of the room was an elderly servant who was desultorily sweeping the floor. She enquired of this menial when the next stage to Bath would leave. He regarded her with a disdain engendered by years of contempt from his betters.

"Be gone half past this hour."

Petty was not quite sure whether he meant that it would be going in half an hour or whether it had just left. However, she deduced from the arm-waving that accompanied the short speech that if she proceeded to the yard she would be just in time. Although consumed by hunger she thought she had better not delay her departure, and she found when she reached the yard that this had been a wise decision as the coachman was about to blow the tin. She climbed aboard and prepared for another day of jolting, bumping discomfort.

The coach set her down in Bath at the White Hart Inn. This was a large bustling hostelry, accommodating the London coaches and possessing at least twenty postillions and several excellent well-matched teams. The establishment was presided over by a large woman who, as the wife of the purveyor of wines and spirits, regarded herself as very much the master, and was regarded by her numerous employees as very much the martinet. Her ideas did not include giving lodging to young females, dressed in dowdy clothes and not being escorted by any older female or abigail.

When Petty, white-faced with tiredness, approached her to beg a room for the night, her first instinct was to send her about her business, but it was her boast that she "knew her oats from her chaff", and she recognised quality, even shabby quality. So, somewhat reluctantly, she agreed to one night's accommodation, paid for in advance. She was mystified by Petty, and when this young lady announced that she was searching for a post as a governess and enquired most politely where she could obtain employment, her amazement was complete, but she directed her towards the registry in Well Street. In spite of her exhaustion Petty decided she must visit this establishment without delay.

The winter sunshine was fading fast and it was becoming very cold as she hurried along the narrow streets. Following the directions given to her by the landlady, eventually, after a few dead ends, she turned into Well Street, coming face to face with the huge red brick registry. She paused, swallowed hard, gave herself a shake and went inside. The hatchet-faced woman behind the desk looked her over with a penetrating stare.

"Yes?" she barked.

Petty, totally unused to being addressed in precisely that kind of tone, stiffened and said politely in her well-bred musical voice, "I am searching for work as a governess."

"Oh yes, and I suppose you have masses of experience and excellent references?" Hatchet Face said sarcastically.

"Well… no…" Petty returned. "But I have been well educated. I can read Latin and Greek and speak them, and French and mathematics…"

"Oh yes," Hatchet Face repeated, "and where is your proof, young lady?" she finished triumphantly.

Petty looked dismayed. It had not previously occurred to her that she would need proof or that she might have to produce references to get a job. She had, naively, imagined that her word would be adequate, and if not she could always demonstrate her literary powers. She now realised, with horror, her stupidity; of course no one would trust her without references. Tears sprang to her eyes.

Hatchet Face stood up. Pointing to the door, and speaking at the top of her hard unpleasant voice, she said, "Go on, get out. Do not waste my time. Stupid girl. Expecting a job, expecting to be a governess. No references. No doubt no experience. Now go, we do not find jobs for the likes of you."

Petty, her eyes clouded with tears and despair, turned blindly towards the door. In her distress she did not realise that a vast woman was blocking her path; she walked straight into her. A steadying hand caught her and a jolly voice asked, "Now, Mrs Friday, what is all this?"

Mrs Friday's, for this is what Hatchet Face was called, attitude changed remarkably. She grovelled ingratiatingly. "Oh, Mrs Lumley, I cannot apologise enough. This wretched girl, they expect everything, wants a job. Go on, get out with you." She waved at Petty, still being firmly held. "I am so sorry, Mrs Lumley, that you should be so inconvenienced."

Petty shot a look at this lady who had produced such a change in Mrs Friday, and in spite of her misery nearly laughed. Mrs Lumley was an amazing sight. She was very plump, dressed in the height of fashion in a most inappropriate gown of bright purple satin. Her pelisse was of bright pink merino, clearly made by a most superior modiste. On her head she wore a creation of flowers, feathers and bows in multi-coloured ribbon. She had a number of blonde curls which bobbed around under this huge cap, surrounded by multitudinous ornaments. Her cheeks were bright red and she possessed more chins than Petty had ever seen on a person before. However, when Petty met her eyes she found them as shrewd as they were kind. She was clearly a woman of some importance in Bath, judging by the change that had come over Mrs Friday when she appeared.

"Well? I asked for an explanation," Mrs Lumley demanded. Her eyes rested on Petty and took in every aspect of her clothing and condition. "It appears that this young lady wants a job."

"It would seem so," Mrs Friday crawled, "but no references, no character, no one will employ her like that."

Mrs Lumley looked at Petty, who was biting her lip trying not to cry and then back to Mrs Friday.

"Well! I will," she pronounced.

"No… please… it is not at all necessary." Mrs Friday was dismayed.

"Yes. I have a mind to have a well-bred companion for my Dora. She could do with a bit of polish, and it is obvious that this… what is your name, dear?"

"Petty," Petty interjected automatically, but as if she had not heard her Mrs Lumley continued, "This young lady is obviously a person of some quality and from what I heard, some education."

"We have only got her word for it," Mrs Friday objected.

"And why should we not believe her word, pray?"

"But I can… truly I can… please believe me I can do mathematics, French, Latin and Greek… only I am not very good at stitching," Petty always honest, admitted.

Mrs Lumley laughed, a deep-throated infectious cackle. "Do not fret, my dear, I am going to employ you. I do not think my

Dora is one for Latin, but if you can give her a touch of your quality, I shall be well satisfied."

"Oh, thank you. Thank you," Petty sniffed. "I am so grateful."

"Well now, do not cry. Would you prefer to come back with me now? Or would you like to start the post in a few days when you have told your family and made arrangements?"

"Oh, please, I would so like to come with you now, I have no family, well none that will be concerned about me," Petty amended. "But I have left my luggage at the White Hart. Maybe I should go first there to retrieve it."

Mrs Lumley's shrewd eyes rested on Petty. They took in her youth, her vulnerability and her obvious exhaustion.

"You look proper done in, my dear," she asserted. "I think it best to send Sam the coachman for them, once he has driven us home. You look in need of a good dinner, a warm fire and a soft bed." There was a slight sound of protest from Mrs Friday, which was quelled with a surprisingly fierce look from Mrs Lumley, who said in a dismissive way, "That will be quite enough from you, Mrs Friday." She then swept up her protégée, taking her arm and making slowly for the door and her waiting carriage.

Petty's eyes opened in astonishment when she saw this equipage. It was painted a violent pink; inside the luxurious upholstery was covered in gold brocade; the windows were garlanded with silk curtains of a red hue. However, these ostentatious deep silk cushions were exceedingly comfortable, and Petty sank back into them with a considerable sense of relief. Mrs Lumley watched her. She asked no questions, that was for the future.

In truth, she needed no companion for Dora but she had been intrigued by Petty. She had immediately understood, as Mrs Friday had not, the background from which Petty had come. She had never been privileged enough to mix in anything approaching that stratum of society herself and indeed would never expect to, but Mrs Lumley, who was in everything else all sense, had one small Achilles heel and that was her daughter. No social aspirations for herself would have entered Mrs Lumley's head but where Dora was concerned it was a different matter. Her overriding ambition, albeit a fairly hopeless one, was that Dora should have a season in London. She knew that it was a fanciful and unrealistic desire and that there really was no chance that it would ever come true, but she did allow herself this one small daydream, and it was this aspiration that had made her employ Petty. Her late husband had much believed in a maxim of readiness. "No good getting a chance if the preparedness was not there," he had been wont to say, and Mrs Lumley knew that he had been correct. Petty, she could see, was no governess, but she had been touched by her directness, by the sweet look in her clear eyes, by her unaffected and yet distinguished manner. Her intelligent face appealed to Mrs Lumley, and she was certainly not prepared to let an obviously innocent well-bred girl be left to the coils of the Mrs Fridays of this world.

The carriage drew up at 24 Laura Place. The house was a handsome six-storey building in the best part of town. Sam the coachman let down the steps and gave his arm to his mistress, who, through a practised procedure, managed to manoeuvre her large bulk out through the coach door and up the steps. The front door of this elegant mansion having been flung open by the butler, Petty jumped agilely down, refusing help, and followed Mrs Lumley into her house.

She entered the hall and looked with some surprise around her. Used to the understated elegance of the haut ton, her visiting confined to houses designed by the foremost artists of the day; Adam, Holland and William Kent; she was quite unprepared for the overdone extravagance that Mrs Lumley considered essential for her comfort. Mr Corringham, who had received the attractive commission of reconstructing the entire edifice on lines which his patron thought befitted a woman of her competence, had spared no expense decking the house in expensive objects, ormolu-decorated furniture and silk frills.

Mrs Lumley turned to her butler. "Hawley, be so good as to arrange a bedchamber for Mrs…" She turned to Petty.

"Blakeston?" Petty supplied quickly. She had had ample time during the journey from Cheltenham to think up a name for herself. She had been going to use Mrs Milton but had fast realised that any name that connected her to her previous life would enable them to trace her, in the unlikely expectation that they might want to find her, she thought, her mouth twisting slightly as she bit back the tears.

"Mrs Blakeston. Yes… tell Mrs Cardy, the Blue Room." Mrs Lumley had not missed the expressive thoughts that passed across Petty's pale face.

"The Blue Room, madam?" Hawley sounded surprised. The choice of the best spare bedchamber for this inconsequential girl astonished him.

He prided himself on his abilities and indeed he was exceptional at his job. Ambitious to a point and determined to finish up as butler in a mansion with a large staff under him, he had not yet had the privilege to work in a noble house in any capacity, and this limited experience meant that he did not instantly recognise Petty's quality, which she was at pains to disguise. Mrs Lumley's experience of the ton was also somewhat narrow but she, older and sharper, saw through Petty, realising that this plain slip of a girl was clearly a scion of distinguished parents.

"Mrs Blakeston is to be a companion to Miss Dora."

Hawley was more surprised than ever, but his mistress's voice was such as to brook no comment, so he merely bowed.

"Follow me please, ma'am."

Petty, lost in her own thoughts, and used all her life to being addressed as "my lady", made no move. This hesitation was not lost on Mrs Lumley who, looking at her shrewdly, merely said, "Do go to your room, my dear, and rest. You look fagged out."

"Oh... yes, how very... I mean... thank you," Petty, suddenly conscious of her mistake, replied in some confusion. Blushing slightly she picked up her skirts and followed Hawley up the imposing staircase.

The Blue Room was an elegant apartment, decorated in Mrs Lumley's inimitable style. Petty looked around her. The room was bright with candles and a large fire burnt in the grate. A huge four-poster bed, piled invitingly with frilled cushions and thick draperies, tempted her tired limbs. She was most appreciative of the unaccustomed luxury but was amused as she gazed around. She had not thought it was possible to have so many frills. When I am in bed I shall have to count them! she found herself giggling for the first time since her precipitate flight from Wakeham. She thought back on that awful morning of her wedding. Could it only have been yesterday? It seemed an age away.

She took off her cloak and pelisse and looked ruefully at her crumpled and travel-stained dress. She did have another but that was reposing in her portmanteau at the White Hart. She was just despairing of presenting a creditable appearance at dinner when there came a quiet scratch at the door. On being bidden to enter, the face of a young girl peeped around.

"I am Dora," she announced. "Please may I come in?"

Petty smiled and nodded. The young damsel who entered was about eighteen. She was not very tall; a small round face with gentle brown eyes sat on a slender neck, on the top of a pleasantly rounded figure. She had a cluster of pale brown curls gathered into a knot on the top of her head. She was dressed quite exquisitely. Mrs Lumley may have worn outfits which could only be considered as unsuitable in one of her bulk and age, but where Dora was concerned her taste was impeccable. She was attired for dinner in a gown which Petty, with her long experience of the duchess's wardrobe, quickly realised was very expensive. A silk overdress, delicately embroidered, covered a frilled muslin underskirt; the whole ensemble was in shades of pink, which set off Dora's fragile beauty to perfection. She was clutching an equally beautiful dress, which she shyly offered to Petty.

"Mama thought you would have nothing to change into, as your baggage is not with you, so we hoped that you would not object to wearing one of mine?" She regarded Petty with some anxiety and then added, "Oh dear, you are so much slimmer than I am, I do hope it will fit."

Petty, long inured to unsuitable and well-worn hand-me-downs from the statuesque members of her family, was grateful that at least Dora was of a height, and as she looked at the gown she was being offered, she realised that not only was it hardly worn, but quite exquisite.

"Please put it on. I will return in just a minute," Dora said shyly. She disappeared.

Petty stepped out of the dirty, ugly cambric, and slid the silk dress over her head. It was the softest, most beautiful thing she had ever worn. Mrs Lumley had chosen this particular dress from Dora's wardrobe with great care. The celestial blue set off Petty's eyes to perfection; the square-cut bodice showed off her delicate shoulders and the puffed sleeves edged with lace complemented her slim arms, enhancing her fragile frame. Dora returned, bringing with her a large bustling woman who looked Petty over suspiciously.

"This is Nurse," Dora explained. "She will alter the dress to fit."

Nurse looked Petty up and down; her face gave nothing away. Petty, well used to the vagaries of servants, held out her hand and said with a sweet smile, "I do hope I am not putting you to any trouble, Nurse." Her smile and the well-bred air won over this redoubtable lady in a trice.

"Not at all, miss, I will just see what can be done to make this acceptable. You is just a bit thinner than Miss Dora, and so pale, we will have to see what we can do to put some roses back in those cheeks."

"Thank you, Nurse," Petty replied with docility. She was used to the members of Nurse's worthy profession treating everyone as if they were still in leading strings. Nurse poked her in the ribs to see how the dress could be altered to fit and ordered Petty out of it. "Now, I will do a rough job on it for tonight and by tomorrow it will be perfect!"

Petty did not doubt it. She smiled at Nurse and Dora. "Thank you! Thank you, both! Thank you for your kindness."

CHAPTER SIX

I t was barely light the next morning when Lord Milton descended into the breakfast parlour, which at this hour was quite deserted. His Lordship rang for a footman, and while he awaited an answer to his summons he stood by the long windows and gazed out at the bare trees that bordered the park; pale pink winter sun cast streaks across the sky.

His Lordship sighed; what a coil he had got himself into, a coil quite of his own making; he did not care if he married the daughter of a duke, but Cuthbert had. He smiled ruefully to himself as he remembered the old man's face when Edward had informed him of his forthcoming nuptials, the beam of pleasure. A slight cough behind him made him turn to see Croft, who stood by the breakfast table escorted by two footmen.

"Good morning, my lord. Breakfast, my lord?" Edward nodded. "Immediately, Your Lordship." He waved to the footmen who proceeded to bring in and lay the covers for a plentiful meal. Croft meanwhile busied himself, supervising his inferiors, then when satisfied that all was to his standard he dismissed the footmen and, pouring His Lordship's tea, enquired: "At what time does Your Lordship plan to leave?"

Edward's mouth twitched. Servants such as Croft knew everything that went on. "As soon as Lord Slaughan is ready."

As he spoke, the marquis strolled into the room. "Good morning, Edward, Croft. What time do we depart?"

"As soon as possible." Edward sat at the table helping himself to the substantial feast that had appeared as if by magic. "Can I cut you some of this excellent tongue, Gideon?"

His new brother-in-law nodded agreement. As he did so, an unexpected arrival brought both men to their feet again. The duke entered. He was wearing a dressing robe of fine embroidered silk and his dark hair was carefully brushed; the blue eyes were warm as he extended his hand to his son-in-law. Nodding dismissal to Croft he sat down at the oval table, signalling as he did so for the marquis and Lord Milton to join him; he appeared faintly embarrassed.

"1 am glad that I caught you before you departed. I want to say how much I appreciate your actions…" He paused. "I think it may be preferable if we keep the story of Petty's disappearance to ourselves…" He poured himself a large cup of coffee and continued, "1 think Petty's wishes must be respected and thus, if you are agreeable, I do not intend to send the announcement to the Morning Post yet."

Lord Milton nodded acquiescence. Until he found Petty it was preferable that no one knew of the marriage.

"Please make sure that you keep me informed, Gidi, send…" he paused, "… as soon as you reach Amelia's, I shall not rest until I know that Perpetua is safe."

"Nor will l, sir," responded Edward. "Come, Gideon, I think the sooner we make a start the better." He shook the duke's hand. "Please do not worry. We will return your daughter with all haste."

Lord Milton drove his own carriage complete with a team of well-matched bays. He was an accomplished whipster, and Gideon, himself a member of the Four-in-Hand Club, found, slightly to his surprise, that he was most impressed by his new brother's handling of the ribbons.

 66

The first part of the journey was accomplished in silence. Edward drove stylishly but lost in thought; he was much regretting his hasty marriage. It had seemed the ideal solution to his need for a wife and an heir. To his need to re-establish his position in society. He had great love and respect for Cuthbert and he accepted that it was his grandfather's dearest wish to see his grandson take his rightful place in the world. Edward was not, personally, sure that this was so important, and comparing his parents' marriage with that of his new wife's parents', he knew which one he would want for himself. Although he now realised, sadly, that through his precipitate stupidity that happy companionship was never going to be his. He felt a deal of anger that he should have allowed himself to be persuaded into his present position. It was not like him, and now here he was chasing across England to try to retrieve a recalcitrant bride!

He was angry with the duke and even more with the indulged duchess, whose unnatural feelings towards her children, and especially Petty, he could neither approve nor respect. The heavy lines on his face grew more marked as he thought on the events of the previous six weeks, and more particularly those of the last twenty-four hours. His visage looked so forbidding and harsh, that Gideon, watching him carefully and comprehending his thoughts, felt moved to comment.

"Sorry you ever set eyes on us, eh?" he, half teasing, remarked. "Regretting your alliance already?"

Lord Milton jumped; a slight red flush coloured his face as he realised how accurately the marquis seemed to have gauged his thoughts. He turned and looked at Gideon in whose laughing deep blue eyes he read real sympathy.

"Damn it, how did you guess?" His Lordship answered wryly.

"It was not hard. My mama has hardly a conciliatory nature. I have rarely enjoyed anything as much as the trimming you gave her. It is about time somebody raked her down. It ought to be Papa but somehow... he just cannot seem to bring himself to..." He stopped.

"It is often very hard to be angry with those we love, even in their best interests," Lord Milton pointed out.

"Yes, but the thing is, I am not sure that he does love her anymore. He did of course. It was such a scandal. The Marquis of Slaughan throwing himself away on a portionless nobody with a beautiful face. He could have married anyone." He paused. "She can be very beguiling when she wants to be, of course."

"I know."

The marquis hooted with laughter. "Oh yes, I saw you being given the full treatment. It is a lesson, not to be taken in by sweet faces and simpering ways. I for one do not intend to fall into that trap."

"I should not have addressed her in that way though. My grandfather, Cuthbert, would have taken me to task if he had thought I had so betrayed my upbringing as to speak to a duchess in such an improper fashion."

Gideon laughed. "Your grandfather?"

"Yes, on my mother's side. My paternal grandfather, Lord Milton, whose name I now bear, would never meet me or my sister. He considered that my father had married to displease him, a girl who could never be regarded as acceptable." His voice was hard and the harsh face inscrutable. "My mother was wonderful, intelligent and beautiful. She doted on my father and he on her. She died when my sister Aurelia was born. I was privileged in that I had such a happy, loving infancy, whereas poor Aurelia never knew her. My father died within months of her. He had been saddened by the attitude adopted by his family towards us, but his love for my mother made up for this loss of family; once she had gone I think he had nothing left to live for. He wrote constantly to Lord Milton but was always repulsed. I am told His Lordship regarded my father as dead. It must have hurt Papa so much. I was fifteen, 1... I do not imagine that I comprehended the depth of the pain caused by my grandfather's intransigence."

Edward, who was usually a reserved character, found himself confiding in Gideon in a most unexpected way. He did not quite know why he was doing it. He liked his new brother and felt a strange closeness to him. Gideon did not find it odd; he was experiencing the same feelings. Edward continued his story.

"Cuthbert brought us up, well, I thought I was grown up, one does at sixteen, but Aurelia was a baby. I am afraid he spoilt her terribly. He loves her so much and could refuse her nothing."

Gideon noticed how his voice had become warmer and the harsh lines softened as he talked of his grandfather and sister. "Tell me about Cuthbert."

Edward smiled. "You really want to know?"

Gideon nodded. Edward paused awhile to negotiate a tricky corner. He kept horses on the road to Yorkshire and the team of greys that had replaced the bays when they changed horses were, the marquis observed, out-and-out goers. Now they were allowed their heads, and Gideon was permitted to see his new brother driving to an inch along the main thoroughfare north.

"Cuthbert? Well, he is a most remarkable person. Gruff, large. Dresses the gentleman, yet his origins always apparent, not that he tries to hide them. Indeed, he is inordinately proud of retelling the story of his rise from humble cottage to possession of half a county. He is blunt, honest; I would trust him above anyone. He adored my mother and I think part of him died when she did, but he would never admit it. He transferred all his love onto us, well, particularly Aurelia, who reminded him so much of my mother. Headstrong, beautiful, beguiling and an heiress! I have my work cut out, I can assure you."

Gideon smiled. "Perhaps I should make her acquaintance?"

Edward gave a crack of laughter. "From what I know of your reputation, young man, I cannot imagine a more disastrous course! I would be then forever hauling you both out of scrapes!"

Gideon, who had had no prior opinions of this new brother found himself liking him and enjoying his company in an entirely unexpected way. The marquis, as most of his class, mixed almost exclusively with members of the ton. Edward most certainly did not. This, and the difference in their ages, meant their paths had not previously crossed, but Gideon was impressed by Edward's honesty and straightness, as well as by his obvious intelligence and humour. He found it as easy to confide in him as Edward had in Gideon.

"Your grandfather seems altogether more desirable than mine, His Grace Gideon Augustus Gillespie Henry Mordaunt, Baron Handley, Earl of Wakeham, Marquis of Slaughan, seventh Duke of Staplefield. Indeed I bear his name!"

He grinned at Edward. "Let me see if I out grandfather you. Mine was quite frankly a blackguard! Immoral, an inveterate gamester, he played high. Invariably lost. If you could have seen the company he kept. The most repellent, odious libertines that have been known this many a year. Added to which he was an intimate of Her Grace the Duchess of Devonshire; they gambled compulsively together. She, I believe, was quite enchanting, and my grandfather developed a tendre for her which seemed to oblige him to lose vast fortunes to her regularly. At least the fair Georgiana was an acceptable liaison. In addition, unfortunately he also maintained a series of undesirable mistresses, whom he indulged with a profligacy which dismayed my aunts, my father, indeed all the family. He could not be brought to any sense of his obligation towards us. He spent liberally on himself, his women, and his gambling. The estates were mismanaged, mortgaged up to the hilt; parts had to be sold. You may think badly of my father but he struggled to keep the family from going quite under."

"Your grandfather died quite recently I believe?" Edward enquired.

"Lor, do you not know what happened?"

Edward shook his head. They had reached a stretch of open country, and skilfully he sprung the greys, increasing their speed effortlessly. Gideon watched in admiration of the choice of cattle and the consummate driving skill, then continued, "My grandfather frequented most gaming houses, not only White's, Brooks', Almack's, Boodle's and Watier's but also many of the latest and less respectable hells, those of an undesirable nature where the object is to fleece green young men and sanguine old ones. It was June, the day had been exceedingly hot, and the customary evening coolness had not been realised. I had spent the evening with Freddie Crespigny Lucy and Hugh Werdon. It had been an entertaining night and we were all thoroughly foxed when Freddie suggested we try Trevor's. It was my first visit to this newest of establishments, we do not favour gaming hells in our house, you understand! I was too disguised to make objection in this case, so off we went to Hill Street, full of gusto, rolling in as merry as a band of Robins.

"My first impression when we entered was of the heat, which was overpowering. It was clear Trevor had spent liberally; the rooms were alight with candles. Floor-length gold mirrors decorated every wall, the hangings and furniture plush in cream brocade. I saw His Grace immediately; he was with Sir Godfrey Webster and Lord Brockleway. The sight of Grandpapa sobered me up in a wink, but naturally his presence did not have the same beneficial effect on Freddie and Hugh. I grabbed Freddie by the arm and vainly tried to make him leave.

"'No, old boy, got to have a bet, got to have a win, good place this, all the go,' he objected.

"'Freddie.' I pulled his arm, desperately signalling to Hugh, who was glassily eyeing the chandeliers, to help me. His Grace had gone into the large saloon where faro was being played. I had just managed to persuade Freddie and Hugh to leave with me, when I heard an altercation taking place in the faro room. It was His Grace's voice and he seemed to be arguing vociferously. I dropped Freddie's arm and changed direction.

"'I say, old boy, I thought you wanted to leave. Make your mind up,' he vouchsafed loudly.

"'Shh… shh… His Grace,' I whispered, pointing at the saloon. He moved unsteadily towards the double doors. I hurriedly followed him, slipping into the rear of the room behind Freddie, who was weaving his way rather precipitously across towards the faro table. Horrified I heard His Grace's voice ring out. He had clearly been imbibing for several hours and was three sheets to the wind, as was his opponent, whom I recognised as Sir Stanley Melville.

"My heart sank. I knew this meant trouble, the enmity between the Melvilles and the Mordaunts goes back ages. No one quite knows how it started but I think my grandfather fought a duel with Sir Stanley Melville years ago. Aunt Elizabeth hints that Sir Stanley tried to elope with my grandmother, which could have been the cause. Grandmama was possessed of a not inconsiderable fortune, and the Melvilles never have a feather to fly with, indeed I believe they are starving off the creditors at this very moment. I understand, when he was young, Grandfather had had an incident with Francis Melville, but the family had hushed it up and I never knew what actually had occurred.

"'How dare you, Sir Stanley. I mark the cards? I cheat? You know not what you say. The honour of the Mordaunts is at stake. Name your seconds.' His Grace pulled out a small pistol and started waving it about in the air. I heard his words with horror. Grandpapa was a rogue, but I do not believe he was a cheat. I pushed my way across the suddenly silent room.

"'Grandpapa,' I pleaded, trying to reach for the gun.

"'Get out of my way.' He was white with anger. He pushed me aside. In spite of his excesses he was still a very strong man and l, a trifle bosky, was unsteady on my feet.

Sir Stanley laughed; the jeering sound echoed across the room; his sneering face contorted with hatred, taunted, 'Cheat! Cheat! You cheat… the cards are marked.'

The excessive heat and the ancient feud between the families had turned him mad with rage. He had lost all sense of control and my grandfather was not much better. They stood like two fighting dogs spitting and snarling at each other.

"'Name your seconds.' Grandfather could hardly speak for the fury that consumed him.

"'No… no… you must not… Grandpapa!' For the second time I tried to intervene. He was far too old for a duel and God knows, we could not afford another scandal to our name. It was now Sir Stanley's turn to push me aside.

"'Out of the way, lying, deceitful, mendacious boy, trying to protect your grandfather. The Mordaunts are cheats, liars, blackguards.' In his anger he had lost control of what he was saying and by this time I was so furious myself, and still not completely sober, that I think I could have strangled him myself."

"Perfectly understandable," murmured His Lordship. By this time the light was fading. It had grown very cold and Edward had decided that they must find lodging for the night, but not before the end of Gideon's story, as he realised the importance of the young man having a chance to unburden himself to a disinterested party. So he slowed the horses and bade Gideon continue.

The marquis did so in strained tones. "Grandfather sprang out onto Sir Stanley, they were grappling like a pair of fighting cocks. 'How dare you! We Mordaunts do not cheat.' He was struggling for breath; I was frantically trying to get free so that I could separate them, but Sir Geoffrey Bone, an unpleasant crony of Sir Stanley's, had me in a vice-like grip. 'Name your seconds. Lord Brock will act for me.' He nodded at the poor Lord Brockleway, who started to protest vociferously.

"'Grandpapa, stop! You cannot… you must not fight a duel… Freddie, Hugh, stop him. Please someone stop him.' Sir Geoffrey had my arms pinioned to my sides. Hugh and Freddie just stood and gaped and the whole company seemed as if struck to stone.

"Grandpapa and Sir Stanley were now struggling in a most undignified fashion, when there was a loud retort. The gun went off. Everyone jumped. His Grace fell to the floor. Sir Geoffrey let me go. I rushed across to Grandfather; he was bleeding copiously and a horrible blue colour seemed to be spreading over him. I clutched his hand.

"'My boy... tell... done for... tell your father... l... had a... time.' He was unable to get any more words out. Then he was gone. I sat stunned, his head in my lap.

"The room, which had been utterly silent, suddenly filled with babble. I was aware that Sir Stanley's friends were hustling him away. Which was probably the best thing to do, matters needed to be hushed up, nothing to be gained by an investigation of the circumstances. They were both idiotic old men. In their cups, behaving as if they were seventeen. The cards were not marked, of course."

"Hard on you." Edward smiled understandingly.

"Yes, I did not like him much... but he was my grandfather. The family were all secretly delighted... but I still feel strange. It was his dying in my lap, I suppose."

A slightly pained look flitted across his face. He screwed up his eyes as if to protect against the rapidly setting sun.

Glancing at Gideon, Edward remarked, "I think we had better stop for the night."

Due to the excellence of His Lordship's driving and the superiority of the cattle which he kept on the route to Yorkshire, the two brothers arrived in record time. As they swept up the drive of Charlsdon House, Edward was conscious of a feeling of anxiety, which he suspected that Gideon shared. He hoped that Petty had arrived here and that she was safe. She seemed so young and inexperienced to travel that distance alone, and in winter. No sooner were they drawn up outside the imposing portals of my Lord Edgerton's house, than Gideon leapt down and hammered on the door. It was opened by an elderly butler, whose face beamed with pleasure as he beheld the young marquis.

"My Lord Gideon…" Words overcame him.

"Hello, Beasely. Where is Petty?" Gideon demanded.

"Lady Perpetua?" The elderly retainer looked perplexed.

At that moment the stately figure of the Lady Edgerton appeared at the top of the impressive stairway. Clearly in her youth she had been a great beauty and the ravages of time had not wrought too heavy a price on her. She was still a very good-looking woman with the Mordaunt eyes and excellent complexion.

"Gideon, my dear boy, quite delightful, how perfectly wonderful to see you. To what do we owe the pleasure of this visit?"

She swept down the stairs holding out her hands to her favourite nephew. As she reached the bottom she was suddenly aware that he was not alone. She raised an enquiring eyebrow at Gideon, whilst her sharp eyes searchingly examined every aspect of Lord Milton.

"Oh, Aunt Amelia. Lady Edgerton, may I present Lord Milton, Petty's husband."

The eyebrows shot up. "Petty's what?"

"Lady Perpetua has done me the honour to become my wife, did she not inform you?" Edward kissed the outstretched hand. "Enchanted to make Your Ladyship's acquaintance. I can see that you must be a Mordaunt, the only family in the land with such looks." He smiled his most appealing smile. The hard textures softened. Aunt Amelia, never impervious to flattery, nodded gracefully.

"Beasely, see that rooms are prepared for my nephews. Bring some refreshments to the library, tell Mrs Beasely to order dinner to be delayed by an hour." Her instructions completed she led the way into the book room.

"Now, you two tell me what this is all about. I want to hear all about this marriage and want to know what brings you all the way into Yorkshire with such speed?"

"We have come for Petty, of course." Gideon's explanation clearly astonished her.

"Petty? Here? Surely, if you have just married her she ought to be with you." She directed a piercing look at Edward.

"Quite true, Your Ladyship."

"I have not seen Perpetua since last year."

"Oh, come, Aunt Amelia, do not hide her. She must be here. She told Anthony she would run away to you."

"Run away to me! What on earth are you talking about? Come, I think some explanations are in order, but first some refreshment." She nodded to Beasely, who had entered with a tray. "Have you driven all the way from Wakeham?"

"Well, Edward drove and damned fine driving it was too." He waited for the old butler to hand him a drink and withdraw and then continued, "But yes, from Wakeham. We... well... I felt convinced that Petty must be here... you see she did not want to be forced into a marriage. It was not you, Edward, she would have felt like that whomsoever Papa made her marry."

"I see," Edward commented, his face grim.

"Anyway, Aunt Amelia, Petty did consent to marry Edward. She really had no choice. You know how Papa puts her in a quake and Mama would be completely unsympathetic if she thought she was going to be better circumstanced by Petty's marriage. Which indeed she was. So she wed Edward and then... well, I fear she must have bolted..."

"I see." Her Ladyship repeated Lord Milton's words, regarding him with some disdain. "And why, may I ask, did you permit an unwilling bride to be forced on you? It sounds most medieval to me."

"You may well ask," Edward started but before he could continue Gideon interrupted.

"No, no, Aunt Amelia, you mistake. You have it wrong. Edward is a prime 'um. He had no idea she felt as she did. Papa told a whole collection of lies about how happy she was to marry Edward... the settlements, you see," he finished, somewhat shamefacedly.

"I am also to blame. I should have tried to set Petty's mind to rest. I had intended to once I got her away from Wakeham, but it seems I made a proper bungle of it."

"Oh no, Lord Milton," Her Ladyship intervened dryly, "it cannot be seen to be your fault. Augustus always lacked for sense, and as for Julia, well, she is a creature quite without compunction, I am afraid." She stopped as she became aware of the fact that although Lord Milton was now her nephew he was also still a comparative stranger. "But I should not talk thus."

"The duchess never thinks of anyone but herself, selfish to a point," the furious bridegroom added helpfully.

"Quite. My sentiments exactly. I see that we shall go on very well. You have my sister-in-law's measure precisely."

"Well, now you know the truth no need to hide Petty from us any longer," said the marquis.

Her Ladyship looked deeply concerned. "I was not hiding anything. Petty did not come here. I wish that she had."

Edward and Gideon exchanged speaking looks. "Indeed," Edward's worried voice continued, "if Petty did not come here, then where did she go?"

CHAPTER SEVEN

Petty woke with a start. She had no idea where she was.
Pale winter sunshine was streaming through a gap in the
ornate curtains. A momentary feeling of unease when she
could not remember what had happened quickly gave way to
amused recognition as her eyes alighted on the opulence of Mrs
Lumley's decor. She stretched pleasurably; the unaccustomed
convenience made her smile to herself; as the eldest daughter
of one of England's premiere dukes she had endured a level of
discomfort that would only be borne by the lowliest of servants in
most households. Now, as a governess, here she was luxuriating
in this most comfortable of beds, a fire burning brightly in the
grate and a room that was as warm as it was welcoming. She
thought briefly of her mama. The duchess would most certainly
not approve of such an indulgence towards her daughter.
Thoughts of her family made a fresh wave of misery waft over
her. She pushed away memories of Wakeham and Fonty and her
brothers; nothing would be served by dwelling on her home;
much better not to think of these individuals, it would only lead
to unhappiness.

Resolutely taking hold of herself she climbed out of bed and
pulled back the curtains; the light made her blink; however, as
she became accustomed to it she peered through the windows.
She had been too tired the night before to take stock of her

surroundings, but now she wanted to see where she was. Her room overlooked Laura Place; this she could see was an elegant thoroughfare, obviously in the best part of town. Mrs Lumley's house stood on the edge of a small but very pretty park, which Petty could see quite clearly. Winter sunshine illuminated the pale, white heads of the early snowdrops which grew in profusion all over the lawns, and bathed in light a small but pleasant summerhouse which nestled in the corner of a copse. It was charming and Petty could imagine very pleasant walks along its paths. She had never visited Bath before but from what she could see of the town she thought it would be delightful. Feeling more cheerful, she decided she had better discover her duties. Glancing at her clock, she was shocked to discover that it was nearly ten o'clock. She had never been allowed such lenience at home; even when she had attended balls her mama insisted that she rise at the usual time. Guiltily she thought she had better dress. The drab cambric had obviously been sponged and pressed. Petty put it on. Shapeless and brown it made her look a dowd, but then, weren't governesses meant to look plain? She sighed, remembering last night's dress, soft silk against her skin. She sighed again.

She peeped out of her room; no one appeared to be about. She found that she was very hungry. As she made her way down the sweeping staircase, sunlight poured from the skylight, making the house seem alive and welcoming. She stood in the hall, uneasily, trying to decide which door would be most likely to lead to the breakfast room, when Hawley appeared. He regarded her haughtily and led her, without words, into the parlour.

"Mrs Lumley requests your attendance at eleven o'clock in the saloon," was his only comment.

He withdrew, leaving her alone. A healthy repast was laid out on the sideboard. Petty helped herself to coffee from a silver urn, sweetmeats from a cut glass bowl, and rolls and buns which were nestling in a china basket. She sat down at the marquetry breakfast table. She found the decoration in Mrs Lumley's house something of a puzzle. Used to the understated taste of the haut ton, she had not as yet encountered the ostentatious ebullience of very rich persons who were not of the first order.

Having made a hearty breakfast, she was just wondering what to do next when the door opened and Dora bounced in. She was enchantingly dressed in a pelisse of aubergine drab, double-caped over a white muslin dress, adorned with knots in pink and green. She wore half boots of the finest green kid, and this elegant toilette was completed by a bonnet which framed her enchanting face. She smiled at Petty.

"I do hope you slept well. I have been out walking with the Simpsons, Cecily is my particular friend, we've been to Hobsons, the lending library, I have two new novels, maybe you have read them?"

She handed them over to Petty, and went on without stopping, "Have you read Waverley? It was most amusing. Cecily has a dear little dog, she's called Dottie, she is so terribly sweet, I cannot wait to show her to you. I must ask Mama if I may have one. Do you have a dog? I have wanted one so much," she bubbled along. "Cecily is to come out this season, her aunt, who is Lady Hamel…"

Encountering a quizzical look from Petty, which she misinterpreted, she apologised. "Oh, listen to me, prattling on about people you could not possibly know. I am so sorry."

But in this she was wrong. Petty remembered well this redoubtable female, blessed with a beak nose and crossed eyes who had looked her over and pronounced to the duchess, "My dear, what a plain girl, a throwback, without doubt. How very strange that you, my dear Julia, and Augustus should have produced such an unexceptional and ordinary girl. No conversation, no looks, no fortune. My dear, how will you make a conformable alliance for her?"

So Petty remembered Lady Hamel very well. So disconcerted had she been by this cruel forthrightness that she had cried for quite a week, realising that her chances were quite hopeless.

She was brought back from her musings by Dora, who continued breathlessly, "Her aunt has asked her to London for her come-out, she is to share a ball with her cousin, The Hon. Sophie. I believe she is a great beauty and Cecily says has the most charming temperament."

"Oh no," Petty protested, "a most ugly and disagreeable girl."

She stopped, perceiving the surprised look on Dora's face. Fortunately for her the haughty Hawley appeared.

"Mrs Lumley will see you now, Mrs Blakeston," he remarked with disdain.

Petty followed his frigid back up the stairs and into the saloon. This was another well-proportioned room, dressed in what Petty was beginning to discover was Mrs Lumley's customary style. The primary colour in this room seemed to be pale green: the walls were pale green silk; all the draperies decorated with the usual frills were another shade of green. The furniture consisted of some exquisite Sheraton side tables and some, to Petty's eyes, very ugly overdone ormolu cabinets. Chairs and chaises were in yet another shade of green silk; the room made Petty feel as if she were in overgrown forest, or perhaps under the sea. She wished she had someone with whom to share her amusement.

"I see that you are admiring my room. Gorgeous, is it not?" Mrs Lumley, resplendent in another creation of cerise and lilac, her vast coiffeur decorated with caps and yet more frills, remarked. She smiled encouragingly at Petty and, patting the sofa, said, "Come, my love, here, sit by me." The warmth and kindness in her voice made a lump come to Petty's throat. People did not usually address her in just such a gentle way. She crossed and sat next to Mrs Lumley's ample form.

"Mrs Lumley," she started, "I do not know how to begin to thank you… I am… really so grateful… I do not know what would have happened to me if you had not come along at that moment," Petty continued in a suffocated voice.

Mrs Lumley pressed her hand. "Well, I did, so no need for you to get worried now. I mean to make sure that you come to no harm, my dear, but have you no family whom you should inform that you are here?" The kind eyes looked keenly at Petty.

"No… no… there is no one. I am a widow. My parents are dead. I have no brothers or sisters," Petty lied unconvincingly.

Mrs Lumley watched her. "Well, if you find you have letters to dispatch, give them to Hawley. He will make sure they are sent immediately."

This gentle suggestion did serve to remind Petty of the problem of her family, how to reassure them, or at least Fonty, that she was safe. She could not write because if she did so, she was sure the duke, or perhaps Lord Milton, would be down upon her, angrily dragging her back to Wakeham and her fate. She shuddered. Mrs Lumley missed nothing of the thoughts that crossed her mobile face, but she made no comment for the present.

To her, Petty seemed like a small, frightened animal. She did not know what it was that made Petty so scared of her family but she meant to find out.

"I think we shall deal very well together," Mrs Lumley continued. "You have met my Dora, the sweetest of girls, but lacks polish, which is where you come in, my love. I do not need you to teach Dora Latin or mathematics. Indeed, I do not think she has the brain to understand those things. No, what I want you to do, is to give her some of what you have, that well-bred quality, that town polish."

Petty started; she just controlled an irrepressible giggle that threatened to pop out. The idea that she could give anyone town polish! How the duchess and her more imposing friends would have sneered at such a preposterous notion.

"As you can see, no bones, my sweet. I am from simple stock. My dear papa was the village schoolmaster. I, though you may find it hard to credit now, was the belle of the village."

Petty tried hard to curb her surprise. Mrs Lumley smiled understandingly.

"Mr Lumley swept me off my feet. My papa did not like me marrying trade. Beneath me, he thought! Did very well for himself Mr Lumley did, I need not tell you, my love, very well for himself. Left me, and his dearest daughter, extremely well provided for. After his untimely demise, I came to Bath, thought it would be a genteel place to bring up Dora, and it is, and it is. She is accepted everywhere, attends all the best parties." She laughed suddenly. "Well, she would of course, all the best parties given by me!"

Her deep-throated chuckle was very infectious and Petty found herself succumbing to a fit of giggles.

"That's the ticket. A bit of merriment bucks up the spirits no end, and yours look as if they could do with a lot of improving." She looked Petty over shrewdly but with such kind eyes that Petty found she could not object. "Looks need improvement too, if you do not mind my saying so. Basic material good, finish awful. You will never be a great beauty, my dear, but when I, Gertrude Lumley, have had the dressing of you, you will do very well."

All this was said with such benevolence that Petty could take no offence; she thought she ought to protest but Mrs Lumley continued, "Now I digress. I will not apologise for that, my dear. If I did every time I went off the thread I would be doing it all my days." She laughed again. "Now, I was telling you what I want from you. Petty, was it? I cannot call you Mrs Blakeston. I think we are going to be great friends."

Petty rather thought they were too. She smiled inwardly to herself. She did not think the duchess would approve of such a friendship, but Petty did not care. No, she did not care at all.

"Let me confide in you, my dear, the dreams of a foolish old woman. No! I am…" she repeated as Petty made to demur, "… a foolish, doting mama! I have a wish, a silly wish… an impossible wish… an improbable dream. We ought to dream. Without dreams mountains are not climbed, battles are not won, states are not freed, music is not written, paintings are not created." She stopped. Petty found her philosophy interesting and endearing. No one at Wakeham would have bothered to think in precisely that way.

"But to my dream. My dearest wish… it is… You see, I would like Dora to have a come-out, to do the season."

Petty was astonished. It was hard to know what she had expected, but certainly not that! A come-out was so automatic in the circles in which she moved that she had never thought of it as anything other than an uncomfortable necessity, to be endured rather than enjoyed, and the idea that anyone could wish that on her daughter seemed faintly absurd.

Mrs Lumley went on. "You see, I love my Dora. Just one season of balls and gaiety. I am so proud of her. Well, all mamas are, I suppose."

Petty grimly thought of her mama. Proud was hardly an adjective she would use to describe the way the duchess felt. Her expression was not lost on Mrs Lumley, but she said nothing, merely continuing, "She is such a lovely girl, it must be thought a pity if the only young men she meets are the gallants in Bath. She has to have… the chance… it is the pinnacle," Petty choked. "Did you have a season, my dear?"

Petty, incurably honest, could not deny that she had.

"I thought so. It will not seem much to you. You've always moved in the best circles… Oh… you cannot fool me, I am not a green girl. Hawley may not recognise it, but I did the instant I set eyes on you. Even in that dreadful dress, all crumpled, your hair dressed goodness knows how. All haggard you were, but it shone through, oh yes it shone through. It is what I want for

Dora. Oh, I realise it will probably never happen but we must be best prepared. Mr Lumley used to say, 'Preparedness is all,' and who am I to deny that my beloved husband was always right! I want you to prepare my Dora. She must know how to behave. She must know who is who. She must know what to do if ever she is lucky enough to be asked to Almack's. You do know that, don't you?"

Petty nodded. She was about to protest that it was all very silly, the season, Almack's. Then she realised for the first time that it was easy for her, who had lived in that world all her life, to despise it, but to others it was all important. She held her tongue.

"Of course I will help Dora," she replied. "It is such a little thing to do in exchange for all your kindness to me." Privately she decided that it would probably be easier to teach Dora about the Lady Hamels, Lady Jerseys and who was who, than it would be to impart a love of the classics to a girl whose intellectual pretensions she guessed would be rather meagre. "Oh yes, I would enjoy that above all things."

She smiled at Mrs Lumley, who responded much surprised. She had seen Petty, as the duchess before her, as a small dab girl, but Petty's smile was unexpectedly enchanting. It lit up her wonderful eyes and her face changed, becoming almost beautiful, full of life and sweetness. Mrs Lumley, never one to miss a challenge quickly, moved to her next point.

"Now we come to the next part of my proposition. I must have the dressing of you, my dear. I cannot permit any companion to Dora to be seen in the shabby vestments that seem to compose your wardrobe. You will forgive me, but as Mr L. said, I call a spade a spade. You must be dressed in the height of fashion."

Petty made to protest, but was cut short by Mrs Lumley.

"I insist, my dear! Call it a uniform for the job. Or perhaps you prefer to return to Mrs Friday?" Her voice sounded severe but when Petty looked into her eyes she saw that they were twinkling. Smiling, she shook her head.

"That's the ticket. I like beautiful things around me. At my time of life I do not want to be seeing shabby brown merino. It gives me no pleasure!" Petty burst out laughing. "I love new clothes, don't you?"

"I do not know," Petty replied truthfully. "I have never had anything new made for me."

Mrs Lumley's eyes opened with genuine shock. "What!" She reached for her fan, fanning herself hard. "Well, it is about time you did. No time like the present. Ring for Hawley, my love, and ask him to order the carriage, we are going shopping!"

The projected trip to Madame Camille was wonderful to Petty. Not being privy to the duchess's shopping trips, she had never experienced anything like it herself. They were ushered into an expensive-looking salon in Milsom Street, as if they were royalty. Madame Camille, curtseying low, was clearly somewhat surprised when she heard what her commission was to be.

However, when she discovered the extent of the wardrobe she was to provide for Petty, she became all compliance and entered wholeheartedly into the scheme. Numerous day and evening dresses were paraded before Petty's eyes and she discovered that whatever mistakes Mrs Lumley may have made about her own dressing, she had immaculate taste where Petty and Dora were concerned. Anything in yellow or red was dismissed with a wave, and Mrs Lumley concentrated on blues and greens. Petty, trying several times to protest as yet more dresses were added to the pile, was merely questioned about a return to Mrs Friday. In the end she abandoned further attempts and joined in, enjoying herself hugely. When eventually the carriage was summoned there were so many band boxes and parcels that Petty thought she might have to walk, as there seemed no possible way that they could all fit inside. However, Sam managed to see everything safely bestowed and the party returned to Laura Place.

Petty settled happily into life in Bath with the Lumleys. The only flaw in her pleasure was a certain guilt about her family; she would have liked to let them know she was safe, but knew not how to do so. She consoled herself with the thought that they would probably be not much worried about her. *I expect they have forgotten me by now,* she allowed herself to believe. Although in her heart she knew this was not the case, and it nagged at the back of her mind somewhat, but in a round of pleasure it always seemed something to be dealt with tomorrow.

In the meantime, life was so pleasant. Mrs Lumley and Dora led a deliciously indolent life. They spared themselves nothing; no small luxuries were denied to them. They were possessed of a wide acquaintance in Bath and were constantly asked to all the best soirees, concerts and evening parties. Petty accompanied them, attired in the new and extensive wardrobe that had arrived from Madame Camille with all possible speed, her hair dressed in a becoming style arranged by Mrs Lumley's hairdresser.

She soon found herself all the rage. This was a completely new sensation for her. In her London seasons she had been renowned for her lack of success; unbecomingly dressed, watched over and constantly put down by the duchess and her formidable cronies, Petty had become more and more gauche, losing any ability to converse sensibly that she might have possessed, regarding everything she said as idiotic. She became more and more withdrawn, more and more miserable. Every evening was an endurance test which she could not wait to end. But Bath. Oh, how different! She found that she was very popular. No longer inhibited and scared to speak, she found that she could both amuse and interest others through her conversation. It was a new and altogether gratifying sensation. She found she much looked forward to her visits to the pump room and assembly rooms. Mrs Lumley's acquaintances treated her with flattering attention and she was soon a firm favourite with the ladies of Bath.

She found that, contrary to her expectations, she particularly enjoyed the company of Mrs Simpson, who was as different from her sister Lady Hamel as was possible to imagine. She was in her mid-forties but looked much younger. Time had been kind to her, but her own relaxed and amiable nature had no doubt contributed to her considerable good looks. None of this could be said to be true of Her Ladyship, whose authoritarian nature and overinflated idea of her own self-esteem had made her face set in rigid lines, and her mouth fix in an unpleasant line. Mrs Simpson's daughter, Cecily, Dora's friend, was an altogether delightful girl. She had inherited her mother's amiable nature, but in addition to that she had an excellent brain and had been well educated, Mr Simpson believing that all his children should have access to good literature, language, philosophy and a working knowledge of politics. Petty found it a refreshing change to discuss matters with her, for Dora, although blessed with the sweetest of natures, had no intellectual pretentions. She was sorry to see Cecily and her mama depart for the much-regarded season.

Petty had also slowly gathered a small court of admirers around her, not high flyers but most agreeable nonetheless. The principal of these was Mr Gray, a charming man in his early thirties, educated and popular. He was famed for his address. He would stand up with the youngest and shyest girl in need of a partner, rapidly putting her at her ease with his unaffected manners and warm concern. His good breeding, his punctuality and ability to converse with anyone, made him a great favourite with the hostesses. He lived with his ailing mother in Camden Place, and was kindness itself to her, earning praise from all quarters for his heedfulness. He was assiduous in his pursuit of Petty, but as this was executed with such gentleness she never felt intimidated or nervous.

Petty had never enjoyed herself so much before. Her duties were hardly arduous, and one delightful week slipped into another. The bulbs came up, the evenings lengthened, walking in the park the smell of the spring flowers filled the air with a delicate scent. Bath was slowly filling with more visitors; those that were not part of the London season came to Bath.

One particular morning in May, Dora, Mrs Lumley and Petty were in the morning room discussing the previous night's concert.

"I have rarely heard Mozart played as well!" pronounced Mrs Lumley; Petty had been surprised by her obvious pleasure and appreciation of music.

"I do agree," Petty responded. "I do so wish that I could play the piano like that!"

"I like the way you play," Dora responded stoutly. She was by now devoted to Petty and felt that she could do no wrong.

Petty laughed. "Oh, Dora, you are so kind, but indeed I cannot play Mozart as well as that."

"I think you play better."

The outcome of this discussion was postponed by Hawley, who announced the arrival of two popular visitors: "Mrs Darby and Miss Darby."

Emma Darby was a particular friend of Dora's, and the two girls fell upon each other as eighteen-year-old damsels are wont to do, rapidly exchanging opinions on the apparel worn by their close friends at last night's concert, and the plans for the next entertainment.

"I trust I find you in the best of health, Mrs Lumley." Mrs Darby was a thin woman with no shoulders and sharp eyes that did not miss anything. She was dressed in the first stare of fashion and prided herself on the knowledge she possessed of the world and entertainment. She engaged in the friendliest of rivalry with Mrs Lumley to see who could host the best parties. Mrs Lumley usually won, but it must be said that Mrs Darby was a worthy opponent!

"And you, dear Mrs Blakeston, blooming as usual, Bath certainly agrees with you. Or perhaps it is the attentions of our dear Mr Gray?" Petty blushed rosily at this forthright allusion. She was as yet not accomplished enough to depress pretension and was left feeling slightly uneasy by comments such as these.

"Now, I expect you wonder at the reason for my visit, not that I think I need a reason to visit my dear friends. We do not stand on ceremony, do we, my dear Mrs Lumley? But today I do have something special to impart. I am intending to give an evening party next Tuesday for my dear sister who will be staying in the vicinity, and naturally I must insist that you all attend."

No such insistence was necessary, as the occupants of Laura Place would not have missed an evening at Kendlin for anything. Conversation then proceeded to a discussion of which gowns would be suitable. Swiftly followed by an appraisal of everything worn by friends at the various social functions attended by both the ladies. Petty, who derived little pleasure from an analysis of others' foibles, picked up her book and commenced a new chapter.

Tuesday dawned; it was a beautiful day; hot spring weather is certainly the most delightful. The sky was azure, with not a single cloud to sully its blueness. The light was sharp, possessing none of that haziness which can mar the summer. It was warm but not humid, and the evening entertainment promised to be even more agreeable for being able to enjoy the gardens.

Mr and Mrs Darby lived at Kendlin Hall, a small estate a few miles outside Bath. As the carriage drew up outside the hall, Petty was reminded how pretty the house was. It was a square building, the front's delicate proportions centred by a double front door flanked by four windows. The long windows at the back opened onto a most delightful terrace which ran the full length of the house. Sloping down from this main terrace were several smaller terraces, and the view from the house was of a lake and well-laid-out gardens. Mr Darby's father had built the house and indulged his passion for gardens. His son had carried on the tradition and the resulting schemes were some of the most delightful in Wiltshire.

The party seemed to be underway when they arrived. Dora was quickly swept up, her hand immediately solicited for the set just forming. Petty, as soon, found that Mr Gray sought her out.

"Please will you take a turn around the gardens with me?" he requested. "It is such a wonderful evening." Petty agreed happily. They walked companionably, traversing the main terrace and proceeding down the walk which led to the lake. It was a glorious evening. The setting sun suffused a pink glow over the gardens, and the scent of the wisteria which covered the walls wafted sweetly across to them. They made their way down the steps leading to the rose garden, in the middle of which was a small fountain.

"Let us sit for a minute," Mr Gray suggested. Petty nodded; she felt light and carefree. They sat on a wooden seat. Although it was still early in the year, the warm weather had caused the roses to unfurl their petals, mixing their delicate smell with that of the wisteria. Petty sat, content. It was so peaceful. She breathed deeply, enjoying the full beauty of this pure evening.

"Mrs Blakeston, Petty, I have something of the greatest import to say to you."

Petty started; a feeling of disquietude crept over her, interrupting the tranquillity which had enveloped her. "Oh no, please, do not…"

Mr Gray possessed himself of her hands. "I must, you cannot be unaware of my feeling for you. I would regard it as the greatest honour if you would agree to be my wife."

Her peace shattered, Petty came back to reality with a bump. "I cannot. No! I cannot… Oh, please, please do not go on…"

She felt the ready tears at the back of her eyes; jumping to her feet she begged, "Oh, please forgive me, it is impossible… I have been so wrong." As she raised her eyes to his face he was surprised to see how much hurt and pain was in them.

"No! It is I who must apologise. I did not mean to cause you such anguish." The confusion apparent in his voice was repeated in his face. Petty broke from him. With all speed she rushed back towards the house. Pausing outside the open windows which led to the drawing room, she tried to collect herself.

The spell of Bath was broken; how badly she had behaved. It had seemed so enchanted. For the first time in her life she had known what it meant to be happy, but she knew she was not entitled to this happiness. It was bought at the cost of others. As she stood there, Mrs Lumley, at the window, waved at her, gesturing to suggest she came in. With some trepidation she obeyed the summons. The room was hot and crowded, and as she made her way to Mrs Lumley's side, her thoughts were in turmoil.

"There you are, my sweet, we wondered where you had gone."

Petty returned her welcome with an abstracted smile. Petty glanced around the room, trying to collect her jumbled thoughts, but as she did so, she froze, her eyes opening with horror. At the other side of the room conversing amicably with Mr Darby was Lord Milton.

Petty wanted to run, but her legs were jelly. She knew he had not seen her, but at that moment His Lordship looked up; at first as his eyes alighted on her she thought she was safe. He obviously did not recognise her, how could he? She was so different from the plain, silent girl at Wakeham. Unable to stop herself she stared at him, wide-eyed, transfixed with horror. Then he realised who she was. His face seemed to contort with anger, and he slowly moved across the room towards her. Petty stood, unable to move a muscle, the colour draining from her face until he was next to her. His cold, furious voice tore at her. His words were fierce but so quiet that no one but her could hear them.

"So, I find you at last. How unexpected. Your family are sick with worry. We had quite given you up for lost," he hissed.

Petty tried to answer, no words came. She trembled, her knees shook. It was like being at Wakeham all over again. All the old fears came rushing back. The blood drained from her head. Petty fainted.

CHAPTER EIGHT

When Petty came round she found herself in Mrs Lumley's travelling carriage, with no idea of how she had got there. Her limbs felt like jelly, and she knew she would have the greatest difficulty standing. Her brain felt as if it were made of fluff; at the back of her mind was a nagging feeling that something terrible had occurred. She struggled to remember, and then she heard voices outside the coach.

"I so much appreciate your escorting Mrs Blakeston back to Bath for me. I hate to leave her like this. Perhaps I should accompany you?"

"Please, Mrs Blakeston will be quite safe with me, you must not worry," Lord Milton replied reassuringly.

"I suppose so." Mrs Lumley still sounded concerned. "I am grateful to you, Lord Milton."

"It is a pleasure, Mrs Lumley. I would not deprive Dora of her evening for the world."

Petty sank back on the squabs. She was in despair. How had Lord Milton become acquainted with Mrs Lumley and with Dora? He was to drive her back to Laura Place, her worst fears realised! It must be a nightmare, perhaps she would suddenly wake up? Petty clenched her eyes in fear; pain shot across the back of her forehead. Lord Milton here. Lord Milton to spoil her happiness… and then she remembered everything. Mr Gray's proposal. Lord Milton's black eyes boring into her. The horror of discovery. The certainty of being dragged back to Wakeham in disgrace. Oh, why did he have to come? Oh, how had he found her? Tears trickled down her face, dripping onto the pale blue silk dress, so expertly made by Madame Camille. Now she would be hauled back to Wakeham to face the strictures of the duchess, back to drab, worn, ugly cast-offs. She sobbed. Then another thought struck her. It would not be her beloved Wakeham! She sat bolt upright. She was married to Lord Milton; he was entitled to take her wherever he pleased!

The door knob turned. Petty sank back and closed her eyes. She would pretend to be still asleep, it would prevent conversation, and when they reached Laura Place, she could run in and Hawley could protect her from her husband. Edward got in.

"Thank you, thank you again. Please pay me a visit tomorrow and I can thank you properly."

Mrs Lumley held out her hand to him. He raised it to his lips. "Unnecessary, my dear madam, I am only too happy to be of service."

The coach moved off. Sam coachman drove slowly and carefully. Petty hunched in a corner, her eyes firmly closed. Lord Milton sat in the opposite corner. He seemed lost in thought. Petty did not dare to open her eyes to look at him but he said nothing. Thank goodness for Sam, she thought. He cannot upbraid me in front of him; he cannot castigate me as his wife in front of Sam; he cannot expose my perfidy. Another tear escaped from the corner of her eye, running down her face. She hoped desperately that it would be too dark for him to notice it.

Lord Milton watched her. He observed the stray drop of water that coursed down her face. He realised that she was not asleep, but was quite grateful himself for a time to collect his thoughts. He had been astounded when he saw her at Kendlin. He had gone there with Mr Darby's sister, whose husband was an acquaintance of his. He had not immediately recognised the pretty and elegant girl as his wife, and when he did, his first feeling had been one of relief that she was still alive and safe. This was swiftly followed by one of intense anger that she could have been so inconsiderate as not to let anyone at Wakeham know that she was unharmed. It was only the presence of the company that had stopped him tearing at her there and then. This anger was still smoldering inside him, and while he was determined that she should know how he felt, he was equally determined not to lose his temper with her.

The journey seemed interminable to both parties, but eventually the carriage drew up outside number 24, Laura Place. Sam let down the stairs. Before Lord Milton could help her, Petty threw herself down the steps and into the door which had been flung open by Hawley. With great alacrity she was making for the steps to her bedroom when Lord Milton's icy voice stopped her.

"Just a moment, Mrs Blakeston. A word with you."

Petty turned; her petrified eyes just looked at him. He crossed to her as she stared wide-eyed at him. "We can either discuss this in the hall in front of the servants or in private, which would you prefer?" he hissed quietly.

She looked at him blankly. Hawley, to whom she was never a favourite, regarded the interchange with interest. Petty, realising this, nodded acquiescence. She was aware that the confrontation could not be put off forever, and a plan was forming in her mind. She led the way into the book room, firmly closing the door on the interested butler.

She turned and faced a furious Lord Milton.

"So I find you at last. Have you any conception of the anguish and pain that you have caused? Have you any idea of how much time l, and your brothers, have spent chasing about the countryside searching for you? Coming back in despair because we could find no trace of you? How can you have done this? How can anyone behave in such an irresponsible way?"

Petty found her legs trembling. She felt unable to breathe properly and certainly she could find no words to defend herself. Her continuing silence infuriated Lord Milton; his temper burst.

"How dare you? How dare you sit in Bath, clearly in the lap of comfort, without a word, without one word to your poor family nearly sick with worry? How could you marry me and then just disappear? Did you have no thought for anyone but yourself? Your parents arrange an advantageous marriage for you and all you can do to show them your gratitude is to run away?"

Petty, who had never lost her temper in her life, suddenly found strength returning to her legs. She pulled herself up. Words came with a fluency she did not know she possessed. "Advantageous marriage for me? Me? No one cares about me! The only reason that they wanted me to marry you was for themselves! For their ends. So that my mother could have yet more clothes! So that my father did not have to sell his horses. Do you know what it feels like to be sold to the highest bidder?" Facing him, with her brilliant blue eyes flashing, she saw a sudden flicker of understanding in his black ones.

"Do you know, here I am a companion and it is wonderful. Here I am happy. They are kind to me. They care about me, and now you have come to spoil it all; you have to find me out and I suppose you will drag me back to Wakeham. Well, I will not go! I will not."

"Alright, so you prefer to be a governess to being the daughter of a duke, but why did you have to marry me? Have you no idea of the invidious position that I find myself in? I want a wife. I want children, I wanted a friend, I wanted a family life; now I can never have one. You have married me under false pretenses, you deny me a chance."

Petty looked stricken and he knew he had hit home. "No one knows about our marriage. Can you not just find someone else?"

Edward lost his temper completely. "Find someone else? You stupid girl, how could I do that? I can see that I shall have to take you back to your father and see if he can talk some sense into you."

"No! No!" Petty rushed from the room. Picking up her skirts she ran up the stairs towards the sanctuary of her bedroom, leaving Lord Milton white with fury in the hall.

"Can I help you, sir?" Hawley appeared. "Shall I call the carriage for you?"

"No, thank you." Lord Milton made for the door. "I shall walk."

He went out. The night was balmy and the air was filled with the sweet, heavy smell of the spring. He was cross with Petty but he was furious with himself. He had sworn to himself that he would not lose his temper with her if he found her, and yet the first thing he had done was precisely that. He had let her provoke him into betraying himself in a totally unbecoming way. He knew that she hated arguments; he knew that angry words slayed her; he knew that the sarcastic gibes of her family reduced her to a speechless wreck. He had always despised them for their treatment of her and yet here he was behaving in the same way. Now here he was. He, who prided himself on his understanding, behaving worse than the Mordaunts. Yet, the odd thing had been that she had managed to answer him back, and, he smiled ruefully to himself, she had looked quite surprisingly magnificent when she did so.

He decided to go back in the morning and apologise and see if they could start again. Instinctively he felt that they could deal far better than this. Thinking over this strange evening he decided that he rather liked Mrs Lumley. She had amused him and he rather thought that she was probably much cleverer than might at first sight appear, and she had done well by Petty. What a difference she had wrought. Petty was really lovely; he would pay a morning visit.

Petty closed the door of her room leaning against it in relief. She felt terribly tired but surprisingly strong. She was not going back to Wakeham, of that she was sure!

She took out the portmanteau which she had taken from Wakeham on that far-off winter day, and started to pack it. She pulled the drab cambric from the rear of the closet where it had been stuffed, and stared at it dolefully; it was so horribly ugly. She sighed as she ran her eyes over the wardrobe of beautiful clothes that Mrs Lumley had bought her.

"A uniform for the job," Mrs Lumley had called it and, as Petty would no longer be doing the job, she could not take any with her. The problem was that not only were her clothes from home plain and unflattering, but also everything she had taken from Wakeham was thick and suitable for winter weather. She must have something cooler. Luckily she had spent very little of the one hundred pounds she had taken from her father, so she had the means to purchase some thin muslin and make a dress. The problem was that she had not lied to Lord Milton when she said she could not sew. In a dress of my making I am going to look such a dowd, she thought wryly. In the end she decided to borrow one of the dresses supplied by Mrs Lumley.

When she had packed, she sat down and wrote a note to Dora and her mother, thanking them for their kindnesses and begging their forgiveness for taking the dress.

She then got into her comfortable bed, but sleep would not come. She tossed and turned, the events of the night churning around her mind until eventually she fell into a fitful doze.

At 5.30, she awoke, dressed, and slipped downstairs. She tiptoed across the hall, nervously approaching the bolts of the front door. She knew it would be half an hour before the servants were stirring but as she drew back the bolts, the screeching sound they made caused her to look behind her, half expecting to see an irate Hawley in his night cap emerging from the top of the stairs. No such vision occurred, however. She heaved a sigh of relief. The door open, she bounded out into the street, closing it behind her as quietly as she was able.

The sun was just beginning to come up, heralding another lovely day; the tops of the houses in Laura Place and the trees in the small park opposite were bathed in early sunlight, the air was fresh and, although it was so early, quite warm. Petty, as she turned out of Laura Place, looked back. The houses were bright and pretty. She felt very sad; she had loved Bath.

She sighed and made her way towards the White Hart Inn. She knew that all the stages left from there. She was not sure where to go next; she thought of London, but felt scared of trying the metropolis, after all she knew no one in London; she grinned at her stupidity. In truth I have a vast acquaintance in London. For example, there is Aunt Hortense – I can imagine her face if I turn up as a subservient governess and Mama's friends; they would be beside themselves with horror, thinking of these illustrious ladies who had made her seasons so miserable. She would almost have liked to have done it just to see their faces. She laughed out loud. That's better, she told herself. The fact remained that she had no idea how to get a job in London and the city was so intimidating. She shivered. Tempting though it was, she could not in reality approach Lady Cowper or Lady Jersey or the Duchess of Afton or any other of her mother's close friends to ask for a position as governess to their children or grandchildren. Although the thought of doing so was almost irresistible. She giggled again. Perhaps London was not the best idea.

She would, in any case, have to buy a ticket for the first stage leaving Bath, as she must assume that Lord Milton would come after her as soon as her absence was discovered. Relying on the fact that the Lumleys did not keep early hours would not be enough. She must leave at the first possible moment. On reaching the White Hart she found that the first coach to depart left for Tonbridge at six o'clock. She was in luck, as, when she approached the coachman, she found the waybills had not been made up and a ticket could still be purchased. As she now was an experienced stage-coach traveller, she had demanded a corner seat. She clambered on board, settling herself nervously in her corner. She could not be happy until the stage rumbled out of the yard of the White Hart and she was leaving Bath and Lord Milton.

Dora and Mrs Lumley did not leave their rooms early on the morning after the fateful party at Mrs Darby's, and they were just finishing a late breakfast when Lord Milton's card was sent in. When Hawley had opened the door, following an imperative summons upon it, he had been unsure of how to treat the man who stood there demanding admittance. He had disapproved of the little that he had overheard the night before. Underestimating His Lordship's understated air of elegance, he mistakenly decided that Lord Milton was to be treated with haughty disdain.

"Mrs Lumley is at breakfast," he pronounced dismissively in lofty accents.

Lord Milton, quite unaccustomed to such pretension, lifted his glass and steadily regarded the butler through it.

"Inform Mrs Lumley that I am here," he returned in an icy voice. Disconcerted and recognising his error, Hawley scuttled to obey, returning a few seconds later to show Lord Milton into the elegant breakfast parlour.

"Please excuse us, Your Lordship, but we do not stand on ceremony here. I hope you will join us?" Mrs Lumley greeted him warmly.

His Lordship declined. "I have already partaken of an excellent repast at York House, but I must apologise for interrupting you." He waited until the servants had withdrawn and then enquired offhandedly, "I hope that Mrs Blakeston has recovered her spirits and her health this morning?"

"I must admit I do not know. Have you seen Petty this morning, Dora?"

Dora shook her head. She kept her eyes fastened on her plate. She was much in awe of His Lordship; his dark looks frightened her.

"Come, my love," her mother reproved her gently. "Look up, His Lordship will not eat you." Dora blushed a bright pink; her eyes fluttered nervously up to Edward, who smiled his warmest and most charming smile, to which Dora found herself responding, in spite of her fears.

"Miss Lumley, I would be much in your debt if you would go to check that Mrs Blakeston has recovered. I am, you see, most particularly concerned about her." This request, in a gentle voice, was accompanied by another smile.

Dora smiled back; any apprehensions she had possessed had vanished. "Certainly, Your Lordship, it will give me great pleasure."

She darted off on her mission, leaving Mrs Lumley to suggest that as breakfast was finished they adjourned to the saloon. Lord Milton followed her into the saloon. She was, as usual, dressed in her matchless way. A violent yellow pelisse was perched over a jonquil underdress, adorned with a multitude of her beloved frills. On her head was a huge cap, every inch blessed again with frills and furbelows. His Lordship, far too well bred to raise a smile, was nevertheless a trifle amazed by the sight she presented, especially when set in the green drawing room.

"I know I am a fair sight," she pronounced and as he made to demur, "No! No! But I do like bright colours and at my time of life I see no reason not to indulge my fancy. Pray, won't you be seated?"

Lord Milton seated himself opposite her on the green sofa. "Indeed, madam, I see no reason at all for denying yourself." He smiled.

"Now, you must tell me about Mrs Blakeston, but before you do I must tell you that we are extraordinarily fond of Petty, and I for one do not intend that she shall be further hurt!" She looked at him challengingly. He returned her look slightly restrained. She nodded at him, the amazing creation on her head bobbing in time to her nods.

"I may be an old woman but you cannot put one over on Gertrude Lumley! I saw her face last night when she saw you, and I must say that after you had gone with her I did consider whether I had done right. As the evening wore on I must admit that I grew less and less happy that I should have let her go with you."

"You were right," he interposed. "My damnable.. I apologise, ma'am temper."

"Oh, you must not mind me, I have heard worse in my day. Now, I know that our Petty was no governess, for all she was so good at the Latin and Greek."

"Bookish…" Edward remembered quietly to himself.

"Not that I wanted her for the classics, my Dora was no scholar," Mrs Lumley went on. "Town polish, that is what I wanted, and very good at that she was too." She continued in response to his surprised look, "Oh, very good at it she was. Knew everyone; her descriptions of all those earls and dukes and lords, had me fair in stitches she did, such a humour. That Lady Jersey who never stops talking, and the doll-like Lady Caroline Limb."

"Lamb," he corrected mildly.

"Well, that mad one who loved that poet chap. She took off Lady Hamel, well, I thought I would split my frock. You see Lady H. is the aunt to Dora's friend Cecily Simpson, and Mrs Simpson, an encroaching old know-it-all, is forever boasting of the acquaintance. Petty pulled her pretty face into the ugliest of expressions and assumed the most strident, rasping voice and showed us just what were my Lady Hamel's true colours. I know who I would believe any day. Oh, I cannot describe to you the fun we have had with that young lady of yours. I am not wrong, am l? She is somehow your young lady?"

"My wife."

"Your wife! Well... l... mean... how? What? I am fair flummoxed..." Mrs Lumley, not often at a loss for words, looked dumbfounded.

"Yes. I think I can trust you with the truth?" He regarded her keenly. She nodded seriously.

"It is a story that does me little credit, I am afraid. I come from ordinary stock myself." She looked at him questioningly. "Oh, I know I have a title, but that was by default."

He went on to explain how he came to be married to Petty. She did not interrupt him, except to exclaim when he told her who were Petty's parents. "The daughter of a duke, here!" He told her about Cuthbert, whom he privately thought would much appreciate Mrs Lumley and vice versa; he told her about the duchess and her treatment of her eldest daughter. She tutted angrily at his description of this spoilt and domineering character. He finished with his description of what had occurred in the book room last night and how ashamed he felt for his unwarranted loss of temper. Mrs Lumley heard him out; she nodded sagely at the end of the story.

"You must not reproach yourself too much. It is a common enough fault to lose temper at such a time as this. I do not think that Petty, I am sorry, Lady Perpetua or Lady Milton, has been harmed by her experience, it could well be the making of her. But where are they? Perhaps you would be good enough to ring the bell and let us discover what has happened to them?"

He crossed to do her bidding, but before he could do so the door opened and a bewildered Dora rushed in.

"Petty is not in her room, Mama. I thought at first maybe she had gone for a walk, but Hawley says she did not go out and then I found this note." She held out the piece of paper in the manner of an actress declaiming in a play.

"Let me see," Lord Milton snapped. Her surprised look stopped him. "Please, may I see it?" he added.

"But it is addressed to Mama," Dora pointed out.

"Give the letter to Lord Milton, Dora, I am convinced that it will be material that he should know its contents."

Dora looked somewhat surprised but did as she was bid. Edward broke the wafer and read:

Dearest Mrs Lumley and Dora,

Something has occurred that makes it imperative that I leave you. I will never forget your kindness to me, I have been happy with you as never in my life before. Indeed yours has been the only true kindness I have ever experienced. Please believe me, I am desolated to go, but I have no choice. I apologise that I have taken the blue flowery muslin dress. I hope that you will not mind if I borrow it for a few days. I will of course return it as soon as I can.

Thank you, and bless you.
Petty

He stopped. He and Mrs Lumley looked at each other. It was Dora who broke the silence. "But where has she gone? And why has she gone? Surely she loved us enough to tell us why she left so hurriedly? Will she come back, Mama?"

"I do not know, Dora." Mrs Lumley's voice sounded so worried that Dora looked at her, concerned.

"Mama, she will be alright?" She looked from her mama to Lord Milton.

"Yes… Yes, she will, Dora. I shall go and look for her now. It is my fault. This time it is all my fault," he said angrily.

"Do not reproach yourself, Lord Milton," Mrs Lumley remarked, her eyes full of understanding. "She runs because, so far, when the going gets difficult she cannot as yet face up to it. She will, she stood up to you last night. We will find her again, do not fear."

Lord Milton kissed her hand. "Thank you, ma'am. I hope that you are correct. I will go to discover if she hired a coach."

"I think you should try the stage. They leave from the White Hart Inn, in Ship Street."

"The stage?" His Lordship looked amazed.

"Oh, did Her Ladyship not tell you that she came here on the common stage?"

Lord Milton laughed. "No… I find it hard to countenance."

"Nevertheless true." Mrs Lumley smiled. "Please keep us informed of your progress. Oh, and if you find her, tell the silly child that the dresses I bought were hers, I did not want to keep them."

"I shall, of course, reimburse you for them," His Lordship pointed out stiffly.

"You will not. Don't you get stuffy with me," Mrs Lumley, equally firm, replied. They stared at each other.

"We shall see."

"We shall not." Mrs Lumley grinned. "I am an old woman. You would not want me to get cross and suffer an apoplectic stroke."

He kissed her hand. "Blackmailer," he returned, his eyes brimming with laughter. "Now I must go with all speed."

"Good luck."

Chapter Nine

It was unbearably hot on the coach. Petty's spirits were so downcast that she was unable to enjoy the beauty of the countryside through which she was passing. Her thoughts, as they went through small pretty villages whose cottages were garlanded with roses, were unpleasant. She felt Lord Milton on her tail. She wondered what was going to become of her, as she knew that she could not be as lucky as she had been in meeting Mrs Lumley. As the journey progressed she became steadily more miserable, and it was a relief when they at last reached Tonbridge where they were to stop and spend the night. The heat of the day was giving way to a cooler evening as she alighted and went into the Dog and Goose.

The landlady came bustling out. "A room for the night and a private parlour, if you please," Petty asked politely. Mrs Sowerby looked her over. Petty knew that she must look dishevelled and untidy, and she suspected her face was streaked with dust.

"Oh," the landlady replied knowingly, "and your maid, miss?"

"I do not have a maid. I am travelling alone."

"Then I must tell you that I have no room. I do not let rooms to the likes of you."

Petty drew herself up and repeated firmly, "A room and a private parlour."

"I… We…" Mrs Sowerby was perplexed; she prided herself that she had the measure of most travellers, and those young ladies who arrived in badly cut clothes, unaccompanied by an abigail or escorted by a gentleman, were to be turned from her door, but something in the commanding quality of the girl's well-bred voice and the imperious look in her eyes made her for once doubt the validity of her opinions. She found herself dropping a slight curtsey.

"If you would be so good as to come with me."

Petty followed her up the steep stairs to what she quickly realised must be one of the best bedchambers. Inwardly congratulating herself on the ease with which she had managed this landlady, she reflected on how astonished the duchess and the incumbents of Wakeham would be if they could see her, and yet how simple it had actually been. She suppressed a stray giggle, and fixed Mrs Sowerby with a beady stare. "Some water, please. I will dine at six," Petty, secretly very pleased with herself, demanded.

"Yes, miss. You will be wanting to wash, that hot it is for this time of year. I have not known a May like this…" Petty could see a discourse on the weather that was going to last at least an hour.

"Quite." She assumed the tone of voice that her mama used to depress pretension. Dropping another curtsey, Mrs Sowerby hurried away to fulfil her orders.

As she closed the door Petty hugged herself and grinned. Was it really that easy? She whirled around; finding she had made herself quite dizzy she sat at the dressing table and regarded herself in the glass. The face that stared back at her was pale and wan, the eyes dark-rimmed and still swollen from the tears that had been shed into her pillow the previous night. Lord Milton's words echoed in her brain. Incurably honest she was now forced to face an unpleasant truth which previously she had been able to ignore. She had used him hardly; she finally understood how unfair she had been. Overwhelmed by the strictures of her father, by the reproaches of her mother, by his own unsympathetic and detached manner, she had only thought of a way of escape for herself; she had not considered his feelings, indeed she had never, until last night, thought of him as a person at all. She tried to think of how she could make amends. Annulment? Divorce? She had no idea of how these appalling things worked. She did see clearly that either of these options would produce a terrible scandal which, at the moment, seemed to have been averted. She would think of something. She would find a solution. As she ruminated on these matters there was a knock on the door and Mrs Sowerby returned, bearing a large bowl of water.

"You look right done in, miss. Why don't you have a lie down? I have put a couple of hens on for your dinner... and if you would like, I could sponge and press your dress." She pointed to the muslin which, after its hot hours in the stage, looked creased and grubby.

"Thank you. I will have a rest." Petty dismissed her and lay down on the bed, and, contrary to her expectations, fell asleep.

It was past six when she was awoken by the tentative knock of a chambermaid who brought in her dress beautifully pressed. She was a plump, pretty girl who strongly resembled Mrs Sowerby, and would by middle age be an exact copy of her mama.

"Will there be owt else, miss?" she asked with a friendly grin.

"No, thank you. You must be Mrs Sowerby's daughter. What is your name?"

The girl hooted with laughter. "Lor, miss... how did yer know? I do look right like my ma... everyone remarks on't... and it's Lucy, miss, Lucy Sowerby." She beamed with good-natured pleasure. "I was sixteen last birthday, my young man, he is called Ben, he drives a..." She seemed to be about to enlarge on the minutiae of her life when an imperious "Lucy!" from below made her bob a curtsey. "I'd best go, miss, we've a quantity of things to do. We've quality staying in the house, and we are

108

that full…" She beamed again. "I have to lay the covers for your dinner, which will be served as soon as you are ready, miss." She flustered out.

Petty, much amused by this artless speech, scrambled out of bed, pulled a brush through her tumbled locks, and, attired in Mrs Sowerby's handiwork, prepared to go downstairs. She discovered that she was ravenously hungry and hoped that the dinner she had bespoken would be good. As she opened her door and looked about, trying to decide which was the way down, her attention was caught by a commotion that seemed to be coming from the room opposite. She could hear voices arguing bitterly. As she paused, unsure of whether to continue, the door was flung open and a young girl rushed precipitously out.

She was shaking all over and crying copiously.

"Stop… oh, stop… oh, please, please leave me alone… do not touch me… do not hurt me…"

Seeing Petty in front of her, she flung herself into Petty's arms. "P… Pl… Please help me… do not let him hurt me." The panic in her voice touched Petty. She patted the golden head resting on her shoulder.

"Shh… I will help you. You have no need to be afraid." The small frame shuddered convulsively.

"Do not let him, I… oh, please, oh, pl… p… p…" she sobbed, her words lost in the tears. "I… He… He…"

Petty was suddenly aware that someone had followed the girl out of the room. She looked up and found herself staring straight into the furious eyes of a man. He was tall; on first appearance he seemed very good looking, but that impression was fleeting. On closer examination, Petty discovered that his face was hard and cruel. As he regarded her, his cold eyes narrow with anger, she felt a shiver of fear run down her spine. He was fashionably dressed, although his well-cut coat was a trifle too nipped in at the waist for Petty's taste, and his waistcoat of bright silk and his exaggerated shirt points proclaimed the dandy. Petty had the odd sensation that she knew him and yet she could not place him at all.

"Verity! My love! Come back." The voice was honeyed but extremely unpleasant.

Another shiver overtook Petty.

"No! No! Do not make me..." the damsel responded, clinging onto Petty desperately. "Please, please... no... no." She burst into a paroxysm of crying.

Petty felt at a loss; she did not know what to do. The girl was very young and very scared; Petty herself felt terrified. She took a breath and said with a conviction she did not feel, "Shh... do not cry. You do not have to do anything you do not want to do." She accompanied this statement with a challenging look at the man, who returned her stare as if he might grab her at any minute and tear her into bits.

"I do not know what makes you think that you have any right to interfere," the unpleasant voice continued, a shade too quietly for comfort, the menace in it unmistakable.

Petty quaked, then chiding herself for her want of courage, she put up her chin and regarded him defiantly.

"I have every right to interfere. It is clear to me that this young lady finds your attentions not at all to her taste."

"Oh! And what, pray, do you consider you know about what is to her taste? She was happy enough to come with me."

"Well, it is clear to me that she is not at all happy now." Petty bit her tongue and tried not to let her apprehension show.

The man took her arm and held it in a fierce grip. "Let her go and leave us alone," his vicious voice hissed in her ear. "Verity, come with me!" he demanded. Letting Petty go, he grabbed hold of Verity and started to pull her towards him.

"Stop! Stop! Let her go!" Petty commanded. She pushed herself between them and stood facing him, her eyes blazing with anger.

"How dare you! Leave her alone! How dare you attack a mere child! You wear the clothes of a gentleman but I can see that you are nothing but a beast."

He looked at her somewhat surprised. He had taken her for a chambermaid or perhaps a local farmer's daughter, but he now realised that he had been mistaken and that this small girl who stood facing him, rigid with fury, was actually a person of quality; he changed his tactics.

"l apologise, Verity, I do not mean to harm you, my dear, come back into the room," he whined in an ingratiatingly awful voice. Verity, who by this time was so distraught, was quite unable to answer. So Petty responded for her.

"I see no desirability in her returning with you," she replied in a haughty voice. She now found that the years of observing the manners of her mama's friends was highly efficacious. By copying the demeanour of the grandest of these formidable dames, she thought it might be possible to be rid of this undesirable man.

She pushed Verity in the direction of her room and stood firmly between her and this irate gentleman. Having made the discovery that she was not, as he had previously believed, a nobody, he was a little unsure of quite how to proceed He had absolutely no idea who she was and yet there was something about her which was familiar. If she was of gentle birth, what was she doing travelling alone? Or perhaps she was not alone? Maybe there was an aunt or chaperone or someone? He decided he had better be careful. He bowed to her and said in a casually studied voice, "As you wish, Miss…?"

Petty, had no intention of letting him know her name and desired nothing better than to get away from him as fast as possible, merely nodded dismissal, turned and walked slowly with as much dignity as she could muster, back into her room. Once inside, she closed the door firmly, heaved a sigh of relief and turned to face Verity.

The girl was crouched down beside the bed. She was sobbing uncontrollably, and shaking all over. Petty realised that before she could find out anything about her she was going to have to try to calm her down. She took her hand, leading her to the chair, saying in her quiet, gentle voice, "Come, you have nothing to fear, no one can hurt you now."

The girl shot an agitated look at the door. "I… He…" Her small body shuddered convulsively, her hands clung to Petty.

"Shh… Do not cry. Try not to cry anymore." Petty realised that she was exquisitely beautiful, but very young. Her heart-shaped lace was framed by golden curls; her eyes were deep green; she had a tiny snub nose, and a full generous mouth. She was dressed in a round gown of muslin, with a half robe of dark blue sarcenet trimmed with gold lace. On her feet she wore pale blue kid slippers. She was hatless and Petty thought that quite probably her bonnet had been flung off in the gentleman's room. She wondered what such a young and clearly innocent girl was doing with such an obvious rake. Why had she no chaperone? What had happened? Had she gone with him willingly? That seemed unlikely. Had he abducted her? Petty shivered. Verity was clearly gently bred and her clothes were expensive. She must try to stop the girl's tears; she needed some answers.

"Stop crying. It is important that you stop now," Petty commanded. Her voice, surprisingly firm, had the desired effect. Verity took a tumultuous breath, swallowed hard, rubbed her hand across her eyes, and ceased crying. She still shook with the effects of her sobs but seemed altogether more rational.

"I must ask you some questions," Petty responded gently. "You do understand that, don't you?" Verity nodded. "How came you to be here with that awful man? Who is he?"

Verity hung her head and said nothing. "Please, you must trust me," Petty went on, somewhat desperately. "We need to make sure that he does not hurt you anymore, I must get you away from here. Your family, will they not be worried? Your mama? Your papa?"

Verity gave another sob. Petty thought she would cry again. "Nothing is so bad. Please, I can help you but only if you tell me what happened. I will not be cross, I will understand, whatever it is." Verity looked at her, her green eyes swimming with tears. Petty smiled, her smile so sweet and reassuring, that Verity obviously decided that Petty was telling the truth.

"I… you see, have been so wrong!" More tears overflowed from the green eyes and ran down her face.

"We all do things that are wrong, we all make mistakes. You must, well, we must, make sure that your reputation is not damaged irreparably," Petty replied comfortingly.

"You are so kind… I am so very grateful."

"Please tell me, what happened?"

"The gentleman with me is called Bertram Melville."

Petty gave a start. That was why he looked so familiar. Of course, she should have known.

"I met him with Papa. My papa is Sir Hugo Croisthwaite." Verity's papa was unknown to Petty, which meant that he probably did not move in the first circles. "We are very rich. My mama died when I was born, Papa looked after me. I had a governess, Miss Pleasty, but last year I decided that I was far too old to have a governess anymore."

"Oh," said Petty. "And how old are you?"

"I am seventeen," Verity confided artlessly.

Petty kept the thoughts of the desirability of a girl of only seventeen being without a companion to herself; she deduced that Sir Hugo probably adored his daughter. She could probably twist him around her little finger, Petty imagined.

"So Miss Pleasty went. She was always telling me how young ladies should behave. I got very bored with her."

Petty felt tempted to ask if Miss Pleasty included the lack of desirability of running off with men in her strictures but decided against mentioning it at this point. Verity, who was fast recovering her composure, continued, "Papa is a Member of Parliament and quite often Mr Melville came to the house to see him. Mr Melville was all attention. He seemed so kind. He said I was very beautiful. He said I was the moon and stars to him. He wanted to marry me. I did not know if I wanted to get married yet, you see I am only out this year, and although I liked Mr Melville…" she paused, thinking, "I was never so taken in in my life. He is of all things most unlikeable," she added.

Petty laughed at the expression on the beauty's face as she said this. "Indeed the whole family is not what one would desire to know," she commented. Verity looked at her.

"Do you know him?" she asked.

"Uh… well… no… that is only by repute," Petty remarked quickly.

Verity accepted this without a murmur. Petty had the impression that although she was a very beautiful girl she was not maybe a very clever one, and thoroughly self-centered. She went on, "I told him that I did not want to marry him yet, that I wanted to have some fun first. He seemed very happy with that at first, but suddenly over the last two weeks he kept pressing me to marry him."

Petty privately thought that something must have occurred recently in the Melvilles' fortunes to make his demands suddenly become so urgent.

"He was so particular in his attentions, but the more he pressed me the more I just did not want to marry him. He asked me to meet him in the park this morning."

"Did you go unchaperoned?" Petty asked, quite shocked. "Were you alone?"

Verity blushed. "I… well… you see, I told Papa that I was going for a walk with Jane and Matty Locke; they are friends of mine. I introduced Mr Melville to them. They all got on extremely well. It is very pleasant to introduce friends to each

114

other and discover that they like each other, is it not?" Verity said artlessly. "So I often met him when I was supposed to be with them..."

"But did they not have a mama or governess to supervise them?" Petty enquired. She sensed that Verity had not been strictly brought up, and if her father was not careful she was going to be in real trouble. Verity blushed.

"Yes... well, not exactly... they..." She turned to Petty, a pleading look in her eyes. ."1 know now it was wrong. It just seemed such fun, I never thought that it could be dangerous. 1... well, this morning I went to meet Mr Melville to tell him that I did not want to marry him, and that we must desist from meeting like this anymore." Her eyes filled with more tears as she recounted the events of the morning to Petty. "We had arranged to meet in the secluded bower near the rose garden. When I got there I told him that I must never see him in this way again. He would not accept it. It appeared that he had come in his chaise, I did not know why. He grabbed me, I tried to yell, but he put his hand over my mouth. He bundled me into the chaise, tied a handkerchief around me so that I could not protest, and drove off. He brought me here. He told..." She gave a sniff and a stifled sob. "He... told... told me that I would have to marry him, that I would have no choice... I said that Papa would never permit it, but he said that my reputation would be ruined, and that Papa would be pleased to marry me to anyone..." She burst out crying again. "Is it true? Oh, please, it cannot be true..."

Petty patted the golden curls. "No, you are with me, you are safe with me," she reassured Verity with a confidence she did not feel.

The girl had behaved with a great want of conduct, but she was very young and obviously no proper direction had been given her. Petty wondered what kind of a man her father was that he could be so negligent with a daughter both as beautiful as Verity and as rich. The Melvilles were gazetted fortune hunters and rakes. How could any father of a gently brought-up girl expose his daughter to their dangerous wiles? Meanwhile, what was to be done? How best to manage? Petty realised that she would have to convey Verity home on the morrow and for tonight she had best share her chamber. Petty would get Mrs Sowerby to make up a truckle for her. That thought brought her to the next problem: how to get around the chagrin that she was sure that that redoubtable woman would show?

"Verity?" Petty enquired. "How did Mr Melville explain you to the landlady?"

Verity sniffed. "He… he said I was his wife." She let out another wail, and Petty, her worst fears realised, tried in vain to think of an explanation that would satisfy Mrs Sowerby and protect Verity. None came to her, and in the end she decided that a slightly embroidered version of the truth would have to suffice.

Charging Verity to stay in the bedchamber and to lock the door behind her and not to open it to anyone but herself, she prepared to go downstairs and face Mrs Sowerby. Verity, on discovering that her protector was to leave her alone, immediately became very tearful and begged Petty not to desert her. Petty, with her usual inexhaustible forbearance beginning to wear thin, explained in patient tones that she had to talk to the landlady; that as long as Verity kept the door locked she had nothing to fear.

Eventually she managed to escape. As she made her way down, she felt quite faint. She was by now quite weak from lack of food, and the unaccustomed fight with Bertram Melville had left her feeling trembly inside. She hoped that Mrs Sowerby would be reasonable. Her hope was not to be realised. Entering the private parlour she had bespoken, she rang for that good lady. It was Lucy who answered her summons.

"Thank goodness you are here, Miss, Ma is in a pother, your dinner is a'ruined, and she don't like that, it gives the house a bad name!"

"Please could you ask your mama to step up here for a moment. I desire to have some conversation with her."

"Lor, miss, she is a'too busy to come to see you now… I will lay your covers and bring your dinner directly."

"Please will you request that your mother attends me immediately?" Petty, exhausted, with her patience tried to its limits, replied with an unaccustomed sternness.

Lucy looked surprised and not a little frightened, her impressions of Petty altered by the severity in her tone. She bobbed a curtsey and said in quite a different voice, "Yes, of course, miss."

Petty sat down to await Mrs Sowerby. She did not have to wait long; the landlady bustled in angrily.

"Now, what is all this? Your dinner is quite a ruin. I am not used to this."

Petty looked her straight in the eye. Ignoring her incivility, she commanded, "Sit down, Mrs Sowerby, and please listen to me." Mrs Sowerby looked at her again. There was something about this girl, something which made Mrs Sowerby reluctant to argue with her, something in her mien which made Mrs Sowerby feel she was in the presence of real quality. She did not know exactly what it was that stopped her in her tracks, it was intangible, but there all the same. She sat down.

"That is better," Petty said in a much warmer voice. "I need your help."

"My help?"

"Yes." She paused. She was not quite sure how to explain Verity's predicament; eventually she decided to appeal to Mrs Sowerby's motherly instincts.

"I have a young girl in my room. She came here with a gentleman who told you that she was his wife. This was not true."

"What! I will not have hussies in my house. This is a good house, we do not have any of those carry-ons here. She must go now…" She got up to leave.

"Just a moment," Petty forcefully exclaimed. "Mrs Sowerby, I appeal to you as a mother. This poor girl was abducted. She was brought here against her will."

"What!" Mrs Sowerby sank back into her chair. Petty, quick to sense her advantage, continued, "She is distraught, terrified, she is only seventeen..."

"How did he manage to abduct her? That is what I want to know." Mrs Sowerby folded her arms across her ample chest and looked Petty in the eye. "Where was her governess while all this abducting was a'going on, that is what I asks meself?"

Petty assumed a tone of confidentiality. "I realise that she has been very unwise."

"More than unwise if I may say so, no better than she should be. I do not open my doors to girls like that and if you want my advice you will steer clear of her too..."

"When I require your advice I will ask for it," Petty replied in measured tones, assuming her grandest expression.

"Beg pardon, miss."

"As I said she has been very foolish, but she is very young and girls of her age do get themselves into scrapes."

"Huh... unlikely," was all that Mrs Sowerby would vouchsafe.

"Come, Mrs Sowerby," Petty said coaxingly, "think of your Lucy. Has she not done some silly things in her time?" She smiled sweetly. She saw by the expression on Mrs Sowerby's face that she had hit the mark.

"She has been foolish beyond permission but that is no reason for her reputation to be spoiled. She is too young and innocent to be ruined by her folly at seventeen. We must help her, as you must hope that someone would come to the aid of your Lucy if it were necessary."

"T'would not be..." Petty gave her a quizzical look. "Well, I supposes they can all be dizzy dolts at times."

Petty gave a sigh of relief. "She is very scared. I understand that she is a great heiress. Mr Mel.... the gentleman took her quite against her will. His family are very short of funds and I believe he meant to terrify the poor child into consenting to marry him."

"Tut, tut." Mrs Sowerby shook her head. "It is not right, that is what I say…"

"Quite. Now, do you think you could undertake to get rid of the gentleman? I know that it is a task far beyond my limited abilities." She smiled.

"You leave him to me, miss, I will get rid of that nasty abductor in the whisk of a lamb's tail." She got up to go.

"Just a moment, Mrs Sowerby. I think it would be better if I shared a room with Verity. Would you be so good as to arrange for a truckle to be set up in my room?" Petty, who looked pale as a sheet by now, unconsciously passed her hand over her brow.

"Lucy shall do it now." She cast a shrewd glance at Petty. "Now, miss, you look right fagged. When did you last eat?"

Petty felt the world spin round; she must not faint, she must not. Mrs Sowerby's motherly instincts were aroused. She put her arm around Petty and helped her to the sofa, calling for Lucy in strident tones. When this damsel appeared, she ordered her to make haste and procure a draught of lemonade and a wafer. This refreshing beverage and the biscuit having been consumed by Petty, she had the satisfaction of seeing the colour return to her cheeks.

"That's it! You will be right as a trivet. You just rest here."

"But, Verity…"

"I'll attend to her…"

"No, you see, I said not to open the door except to me." She tried to rise and found the world spinning again… She was forced back onto the cushions.

"Don't you worrit your head, you leave it to Ma Sowerby. I'll just deal with that gentleman first." She bustled out of the room. Petty felt relieved that she seemed to have found an ally. She lay back and tried to consider how best to proceed.

 119

CHAPTER TEN

M rs Sowerby was as good as her word. She came back into the private parlour about half an hour later, accompanied by Verity who, having regained her composure, was chattering animatedly and appeared on excellent terms with the landlady.

"Oh, it is everything that is wonderful," she chortled to Petty, who by this time had sufficiently recovered herself to be able to sit at the table and enjoy a dinner composed of duck removed by a turtle pie, cream of halibut, all followed by an excellent syllabub. "Mrs Sowerby told Mr Melville to be gone, in no uncertain terms. Apparently she threatened him with the runners if he did not leave her establishment immediately," she prattled on, perfectly happily.

Petty, whose mind was preoccupied with various unpleasant thoughts concerning the problems of conveying Verity home and her own predicament, responded very little. She sat in a blue study, eating automatically. Verity was perfectly content with an occasional nod in response to her chatter. When they had finished, Petty decided it was time to interrogate Verity further. Interrupting her flow of inconsequential thoughts, Petty demanded, "Now we must make some kind of plan..."

"Plan? Why?"

"Well, I must endeavour to return you to your papa, and I do not even know where you live."

"Oh, do not worry your head about returning with me, if you could just arrange for a post-chaise to collect me in the morning, I can repair home," the girl replied flippantly.

Petty, whose patience with this spoilt young lady was beginning to wear a little thin, started to point out the impropriety of such a journey.

"You cannot, I am sure, intend to travel alone."

"Well, it seems you are." Petty had privately to acknowledge the veracity of this remark, but hurried to demonstrate the difference in their cases.

"I am very much older than you, and I am a widow. I am on my way to search for a post as a governess, so our situations cannot in any particular be seen to be the same." To her relief Verity appeared to accept this explanation. "In any case do you have the funds for hiring a chaise?"

"Oh, you can advance them to me. Papa will repay you when I get home," Verity replied airily.

"Even if I possessed enough to send you by post, I do not know where I shall be situated next, so how could your papa repay me?" asked Petty, privately deciding that it would do the beauty good to travel on the stage! "Now, please give me your address so that I may make enquiries as to when the stage leaves."

"The stage?" Verity looked amazed.

"Yes, the stage," Petty said firmly.

"What an adventure, wait till I tell Matty I went on a stage coach." Petty had to laugh at this ingenuous comment.

"My address is 38 Portman Square. Well, that is one of my addresses. I was born in Yorkshire. We have estates near Yedingham. Do you know Yorkshire?"

"Oh! Yes… My best aunt comes from…" Petty started, then she thought better of continuing. Luckily for her, Verity went on as if she had not heard her.

"My mama's family come from Gainsborough, but Papa is in London at the moment. He is writing a book. He is always in his library," she said in a resigned voice which made Petty laugh again. Then she stopped and thought a moment. "Do you think he will be very angry with me?"

"I think he will be very happy that you come back unscathed, but I do not know your papa, is he given to tempers?"

"Well, no, he is not really; he is always reading and thinking about Parliament, but he might not like my getting myself in… in a position… where…"

"No, I think he might not like it," Petty said firmly. "But I will try to explain."

"I think it is a very good idea that you accompany me home," Verity said in a determined tone. Petty was much amused and suggested that they repair to bed.

She rang the bell to discover when the stage left for London and whether there were places on the waybill, and to give instructions to Mrs Sowerby to awake them. When they reached the bedchamber, Verity got undressed and climbed without thought into the bed. Petty sighed and prepared for an uncomfortable and cold night on the truckle.

Lord Milton came out of Mrs Lumley's house prey to uncomfortable thoughts; his face was harsh and his dark eyes angry. Hardwick, waiting at the bays' heads, had seen that look on his master's face before. It did not bode well. His Lordship jumped up onto the box of the curricle; taking the ribbons in his capable hands, he commanded: "Let go of their heads!" The horses sprang forward, and as the old groom clambered hurriedly onto the box behind His Lordship, the curricle sped down the streets towards the White Hart. Lord Milton's face remained hard and unrelenting. Hardwick, who knew his master too well to try to make any conversation, clung on determinedly as the curricle swung at top speed along the narrow streets. As he held on, he had time to observe the amazed admiration on the faces of the passers-by as they observed the skill with which His Lordship manoeuvred his horses around a difficult corner.

On reaching the yard of the White Hart, he flung the reins at Hardwick and jumped down, striding purposefully into the inn, which was unexpectedly quiet at this time of the day, as most mails left early morning or evening. The landlord, facing a stiff, irate gentleman of quality, grovelled hard but was unable to help. He begged pardon but they had been so busy that morning that he could not recall a girl answering Petty's description. On being commanded to request of his staff to see if any of them could remember her, he replied ingratiatingly that he would.

Suggesting to His Lordship that he take a seat, he returned having consulted with his soulmate, who had told him roundly not to waste his time helping decadent blades find their fancy ladies, and informed Lord Milton that they were sorry but unable to help. His Lordship tossed a few coins onto the counter and flung out of the room. Regarding the largesse, the landlord was heard to remark to his devoted spouse that he was quite sorry not to have been able to help, for he was sure that had he been able to, His Lordship may have been even more generous. However, he was soon put in his place by his good lady, who told him soundly that girls who were no better than they should be and rakes were not deserving of help. In truth, she did remember Petty, but she had not liked what she had seen of Lord Milton who appeared to her to be arrogant and supercilious. She was not going to help men of his stamp. Had he displayed the more conciliatory manners and had he exerted the charm of Lord Slaughan or Captain Braybrooke she would, most probably, have told him what she knew, which was that a girl answering Petty's description and name had boarded the Tonbridge stage that morning. But faced with a stern, unrelenting gentleman, she was not about to give anything away.

Hardwick, who was of an altogether different turn of character, had managed to glean a little information.

"Your Lordship, it would seem that Her Ladyship was 'ere, that 'er groom... well, if yous a'could of called 'im that, in my thoughts he don't know a horse from a bullock." His Lordship smiled as his devoted retainer went on, "Well, 'is as 'as the looking after of the 'osses, he says a young girl was 'ere wot sounds like she was 'er Ladyship."

"Where did she go?"

"Well, that's as is the trouble, my lord, he don't know. He jes' says she was 'ere." He shrugged his shoulders. "I'm sorry, my lord, I can't get anything more out of him."

His Lordship sighed. "What to do next, Hardwick?" Although he spoke to the groom, his musings were in part to himself. "Do I go to Wakeham to tell them?" He paused. "I think not."

The characters of the duke and the duchess returning forcefully to his thoughts decided him against it. They would not understand how he had managed to find Petty and then just as swiftly lose her again; he was not, in truth, proud of himself, but to have to face their censure after the way they behaved to Petty would put him out of humour and he might be betrayed into telling them what he thought of them and, tempting as this was, he knew that at the present time it would not help the situation!

"No, Hardwick! Not Wakeham, London. Yes, Grafton Street. Immediately! See the bags packed and disposed and the horses put to. While you see to that, I must pay my respects to Mrs Lumley."

"Yes, Your Lordship," the old groom said wearily. He knew his master well and was sure that he would drive up to the limit back to London.

The visit to Mrs Lumley was quickly paid. She was deeply concerned that he had not managed to find a trace of Petty. He thought at the moment it was better not to divulge that a girl who might be Petty had been seen at the White Hart. He did not wish to raise her hopes. He bade her farewell, reassured her that he would continue his search, and that he would keep in touch with her. Kissing her hand, he smiled.

"Now, get along with you, my lord," she replied, plainly pleased with his attention. "Just you tell me that you are going to find my Petty, I am fair worried about her, don't mind if I tell you."

His face grew serious. "I am very concerned myself, perhaps she will have gone to London?"

"Do you think so? She did not seem to like London much. She always said she did not want to go there."

"I was going to take her myself," he said wryly. "I did not even ask her if she wanted to go." He hesitated. "I just wanted to get her away from those people... I was as bad as them, it seems," he finished harshly.

"You must not go on blaming yourself," Mrs Lumley continued sagely. "It will not help matters."

"I know... I know. I will send the instant I find out anything."

Lord Milton drove, as the old groom had predicted, at a scorching pace, arriving in Grafton Street late that night. As he trod up the steps he realised that the house was ablaze with lights. He had not time to question this, when the door was flung open by the butler.

"I am glad to see, Your Lordship."

"Yes, Penn," his master replied somewhat impatiently. "But what is all this? Burning candles most wastefully? Are you trying to bankrupt me?" There was a smile in his voice as he looked at his butler quizzically.

"No, my lord," he started, but at that moment the grizzled head of Cuthbert appeared around the library door.

"Edward, my boy, and why were you not here to welcome us?"

"Simple." He wrung his grandfather's hand, beaming with appreciation. "Because I had no notion that you were coming, and who is we?"

"I brought your sister, thought it about time Aurelia had a bit of town polish."

"Oh, it is so good to see you." Edward embraced the old man warmly. "I am so delighted that you are here. I need your advice. I need your counsel."

"Only too pleased, my boy." It was his grandfather's turn to beam with pleasure. "But not tonight, I think. You look quite done in. From whence did you come?"

"Bath."

"Bath, in one day, you driving? Now, in my day the journey took three."

"Yes, but things are different now. Life has moved on." He smiled broadly at his grandfather. "Penn, I have not dined. Please arrange for something to be sent to the book room.

"Immediately, my lord."

"Will you join me while I eat? We can talk then."

Cuthbert nodded, and whilst the underlings scurried away on their tasks, Edward followed his grandfather into the library. This was a beautiful room, elegantly decorated, the Chippendale and Sheraton furniture setting off the carefully collected pieces.

The heat of the previous few days had given place to a windy, chilly evening, and a small fire had been laid in the grate. Cuthbert made his way to it, and as he stood warming his hands, he watched Edward intensely, taking in the stricken look in his eyes. As if unaware, Edward paced up and down the room.

"Oh, Grandpapa," he started angrily, "I have made such a botch of it." He went on to describe briefly what had happened. Cuthbert listened in silence. He knew his grandson well, and it was unlike him to be either out of control of a situation or so dissatisfied with his behaviour; possessed of a natural reserve

 126

combined with a reluctance to commit himself meant that it was unlikely that he would easily give his heart away.

Cuthbert did not in truth think that this was the cause of his obvious unhappiness with his conduct, but he felt that there was more to it than just his wife's disappearance that was making Edward so vexed. He thought for a moment and then enquired in his straightforward way, "Why are you so out of humour, my boy?"

Edward was not normally forthcoming so he was not really expecting a reply, but he was wise enough to know that direct questions did sometimes produce honest answers and he was hoping that perhaps in this case his strategy might work. It did not.

"Out of humour?" Edward grinned, his face relaxing. "Oh dear, I suppose I am. I feel very responsible for Petty. She is little more than a child and is, after all, my wife. Whereas the first time she fled I could blame the duchess, this time I can only blame myself. I should have behaved better. Having been fortunate enough to find her, I should have been a great deal more careful not to let her slip through my fingers again." The look that had worried Cuthbert had gone and Edward seemed back in control of himself. "I do not think I will find her again that easily."

"Where will you start?"

"I do not know. I will have to consider tomorrow. But now will you join me in a glass of wine as I eat, and tell me what that sister of mine proposes to do?"

His grandfather had to be content with that but was left feeling that somehow he had not quite taken the proper advantage of the chink in his grandson's armour which he had revealed, and the feeling of slight unease remained.

"Oh, that naughty puss, she has been nagging me to bring her to town. Apparently the beaux of Harrogate are not enough for her, she must needs meet the London set."

"I hoped that she might be presented next season. One of the reasons for marriage was that there would be someone to chaperone her and organise her come-out." He smiled ruefully. "Not that I think Petty would be much up to the task."

"Well, it would seem that Aurelia has a school friend in London who has written enumerating the delights of Ashley's Amphitheatre..."

"Astley's," Edward interjected.

"Astley's then. You know she's a one for horses and it would be that the spectacle of some Louisa girl dancing on a white circus horse she must see and then it is Vauxhall Gardens and the fireworks and nothing would content that minx but that I bring her..."

Edward laughed again. He understood perfectly the wiles that had been employed to convince Cuthbert to bring Aurelia to London. In truth it would be no bad thing. The season was well advanced now, and if she were to come out next year it would not go amiss that she acquire a small measure of knowledge of London. He had seen too many overprotected tongue-tied country girls brought to London for their first season totally out of their depths, and he did not wish his sister to join their number. Although he did not anticipate that his bouncy Aurelia would be short of conversation, nevertheless, she was still very inexperienced in the ways of the world, and a few weeks finding her way about could only be a good thing.

The only problem was, who was to chaperone her? It was out of the question that she could go out without a proper person to accompany her. Perhaps this friend would have a suitable governess? He thought of Petty. It was strange how she kept intruding into his thoughts. He smiled to himself. She must indeed have been one of those country girls, with stilted speech, gauche and awkward. He wondered where she was and if she were safe.

"I think on balance that it will be no bad thing that Aurelia is here." He smiled affectionately at his grandfather. "Now, it has been a tiring day, let us retire."

When Lord Milton left her, Mrs Lumley sat bathed in thought. Then she rang for Hawley and ordered her carriage. She told Dora that she was going out and that if anyone called, to tell them that Mrs Blakeston had been unexpectedly called away. She drove at a stately pace to the White Hart. On her arrival she summoned the landlady, to whom she was well known.

"Mrs Lumley... oh, ma'am, what can I do to help you?"

Mrs Lumley smiled her most charming smile. "First, some refreshment, and then, my dear Mrs Pickwick, I need your help." The refreshment was quickly brought and the information that Mrs Lumley needed as quickly elicited.

"Tonbridge? I wonder why Tonbridge?"

"Begging your pardon, Mrs Lumley, but I 'as 'ad the notion that she did not want Tonbridge so much as it was the first stage out of here. She did not seem to mind where she went."

"Yes... I suspect you are right." Mrs Pickwick, amply rewarded for her pains, ushered Mrs Lumley to her carriage.

On reaching home, Mrs Lumley summoned her maid and her groom, informing them that they were to start for Tonbridge as soon as nuncheon had been consumed. Dora was to be sent to stay with the Darbys, but here she met her first setback. Dora was determined to go with her, and try as she might, she could not persuade her usually biddable daughter to change her mind. So it was agreed that Dora would company her mama, and her maid was sent to pack.

Petty passed a sleepless night on the truckle. The weather having changed, she found that not only was the truckle hard but she was also cold; her thoughts as she lay awake trying to get comfortable, were not pleasant. She wished she were in Bath.

She wondered if Mrs Lumley was so disgusted with her that she would wash her hands of her. It was not like Mrs Lumley, but she had let them down very badly. Tears ran down her face and onto the pillow. In the large four-poster Verity slept peacefully. Eventually the dawn broke; Petty dozed off, only to be awoken about one hour later by Lucy.

"Good morning, miss, you'd best make haste, you will miss the stage. I have brought you water." She nodded to Verity who was stretching sleepily.

"Oh, what an awful hour. At home I do not have to rise until at least ten."

"Well, you are not at home now, and if we are to catch the stage we must make haste," Petty returned tartly.

"Oh, I suppose so." Verity climbed out of bed reluctantly.

"Hurry and get dressed," Petty expostulated.

"Have you laid out my clothes, and are you going to help me?" Verity demanded.

"Goodness me, can you not dress yourself?" Petty remarked with some asperity. It was one of Fonty's maxims that, however high born you might be, you must be able to do things for yourself, and all the Mordaunt children were trained to be able to care for themselves.

"I do not have to, I have servants."

"Well, I am not your servant, and as you chose to leave home without a maid, you had better learn to put your own clothes on."

In the end, however, she was forced by the necessity for speed to help. When they were ready, Petty packed their bags. Verity had brought nothing with her from home, but apparently Bertram had purchased various articles for her. He obviously understood women, for she was well equipped. She hurried Verity down, paid their shot, and pushed her onto the stage, complaining vociferously about her lack of breakfast.

"You can have some when we stop to change horses."

Once on the coach Verity continued to complain: the swaying made her sick, she was squashed, she was cold, the coach went too slowly, she was not used to travel in this way. Petty resisted the temptation to tell her sharply to be quiet, but she was even more exhausted by the time the coach drew up at the Swan With Two Necks in Lad Lane.

They clambered stiffly down from the coach and asked the ostler to tell them where they could obtain a hackney carriage. Petty had spent two seasons in London but had never moved outside a select area. If she had not felt so stupid with fatigue she would have been intrigued by the bustling life of the city. Verity, who had been allowed to explore far more of London, was not at all interested in the scuttling ostlers, the post boys in their blue jackets and bright buttons, or the numerous cooks, porters, storekeepers and the other members of the 2,000 staff employed by William Chaplin.

They found a shabby hackney carriage and climbed wearily in. Petty gave the direction, and they lay back against the squabs.

CHAPTER ELEVEN

As the hackney made its way through the streets, Petty peered out of the window; she recognised nothing, which was not altogether surprising for her knowledge of London was very limited, bounded as it was by Berkeley Square and its environs. Indeed, in her two seasons Petty had never moved outside the fashionable part frequented by members of the ton. She was familiar with the shops on Bond and St James's Streets, and she had been carefully schooled only to visit these in the mornings, accompanied by Holtby and a maid. No well-bred lady would have dreamt of risking her reputation by paying visits to Bond Street in the afternoon when they might have been subjected to the lascivious leers of the rakes and dandies. She was, also, well versed in the haunts of the top echelon: Almack's, where she had spent many endless evenings trying to hide her awkwardness in corners; presentations at Carlton House hosted by the Prince Regent, where her gawky shyness had left her ignored by accomplished society; numerous miserable balls and routs given by high-born ladies, designed to enhance their standing as hostesses. These made up Petty's experience of life in London! Although her experience was confined she was quick enough to realise, not without relief, that Portman Square was quite alien to her and was glad to assure herself that she had been correct in her surmise that Verity's papa did not move in the higher ranks of society. She would not encounter the Ladies Jersey or Hamel here!

The hackney drew up outside number 38. It was an imposing stuccoed mansion built on six floors, with a porticoed doorway framed by the Corinthian pilasters made so fashionable by Mr Nash. Hardly waiting for the carriage to stop, Verity tumbled out and dashed up the steps, banging on the knocker as hard as she could. The door was opened by an elderly butler who seemed overcome when he saw Verity.

"Oh… miss… oh… Miss Verity." He seemed about to cry. "Oh, miss, oh, you have come back. We thought… we thought… Oh, miss, we thought we might never see you again…"

"Well, I am here, Drake. I am back. Where is Papa?"

Petty, left paying the coachman, was seemingly forgotten. Verity bounded into the house, ignoring her. The old butler, however, looked at her questioningly. She moved up the steps.

"You see, I have brought back Miss Verity quite safely. Please see that the bags are unloaded." She made to follow Verity into the house. Drake appeared to be about to stop her but Petty fixed him with her grandest look and said in her well-bred voice, "I do think it is important that I see Sir Hugo to explain, do you not?"

"Yes. Yes, of course, miss, I am so sorry." He ushered her into the hall, a sombre area panelled in dark and heavy wood.

A man came out of the door on the left, which was obviously the library; he was tall with wispy sandy hair, slightly thinning on top. He was dressed without much elegance in clothes which became a country squire; his eyes were a very pale blue and they peered short-sightedly over the small glasses which perched on the end of his nose. He looked somewhat distracted.

When he saw Verity, however, his face lit up with relief. She ran to him.

"Papa! Papa! I am back! Oh, Papa, it was so awful… he took me…" She flung her arms around him.

"Shh, my dear, what happened? What happened?" His voice had a slight Yorkshire tinge.

"Oh, Papa, it was so awful. I was so scared… Mrs Blakeston rescued me…"

For the first time her father seemed to become aware of Petty standing uneasily in the hall. She was by this time so tired and dispirited it was as much as she could do not to sink to the floor. He looked at her in an absentminded way then inclined his head slightly and asked, "Mrs Blakeston?" Petty nodded slightly. "Is it true that it is you whom I have to thank for my daughter's safe return?"

Petty nodded again. Although he had glanced in her direction he hardly seemed to see her for he was unable to take his eyes off his daughter.

"You had best come into the library, where you may tell me about it." He tucked Verity's arm into his and returned to the library.

Petty, left standing awkwardly in the middle of the hall, not quite knowing what to do next, found unwelcome tears starting in her eyes at this cavalier treatment. She did not know what she had expected, but being disregarded had certainly not occurred to her as a possibility. By this time, however, the news of Verity's return had permeated the servants' hall and a quantity of servants appeared, ostensibly hurrying about their business. Among them Petty noticed a tiny lady with an unmistakable air of command. She had snow-white hair which she wore tucked into a spotless white cap, twinkling brown eyes which were surprisingly youthful; her grey dress betokened a housekeeper. A quick glance sufficed to apprise her of the situation. She dismissed the interested servants with a wave of her hands and turned her attention to the butler.

"Well, Mr Drake?" she enquired.

"This young lady has brought back Miss Verity, Mrs Drake," he replied.

His excellent spouse smiled at Petty. "Thank you. Thank you, Mrs..." Mrs Drake started, then suddenly realising how close Petty was to collapse, she moved quickly to her side, taking her firmly by the arm and propelling her into the library, where she pushed her into a huge leather armchair by the fire. She fixed her employer with a fierce glare and ordered, "You sit there, Mrs Blakeston. I am going to fetch you some refreshment. Now, Miss Verity, are you hungry?"

Verity turned to the housekeeper, throwing her arms around her neck. "Darling Drakey, I am, oh yes, I am. Can I have one of your milky specials, please?"

Mrs Drake cast a shrewd look at Petty and then at her master. "Come, Miss Verity. Let us go and see Cook and see what she has prepared," she stated and whisked her out of the room.

Petty looked around her; the library was a vast gloomy room. It was very untidy; there were dusty books and piles of papers all over the floor; the whole place smelt musty and stale.

Petty had an overwhelming desire to fling open the windows and let in some fresh air. At one end of the room stood a huge desk. It too was covered with books, papers, newspapers and files. How Sir Hugo could find anything there Petty was at a loss to understand and she could not conceive how anyone managed to work in such a mess; privately she thought that it was impossible!

"Perhaps you would be good enough to explain what, apparently, happened to my daughter and how you came to be involved?" Sir Hugo started. He seemed unsure of whether to thank her or rebuke her. Petty, utterly fatigued by this time, felt tears at the back of her eyes; she had nowhere to go, it was late and her slender emotional resources were quite depleted, her energy expended.

She did not quite know what she had expected from Sir Hugo, but if she had had time to think about it she would have expected some gratitude. A stray tear slipped down a cheek. Sir

Hugo, whose demeanour was fairly abstracted, saw her for the first time. He regarded the tear and realised that she was very young. He smiled rather more kindly.

"Come, please tell me what part you played in my Verity's flight. You must know we have all been worried stiff."

"I played no part in your daughter's 'flight' as you call it. I did not meet Verity until last night," Petty replied with some asperity. "And without conceit I have to tell you that had it not been for me she would have been spirited away by as nasty a gentleman as I hope I will ever meet." Her aggrieved tone had its effect.

"I apologise. Please explain to me what happened."

"It would appear that Verity has some unsuitable and very silly friends, the Misses Locke. They have helped her to dispense with the services of a respectable governess and encouraged her to meet a very undesirable young man." Sir Hugo had the grace to look somewhat shamefaced. "This young man, one Bertram Melville."

Sir Hugo looked very surprised. "Mr M... Melville?"

"He's a well-known fortune hunter. I'm afraid he has been arranging to meet your daughter alone in the park, apparently urging her to marry him. Yesterday she refused so he abducted her..."

"What!" Sir Hugo had the grace to look appalled.

Petty nodded. "Apparently he bundled her into a coach, and took her to an inn in Tonbridge, which is where I heard her pleas. I managed, admittedly with the landlady's help, to get rid of him. I brought her back to you, her reputation untarnished, but not, if I may say so, because of your good offices. It is clear to me that for a girl as beautiful as she is, and as wealthy, she has been very inadequately chaperoned." She was so tired that it was impossible to cover her words in polite platitudes.

He smiled vaguely at her. "I owe you an apology and a great debt of gratitude. It was I who introduced her to Mr Melville but I had no idea he would behave thus. I believed him to be a gentleman."

"He is well born but I am afraid he has none of the manners that characterize a true gentleman. I gather he is on the search for a rich wife and I imagine that Verity fitted the bill."

Sir Hugo looked worried. "What do you think I should do… call him out?"

Petty was amazed that a man should not know how to avenge his daughter's honour. She did not think, however, that it would be desirable for a duel to be fought over Verity, as this would only draw attention to the girl's folly.

"No… I do not think that would be a very satisfactory end, think of the scandal… He will of course never be admitted to your house again."

Sir Hugo sighed with relief. He clearly wanted no part in any kind of confrontation with Melville. "Good, then that is settled." He regarded Petty guiltily. "I know I am remiss as a parent, I am very involved at the moment in Parliamentary reform; Equality, the Rights of Man, the Principle of Utility; these are the issues that are important for the future of the working man in England. If we are to go forward we must readjust the balance of government in their favour. They must now have a voice in government proportionate to their economic influence. It is of the most enormous importance. I think only of this."

He ran his hand through his sandy hair. The ideas he propounded were new to Petty; she had been brought up surrounded by the principles put forward by the aristocratic Whigs. Her father was one of Lady Melbourne's favourites, and she knew that until his death six years earlier, Fox too had been one of the duke's intimates. She was, however, too tired and too concerned about her own future to enquire too carefully into these new thoughts. Sir Hugo looked worried.

"I do not know what to do. Since my wife died we have had a series of governesses, none of whom has been very satisfactory, I am afraid… They do not seem to be able to control her."

Petty saw her chance. "May I have a go? May I come and be

Verity's companion? I think she is too old for a governess. I am searching for a new post. I have been working in Bath for Mrs Lumley, I am sure she will give you a reference, if you consider it to be a necessity."

He looked her over in a strange way.

"Yes, I suppose it would answer... yes... yes, you can stay. It will solve the problem. Now that that is arranged I can return to my work." He rang the bell.

Then he crossed to his desk and was immediately lost in a thick document. Petty sat in the leather chair. She was cold and miserable. She felt lost and she longed for the cheerful company of Mrs Lumley and Dora; she did not feel welcome here, it was an ugly house. Verity was spoilt and as unlike the adorable Dora as it was possible to imagine; Sir Hugo was rude, unfriendly and very ungrateful. Lord Milton was beastly to have found her congenial hiding place and to have ruined her happiness, not once but twice. Petty gave a small sob. She felt very sorry for herself. The bell was answered by Mrs Drake. Sir Hugo looked up; clearly he had forgotten Petty quiet in the chair and was annoyed to be interrupted.

"Yes!" he said impatiently.

"You rang, Sir Hugo." Mrs Drake, long inured to the vagaries of her employer, looked questioningly at him.

"Yes... Mrs Blakeston there." He waved in Petty's direction. "Going to be a companion to Verity, see she has a room." Then he turned back to his books and was again lost.

Mrs Drake smiled at Petty. "You come with me, you look ready to drop." She scooped Petty up and bore her up to the top floor, showing her into a plain, serviceable bedchamber. A narrow bed made up with spotless sheets lay against one wall. Opposite was a bare wardrobe; a small bedside table completed the furniture. Mrs Drake crossed to the windows and drew the dimity curtains.

"I... I... just... well, that is, we... the staff... well, particularly my husband and me… we want to thank you for what you done for Miss Verity." She shot Petty a slightly embarrassed glance. "She don't mean harm, miss, it's that she is a bit silly."

Petty raised an eyebrow slightly.

"l know it was very silly, going off like that." She looked despairing. "She is a good girl… but her mama died when she was tiny and Sir Hugo… he…" She stopped, at a loss for words.

"He is most preoccupied with his work, is he not? She is too much allowed her own way, I suspect. Does she not have a female relative who could have come to chaperone her?"

"Well, there is Sir Hugo's sister, miss, but she did not approve of her brother's politics. She don't approve of Miss Verity at all, in fact she don't approve of nothing!" She finished with a laugh. "She said she would not come to this house if it was the last house on God's Earth!"

Petty had a clear picture of an embittered spinster who no doubt hated Verity's beauty, a Great-Aunt Elizabeth, without the humour. Petty suddenly had a pang of longing for her own family, and an ache for Wakeham that was so strong it was almost physical. She pushed it away.

"I see."

"You will be so good… for Miss Verity… It did not take a moment for Drake to see that… We are so pleased you are staying."

This was said so simply and honestly that Petty was touched. "l hope I can live up to your expectations." She smiled.

Mrs Drake sniffed. "No doubt of that! But now, why don't you unpack and come down for some supper?"

Petty slept much better than she had anticipated and rose the next day to take up her new duties in a far more cheerful frame of mind. As they breakfasted, she asked Verity how her time was occupied.

"Well," replied the girl, "l do have a very good time. I go shopping with Matty and Jane, I walk in the park with Matty and

Jane, we have evening parties, they have all kinds of friends. Last week Matty formed a party and took me to the theatre, we saw Eliza Vestris, she was the most exciting woman, she danced like a sylph, and guess what? She dressed in breeches! Have you ever thought of anything so thrilling!"

"Breeches!" Petty found herself far from thrilled; in truth, Verity's answers dismayed her.

She was beginning to be very suspicious as to exactly what kind of women Matty and Jane were; Petty had been brought up in a very narrow social sphere and carefully shielded from demi reps and the professional courtesans known as 'Fashionable Impures'. She was not, however, so innocent or naive not to understand that such women existed, indeed having been privy at an early age to hushed conversations about the exploits of her grandfather, she and all her sisters understood far more of what went on than the duchess would have deemed acceptable.

Petty had been educated to be rigorous in thought. Fonty did not believe in preconceived prejudice and passed this important discipline on to her charges. Therefore, although she was uncertain as to the respectability of Matty and Jane, she refused to prejudge them for she had not yet met them; however, they did not sound desirable friends for Verity; she must question her further.

"I see," she replied kindly to Verity's observation. "Tell me who presented Miss Locke and her sister to you?"

"Oh! I have known them for an age… you know how it is…"

Petty did know 'how it is'. She had many acquaintances, the children of her parents' friends whom she had known all her life. "Oh! I see. Your papa is a friend of Mr and Mrs Locke?"

"Well… not exactly… I have not the pleasure of an acquaintance with Matty's mama and papa, but I am sure that they are everything that is respectable," Verity replied airily.

"Yes, but who introduced you?" Petty was not prepared to be fobbed off.

"Oh! Stop interrogating me… you are not my keeper, I cannot remember exactly who introduced me to whom. I have lots of friends." She resorted to anger to try to deflect Petty from her very proper questions, and, having finished, rose from the breakfast table and was about to leave the room.

Petty, however, well used to the foibles of spoilt beauties, was not turned from her purpose that easily by either anger or rudeness. "Just a moment, Verity! Please sit down again, I have not finished."

Verity pulled a sullen face but she obeyed Petty.

"Thank you!" Petty smiled sweetly and put out her hand. "Come, Verity, let us not quarrel, truly I meant no harm. I have no acquaintance in London myself, and I am so keen to make some new friends, so please will you not tell me about Matty and Jane and your other friends? I am so keen to meet them." She smiled beguilingly.

Verity, too stupid not to walk into the trap set for her, responded to the smile, giggled delightedly, took Petty's hand and told her about her meeting with Matty and Jane.

"Oh, dearest Petty, you will not be cross with me, will you?" Petty shook her head. "You see, Papa is so occupied. When we came to London I thought that he would introduce me to lots of people. I thought I would go to lots of parties with him, but he is too busy. The only person who came to the house was Bertram Melville and I am not really sure how Papa met him. Oh, and lots of very dull political people. I understand that Papa's work is very, very important." She sighed. "But here I was in London and every day all I did was to walk in the park with Miss Pleasty; it was so boring. While we paraded up the same paths every day I noticed Matty and Jane. They were always escorted by good-looking young men. I did envy them, then one day Miss Pleasty did not feel well so I left her on a seat and I went on alone. Matty was there with a Mr Harding. I smiled at them." She looked at Petty, her blue eyes pleading. "I know I should have waited until I was introduced… but…" Petty found herself for the first time feeling rather sorry for the girl. Her father should have arranged something for her; she was young and so pretty. Petty could understand that she wanted a little fun, not that she could approve of her way of going about it.

"Anyway, Matty returned my smile, she said farewell to Mr Harding and got into step with me. She was so friendly, I told her all about Papa, and that my mama was dead and no chaperone except the dreary Miss Pleasty and how I had come from the estates in Yorkshire to London and how I so much wanted to go to parties, and she said perhaps she could help me." Verity looked at Petty defiantly. "And that is what she has done. They have been so kind, they have included me in all their outings, they have introduced me to all kinds of people, and I was only able to introduce them to Mr Melville, for he was the only person I knew, but Matty seemed to be very pleased to make his acquaintance, and they became close friends."

Privately Petty thought she was not surprised that Matty had been pleased about Bertram; she was starting to understand how he had managed to run away with Verity. She was not sure what his intentions had been but she was sure that the outcome would have resulted in financial gain for the Melvilles.

Verity's innocent confidences had given her much food for thought. It was clear that Verity had no structure to her day; she spent no time on any pursuits which would enlarge her mind. This lack of supervision had resulted in a total lack of purpose. Petty could see that she would have her work cut out if she was to restore some structure and order to Verity's life. It would probably be necessary to introduce some morning lessons to the girl, although how she would take to a restoration of the schoolroom, Petty was not sure, but it must be achieved. She sighed; this was a task that had been quite unnecessary at Mrs Lumley's, as Dora had been so carefully brought up and well understood the importance of discipline.

She was quite unsure as to whether she was equal to the task of controlling Verity; she had no experience in these matters; Fonty would have known what to do. Thinking of her governess reminded Petty of one of Miss Chalfont's maxims: "You can do anything you want if you apply your brain to the problem in question." She took a deep breath. It was a challenge. She did not shirk challenges, at least not intellectual ones, so now she must face this one.

She decided that the first priority must be a meeting with Matty and Jane; maybe her suspicions would be unfounded? She did not have to wait long for this, as the meeting with these girls took place on the very afternoon following her conversation with Verity.

It was a cloudless spring day and Petty, whose limbs were still stiff from her various journeys on the stages, was longing to get out into the air to stretch her legs, so as soon as nuncheon was over she suggested they walk in the nearest park.

Verity was enthusiastic. "Oh, indeed, I would like that above everything. I am sure that Matty and Jane will be in Hyde Park this afternoon and I am dying to see them and tell them about my abduction."

Her words filled Petty with horror on two counts. Firstly her abiding nightmare was that now she was back in London she would bump into someone she knew, and Hyde Park was just the venue where this might happen. She would have liked to believe that they would not recognise her in her drab brown dress, but she knew that she had looked a poor dab of a thing during her seasons and it was more likely that they would not have discovered her in Bath where she had been so much more elegant than here! As they started to walk towards the park she realised that this first fear was groundless. Matty and Jane knew their place; they did not choose to parade in the part of Hyde Park which was tacitly accepted as only for persons of rank and fashion, but in the more secluded areas to the north.

Her second concern was not so satisfactorily resolved. Petty, privately thought that the fewer people who knew about Verity's misadventure the better, tried to suggest circumspection as they walked up from Portman Square.

"Do you think that it is wise to tell anyone about your unfortunate experience? You do not want to be gossiped about, you know."

"Oh, Matty would not tell anyone, she would think it is so exciting to be abducted! A brilliant adventure!" she laughed.

"Verity! I must try to bring you to some sense of what is right. You know it is not an adventure to be kidnapped, it is the height of folly to want to boast of it to your friend. Do you not know that you could have been in real danger?"

"Foo! I would have escaped, or if I did not escape I would have been rescued by a dashing cavalier." She smiled beatifically.

It appeared to Petty that the true facts of what had occurred had been put aside in favour of a fanciful dream. Again she faced her own inadequacy in bringing the girl to a proper recognition of the undesirability of her conduct. How to bring the girl to a sense of what was right and proper? She was musing on this problem when they reached the park, entering by a gate that was unfamiliar to her.

Petty took a deep breath, her spirits rose. It was too beautiful an afternoon to worry about anything; the sky was a deep blue, the light so clear that the colours of the flowers seemed all the more brilliant. Verity led the way through a delightful small garden, the paths bordered by the prettiest of pink and yellow blooms. A gentle breeze wafted from across the tops of the trees, stopping it from feeling too hot. Petty felt more content than at any point since her flight from Bath. Soon they came to a path between some tall trees. It was very shady and looked most inviting. As they started down it Verity gave a hoot of delight and ran towards two girls who were approaching them. When they saw Verity, Petty noticed that they exchanged slightly surprised glances.

"Matty! Jane!" she cried. "How wonderful to see you. I have so much to tell you." As she looked at them Petty shuddered inwardly, her worst fears realised. Although the girls who came to greet Verity were of a type that she, with her sheltered upbringing, had never before encountered she was quick to recognise their lack of respectability.

They were dressed in a bold fashion in gowns which clung to their figures in a most unbecoming way; they were both very pretty but when they spoke it was with an artificial and ugly tone.

"La, Verity! You here! My sweet girl! How you pass current. La, dearest one, what a belle you are to be sure." Matty gave a peal of laughter and grabbed Verity's arm. Petty did not think she had ever seen anyone so vulgar. "Sweetest one... I have seen a certain buck over by the rose garden searching for a certain little fairy queen." She gave another of her hideous laughs, and squeezed Verity's hand.

"Oh, Matty, truly, is he here?" Verity's normally pretty voice seemed to be taking on the characteristics of her unsavory friends.

Petty wondered who he was. It was hard to credit the fact that only the day before yesterday Verity had been off with Bertram Melville; perhaps this 'buck' was he; she hoped not, and if not he, it seemed that there was another gallant. It was all most perplexing.

"La, La... come, come... your swain awaits." Jane took Verity's arm and propelled her in the direction of a garden in a small clearing just visible in between the trees.

"Just a minute! Stop." Petty sounded stiffer than she meant to.

"La, who is this Miss Prim?" Matty sniggered. "Take not a whit of notice of Miss Proper, Verity. Leave us alone!" she demanded.

Petty's temper snapped. "How dare you be so rude! I am Verity's companion and I do not intend to "leave her alone." She sounded braver than she felt.

Matty and Jane exchanged looks. Petty was far too inexperienced in the ways of the world to have any idea of what these two girls were up to; she just knew that she loathed them, and that she wished with all her heart that she were away from here and back in Bath.

"Oh, Verity, don't listen to that old killjoy. Go away! Verity does not need you. We can chaperone her."

Matty waved an arm in Petty's direction, while Jane continued to pull Verity towards the rose garden, where the shady figure of a man was just visible.

"Oh, Matty, Jane, I have so much to tell you. Guess what happened?"

Petty was not going to be put off so easily. "Stop! Verity! Stop it now," she commanded. "Do be sensible…" She tugged at her other arm, turning her away from Jane so that the girl was looking directly in her eyes.

"Please, Verity, come back with me now. I do not want to tell your papa." The girl stopped. "Your papa would not be pleased… He wants me to care for you…" Petty continued somewhat desperately. The threat of her papa obviously brought Verity momentarily to her senses.

"I had better not, another day perhaps." She turned to the sisters, and as she did so Petty noticed that Matty looked most disgruntled and was about to say something when a speaking look from her sister silenced her.

Petty took hold of Verity and left with all haste. She knew that she had alienated Matty and Jane, and as they hurried home she chastised herself for not handling it better. She felt that she was just not capable of dealing with this. Fonty would have known what to do. Oh, how she longed for Fonty.

Petty hurried Verity back to Portman Square. She decided that she must instantly see her new employer and consult with him about the extraordinary happenings in the park, so, before even taking off her bonnet, she tapped at the library door. On being commanded to enter, Petty hurried in. The figure behind the huge desk looked up most unencouragingly.

"Well! What do you want? I really cannot be interrupted, you know!"

Petty started to explain. "You see, Sir Hugo, I took Verity to the park this afternoon and…"

"I do not see. Please do not bother me with these trivia. I thought I had made it very clear that I have important matters to consider. Do you not understand, my girl, how vital it is that we change the power structure? I explained to you we must give more…" He sounded exasperated.

Petty felt all the old insecurities returning; the unpleasantness of his tone, the dismissiveness in his demeanour seemed to render her incapable of coherent speech.

"I do not understand why you see fit to bother me with your problems. You requested the job of companion to Verity; if you cannot do it then you should not have asked for the position. I employ you to take care of Verity and I expect you to do it properly. Now, please leave me."

"But…"

"Mrs Blakeston, I have work to do."

Petty nodded and went to leave. She felt defeated by her own inability to answer him in a way that would make him listen. I thought I was better, she reprimanded herself. I stood up to Lord Milton and Bertram in the inn, but then why am I so daunted by his irritability?

As she went to her room to take off her hat, she felt utterly wretched. Tears ran down her face; she so wished she was back in Bath. She knew she had flourished in the love and approbation that had been shown her there. Being in Sir Hugo's household was like being at Wakeham, only worse. Suddenly she shook herself. She made a decision. She would write to Mrs Lumley. I will ask for their forgiveness, I will ask if I may return to Bath, I will not be taken away by Lord Milton. I will not be forced to return to Wakeham. I will stay with Dora. If they will have me. These thoughts made her feel much happier; she would not have to remain in this place a day longer than was absolutely necessary. She wiped her eyes, brushed her hair, and went to find Verity in an altogether more cheerful frame of mind. As she came downstairs she met Drake who informed her: "Miss Verity has visitors, she is in the drawing room."

Petty's heart sank again as she wondered if all Verity's friends were as appalling as the Misses Locke.

The drawing room was on the first floor of the house; it could have been elegant, but it was decorated in shades of mustard. The three long windows which overlooked the thoroughfare of the square were shrouded in brown drapes. The furniture was made of heavy dark oak, carved with mythological scenes, the sofa upholstered in brown velvet.

Petty entered. After the brightness of the sun which poured into the windows in her small bedroom, the room seemed even gloomier. Verity rose and crossed towards her.

"This is my friend Mary and her mama, Mrs Cornwall. Mary was at school with me in Yorkshire. She is quite my best friend. I am so excited, I did not realise that they were in London," Verity burbled.

Petty shook hands with Mary, who seemed a most unexceptional girl, and her mama who was a rather plump woman, very conservatively dressed in a maroon merino pelisse, matched with a simple high-crowned hat. She smiled warmly at Petty and bade her come and sit next to her.

"I am so pleased that you are with Verity. I have worried about her so much. She means well but I am afraid she lacks for sense. Well, it is what one would expect, having no mama and a father who… Oh, please do not misunderstand me, I do not mean to criticize. I know how difficult it has been for Sir Hugo." She stopped, slightly confused. Petty smiled.

"Quite. It is hard when one is so busy and has no time."

Meeting Mrs Cornwall's eyes she found that they understood each other perfectly. Mrs Cornwall patted her hand.

"I come to bid you both to an evening party that I am giving next Saturday."

This kind invitation was quickly accepted, and the Cornwalls left after Verity had extracted a promise that Mary would be allowed to walk with them the next day. Petty was secretly pleased that her thoughts had been given another direction. She felt much better after her meeting with Mrs Cornwall, as in her she felt she had an ally. She knew that Verity needed her, and much as she wanted to return to Bath, she thought she ought to remain if only for a short while. She still intended to write to Mrs Lumley, but her note now would only contain the information that she was safe.

CHAPTER TWELVE

Mrs Lumley arrived in Tonbridge at lunchtime the next day. She had not enjoyed her journey. She was hot, harassed and very irritable. It was a measure of her regard for Petty that she was prepared to make the journey at all, particularly in the heat, although to their relief when they stopped to spend the night, the evening turned cooler.

Mrs Lumley had taken the precaution of making sure that she had elicited all the necessary information from Mrs Pickwick, they therefore made straight for the Dog and Goose. As she moved slowly into the inn followed by her maid and Dora, Mrs Sowerby bustled out to greet her.

"Good day, I would like a private parlour and some refreshment for my daughter and myself, and please see that my groom and maid are comfortable."

Mrs Sowerby, who had taken one look at the expensive if somewhat outrageous equipage that had brought Mrs Lumley to her door, hurried to obey. On being shown into the parlour, she was about to leave when Mrs Lumley stopped her. "A word please, Mrs…"

"Sowerby, ma'am, how can I help you?"

"I am searching for… for a young girl… She has been staying with me and she was…" She hesitated, she did not want to expose Petty. "She was chased away from me. I have reason to believe that she caught the Tonbridge stage and would have overnighted here. She is…" again she paused, "… a slight girl with very beautiful eyes and…"

"Oh, ma'am, you mean that stately girl with the blue eyes. She was more than a match for that crimping man, told him where to go, she did. I mean, it is not right running off with a young girl, it is what I do not hold with."

"Running off? Did someone run off with Petty?" Encountering a bemused look from the landlady she added, "With the blue-eyed girl?"

"Lord love you… no! No one could run off with that one, far too grand is that one. One look from her and she would see them off, I tell you."

This seemed such an unlikely description of Petty that Mrs Lumley thought that perhaps they were not discussing the same girl, however she nodded encouragingly to Mrs Sowerby who continued, "Mind you, she 'ad to ask my help to get rid of him. I threated the runners and he were gone in the wink of an eye. I think she could have done it, but she had 'er hands full trying to get that Verity from crying."

"Verity?"

"Yes, the girl who had been taken, like. No better than she ought to be in my opinion but when your young lady pointed out that they all gets into trouble and it could have been Lucy…"

"Lucy?"

"Yes, oh, Lucy is my daughter. Not that I have not brought her up proper and she would not be abused or whatever…"

"Quite. Now, do I understand correctly…? Petty found a young girl who had been abducted?" Mrs Sowerby nodded vigorously.

"She rescued… this young girl?"

"Yes, that's it. That's it. Silly young miss, but your young lady, well, she is real quality, she is. I could tell the moment I set eyes on her."

"Do you happen to know where Petty went?"

"Oh yes... she took that young minx to London to her father," the landlady finished triumphantly.

"And do you by any chance know exactly where this Verity lived?" Mrs Sowerby shook her head. "Or even her name?"

Again Mrs Sowerby shook her head. Mrs Lumley thought a moment, and then asked for some refreshment. When the landlady had gone she told Dora that she thought they had better follow Petty to London. She would send ahead and reserve rooms in St James's Royal Hotel.

Although they travelled to London in very easy stages, Mrs Lumley was greatly fatigued by the time they reached the metropolis, and it was with a deal of relief that they reached their destination. Mr English rushed out to greet his guests, ushering them inside quickly to the best suite of rooms that the St James's possessed. Mrs Lumley retired immediately, and it took until late morning on Saturday before she was ready to sally forth to pay a call on Lord Milton, to inform him of what she had discovered.

Arriving at the elegant abode in Grafton Street, she was shown into the drawing room on the first floor. This was an enchanting room, delicately proportioned with fine ceilings and decorated in subtle hues of cream; the hangings were of a pale green and apricot toile; four long windows were open onto a small flower-laden balcony which ran the length of the house.

The furniture was Sheraton. It was mostly rosewood and had been chosen wisely to complement the shape of the room; the pictures were by Dutch masters such as Rembrandt, as well as by modern artists Reynolds, Hoppner and Gainsborough. The whole room was filled with summer blossoms whose scent sweetened the air with a soft fragrance.

The only occupant of the room jumped up as they were announced. She was a slender girl whose beauty was so breathtaking that it made Mrs Lumley stop where she was and stare. She seemed completely unaware of the picture she presented, holding out her hands in an unselfconscious way.

"I am Aurelia Milton," she said with a radiant smile. "I am Edward's sister."

Dora thought she had never seen anyone so beautiful. The Hon. Aurelia Milton had hair that was so dark that it was almost black, very pale crystal clear blue eyes, framed by long dark lashes; her complexion was creamy white, her high cheekbones delicately tinged with pink. Mrs Lumley quickly recovered herself.

"How do you do, my dear, I am Gertrude Lumley and this is my daughter Dora." Dora curtsied smiling shyly, her reward being a responsive look from those dancing luminous eyes.

"I have come to visit your brother. Is he at home?" Mrs Lumley continued. Aurelia made to answer, but before she could do so the door opened and an elderly man came in. He seemed slightly surprised when he observed Mrs Lumley, who was dressed in her usual original style. However, he quickly recovered himself and went across and warmly shook her hand.

"I am Cuthbert Philipson," he said, his voice having a distinct Yorkshire burr to it. "I am delighted to welcome you. Please sit down and we will see how I can be of assistance to you."

"I am Gertrude Lumley. I have come from Bath. I need to see Lord Milton rather urgently."

"My grandson has stepped out, but I do expect him back henceforth. In the meantime, may I offer you refreshment?"

By this time the two had summed each other up and both liked what they saw. Mrs Lumley sat herself on an ample sofa and Cuthbert placed himself opposite her. A few minutes' conversation convinced them that they thought alike on any number of important matters, and they were set for a comfortable prose. Dora looked admiringly at Aurelia, who, blessed with a total lack of vanity, was unaware of her extraordinary looks; this made her a most charming and appealing girl, and it did not take long for the two girls to be sitting down exchanging confidences.

"I must confess that I have never been to London before," Dora vouchsafed shyly.

"Oh, please do not think that I have any experience of the city, for I have not, I have only been to London once and I was so little that I do not remember it at all. I have persuaded Grandpapa to take me to Astley's and Vauxhall Gardens! Are you out yet? I am to come out next year if Edward can find some high-born boring lady to present me!"

Dora giggled. "I am out in Bath," she replied. "But, of course, we do not have any acquaintance in London who could bring me out here. My best friend, Cecily Simpson, is in London. She is here for the season, with her aunt, Lady Hamel, who has presented Cecily and her daughter Sophie. They are to share a ball in two weeks. I have had a letter from Cecily. It appears she is having a wonderful time, balls every night. Lady Hamel even procured vouchers for her to attend an assembly at Almack's! Imagine the honour."

"What is Almack's and why is it such an honour?"

"Oh." Dora sounded quite shocked. "Do you know nothing? Mama has told me all about Almack's. It is her dream that one day I shall attend a Wednesday assembly there."

"But why do you not just go?" Aurelia asked, puzzled.

"Oh, you do not just go. It is the most exclusive place in the world. You have to have a voucher given to you by one of the patronesses. There are seven of these: Lady Sefton, Lady Jersey, Lady Cowper, Lady Castlereagh, Mrs Drummond Burrell, Princess Esterhazy and the Countess Lieven," she recited.

"It all sounds rather silly to me," pronounced the down-to-earth Aurelia. "Are the assemblies particularly exciting?"

"Oh no, Petty says they are exceedingly dull, only lemonade and stale cake, and some dancing. Petty says they do the waltz!"

"Who is Petty? Why does she know so much?"

Dora looked slightly puzzled. "To tell you the truth I do not know how she knew so much. She was my companion. Mama hired her to give me some 'polish'. It's her greatest wish that I shall come out in London. Petty was so very kind, I loved her above everything. The reason we are here now is that we have lost her..."

She stopped, unsure of how to proceed. She could hardly say that Aurelia's brother had scared her away, and in any case she was not quite sure why Petty had run herself. Mrs Lumley thought it better for her to remain in ignorance of the finer details of Petty's marriage.

"Lost her? How did you lose her?"

"Well, it seems she went to London..."

"Well, where is she?"

"We do not know."

"Oh!" Aurelia looked even more perplexed and was about to ask more when the door opened and Edward came in. Immediately he crossed to Mrs Lumley and clasped her hands.

"My dear ma'am, I am so pleased to see you in London, so soon. What brings you here?" Mrs Lumley raised her eyes very slightly in the direction of the girls. Edward turned, greeted Dora, kissed his sister on her cheek and suggested that Aurelia take Dora to the morning room while he talked to Mrs Lumley. Having curtsied prettily, the two girls left and His Lordship turned to Mrs Lumley and Cuthbert.

"Now, what news do you have for me?" His Lordship demanded somewhat impatiently.

"Well, after you left I went back to the White Hart. I am on good terms with Mrs Pickwick." She shot a glance at Lord Milton and then grinned. "I thought that perhaps I could obtain information that had not been forthcoming to you! I discovered that a girl answering Petty's description had boarded the Tonbridge stage."

"Why did she not tell me that? I asked her most particularly."

Cuthbert smiled. "My dear Edward, were you friendly? Were you obliging? Or were you merely high-handed?"

Lord Milton sighed. "Alright I admit probably the latter! But if only she might have told me the truth, I could have caught up with Petty. It is my fault, Grandfather. I worry so much about her. She is such a little thing, so innocent, so unable to care for herself. I pray that some misfortune has not overtaken her."

"I think the landlady at the Dog and Goose in Tonbridge, which is where I went next, would be hard pushed to recognise your description of Petty. She described her to me as grand, stately, very well able to see off some out-and-out villain who appears to have run off with a girl called Verity!" She had the pleasure of seeing both Edward and Cuthbert look amazed.

"Verity! Who is Verity?" Cuthbert enquired.

"I do not know. That is the conundrum. If we knew who Verity is, we would be able to find Petty, for apparently she escorted her back to London to return the girl to her papa."

"We must find out. I shall go immediately to Tonbridge to question the landlady further. She must know something." Lord Milton jumped to his feet.

Mrs Lumley looked quizzically at Cuthbert who said firmly, "Now, Edward, wait. If you think your ability to elicit information is greater than Gertrude's here, you are a greater fool than I take you for."

Edward smiled ruefully. "Touché! But I cannot sit and do nothing..." He paced the room.

"No. I agree," said Mrs Lumley. "But I think we must think carefully about what our next move should be. Petty may go to look for another post as a governess, and think we must make discreet enquiries at the registry offices, but we must take care not to scare her off. I intend to visit my friend Mrs Simpson, she has brought her daughter out this season and Petty particularly liked them. I do not hold up much hope that Petty visited them, for she took a decided dislike to Mrs Simpson's sister, one Lady Hamel! But I should pay a call in any case. I have sent to Bath for our things. Dora and I will remain in London for the present."

"You must of course stay here," invited Lord Milton immediately.

"Oh, I could not put you to so much trouble."

"No trouble, in fact you will be doing me a great favour. I need someone to chaperone Aurelia, and if you and Dora stay here I know she will be in excellent company."

"Well, that is mighty kind of you, Your Lordship. I must declare that am very flattered that you consider us suitable companions for your sister." Mrs Lumley beamed.

"Why shouldn't he? You appear a woman of great good sense to me," Cuthbert pointed out quickly.

"Thank you, Cuthbert."

Lord Milton smiled at the obvious signs of great intimacy between his grandfather and Mrs Lumley. If he had thought about it he would have guessed that they would get on well.

"So it is settled. I will order rooms to be prepared for you."

Petty was not happy in Portman Square. Try as she might she did not like Verity, who reminded her of her sister Lottie, except that of course she loved the Lady Charlotte, and even Lottie would not behave with the lack of propriety exhibited by Verity. She found herself wondering constantly how they did at Wakeham. She longed for the house, the walks, Fonty, her brothers and sisters; she even missed the duke. In spite of the kindness of Mr and Mrs Drake, she was generally treated as an inferior to Sir Hugo and Verity, and this was an experience she did not relish. *Perhaps I have more of Mama in me than I realised,* she caught herself thinking ruefully.

She felt the strongest resentment against the Misses Locke, whose attitude she found particularly unpleasant and patronising. She found herself tempted to give this awful pair a severe setdown, and was quite pleased to acknowledge to herself that she now felt quite capable of doing so. She was, however, wise enough to know that if she gave them the trimming they so richly deserved, they would dislike her even more and she would lose the chance to observe them. She was sure that something was amiss! It seemed that whenever they went to the park, Matty and Jane would appear. Petty had no idea what they wanted from Verity, so after much deliberation she decided that the best policy must be to bide her time and try to gain their confidence.

She had noticed Matty and Jane in the distance on the day that the planned expedition to the park with Mary took place, but they did not come up to speak to them, and Verity, who Petty guessed had also seen them, made no effort to converse with them or even to wave a greeting. This circumstance made Petty even more uneasy.

The day following this visit to the park with Mary, she found that she must needs do a little shopping for herself. She suggested to Verity that she accompany her, but the girl claimed a headache and said that she must lie down, as she did not wish to walk in the heat. Petty sympathised, and said that she would take Sukey, the maid, instead.

When Petty returned to the house, Mrs Drake informed her, in some agitation, that as soon as they had gone out, Verity had declared that she was better and was going out for a walk. She had not yet returned. Petty was furious, but a few minutes' reflection in her room convinced her that the worst thing she could do now was to be angry with Verity. She must find out what was happening. It seemed the only answer, unappealing though it was, was to make friends with Matty and Jane in order to allay their suspicions of her. So when Verity returned, Petty merely said, in her most amiable tone, "I am so glad to see that you are recovered, Verity. Did you have a pleasant afternoon?"

"Indeed I did, the park was so tempting and I knew that my head would be better if I had some fresh air."

Verity, pleased to have escaped the expected trimming, clapped her hands together delightedly. Petty smiled sweetly.

"I am so pleased to see you so merry, it must have been a most enjoyable walk."

Verity sighed, hugged herself, and twirled around. "Oh yes! Oh yes! It was wonderful!" she exclaimed blissfully.

Petty knew that this exultation of spirits could not have been caused by a mere walk! She was determined to escort Verity in the future. The next day they set off for the park; the weather was still hot, but luckily the part of the park they frequented was full of shady paths. Matty and Jane appeared as soon as they entered the gates. Verity was effusive in her greeting and Petty smiled at them sweetly.

"How do you go on, Miss Matty and Miss Jane?" she asked pleasantly. "What hot weather we are having." She put up her parasol. Matty looked slightly surprised at the friendliness in Petty's voice, but responded in kind.

"La, I declare, Mrs Blakeston, it is indeed… Why do we not seat ourselves by the fountain in the shade?"

"What an excellent idea," returned Petty in what she hoped was an ingratiatingly winning way. "What a delightful dress, Miss Jane, that pink becomes you so well."

"Oh, do you think so. I declare I paid over 14/- shillings a yard for this Japanned muslin. Such a price, do you not think?"

Petty had no opinion, but she wiped the shocked look off her face and giggled heartily. "Indeed, yes! Oh yes, what a price!"

It was a good thing that at that moment Verity was deep in conversation with Matty, as even she might have wondered at Petty's uncharacteristic behaviour.

They reached the benches beside a small fountain and sat down.

"La! Dearest Mrs Blakeston," said Matty, encouraged by the warm look on Petty's face, "why do you not rest here and Verity can continue to walk with us?"

Petty opened her mouth to say a firm no. Then she realised that if she let them go she could follow unobserved and see what was going on. So she smiled again and said, "Oh, dear Miss Matty, I would so love to rest. I am sure that Verity will be perfectly safe with you."

"Shall I stay and keep you company?" asked Jane.

Petty thought fast. "Oh no, I would not dream of depriving you of your walk, Miss Jane. Do go," she said in a voice not to brook disagreement.

She lay back, trying to seem exhausted, and watched under her eyelids as the group disappeared around the corner. As soon as she deduced it was safe, she quietly slipped behind them. They were walking very fast and talking animatedly. Suddenly they came into a clearing; Petty stopped just in time and slid behind a convenient tree. As she peeped carefully around it, she could see a man on a grey horse who stood waiting. When he saw them, he dismounted. Verity obviously did not know him, for Petty could see that Matty introduced them.

She was too far away to hear what was said, but he seemed to be kissing Verity's hand in a disgustingly obsequious way. He removed with Verity a little way from the others and ogled her. From what Petty could see he was dressed in the high shirt points, extravagant waistcoat and tight coat of the dandy; she did not recognise him but as they had moved to the other side of the clearing they were really too far to see any of his features.

She wondered what to do next. Verity did not seem to be adverse to his attentions, and seemed to be flirting in a shocking way. As Petty watched in horror, the man bent over and kissed Verity's face. At that moment she knew she must do something, but she was quite unable to move because Matty and Jane were facing her tree.

Finally they turned so that their backs were to her, so, grasping her opportunity, she slipped away from her hiding place and, moving as quickly as she could, retraced her steps towards the fountain. When she was about halfway she called, "Verity! Verity! Matty! Jane!" at the top of her voice, then she got hold of her parasol and banged the undergrowth with it, creating a regular stir. As she rounded the bend in the clearing she saw the man jump on his horse and canter away.

"Hello, Verity!" she called again. "I feel so much recovered I thought I would join you."

The girls exchanged glances, which Petty pretended not to notice. Matty shot a quick look in the direction on the departing horseman and Petty knelt down and as a pretext examined the flounce of Verity's dress.

"Oh dear, I think there is a little tear here," she pronounced in a worried tone. "Never mind. I am sure we can mend it. Shall we continue our walk?"

All three girls seemed relieved and chatted happily about all sorts of inconsequential matters. Petty, although her mind was in a whirl, listened carefully to what was said as she hoped that one of them might let something drop which might give her a clue as to who the horseman had been, and to what Matty and Jane were trying to do.

CHAPTER THIRTEEN

etty came down the next morning to find Verity up and sitting at the breakfast table. She looked extremely pleased with herself, and Petty's heart sank.

"Good morning, Verity. You are up early, have you plans for today?" she asked firmly.

"Oh yes. I have realised that Mary's party is only two days away. We must go shopping, I do not have a suitable dress. I need gloves, stockings, perhaps some new shoes..."

Petty heaved a sigh of relief. "What an excellent idea, I had not given a thought about what to wear myself."

This was the truth, and as soon as she thought about it she realised her problem, for the only pretty dress she possessed was the muslin taken from Laura Place and it was hardly appropriate for an evening party. Verity, on the other hand, had wardrobes full of clothes, but if the idea of Mrs Cornwall's party kept her mind off the Lockes and the mysterious horseman, Petty was prepared for her to buy any number of dresses. "Indeed, I have no evening dresses with me... I do not quite know what to do."

"Well, just come with me and you can buy one this afternoon," Verity pointed out with the sublime disregard of the rich for the pecunious position of their subordinates.

"I wish that it were that simple, Verity, but I just do not have the funds to allow me to purchase a new frock."

Verity looked surprised. "Oh dear, what shall we do? You cannot possibly accompany me in that muslin… I will have to go without you."

At that moment Mrs Drake, who was busy clearing the table, intervened. "Miss Verity! You lend Mrs Blakeston a dress; you are much of a size and you have dozens in your cupboard."

"Oh, I cannot do that, they will not fit… in any case they are mine, I might want them," was Verity's reply.

"Miss Verity!" Mrs Drake sounded shocked. "Do not be so mean-spirited. You can only wear one dress at a time. If Mrs Blakeston has nothing to wear she cannot accompany you, and you will not be permitted to go unchaperoned."

Verity pulled a face. Petty came in quickly, "My dear Verity, I would be so grateful. I know you to be such a generous person."

She did not need to say more; Verity brightened. Like many egotistical people she liked to be thought unselfish and helpful. "It will be my pleasure to lend you a dress for Saturday, but only for the evening, I must have it back that night after the party." Mrs Drake and Petty exchanged glances.

"Oh of course. Thank you, my dear," said Petty soothingly.

"Come, we will go and find one immediately." Verity, carried away by her generosity, jumped out of her chair and pulled Petty impatiently up towards her dressing room.

The dress was duly borrowed; it was one of the least pretty dresses that Verity possessed, a round gown of dull yellow brocade with a green net curricle. The colour did nothing for Petty's slightly sallow complexion and the style dwarfed her slim figure. She thought sadly of the exquisite clothes bought for her by Mrs Lumley. However, it was an evening gown and Petty decided that if she bought a few new accessories it might be made to look at least respectable, and it was not as if anyone would really be looking at her. Verity declared herself ready to depart, the carriage was duly summoned and, climbing into it, they set off.

"Please go to Bond Street," Verity demanded of the coachman. Petty inwardly groaned. Bond Street, at the most fashionable hour, ladies of rank only visited the shops along this famous street in the morning, before the bucks were up to ogle them, and here was Petty being driven into the lions' den of her mama's friends! She need not have had any concern; although she saw my Lady Foley, Louisa Lambton and her mama's dearest friend, the Duchess of Gordon, none of them recognised her. She trod docilely and servilely behind Verity, and their eyes passed over her as if she did not exist. Petty giggled. *"Oh, the anonymity of a servant! I need not have worried."*

Eventually, their purchases completed, they were driven back to Portman Square. Verity had decided that she must have a new dress, and had ordered a ravishing garment in pale blue sarcenet and muslin which complemented her angelic beauty perfectly. Petty was relieved to discover that it was necessary for her to return the next day to try it on. Another visit to the dressmaker in Covent Garden meant another day that they would not be in the park with Matty and Jane, and she was hopeful that Mary's party might turn her mind into more suitable channels.

Saturday evening came. Petty arrayed herself in the yellow brocade; she had bought herself a very pretty shawl and some new kid gloves, and with her hair done in the style taught her by Mrs Lumley's excellent hairdresser in Bath, she hoped her appearance would be credible. She went down and seated herself in the hall and awaited Verity. As the girl came down the stairs, Petty took a quick intake of breath; she looked so beautiful. Her dress was exquisite, her blonde hair piled on the top was interlaced with tiny blue flowers, her luscious eyes sparkled with excitement, a delicate flush touched her cheeks.

"You look so lovely, Verity," Petty said simply. Verity gave an enchanting smile.

"Thank you. Thank you. I know I am going to enjoy myself," she bounced. Petty fervently hoped that this would be the case.

The carriage which was going to convey them to Harley Street duly arrived, and during the short journey Verity bubbled with excitement, chattering about how many dances she would enjoy, whether Petty thought they would dance the waltz.

The house that Mrs Cornwall had rented was not in the most fashionable part of town, but it had large rooms and was well appointed. When they arrived they found the party in full swing. Mary ran excitedly to greet them.

"Verity, my sweet, my dearest friend, I am so pleased you have come. May I make you known to my cousin Harry Trevellyan. Harry, this is Miss Croisthwaite."

"Delighted." Harry bowed politely. He was a good-looking boy with brown hair and the shoulders of a sportsman. Verity smiled her most beguiling smile and extended a small gloved hand. He bent over it, hardly taking his eyes off her exquisite face.

"Please will you do me the honour of the next dance?" he pleaded.

"Indeed, yes." Her brilliant eyes danced at the blatant admiration in the look he gave her. He put out his arm and bore her away. Seeing her thus safely bestowed, Petty wondered where she should go. From the sound of the music, the dancing was clearly upstairs in the drawing room. As she followed the sounds of merriment, she had a sudden irrational desire to dance herself. It had been so long. In her season, feeling gauche and awkward, she had hated it, but in Bath she had loved the sensation of being whirled around the floor. She sighed. I am not made for this life, she thought. I do not like this position.

She followed the noise into the drawing room which was ablaze with candles; a group of older people stood at the far end; she went quietly up to join them. Mrs Cornwall saw her and brought her into the group, introducing her to its various members. She did not know any of the people present but, since Bath, her social graces had increased to such a degree that she found it easy to converse amicably to a Mrs Arbuthnot, who lost no time in telling her at length about her children, ten in all.

As she listened politely she let her eyes wander over the room and they were immediately caught by a young girl who entered the double doors. She was a girl of such extraordinary beauty that Petty just stood and gazed at her. She made Verity, by far the prettiest girl in the room till that moment, look almost plain. She appeared completely unaffected, coming forward to greet the outstretched hands of Mrs Cornwall and Mary. Petty was so absorbed watching this beauty that she was quite unaware of the man who followed her. It was only as he too greeted Mrs Cornwall that Petty froze. It was Lord Milton.

"Aurelia, how beautiful you look and how delightful to see you again." Mrs Cornwall smiled on her exquisite guest.

"Mary, Mrs Cornwall, thank you so much for inviting us."

"My dear, it is a pleasure. Mary, why do you not take Aurelia and introduce her to some of the young? You will find Verity, whom you know and some others."

Lord Milton jumped at the name Verity. He looked up and straight at Petty, standing icy with horror at the other end of the room. He stared and stared at her. Petty's heart beat faster and faster, she felt as if it was going to burst. How could he be here? How could he have found her yet again? It appeared that every party she went to he was going to be there. She saw that he was approaching her; her head whirled, she felt her knees giving way underneath her. His Lordship took one quick step next to her and held her in a firm grasp, preventing her from toppling over.

"Perhaps you had better sit down, Mrs Blakeston," he said in a gentle voice, which was as far removed from the harsh tones she had remembered as was the concern in his face. "It is very warm in here, come a little closer to the window. May I obtain a drink for you?"

Petty shook her head. Lord Milton propelled her gently to a small sofa in an alcove at the end of the room, slightly removed from the chatter of the other guests. She sat down gratefully. Her mind in turmoil, she had no idea what to expect next.

"Please do not run away again." Petty looked up, surprised; whatever she had expected him to say it was not that.

"It would appear that my arrival is a signal for you to take to your heels and run," he explained. To her surprise, Petty suddenly found herself laughing. She looked up into his eyes for the first time and found them smiling down at her in a most disturbing way. She looked down at her hands in her lap.

"Well, to tell you the truth, I am getting extremely tired of journeys by stage coach. It is not at all a comfortable way to travel, very bumpy, hot and filled with people who smell and complain." He laughed and she found herself giggling with him. "Oh dear, I sound rather like my mama!"

"You could never sound like your mama," he replied firmly.

"Oh, Lord Milton," she looked up at him again, "how are they all? I have missed them so much. Are they all well?"

"Certainly last time I was at Wakeham they were all in the most excellent health, but worried about you." He met her eyes, which suddenly and inexplicably filled with tears. Possessing himself of both her hands he continued, "Petty, I am so sorry. It is my fault." She shook her head. "All my fault. How can I ever make it up to you? I should not have married you. It was not fair on you. I have been so worried about you. Please, now that we have found you again, do not run. I do not expect anything from you. Please, please stay here in London. Please stay where you are safe. Mrs Lumley and Dora have been worried sick about you. I should not have lost my temper with you in Bath. I…"

"No! No! It is my fault," Petty interrupted. "I did not think of you, I was selfish. You need a wife, I see that. I am so sorry to have caused you pain…" She raised her eyes to his face; two tiny tears slid down her cheeks. He took out her handkerchief and gently dried them. At that moment Verity appeared.

"Petty, where are you? You are supposed to be with me. I want you to help me loop up my flounce, it is torn."

"I am sorry, Verity! Let me present Lord Milton to you." The introductions made, Petty turned to Edward. "I had better deal with the flounce."

"Of course. Your duty calls. But I must beg a dance later. Please."

Petty blushed. "Oh yes, thank you, I should like that above everything."

"You cannot dance. You are my governess," Verity pointed out crossly.

Lord Milton picked up her chin and looked wickedly into her eyes. "You, young lady, sound like a spoilt brat," he commented. Verity, so surprised, flushed bright pink, and stomped noisily away.

Petty giggled. "Oh, Edward," she said, "you should not talk to her like that."

"But that is what she is," he returned.

"Quite. Also capable of throwing a nasty tantrum when crossed."

"Yes. But not with me, you will find." Petty giggled again. "Who is she?"

"Oh, that is Verity I found her... well, I rescued her in an inn in Tonbridge."

"So Mrs Lumley was right."

"Mrs Lumley?"

"Yes. When you ran away from Bath, I went to the White Hart to try find a trace of you. I was not very successful." He smiled ruefully. "After I had left Bath, Mrs Lumley went to see the landlady. She managed to discover that you had gone to Tonbridge. She followed you there and encountered a Mrs Sowerby."

Petty giggled. "A redoubtable woman, she and Mrs Lumley would have been well matched."

"I gather that that was indeed the case. She discovered that you had saved a 'Verity' and that you were returning her to her

168

papa, but we did not know where her father resided." He was suddenly serious again. "She brought the news to me in Grafton Street but we did not know where to look for you. I have been in despair. I know that it was because of me that you ran… I can only apologise again. Are you indeed now working for Verity's father, are you truly her governess?"

"Yes. It is not easy," she sighed. "Sir Hugo is a Member of Parliament and obsessed with reform, it is all he is concerned with, and as you observed, Verity is very spoilt, and very selfish."

"You do not have to stay with them, Petty, it is not fitting that one of your ton should be a governess. I promise I will not ask anything of you. You may return to Wakeham without fear."

The thought was very appealing, but now that she had the much wished for opportunity to go home, Petty found that she didn't want to, she felt responsible for Verity. She knew she had to work out what the Lockes intended for her; she could not just go and abandon her.

"I do not want to leave yet…" she pondered.

Lord Milton looked at her questioningly, a smile in his eyes. Petty felt tempted to take him into her confidence, but was not sure that he would approve of her determination to solve the mystery. She was still not confident that he would not just whisk her away. Swiftly she peeped at him and remarked, "Is it true that Mrs Lumley and Dora are in London?"

Edward, who had watched her expressive face carefully, did not miss the abrupt change of subject. He smiled and nodded.

"Certainly, and they intend to remain for some time. They are staying with Aurelia and myself in Grafton Street, you must come and see us. Please bring Verity, I gather that she, Mary and Aurelia were at school together in Yorkshire."

Petty blushed slightly at the mention of Grafton Street. It seemed absurd now that she had ever been so scared of a house. Lord Milton picked up her hand.

"Come, you promised me a dance."

Petty rose, putting her hand in his. He led her onto the floor. They were playing a waltz; Petty had danced the waltz before. Since it had been danced at Almack's, it had become all the rage and was quite acceptable, if the patronesses permitted, but on previous occasions she had not much enjoyed it. His Lordship's arm encircled her waist lightly, his other hand clasped her hand; he smiled down into her face. She felt light, her body moved perfectly in time to his; they did not speak, there seemed no need. As he twirled her around she felt a thrill of pleasure. She could have danced all night; regretfully it was all too soon over.

"Thank you," was all he said as he returned her to her seat.

Later that evening she saw him again when he brought Aurelia across to be introduced to her. Petty thought she had never encountered a girl who was so utterly beautiful, both in mien and in temperament. Aurelia was one of those rare magical people who possess a charm which makes them instantly appealing to everyone they meet. She was modest and quite unaware of her magnetism. Petty found her enchanting. Soon after that she noticed that they had left. The party felt very flat. Verity, enjoying herself hugely, was determined to stay until the very end, and Petty resigned herself to a long wait.

Petty was up far earlier than Verity the next day and was sitting in the only sunny corner of the morning room reading a book by a new unknown author, called Sense and Sensibility. She was so absorbed in the book that she did not hear Verity come in. Verity crossed to her and yawned noisily. Petty looked up from her page to enquire, "Well, Verity, did the party live up to your expectations?"

"Oh yes. Yes, it was wonderful. Do you not think that Mr Trevellyan is quite the most handsome of men?"

"I do, most definitely." Petty was effusive of her praise for this unexceptional young man.

"He asked me to drive in the park this afternoon. But I am not sure whether I shall go," she remarked provokingly. Petty, too clever to rise to the bait, merely replied generally.

"As you wish. I intend to pay a visit to Lord Milton this morning. My friend from Bath, Mrs Lumley, is staying with him and I so very much wish to see her."

"Oh, that sounds most tedious. I do not think that I shall accompany you."

Petty, aware that she could not at the moment go and leave Verity, merely answered, "Well, of course, I see that it is up to you. Lord Milton told me that Dora and Aurelia planned a visit to Hyde Park to see the balloon site being erected, but I imagine that it will take place whether you go with them or not," she remarked casually, closing her book. She rose to leave the room. "I shall just go and prepare myself."

"Oh! I think, perhaps, I should come with you, Petty, after all it would be most impolite not to pay my respects to Aurelia and her grandfather."

"Quite. I am glad that you have such a regard for the courtesy owed to your friends."

"Oh yes, I pride myself on my conduct," Verity returned airily with a total disregard for the slightly sardonic undertones in Petty's comment, "but what of Mr Trevellyan?"

"I am delighted that you will come with me." Petty smiled sweetly, guilty about her sarcasm. "We shall leave a message for young Mr Trevellyan, in case he should arrive before we return, but I think you will find that we shall be back in good time for your drive in the park, and it is such a lovely day for it after all."

During the short journey to Grafton Street, Petty sat in the corner of the carriage, a prey to complicated thoughts and for once glad of Verity's inconsequential self-centred chatter. She was very inquisitive about the house they were going to. If she had not run away it would have been her home; she found that whilst she felt very curious she was also intensely nervous about the visit. Her heart beat furiously as they drew up outside number 17, and as she climbed down, her knees felt quite wobbly.

The house was one of the most elegant of town mansions that Petty remembered seeing; it was very imposing but so beautifully proportioned that she felt she was looking at a work of art. It was double-fronted with a graceful arched front door. It had four long arched windows on the first floor, which obviously led into the saloon. A small balcony loaded with pretty flowers ran the length of the first-floor windows. It was built of delicate red brick, and the windows and door were framed by carved porticoes.

Verity, oblivious to both her surroundings and Petty's tremulous state, bounded up to the door and banged on it. It was opened by Penn, the most impeccable of butlers, who maintained a welcoming but incurious demeanour. The inside of the house was as attractive as the outside; the hall was open and very light; at the far end a staircase with beautifully turned balustrades curved its way upwards. The interior walls were decorated in the lightest tint of green. Set in these painted walls were beautiful mahogany doors decorated with gilt patterns. The walls were covered with paintings which Petty longed to examine in detail. The house was welcoming and quite appealing. She could not understand how she could ever have been apprehensive about living here, and the contrast between this and the dingy brown spaces at Portman Square seemed almost too much to bear.

She enquired for Mrs Lumley and was informed that she, Miss Dora and Miss Aurelia were in the morning room. Penn took their names and returned a moment later and bade them follow him.

All three occupants of the morning room rose up to greet them. As soon as they entered Dora ran across to Petty and flung her arms around her; Mrs Lumley followed her slowly, the warmest of smiles spreading across her face.

"Oh dearest, dearest Petty, we are so pleased that you are safe. Mama and I were so worried, indeed it is so splendid that we have found you... How fortuitous that Lord Milton and Aurelia went to that party last night. Oh it is so wonderful, so wonderful." Dora clung to Petty's hand.

"Tis true, my love, most true, most excellent, such very, very good news." Mrs Lumley peered at Petty closely. "You look a little haggard, my love, I hope they are taking care of you properly, and, dear heart, I do not want to appear contumacious but that dress, my sweet, where did you get it? It is of all things the most hideous. You know I cannot abide ugly clothes, it must be burnt immediately!"

Petty burst out laughing; it was so good to see Dora and Mrs Lumley again.

Mrs Lumley beamed at her. "My love, I cannot tell you how upset we were that you left us the way you did." She glanced at Petty shrewdly. "Not that I did not understand, my sweet... Lord Milton explained everything." Petty blushed red; she was not quite sure how much 'everything' was but she suspected that Mrs Lumley knew all about her marriage. She was saved from replying by Verity, who was not enjoying not being the centre of attention.

"Mrs Blakeston," she commanded in a squeaky voice, "please remember you are here to take care of me."

Dora looked astonished at this petulant outburst and Petty exchanged glances with Mrs Lumley, who clearly had the measure of Verity in a moment.

"Why does she have to take care of you? She can come to us now, we love her. We shall take care of her, she shall have lovely clothes once more and look smart," Dora pointed out crossly, her love for Petty making her unusually aggressive.

"Hush! Dora," murmured Mrs Lumley. At the same moment Aurelia, who had been observing the interchange closely, intervened, saying soothingly, "How beautiful you look, Verity. I have rarely seen you looking so well. Did you enjoy Mary's party last night?"

"Oh yes, I danced every dance. I had to refuse two young men because my card was so full up, was that not the case, Mrs Blakeston?"

"Indeed it was, Verity, you were exceedingly popular."

Verity brightened and Dora looked at her in disgust. Aurelia then tactfully suggested that they proceed to the breakfast room where a cold collation had been set out.

"Do go, my dear," Petty told Verity. "I shall come in just one minute after I have had a few words with Mrs Lumley."

Verity happily followed Aurelia and Dora out of the room.

Mrs Lumley patted the sofa. "Come, my dear, sit here and tell me about it."

Petty sat down obediently beside her. "I do not know that there is much to tell… but first I… I must apologise for leaving as I did, it was most ungracious and ungrateful of me… I do not quite know why I ran away."

"You ran because His Lordship was enraged with you, and you thought he would remove you to your papa."

"You do know everything then?"

"Yes, my lady."

"Oh, that too… you must have the lowest of opinions of me."

"I do not judge, my dear. I know that life does not slide like a marble along a smooth passage. It is filled with bumps and hillocks, wrong turnings and unpleasant sticky objects that impede our way."

Petty laughed. "Oh, Mrs Lumley, I have missed you so much."

Mrs Lumley observed her. "It would appear to me, dear heart, but correct me if I am wrong, that having that spoilt child to supervise is not a time of unmitigated pleasure!"

Petty giggled. "Oh indeed, indeed you are most perspicacious as usual."

"Does she have a mama?" Petty shook her head.

"Papa?"

"Yes… she does…"

Her disconsolate tone made Mrs Lumley watch her closely. "I see," was all she vouchsafed.

Petty unconsciously sighed. "When I see you and dearest Dora…" She stopped. "And this house, it is so lovely." She glanced around the room. "You should see Verity's house it is so brown… so ugly…" Suddenly she looked at Mrs Lumley and grinned. "No! No! I am quite remiss. You must not see it. It is everything that would offend you… quite the least attractive place in the world!"

"Then now that you have found us again, why do you not leave? You do not have to stay there, surely… Come to us."

Petty brightened, then she remembered Verity. She was hardly more than a child. She shook her head. "I cannot."

"Why not?"

Petty looked up sadly. "It is impossible."

At that moment the door opened and Lord Milton came in. Mrs Lumley watched his face light up as he crossed to greet Petty.

"Oh, I must apologise that I was not here to greet you. I do hope that they have taken proper care of you." He took her hand and lifted it to his lips. Petty felt a quiver of excitement run through her. She raised her eyes to his. He was smiling at her with such warmth that she felt quite trembly; she smiled back at him.

"Oh yes, indeed. Your house is so beautiful I do not know when I have seen so elegant a mansion," she enthused.

"I was just telling Petty, that now that we have found her again she must come back to us," Mrs Lumley beamed good-naturedly.

"Oh! Ma'am, I have said it is impossible…" She glanced at Lord Milton. "I cannot… I must stay with Verity… I cannot come here."

His Lordship's expression changed imperceptibly; he drew back a little. "As you wish…" he said stiffly.

Mrs Lumley glanced from one to the other; she could have bitten her tongue off. Usually so perceptive, she realized that there was something which she did not as yet comprehend.

"Well, now," she said brightly, "I think we should see how those young creatures are getting on. Will you not join us for nuncheon?"

"Oh yes," Petty replied gratefully.

Lord Milton, having recovered his demeanour, merely asked pleasantly, "May I offer you my arm?" He led her out of the room and down to the morning room. Mrs Lumley followed, her active mind racing as she pondered on what she had noticed.

Petty and Verity arrived back in good time for the projected visit to the park with Harry Trevellyan. Petty, who had taken rather less notice of the young man on the previous night than she might have normally done, had things not been so confusing, was agreeably surprised. Harry was a large young man; the shoulders of his well-cut coat seemed to stretch across his muscular back. He was dressed with propriety, although not fashionably; the points of his spotless neck cloth were not such as to preclude him turning his head, but in spite of this Petty got the impression that he was slightly uncomfortable in town clothes and would have been happier dressed for country pursuits. In fact he would probably look out of place in the drawing rooms of the ton. He had a fresh, open face, covered with freckles, a quantity of curly reddish hair, blue eyes surrounded by tiny wrinkles denoting a man who spent much time outside.

He was driving a curricle with a team of well-matched bays. Petty, who in spite of her protestations to Lord Milton to the contrary was an excellent judge of horseflesh, realized that although they were not out-and-outers nor were they knocked in the wind, or too high in the shoulders.

He greeted Verity with blatant admiration in his eyes, handing her into the curricle as if she were a piece of porcelain. Petty clambered aboard, squashing herself to one side. Harry drove well; he was not an accomplished whipster in the way of her brother or Lord Milton but he drove as Petty imagined he did everything, with a high degree of competence.

"Where do you come from, Mr Trevellyan?" Petty enquired cordially.

"Why from Yaxley, in Huntingdon. My mama has an estate there."

"And your papa?"

"My mama is a widow, Miss Croisthwaite."

"Why, then you are just like me! I have only one parent. Do you have any brothers or sisters?" Verity demanded.

Harry negotiated a difficult corner and turned, smiling to Verity. "No, I am the only one, my mama sent me to London for some town polish, but I have to admit to you, Miss Croisthwaite, that until last night I was not enjoying it much!"

"Oh, and what changed last night, if I may ask?" Verity replied coquettishly.

Harry blushed slightly but answered in his straightforward way, "Why, meeting you."

Verity giggled delightedly. "Oh, Mr Trevellyan, what a gentleman you are! I have no brothers or sisters, it is sad to be only one, is it not?"

He nodded vigorously. "Yes, but I do have a quantity of cousins, Mary and Georgiana and... oh, lots that you do not know and often they feel like sisters or brothers. I do not feel deprived."

An expression of sadness flitted across Verity's mobile face, clearly observed by Harry. He smiled encouragingly at her, covering her hand with his gently; she grinned back.

Petty suddenly noted, with some horror, that they were approaching the fashionable ride of Rotten Row; she shrank further into her corner, hoping that she would become invisible, as indeed she was to Harry and Verity, who were lost, as those who are enchanted with each other, in a happy dream.

Their inconsequential chatter was a blur for Petty, so concerned was she to hide. Suddenly Harry slowed the carriage and she heard her name called; her heart sank, this was it, one of her mama's friends. She looked up expecting to see Lady Hamel, at least, straight into the dancing eyes of Lord Milton!

"Trying to appear invisible, Mrs Blakeston!" he teased.

"Now, Edward, why would she want to disappear?" the melodious tones of Aurelia interrupted. "How are you, Harry?" She held out her hand to him; he jumped down politely. "I did not think that driving in the park held much interest for you! Verity! How pretty you look." She turned her attention to her friend. "We are on our way to see the erection of the balloon site, are we not, Dora?" And with her unselfconscious grace she presented Dora to Harry, confining their conversation to the projected balloon ascent.

"Oh! How pleased I am that it is you," Petty said to His Lordship impetuously. "I thought it must be…" She stopped, blushing prettily.

His Lordship laughed. "My Lady Leiven or the duchess perhaps…" His eyes teased her.

"Yes… well… it would have been rather undesirable to meet them, do you not agree?" He nodded, laughing. "What a very well-matched pair!" She ran her eyes over the elegant greys which pulled his high-perch phaeton. "I expect they are real goers." He laughed again at her boyish remark. She sighed longingly, "I imagine they are wonderful to drive."

"But I thought you did not drive, Mrs Blakeston?" Edward's eyebrows lifted questioningly.

Petty put up her chin slightly and sucked her lips. She looked him straight in the eye. "Well…" was her only reply.

"Oh, Lord Milton. It is so delightful to drive in the park," Verity interrupted.

"But rather restricted when you have a team such as that," Harry pointed out, waving his hand in the direction of the greys. "I say, sir, they are top-notch steppers. I should like to see them when they could really go!"

"Well, and why not. Let us all go on an outing, a drive and a picnic, how does that appeal?"

All three young girls nodded vigorously.

"Oh yes! Yes! Altogether a gorgeous proposition," Verity bounced.

"Good. I can see that you have gentle hands, young man," His Lordship said to Harry. "You may drive them, if you wish."

"I should say so, sir."

"Lucky Mr Trevellyan," Petty interjected unthinkingly.

"You may drive them as well, if you think you can hold them, Mrs Blakeston," said His Lordship, very seriously, but with his eyes brimming with laughter. Petty looked at him.

"I think that I can," she pronounced equally sagely.

"Then it is agreed. We have only to set the date." He nodded farewell and they vanished in the direction of the balloons.

CHAPTER FOURTEEN

Miss Chalfont sat at the table in the schoolroom at Wakeham. She was assisting Marcus in his first foray into the conjugation of Latin verbs. The sun poured into the shabby room, its rays falling onto Petty's dolls' house, in her absence lovingly cared for by Fonty, who dusted each piece of tiny furniture, so painstakingly assembled, herself. As if by the act of touching these exact replicas she would be close to their creator. She had aged since Petty's departure; her step was not so sprightly and her face looked careworn; in truth she had a constant knot of misery in the pit of her body which never left her.

She was now beginning to believe that they would never see Petty again; her heart had lifted and her spirits had soared when the news had come from Lord Milton that he had seen Petty in Bath, only to be dashed again when he informed them that she had run away again. She had liked the sound of Mrs Lumley, who seemed to think as she ought on many important topics, although the duchess had been so appalled at the idea that her daughter was working for a woman of Mrs Lumley's ilk that she had had to take to her bed for a week.

Fonty had treasured the letter that that good lady had sent them, extolling Petty's virtue. She hoped against hope that some trace of Petty would be found, but as the days turned to weeks she was losing expectation that the outcome would be as she wished. Her heart felt broken; she blamed the duchess for the loss of her daughter, and found it hard at times to be civil to that lady. She tried to concentrate on her other charges, but the truth was that she had loved Petty almost as her own child and her loss seemed at moments unbearable.

Marina sat opposite to Marcus; she was busy with a French translation. She too felt keenly the loss of her sister; she was paler and thinner, and her unhappiness showed in the turned-down corners of her small mouth.

The duchess complained the most. The invective about the pain her daughter had caused her went on unceasingly. She took great pleasure in demanding constant support from the rest of the family. It had become her wont to spend every day lying on a chaise in her day room, Holtby beside her, a handkerchief always to the ready, the affecting pose of the distraught mother, mourning her child.

The lines on the duke's face had become more marked; he did not share his thoughts with anyone, and only Fonty guessed the extent of his grief. He felt guilty as he never had before; the pleasure that he should have taken in the solution of their financial problems was in truth non-existent. He discovered that he did not now care whether Wakeham was saved or not, his only thought was what he had done to his daughter. In his mind he went over and over his conversation with her. If only he had listened to her; a constant image of her face as she pleaded with him was with him always.

He found it almost impossible to communicate with the duchess. He did not believe it was her fault. Oh no. He knew where the blame lay, but her unnatural feelings towards her children sickened him now. He did not understand how he had loved her so much; all that had gone now. He felt nothing, not even pity.

Lord Anthony had returned to Oxford, his life too shattered by the loss of Petty. Closest to her in age, he had also been her dearest friend. She had loved him deeply and he in his turn had adored her in a brotherly way. They had romped together as children. They had learnt together, gently competing against one another academically. Since infancy they had exchanged secrets. With Anthony, Petty had never felt shy and withdrawn, she had made him laugh; he in his turn had reduced her to fits of giggles. It was with Anthony that Petty had perfected her talent for mimicry, taking off anyone who came within her sphere, constantly encouraged by a mischievous brother.

Apart from Miss Chalfont, Gideon best understood the disintegration and change in his family. He felt powerless to restore equanimity. He tried without success to persuade His Grace that the marriage he had arranged for Petty was not a wicked act of an uncaring father. Having spent some time with Edward, his liking and respect for him growing by the hour, he could only repeat that he could not think of a more admirable partner for Petty. His Grace remained unconvinced, not about Edward's merits, but by his own intransigence and lack of care. Wakeham had become a miserable household.

The day after Petty's visit to Grafton Street, as she and Verity occupied themselves in the gloomy morning room, Mrs Lumley, accompanied by Dora and Aurelia, arrived to pay a morning visit to Portman Square. Drake showed them into the drawing room and went to fetch Verity and Petty.

"My dear, how right you were." Mrs Lumley's first words to Petty were uttered in sepulchral tones. "You were only too accurate, this is quite the ugliest room I have ever had to sit in." Petty smiled inwardly; it was so good to have Mrs Lumley with her again. Noticing Verity, Mrs Lumley turned to her. "Oh, I beg pardon, Verity my dear, you must not mind me. I know it is your home, but truly, no one should be surrounded by such ugliness, it is bad for the soul."

"Well, you see, Mama died, and Papa has no heart for anything, except for his constituency and his passion for making it better for the common man," explained Verity. Mrs Lumley nodded.

"I see. Well, when you are a little older I think you must take it in hand. Now, be a good girl and take Dora and Aurelia, while I have a few words with Petty."

Petty wondered what she was going to say; she hoped that she was not going to repeat the suggestion that Petty now return to her, as, even though she would dearly love to have done so, it was impossible.

"Now, my love, I expect you are wondering what I came to say. I will not mince words. Now that I know that you have a family and who they are, I do not think you can leave it any longer without telling them that you are safe. When His Lordship told me about them, I took the liberty of writing to Miss Chalfont to tell her how I had found you, and I received the most charming reply but she is clearly very unhappy. I think in truth they are all desperate with worry about you. Oh no, she did not precisely write that, but you cannot fool Gertrude Lumley, I can read between the lines with the best of them."

Petty's eyes filled with tears. "Oh, Mrs Lumley, I so want to write to them but I have not, for I was so scared they would make me return to Wakeham in disgrace. Or worse that they would have handed me over to Lord Milton." Mrs Lumley looked surprised.

"But His Lordship is not a monster, my dear, he is a very cultured gentleman."

"I see that now… but… you see, at Wakeham, in Bath…" She wrung her hands. "I… he… was so fiercely angry… I am not very good with angry people. Well, that is not entirely true now… but it was then… Oh, I am explaining so badly."

Mrs Lumley smiled. "No one is going to make you go anywhere, my sweet, you can be sure of that, but I do think you must write to your poor family."

Petty nodded vigorously. "Oh! Indeed that is what I would like above everything."

The letter was written that afternoon. It was duly dispatched post haste. As she sealed the epistle Petty felt as though an enormous load had been lifted from her heart. It had cost her much anguish, as she was unsure of exactly what she wanted to say, or how she wanted it to sound. In the end, after tearing up several attempts which included trying to explain her behaviour, she kept it simple.

Portman Square

Dearest Papa and Mama,

I have wanted to write to you all so many times to tell you that I am safe and well. I understand that I have caused you distress, and I am truly sorry for it, it was never my intention to worry you. Oh, that sounds very silly. Of course, my disappearance must have caused you to be anxious, but I felt I had no choice.

I am working as a companion to Sir Hugo Croisthwaite's daughter.

Before that I worked for Mrs Lumley in Bath. I understand from her that she was in contact with you, and it is she who has impressed upon me the importance of setting your minds at rest. I am well, I am quite happy. Please do not ask me to return to you or my previous situation. I cannot. I again apologise for the distress I caused you. Please forgive me. Please give Marina and Marcus a kiss for me, and my dearest love to Fonty and you all.

Your dutiful daughter,
Perpetua

Thanks to the good offices of John Palmer and his mail coaches, the letter reached Wakeham the next day. Petty had addressed it to her father and it was to His Grace, as he sat in seclusion in his library, that it was brought.

It had become the duke's habit to spend the greater part of his days either riding alone around his estates or isolated in his book room. The unwelcome thoughts about his behaviour, which obtruded into all his waking moments, alleviated somewhat by the beauties of Latin verse, of Shakespeare, Milton, the sermons of John Donne and other of his favourite books.

This afternoon, after a particularly unpleasant session with his wife, he had retreated to try to find solace in the philosophy of Aristotle, but for once even the words of this erudite Greek failed to ameliorate his lowness of spirit. The rain, which had made it impossible for him to ride, poured relentlessly from a dark, heavy sky. Restlessly he paced the long room. He stopped, rapt in his thoughts by the window, gazing unseeingly at the sodden park. An intense melancholy overtook him as his eyes caught the brilliant pink of the rose petals dashed to the ground, while in full bloom, by the pelting water.

He thought of his own life. He was approaching fifty; he, like the roses, had been destroyed in his prime, by the unpardonable excesses of his father, by the selfish beauty to whom he had harnessed his hopes in the innocent days of his youth. He sighed. What was there left for him? He had vast estates. He had a great and illustrious title, but what was that worth? Petty's disappearance had sharply focused on what to him now seemed a pointless existence. There was a knock at the door.

"Yes?" he barked.

John came in; he too had been prey to uncomfortable thoughts since Petty's departure. He had kept his own part in her escape to himself, but he occasionally questioned whether she would have been able to leave if he had not helped her, but then she had told him she was going to her aunt. He liked to think he would not have assisted her if he had known she was just running away. He carried a silver platter. He bowed. "The letters, Your Grace."

"Thank you, John. Put them on the desk."

"Very good, Your Grace." John bowed again and left.

The duke turned from the window and addressed himself to his correspondence. Most of it concerned mundane matters to do with the management of the estates. The Whig party. Invitations and letters of a social nature being addressed to the duchess.

He came upon Petty's letter at the bottom of the pile. As he picked it up he found that he was unaccountably trembling. He thought he recognised the writing; hope leapt into his heart. But was it possible? Was it just a mirage? Maybe it was not her writing? Perhaps it just resembled hers?

He broke the seal with shaking hands and read her few lines. Relief flooded through him; Petty was alive and well. She was safe. She had asked for forgiveness, but it was he who must be forgiven.

His first instinct was to go with all possible speed to London to see her, but he then realised that this would be inadvisable. He remembered what Edward had said about his own precipitate handling of Petty in Bath; he must not make that mistake. He rose and went to the schoolroom. As he entered, Marcus was demanding release from Latin verbs.

"Please, Fonty! Please, please may I stop now?" he wheedled, then seeing his father he froze. Miss Chalfont stood up.

"Good morning, Your Grace. An unexpected pleasure. Lord Marcus was just requesting a walk in the gardens. I am having the greatest problem persuading him that it is far too wet to play outside." She twinkled. "He does not escape his conjugations that easily."

His Grace laughed. Patting his youngest son on the head affectionately, he pronounced, "If Fonty is agreeable, I think you should have the rest of the day off."

The governess's eyes flew to his face; the strained look that he had worn since the awful night of Petty's wedding had gone, his eyes were bright, he looked extraordinarily happy, he smiled uncontrollably.

"And me! May I have the day off too?" Marina's anxious voice broke into Fonty's observations. She glanced at the duke, who nodded. Crossing to Marina he caught his little daughter up into his arms and hugged her, an action that was so unlikely that Fonty knew something wonderful had happened, and she knew just what it was. There could be only one cause for the complete change in His Grace. She caught his mood. Grinning broadly she caught Marcus and whirled him around. Both children looked confused at the sudden joyous mood of their normally staid elders.

"She is safe, Fonty, she is safe!" His voice broke and the governess noticed that his eyes were shining with tears. He released Marina. "She is in London, Mrs Lumley has found her. Well, I assume that she found her... Petty says... but here, you had better read for yourself." He handed Petty's letter to the governess, who eagerly perused the few lines.

"My first desire was, of course, to go straight to London and bring her home, but on second thoughts, that may not be the best course to follow. You know Petty better than anyone, what is your opinion?"

"Well, as she says that she does not want to return to us, I do not think that you should make her." Fonty looked doubtfully at her employer.

"Oh! I do not mean to compel her to do anything. I am just so glad that she is unharmed." He met Miss Chalfont's eyes, which were filled with tears. Catching her hand he kissed it, unable to speak.

"Is Petty really in London?" Marina demanded. "Oh, is she really alright?"

The duke nodded again. Fonty gulped, pushed back her

tears, and said in a practical tone of voice, "Yes, my dears, your sister is unscathed and in London." She brushed away a tear. "With regard to the best action, what does Her Grace think?"

The duke stopped. Looking at Fonty guiltily, he raised his eyebrows and said, "Well, I thought I…"

"I think you must tell her as soon as possible," suggested Miss Chalfont understandingly.

"Yes! Yes. Immediately."

Fonty dropped a slight curtsey; she opened the door for the duke and as he passed through she caught his eye. They smiled delightedly at each other, neither being able to contain the relief that overwhelmed them.

The duke made his way slowly to the duchess; his initial exhilaration had given way to a realisation that he must think carefully about Petty's situation. He was as aware as Fonty of the impropriety of her position as companion to Miss Croisthwaite; she was a duke's eldest daughter, and, he acknowledged ruefully, the wife of a wealthy peer. She clearly could not remain as a governess to a nobody.

On the other hand he must take the greatest care not to frighten her; better that she remained in an inappropriate post than that the misery of the last five months were to be repeated. He knew that one of his main problems would be the duchess. He could not imagine her accepting Petty's position; it would, he realised, reflect badly upon her and she would never accept that. How she appeared to her friends was of the utmost importance to her; it was, therefore, with a certain degree of trepidation that he approached his wife's rooms.

Although the day was gloomy the duchess's chambers seemed filled with light. Her Grace lay in an affecting pose surrounded by blooms. Holtby was at her side, holding bottles of Hartshorn and smelling salts. The duke was struck again by his wife's physical beauty, the aura of perfection that she exuded. It was not hard to understand how his young self, emerging into adulthood, escaping from the rigid miserable family that had surrounded the seventh duke, was bowled over by so much pulchritude. He sighed. She, aware somehow that she had lost some of the adoration which she knew to be her due, stretched out her hand voluptuously. She nodded dismissal to Holtby.

"Come, my dearest, come sit beside me," she commanded. "We must be together in our time of trouble." She smiled radiantly at him, a smile of such beauty that he almost wanted to catch her into his arms. He bent and kissed her gently; she felt that her power over him was still complete.

"Our 'trouble' is over." He chose his words carefully. "I have this morning received a letter from Petty, she is in London but safe and well." He turned slightly from her.

"Oh! Oh, I thank God!" It was the reaction he had longed for; perhaps his reservations about her were misplaced? Perhaps she was as he had hoped in those far-off days?

"Where is she? Where is the letter? May I read it?" She rose from her chaise and clasped his hands to her, her pale blue eyes held his; again he had an almost irresistible desire to crush her to him. To capture for a second the fragile past and postpone for a minute the disclosures of Petty's letter.

"Augustus! Where is she? What is she doing?"

He turned slightly from her. "Julia, we must be glad that she is safe, that is all that matters. Is it not?"

She stiffened slightly, her voice changed. "Tell me! Tell me where she is."

"She is working for Sir Hugo Croisthwaite. She is a companion to his daughter." Moving away from her he held out Petty's letter; she took it and read it without comment.

Then she raised her face. "This is impossible. It is a disgrace. I cannot countenance this. That a child of mine should so dishonour the family! She must be brought back immediately. A governess! A governess! How can she do this to me? How can she, and in London too, why, she might meet any of my acquaintances, I have never been so let down. She really is the most selfish of creatures." She gave a small sob, and sank back down onto the chaise. "After all that I have done for her, how could she? We have all worried and worried, I have been distraught, I have been laid low by her disappearance and here she is after all that, alive, well, living in London and not a word! I shall summon Lord Milton. He shall deal with his bride! It is too bad, really it is. She has no thought for anyone but herself! No thought!" She lay back on her pillows.

The duke, saddened by the reaction, which he had anticipated but had hoped would not happen, turned from her in disgust. "You will do nothing of the sort, Julia. She asks that we do not summon her to come back and we shall not."

"Certainly she must come back! How can you suggest that she should stay in such an unworthy post? It is quite unacceptable, I shall summon Gideon. He must go and retrieve her tomorrow. You must punish her accordingly. No. Lord Milton must punish her, she must be locked in her room." She rose furiously and rang the bell.

"Be quiet! Julia! Stop it! You will do nothing of the sort." His voice whipped across the room; all his disappointed hopes found expression in his fury as he grabbed her arm and pushed her roughly onto the chaise. "Now listen to me! You will do nothing! Nothing! Do I make myself clear? Leave Petty alone!" They faced each other, he white with anger, she equally furious.

Holtby, arriving in answer to the bell, stood outside the door listening to the angry voices. She heard enough to know that Petty had been found. In truth, the girl had never been a favourite of hers and she was not best pleased that she was safe, particularly as the duke now seemed to be showing a marked predilection for preferring his daughter to his wife, and this rejection of her beloved mistress did little to endear Holtby to Petty. She paused outside the room, unsure of whether to go in, but her courage failed at the thought of confronting the duke and duchess.

She found Gideon in the gun room. He was unwrapping a parcel that had arrived that morning from Manton's and which, as expected, contained a new pair of pistols that he had recently ordered.

"My lord! My lord!" Holtby breathlessly pleaded. "Please come, Gideon, put down the parcel."

"What is it, Holtby?"

"His Grace. Her..." she gulped, "... Grace... fighting... arguing. Lady Perpetua... all her fault."

Gideon put down the gun and wheeled around upon her, grasping her shoulders. "What are you talking about? Petty? What has she to do with it? How could anything be her fault?"

"Better come and see, my lord." She pulled herself free of him, rubbed her shoulder and, sniffing crossly, left the room.

Gideon followed slowly. He was perplexed; it was unlike his father to bother to quarrel with his mother. Gideon knew that all His Grace's illusions about his wife had been shattered, not only since Petty's disappearance but also increasingly over the last few years. But to shout at her, to be riled by her, it seemed as unlikely as that he loved her.

As he reached Her Grace's chamber he heard the raised voices of his parents. So it was true, Holtby was correct. He did not like his mother's dresser, indeed none of the duchess's children had a particular fondness for the woman who indulged their mama in the overprotective and damaging way that was Miss Holtby's wont. Gideon tapped loudly on the door and then went in. The duke stood facing the window, his back rigid with anger; the duchess had collapsed onto the chaise longue; she was crying affectedly. Holtby was bathing her head.

"What is it? Papa?" the marquis asked.

His father turned, smiled. "Oh! Gideon, I am glad you have come. Petty is safe! I have this morning received the following note from her." He held out Petty's letter.

Gideon's face broke into smiles. "Petty! Petty! How wonderful! I am so pleased. But why do you both look so disconcerted, is it not the best of news?"

"Indeed it is!" The duke grinned at his son and shook his hand. "The argument with your mama is what to do with Petty. She, as you can see from her letter, wishes merely to let us know that nothing has happened to her, she does not wish to come home. Your mother…" here he shot an antagonistic look at his wife, "… wants her brought home in disgrace. I will not permit it." On these words the duke drew himself up and said in an imposing fashion, "l will not permit your mother to harass Lady Perpetua in any way whatsoever."

"Of course, her wishes must be respected," Gideon decreed. "But I must admit that I would like to see her."

"I agree, and we must be at pains to reassure her. I would wish you to go to her, Gidi." His use of Gideon's pet name meant that His Grace was much moved. "Tell her that we love her, we do not wish her to do anything she does not wish to do."

"Oh, very fine, Your Grace." Her Ladyship rose from her couch. "And what about our disgrace? What about her husband? Have you forgotten him? He must have some say in the matter."

"But I do not think that Edward will want to interfere either. He feels very responsible for what has happened and he has been much shocked and worried by Petty's running away, he will not want to scare her," Gideon observed.

"Nonsense," Her Grace snapped. "He will be as eager as we are to bring her to a sense of what is due to her parents and her husband. She must not be allowed to believe that it is acceptable to behave in this unwarranted fashion."

"Eager? Eager? But I am not eager to do anything to my daughter that will increase the distress that I have already promulgated by my neglect of her feelings." The duke, exasperated to the point of fury by his wife's ability to totally ignore his words, nearly shouted these last words, but taking a grip on himself he turned to Gideon and repeated, "I want you to go to London, see Petty and reassure her. If she wants to come home we will, of course, receive her with great joy. If, however, she desires to remain where she is we will respect her wishes."

His wife, white with anger, turned on him. "How can you! How can you, Augustus, disregard my sentiments in this unfeeling way?"

"Your 'sentiments' as you call them are a matter of supreme indifference to me," her husband remarked icily. "Now that that is decided, I shall leave you." He bowed slightly at his livid wife, and left. Gideon, who wisely thought that to remain with his mother in her present mood would be a mistake, followed him.

Chapter Fifteen

etty stood at the window of the gloomy drawing room and watched the endless rivulets of rain run down the window pane. She felt sick; her heart seemed to be jumping around her chest. Brooding over her father's reaction to her letter, she convinced herself that the result of her confession must involve a forcible removal back to Wakeham. All that she could do was to wait for the seemingly inevitable outcome to what she now regarded as the folly of disclosing to her mama and papa her whereabouts.

Whereas her papa may have been persuaded to look leniently on her misdemeanours, her mama most certainly would not. She sighed. Although she was not happy in Portman Square, and part of her longed for the peace and beauty of Wakeham, she knew that to be ignominiously returned home to disgrace and the endless remonstrations of her mama was not to be desired. She supposed that if she were honest they should return her to Lord Milton. She tried to ascertain how she really felt about that prospect. She had known for some time, indeed since the night at Mrs Cornwall's, that she was not as averse to the prospect as she had been previously.

They had met several times since the night of the party and she had found him attentive and the most delightful company; he made her laugh and she seemed to be able to do the same for him. She knew that he was very knowledgeable about any number of things, and was longing to get the opportunity to discuss the political ideas put forward by Sir Hugo with him. She also found that there were all kinds of little things that happened during the course of her day that she knew would amuse or interest Edward, and she found herself storing them up to tell him the next time that they met.

She was unsure of his feelings for her. It was clear, she thought, that he was no longer angry with her, and sometimes his eyes smiled with such warmth that it quite took her breath away, but perhaps he smiled at everyone like that? She did not know.

She peered out onto the square. Although it was only three in the afternoon, it was so dim out there that it appeared almost like night. The sky was a dark blue colour and the wind was whipping the heavy grey clouds, sending them scurrying across the sky; the trees in the middle of the square were being blown almost sideways. She was sure that there was about to be a terrible storm.

She wrung her hands, how had they greeted her letter? She could not stop herself fretting about the repercussions consequent upon her action. During the four days since the letter had been dispatched her thoughts had chased each other around day and night.

Suddenly, as if to echo her worst apprehensions, there came a loud knocking on the front door. Petty jumped; her heart beat fiercely; this was it! She just knew it! This was her papa. He was coming to remove her. She had known that would be the case. She had known it since the letter was sent and yet she had had no choice, she had had to send it. Mrs Lumley had been right about that. She could not let them worry any longer.

A flash of lightning lit up the dark sky. She took a deep breath. Her heart pounding she waited for the inevitable arrival in the drawing room of Drake with her father following. Idly she wondered whether her papa would own to his title; she rather hoped he would not.

She heard Drake coming up the stairs, a loud clap of thunder pealed out as the butler knocked quietly on the door. Petty swallowed hard; all the colour drained out of her face. Deciding, "*At least I must try to be brave.*" She drew herself up and defiantly placed herself in front of the double doors as Drake flung them open.

"Lord Milton to see you, Mrs Blakeston," he announced, shutting the door after His Lordship. Petty looked so surprised and shocked that Edward burst out laughing. He noticed that she was white and shaking. Crossing quickly to her he asked, "What is it? You look as though I were a ghost!" Another peal of thunder and more lightning rang out across the sky, lighting up Petty's pale face. She looked at His Lordship and started to giggle, hysterical with relief.

"I thought…" She struggled to get the words out between her giggles. "I thought you were Papa. I thought you had come to take me away."

"Oh, is that all?"

"All! All! It was the most disagreeable of prospects. No, perhaps not the most, Mama would have been far worse." She plonked herself on the sofa. "I am so glad it is you, Edward, and not Mama."

"So I should think!" he retorted. "Being acquainted with your mama was one of the least agreeable things of our marriage!"

Petty suddenly looked serious, she blushed, her eyes flew to his in consternation; his held hers, smiling tenderly. "I do not want to disconcert you, Petty," he said gently, "but we must talk about it at some time… and now seemed the right time… Mrs Lumley told me you had written to your papa, and that was certainly the right thing to do, but it does mean that the matter of our marriage can no longer be ignored."

Sitting down beside her, he possessed himself of her trembling hands. "Have no fear, no one is going to hurt you or upset you. I promise." She raised her eyes to his and looked into them, smiling tremulously. His smiled back reassuringly. She felt light and as if she were going to float away; he leant towards her and she had an almost overwhelming desire just to melt into his arms, to be cherished and loved. At that moment the door opened and Verity strode in.

"Petty," she demanded. Lord Milton dropped Petty's hands.

"Good afternoon, Verity," he said in his most dismissive voice. "I was just offering Mrs Blakeston some comfort; she is scared of the storm."

Petty spluttered and, meeting his eyes, made to protest but a quick speaking look from him silenced her. She caught his eye, her own dancing. "Indeed yes, I am so frightened of the thunder. Is it not loud and terrifying?"

"Foo!" pronounced Verity. "How silly you are. For my part I love to look at the storm, and even more to walk in it. I want to go out to the park. It has been raining for three days and I am bored!" Her voice rose. "I want to go out, I want to go to the park. I have not seen any of…" she corrected herself, "… anyone for days. It is most tedious to be stuck here!"

Lord Milton laughed. "Indeed, one of my tasks today was to bid you to come to dine with me tomorrow. I have some guests staying with me." He tried to catch Petty's eyes but she was gazing into space, her thoughts racing. What would have happened if Verity had not come in? Bother the girl and bother her for still wanting to meet Matty and Jane, which she knew was the real cause of her restlessness. His Lordship continued, "Captain Braybrooke and Gideon Mordaunt."

Petty turned, her eyes open with horror. "Oh I… do… not… think… we are free," she started.

"Oh, how delightful! I should like it above everything," said Verity. "We accept. At what time would you like us?"

His Lordship looked at Petty, frozen with fear. He took her hand. "You have nothing to fear, my dear Mrs Blakeston… no thunder or lightning is going to take you away… everything will be calm and sunny tomorrow." He kissed her hand and squeezed it comfortingly. She, quickly grasping his meaning, heaved a sigh of relief, and managed a wobbly grin. He smiled back at her, nodding slightly, a look of understanding in his dark eyes. In the meantime Verity was cavorting around the room. "Oh, Lord Milton, I am so looking forward to that. May we have dancing after dinner?"

"Verity!" Petty was shocked.

But His Lordship merely laughed. "I do not think so, Verity, unless we can find some music from somewhere."

"Oh, Petty can play, she plays very well," Verity said airily.

His Lordship caught Petty's eyes again. "So I gather…" he replied. "But I thought she only played sonatas by… was it Beethoven and Brahms?"

Petty giggled. "Mozart, I think," she replied, smiling. "But of course I can play, if you so wish it?"

"Excellent! Then I think we shall have an enjoyable evening."

He crossed to the window; the storm seemed to be ceasing, the wind had dropped as quickly as it had come up, the sky was brightening and a watery sun seemed to be breaking through.

"Come, see the rainbow," His Lordship suggested. Petty and Verity joined him at the window and indeed the brightest rainbow Petty had ever seen was arched over the houses on the opposite side of the square. Straggling raindrops were still falling slowly onto number 38 and the sky was still dark on their side but the sun was coming out, making the raindrops sparkle.

"I think I may safely go now." His Lordship kissed Petty's hand again and bowed to Verity, who was still dancing about with excitement about tomorrow.

As soon as Drake had shown him out, Verity started to discuss what she should wear. Petty listened with half her mind, nodding at the appropriate places, her own thoughts plunged into turmoil; had she been mistaken? It all seemed like a dream;

she was not sure about His Lordship. Part of her felt excited; she was looking forward to seeing him again tomorrow. Then she remembered her brother and Captain Braybrooke! Oh well, Edward seemed to have everything under control. Verity broke into her thoughts.

"Petty! Petty!" she demanded. "Are you listening to me? I said, do you think we can go out?" Petty was about to shake her head when Verity continued, "I have absolutely nothing to wear tomorrow, I must go shopping!"

"Oh! Yes," Petty breathed with relief. As long as they were not going to meet the Lockes anything was acceptable. "Of course, my dear. Will you call the carriage?"

Lord Milton drove home slowly. Hardwick sitting up behind him, unused to such a speed, was bemused. He wondered what was making his master look so tight-lipped. Lord Milton, lost in thought, said not word and hardly seemed to notice the groom's presence; this was very strange for, as Hardwick was wont to boast to his less fortunate colleagues, His Lordship was not one to ignore his servants. He was good to them and concerned about them.

Edward was acknowledging a truth to himself, a truth that he had half known for some time, a truth which in the normal way of things would have made him very happy but which, as things were circumstanced, was making him wretched. The truth, which he now accepted, was that he was in love with Petty. She was as unlike any girl that he had ever imagined falling in love with, as it was possible to credit, and as unlike any of his previous dalliances, all of whom had been very beautiful, very vivacious, very accomplished, possessing both social polish and excellent conversation. But Petty, his dearest Petty, had none of these qualities. She was not beautiful, although he defended her to himself; her eyes were ravishing and her face had a sweetness that none of his previous conquests possessed.

She had no social graces, although, again, he found himself defending her; her manners were impeccable and her lovely nature meant that she listened most attentively and with interest to even the most boring matron.

She had no conversation. No, that just was not true, she was well read and highly intelligent and although shy and slightly self-conscious about her ideas, could never be said not to have any.

He knew that he was surprisingly and deeply in love with her; she was all he wanted, all he loved. He wanted to protect her; he wanted to deal with any problems she might have; he did not want to leave her, he wanted her next to him for the rest of his life. But, but… he was married to her.

Married in a way that now caused him to blush with shame. Before he had loved her so much, it had not seemed to matter, but now, now he wondered how he could have countenanced such behaviour.

He regretted his marriage. Oh yes. He wanted Petty for his wife, he wanted it more than he had ever wanted anything in his whole life, but not in this way, not like this. I have to let her go, he thought, and the realisation brought on a pang of pain so acute it was almost physical. His lips set in a tight line. I have to let her free. I love her too much to trap her in this way, she was married to me without choice.

He whipped his horse almost savagely. The animal, totally unused to such treatment, jumped sharply, and careered across the road.

"Your Lordship, have a care," Hardwick reprimanded gently. Lord Milton, shocked back into a recognition of where he was, quietly brought the pair under control.

On his arrival at Grafton Street, Penn greeted him with the intelligence, "Captain Braybrooke has this moment arrived, my lord. He is with Mr Philipson in the library. Mrs Lumley and Miss Dora have gone shopping."

"Thank you, Penn. I will go to join them. Please send up refreshments."

Penn looked disgruntled. "As if I would not have already done so, my lord," he protested.

Expecting an apology from His Lordship, he was surprised to be greeted only with a blank look from those black eyes. " 'e looked that awful. I declare, Mrs Penn, I do not know as what is wrong," he later disclosed to his good wife. She shook her head sagely and wondered also.

Lord Milton joined his grandfather and his best friend in the library. He had not seen William since they had both left Wakeham in January, as the former had been occupied in Yorkshire setting his new estates in order. As Edward warmly clasped his hand, William was struck by the guarded look in his eyes; Cuthbert too noticed the return of the stricken look that so puzzled him.

"William, you are so welcome. It is too long since I have seen you. Tell me, how goes it? Have you managed to order the estates as you would wish? Come, sit beside me. Tell me your news."

The next day was beautiful; the air was clear and fresh, the oppressive heat having quite disappeared. It was Petty's hope that Verity would be so excited about the projected treat that evening, that she would forget about walking in the park; however, it was not to be. Petty made every excuse she could think of for not going, but Verity remained unconvinced by them all and eventually Petty thought it better to agree; to object more would have made even Verity suspicious, and at that point Petty particularly did not want her to have any idea of what she thought of the Lockes.

The afternoon was lovely; the storm had cleared the air and although it was still somewhat wet underfoot, the sun had started to dry out the flowers which looked as though they had been washed, so bright were their colours. In normal circumstances, Petty would have been so happy to walk in the open air after having to remain inside for three days, but today she was uneasy. She kept hoping that the Lockes would disappear. Deep down inside she knew that that would not happen, that there would have to be some kind of resolution, that this situation would not just solve itself, but unsure of what to do, she hoped it would go away.

As they walked through the gardens, she saw no sight of Matty and Jane, and she thought perhaps her secret desire had been granted and they would not be there, but as they turned into the small copse she observed them approaching. Petty sighed, set her face in what she trusted was a look of welcome and awaited their arrival. They were overdressed as usual, Matty in a clinging dress of a shiny material and Jane in a muslin walking dress of violent hue; their faces were painted, their hair curled and decorated in frills and flowers.

Matty gushed. "Oh, dear one, sweet Verity, how we have missed you. La! It seems an age since we saw you." She tucked her arm into Verity's. "Come, my dearest one, tell all, what have you been doing?"

Verity appeared about to launch into a history of all their activities, information that, if imparted, would be most indiscreet. Petty, who did not consider it at all advisable that the Locke sisters knew anything about Lord Milton, or the name Mordaunt, as she had an unpleasant suspicion that the sisters would be assiduous in their research, caught around for something to deflect Verity.

"Oh, Miss Matty, how stunning you look," she lied. "Tell me, have you visited the theatre recently?"

"La! Mrs Blakeston, you are too kind. We have had a daze of parties, I do not know when I have been so amused!"

"We are going…" started Verity.

"Oh, dear Miss Matty," interrupted Petty, "do tell us with whom."

"Oh, we have made the acquaintance of Sir Godfrey Webster, Lady Holland's son by first marriage… such a distinguished man."

She gave one of her unattractive laughs. Privately Petty was horrified! The most undesirable man. A notorious rake with an appalling reputation. Even the Whips Club would have nothing to do with him. He must not meet Verity. She must bring this unfortunate friendship to a halt. But how? She wondered whether to confide in Lord Milton. She had been tempted to do so, as she was sure that he would deal admirably with her problem, but she was nervous of how he would react and apprehensive that he would condemn her for being negligent in her responsibilities to her charge, in allowing the friendship to continue as it had, and she found herself wanting to appear well in his eyes.

Could she try talking to Verity again? It had been useless in the past; the girl had ignored her advice, and had believed Petty to be against her friends, an undesirable position. Petty thought and thought; suddenly she remembered that Gidi was coming, perhaps he could help? She wished heartily that Harry had not been called away to Huntingdon. He would have kept Verity out of trouble.

"La! Verity, you would enjoy Sir Godfrey, such a true gentleman."

Petty shuddered, a description so far from the truth was hard to imagine. She remembered well, in her first season, the scandal of Sir Godfrey's relationship with Lady Caroline Lamb. "Also we must introduce you to Cedric Scott-Waldor." Petty's heart sank further. Even less desirable than Sir Godfrey. Where were they going? Into what company were they sinking? For the first time Petty felt slightly scared. These two men she knew to be ruthless. A more selfish girl than Petty would have packed her bags and left for Mrs Lumley's without delay, but Petty had been brought up to do her duty and although she saw that Verity was extremely silly, she was young and innocent. Petty could not just abandon Verity to her fate. Jane continued.

"Oh, and, my sweet one, at the opera we have been in Harriette Wilson's box. Such a distinguished lady, such excellent friends: Sir Frederick Bentinck, Lord Alvanley, Mr Brummell. You must meet her."

Petty's heart sank further; this was quite beyond what could be countenanced. She turned to Verity. "Come, Verity, we must make our way home. So pleasant to see you, Miss Matty and Miss Jane." She took Verity's arm firmly, propelling her towards the paths which led to the exit to the park.

"Oh indeed, yes, for we are to go…" Verity started. Petty pinched her. "Ow! Ow! What did you do that for!" She turned on Petty furiously.

"What?" replied Petty innocently, continuing to walk with all speed in the direction of the gates.

"You pinched me! You know you did. Why? You had no right!" By now they were out of earshot of Matty and Jane.

"Right! I had every right." Petty was so perturbed by all that she had heard, that she decided to remonstrate with Verity again. She took a breath and tried to talk sense into the girl, employing moderate tones.

"Verity, my dear, I do not want to appear unkind to your friends but the acquaintances that they were discussing today were not at all suitable. Sir Godfrey is the most terrible rake and Harriette Wilson is… is…" she stopped, not quite sure how to proceed, "… quite improper and not received anywhere."

"How would you know? You know nothing of such things. Matty and Jane know who is acceptable in society. You do not."

"Oh, believe me you are wrong. I do know… I… you must understand. I do not give you these warnings gratuitously… I do know that these people she talks of are not the people that a young girl as you should become acquainted with. Your father, I am persuaded, would not approve," she finished lamely.

"Foo. You are quite wrong. You are a nobody, you do not know the likes of Lord Alvanley or Mr Brummell."

Petty, who knew these two gentlemen very well, and also knew that whereas she was in no danger from them, Verity presented by the Lockes would not be in the same case, felt very much out of her depth. She was beginning to despair.

She stopped and turned Verity to her. "Please, Verity, believe me, please see that you must not continue with these friends. It will end in disaster, I know it will."

"Foo," repeated Verity. "What do you know? You just do not want me to have a good time."

"You know that that is not the case," Petty returned indignantly. "That is most unjust. I have..." she started to say and then she gave up. Trying to suppress her agitation, she turned the conversation to other matters. "Come, we must prepare ourselves for tonight. Have you decided what to wear? I wish I had something more suitable than the old muslin."

"Oh, well do not expect me to lend you anything. I have done it once but that was quite an emergency. You must buy yourself an evening dress out of your wages," Verity remarked ungraciously.

Petty reflected that as she had been paid nothing at all, so far, by Sir Hugo, this was a rather unreal expectation. She had no idea how to ask about her remuneration and he had never brought the matter up. At the moment when he hired her she had been so grateful not to be thrown out on the streets that it had not seemed relevant, but now, she admitted ruefully to herself, it seemed very important. She debated whether to mention it to Verity but thought that this was hardly the appropriate moment to do so, as she did not want to antagonise the girl further!

She sighed. She would have liked to look beautiful for His Lordship. She would have liked to look smart for her brother and the captain, both of whom she was longing to see; however, she also knew that these individuals' primary concern would not be how she was dressed. She sighed again. How surprised her mama would have been at her preoccupation with her outfit. She chuckled to herself. By now they had reached Portman Square. Verity was enthusiastically describing the rival merits of her two prettiest dresses and Petty's musings were interrupted by her demand.

"Why are you laughing at me?" she observed petulantly.

"I was not. I was thinking of my mama…"

"Your mama?" Verity was clearly surprised that Petty possessed such an appendage! "Well, which shall it be? Oh, do answer. Petty, Petty, you seem miles away!"

"I apologise, Verity. What was it you wanted?"

"Which dress? Which dress shall I wear? You do not listen to anything," she muttered crossly.

"Oh, I think the blue…" Petty hoped that this was one of her choices; luckily it was.

"Yes, I rather think the blue. Harry said it becomes me so well. I am sorry that he is in Yexley. I wish he would return."

"Oh, so do I," agreed Petty vehemently. "So do I." Privately she considered it a disaster that had taken such a respectable and devoted swain of Verity's away at this particular moment.

Verity ran up the front steps of number 38. Drake opened the door. "Mrs Blakeston. Mrs Blakeston, your trunk has arrived."

"What trunk?" demanded Verity.

"A trunk for Mrs Blakeston," repeated Drake patiently. By now Petty had trod up the shallow steps and was in the hall. She looked perplexed at the huge trunk which stood in the middle of the hall.

"Shall we have it taken to your room, miss?" enquired Drake.

"Yes, yes please." Petty crossed to examine the trunk. Suddenly it came to her. "Oh, Mrs Lumley… Yes, yes, please take it to my room at once." She turned to Verity, smiling broadly. "I shall have something magnificent to wear tonight. I shall not let you down!"

Petty unpacked the trunk in the privacy of her narrow bedchamber; her dresses carefully cushioned between layers of tissue were not even creased, and as she hung them in the tiny wardrobe, she ran her fingers over the soft silks and muslins. They were so beautiful, these frocks chosen so lovingly.

Which one to wear tonight? She discarded the blue silk; it was infinitely more elegant then the one Verity had bought and she had better not put her charge in the shade, not that she could compete with Verity's beauty. In the end she chose a cream muslin round gown, with a lace and embroidered overdress. It enhanced her face and her slender figure and when she came downstairs in it Drake was fulsome in his praise.

CHAPTER SIXTEEN

She followed Drake and Verity across the dingy halt; the butler's indomitable spouse watching quietly from the shadows thought she had never seen Petty look better: the girl's eyes sparkled; her face glowed. Dusty sunbeams slanting from the fanlight windows tangled in the folds of the pale silk, making her dress almost translucent. Mrs Drake, sighing sentimentally, thought Petty an angel from a painting. Drake, aware that there was something special about this evening, personally threw the door open and handed his ladies into the carriage. Petty climbed aboard Sir Hugo's old-fashioned town coach as the sun was beginning to set, casting its pink tendrils of light across the blue sky and onto the tops of the houses. The summer air was redolent with the sweet perfume of flowers, which were everywhere blossoming in profusion, thriving on the torrents of water that had poured down on them through the previous few days, and the succeeding heat.

Petty sat in the corner of the carriage looking through the tarnished windows. She thought London had never before looked so beautiful; the pink light which suffused the streets added to the natural warmth of the day. She felt supremely happy. Rarely had she contemplated an evening with such pleasure. She was longing to see her brother and she relished the chance of renewing her acquaintance with Captain Braybrooke.

Then, of course, there was Lord Milton. When she thought of that gentleman, a small thrill of anticipation shot through her. She hugged the remembrance of him to herself.

The drive to Grafton Street seemed both very long and very short. She wanted to get there so much and yet she felt nervous and shy about what might happen. Suppose she was wrong about everything? Perhaps Lord Milton was merely being kind? She had no way of knowing what he meant. No experience of these matters. She realised how disappointed she would be if her expectations were proved to be unfounded. But I must not let myself feel like that, she told herself fiercely. I must not rely too much on what may be merely supposition.

Then suppose her brother carried commands from her father to take her back? Could she refuse? She did not think she really had that strength. She knew too that it was essential that Verity did not find out who she was, because if she did, Petty suspected that her position would be in jeopardy, and if she had nowhere else to live she certainly could not refuse to go with Gideon! But surely Mrs Lumley would not let that happen?

The evening suddenly seemed filled with pitfalls.

"We are here at last." Verity's voice broke in on her thoughts. Petty found her heart beating so loudly in her chest she was almost sure that Verity could hear it. "How delightful the house looks to be sure."

Petty, looking up, nodded agreement. In the twilight, it was ablaze with lights; the balcony was entwined with honeysuckle, which filled the air with its fragrance. Petty breathed deeply.

She followed Verity and an impervious footman up the elegant staircase to the saloon. Penn announced them and Petty stepped into the room. She had of course been in the saloon before and had been much impressed by its elegance, but tonight it seemed more beautiful and in a strange way more welcoming. She looked around her and noticed with faint surprise and amusement that her brother was chatting comfortably to

Cuthbert and Mrs Lumley. Dora sat quietly next to her mother, gazing in adoration at Aurelia, who was affectionately sparring with the captain, too close a childhood friend to be treated with any great respect!

She noticed that Lord Milton was talking to a young man whom she did not know. He was tall, with thin sandy hair and pale blue eyes. He was dressed in a slightly old-fashioned way with frock coat and black satin knee breeches. As they entered, Gideon, Cuthbert and the captain rose and His Lordship left the unknown gentleman and crossed quickly to greet his guests. Petty watched him as he came towards her, the look on his face so warm that she perceived with a ripple of happiness that she had not been mistaken.

Far too well bred to outwardly exhibit any preference in his demeanour, he was, however, unable to disguise his feelings completely, and the captain, who was watching carefully to see how Petty had fared since leaving Wakeham, was surprised to observe the expression in his friend's eyes as he greeted his wife. The intense look was not lost on his brother-in-law either. William and Gideon exchanged glances; they had been warned by Edward about the necessary pretence that must be observed for Petty's sake, but neither of them had had until that moment the slightest inkling of His Lordship's feelings for Petty. Or, as William thought sagely to himself, hers for him. Apart from that, the marquis, ever appreciative of female beauty, was delighted by the change in his sister and was just about to leap across and tell her so when he received an admonitory look from Edward. He checked himself.

"Miss Verity, how delightful to see you and in such good looks too. Mrs Blakeston, your servant," His Lordship remarked politely. "Please allow me to present Gideon Mordaunt and Captain Braybrooke."

"How charming to make your acquaintance." Verity held out her small perfect hand and, using her most beguiling smile, had the satisfaction of seeing both the young gentlemen brighten as they observed her beauty. She was in her element.

"How delightful. What an enchanting picture you make," Gideon murmured appreciatively. His eyes met Petty's. They grinned at her but he merely indicated a distant greeting before turning his attention to the ravishing Verity. "Miss Croisthwaite, please allow me to find you a glass of orangeat."

He whisked the beauty away from under William's nose, swiftly leading her to the window seat and sitting firmly next to her. Petty laughed. She caught Edward's eye; taking her arm, he drew her away from her brother.

"Quite!"

Petty found herself slipping her hand into his as it lay on his arm, as if it were the most natural thing in the world. She glanced at her brother gazing admiringly into Verity's face. His Lordship followed her look.

"However, I do not anticipate that Gideon will remain enthralled for very long once he discovers Verity's less attractive characteristics," Petty giggled.

Edward led her across to present her to Horace Appleton–Smythe, who turned out to be a neighbour of his in Yorkshire. Petty curtsied readily, secretly glad that Edward had been tactful enough not to include anyone in his party who might have had any idea of her true identity.

The captain, having been outwitted with the beauty, had made his way to the seat recently vacated by Gideon, next to Mrs Lumley, who was dressed in her usual outrageous manner, and he found himself studying with an amazed interest her overburdened cap, when he caught her eye. He had the grace to blush slightly.

"Admiring me cap, were you?" she remarked with a distinct twinkle.

He laughed. "I must admit, ma'am, that I have rarely seen anything quite like it!"

She chortled. "I like a man who speaks his mind. You'll do!" She patted his knee. Her eyes alighted on Verity. She sniffed. "That one will not. A sillier or more selfish piece I have yet to encounter. I am quite determined to remove Petty from having to suffer her spoilt wiles."

The captain glanced in the direction of Petty and Lord Milton deep in conversation, unconsciously oblivious to those around them. "Perhaps that will not be necessary."

Mrs Lumley followed his glance. "Oh, I do hope you are correct. My dearest wish. But there is something not quite right. Something that is worrying her. I just do not know what it is. What is stopping her?" As she spoke, half to herself, she shook her head, making all the bows and ribbons bob up in such an amusing way that but for his breeding William would have laughed. Mrs Lumley frowned and was about to enlarge upon her concern, when Edward, realising that he might appear to have been monopolising Petty, brought her to them.

Petty curtsied prettily. "Oh, dear Mrs Lumley, I must thank you for the dresses. You are so kind. But really I cannot accept them all."

"Is this one of them?" Edward enquired. "It is most fetching. You can and will accept them. I insist." He spoke in a teasing way but Petty blushed red, realising the implication behind his speech. Her eyes flew to his full of tears.

"I cannot. I must not, Mrs Lumley," she pleaded.

Mrs Lumley patted her hand. "Now, Petty, do not be silly. Uniform for the job, I said. What am I going to do with them?"

"But… but I am not… I cannot work for you," Petty replied somewhat desperately.

Lord Milton watched her, his expression inscrutable. "Excuse me! My guests."

He moved away. Mrs Lumley looked even more perplexed. The captain, equally confused, turned politely to his young neighbour, Dora, who peeped at him from under her lowered lids. He smiled reassuringly at her.

"Verity is very beautiful," Dora vouchsafed shyly.

"Yes!" answered William enthusiastically, following her eyes. He regarded the girl at his side; she did not have Verity or Aurelia's beauty but she had a sweet prettiness that was definitely attractive. He engaged her in conversation, discovering that this was not difficult for Dora had accomplished social manners and a lively tongue.

Petty watched Edward, her thoughts a jumble. She did not quite understand why she said the things she said, she did not quite understand why she drew back from him. It was Verity. She was sure of that, but it was more than just Verity. She was scared. Scared that she would be rebuffed and hurt. Nervous that it was all her imagination. Could she leave Verity and work as Dora's companion? No. She could not bear to be in the same house as Edward, not working for Mrs Lumley! Then she smiled to herself. It was clearly ineligible. Cuthbert broke in on her thoughts.

"Well, my girl! You look in excellent health. I do not know when I have seen you look bonnier!" Petty, relieved, giggled slightly. Aurelia, following him, hugged Petty.

"Oh, how lovely it is to see you. I have the best of news," she bubbled. "What do you think? I have persuaded Edward to take us all to Vauxhall. Is it not exciting? We shall have a box and see the fireworks… You will come, will you not?" Petty looked doubtful. "Oh, but you must… she must." She beckoned to her brother.

"Who must do what, wretch?" He grinned.

"Petty and Verity, they must join our expedition to Vauxhall!"

By this time Verity had heard the discussion and joined in vociferously. "Indeed, we shall come. Of course we will. I have long desired to go there."

Petty's stricken look was seen by His Lordship who, ever aware of her comfort, remarked quickly, "Yes! You shall come but I think it will be jollier if we all go masked." He met her eyes. He thought the relief in them utterly endearing.

"Oh, masks, what fun!" she replied.

"Then it is agreed," pronounced Aurelia firmly.

"Shall we have dancing after dinner?" demanded Verity. "You promised."

His Lordship laughed. "I did and I keep my promises. But now I believe that dinner is served."

He offered his arm to Petty and led her to the dining room. Petty was not the only one whose thoughts were confused. Edward, in love for the first time, was experiencing a heightened sensitivity to his love's moods. He seemed aware of every nuance in her speech, and when she seemed to withdraw from him, he suffered a pang which he could only deal with by retreating behind an icy exterior. He knew, in part, that he was behaving irrationally. Normally very tolerant of the moods of others, the smallest change in Petty found him overreacting. He deplored his behaviour but he did not seem to be able to control it.

At dinner Edward sat Petty at the other end of the table next to Gideon. Verity he sat next to himself. Petty was glad of this, for so far she had had not a moment of speech with her brother.

"You look elegant, dearest mouse, are you happy?"

"Oh, Gidi, it is so good to see you." She grinned at him. "Well, I do not enjoy work as a governess much. I think I have more of Mama in me than I thought! But please tell me how they all go on? I miss them so much."

Gideon looked at her reflectively. He was about to comment that she need not work and that if she missed everyone, why did she not come home, but something in her face restrained him. He merely enlarged upon the antics of her sisters and brothers, conveying all the wishes of Fonty and the duke and duchess. Petty seemed content and she changed the subject.

After dinner Lord Milton was as good as his word, for when they returned to the saloon, the furniture had been moved back at one end for dancing. The Steinway piano had been opened.

Edward came to Petty with a pile of music.

"I did not know what you would wish to play so I have brought all these." He put a quantity of music on the piano. "May I turn for you?"

Petty played, Edward stood close to her. She discovered that he was naturally musical, turning at exactly the right moment for her. She was aware of his presence so close to her, his arm just touching hers, exciting yet comforting. The others danced merrily. Petty met Edward's eyes, alight with laughter as Cuthbert seriously led Mrs Lumley onto the floor. After Petty had played for about an hour, Aurelia approached them.

"Petty! Edward! You too must have a dance. I shall play!" She brushed aside Petty's protestations, sat firmly on the piano and struck up a vigorous waltz.

His Lordship held out his arms to Petty and whirled her around the floor in perfect harmony. As she moved so close to him, his eyes smiling at her, Petty made her decision. "I will not continue to work with Verity. I shall leave. I shall come to Mrs Lumley. I am so happy here I never want to go. This is where I belong."

She looked at him. He wanted to speak, he wanted to tell her he loved her and please come and be his wife. He stopped; he did not want her to withdraw from him again. Petty, sensing his mood, wondered.

"Well! I declare I am fair done in," eventually pronounced Mrs Lumley, bringing the evening to a close. Goodbyes were said and arrangements made between the young for a visit as soon as possible, in addition to the projected trip to Vauxhall.

Verity was unnaturally quiet in the coach on the drive home. "Well, Verity, and did you have a pleasant evening?" Petty enquired.

"Dora is so lucky," the girl replied mournfully.

"Why?" Petty responded, surprised.

"She has such a lovely mama." Petty, thinking of Mrs Lumley, nearly laughed but then restrained herself.

"I wish I had a mama," Verity sighed. 'They all have families."

"Aurelia has no mama either," Petty pointed out.

"I know, but she has a brother who adores her and a grandfather who dotes on her. I do not have anyone." Petty for the first time felt sorry for the girl.

"You have a papa who loves you."

"He does not care what happens to me… really. He is too busy."

"I am…" Petty was about to repudiate this statement but thinking of Sir Hugo, she had her doubts.

"At least I have you." Verity, not normally demonstrative, seemed to snuggle close to Petty. "But I wish I had a family."

Petty, on whom the attractions of the house at Grafton Street had also not been lost, suddenly found that her decision was put in jeopardy. She could not after all leave Verity at this time. The girl, while indubitably silly, was not bad, and she had no one to guide her, no one who truly cared what happened to her and she was such an innocent. Petty felt sad. She did not want to stay, she did not like Verity particularly, but she could not leave her at this time. In addition to her dismay that her plans had been once more put asunder, Petty felt cross that she had been trapped by Sir Hugo, forced to remain with Verity. She found that she resented the way that she seemed to have been manoeuvred into a position of responsibility for Verity; she knew that these feelings were in part irrational; she had been grateful enough for the job when she had had nowhere else to go.

As she lay in the narrow bed, her thoughts chased each other through most of the night and when she arose the next morning, unrefreshed, she found that she was no nearer a solution. She went down to the breakfast parlour, and found it deserted, Verity apparently still firmly asleep.

She rang the bell and Mrs Drake answered. "Did you have a good evening, Mrs Blakeston?" she enquired, looking curiously at Petty, noting her pale face and the blue eyes rimmed with dark circles. "You look rather tired, was you very late?"

"No not very, Mrs Drake… I…" Petty did not quite know how to apprise her of Verity's undesirable friendships, her lack of anyone to care for her, or take her part, her unwanted dependence on Petty. "Please sit down for a moment, I want to… well, I want your advice."

"Advice? I do not know if I can help you."

"You see, it is about Miss Verity. I am concerned. I mean, who would supervise her if I were not here?"

Petty instantly realised that she had approached the problem in the wrong way. Mrs Drake flew up in horror.

"Oh, Mrs Blakeston, you would not leave Verity! You must not, she needs you so much. You have done so much for her. She is kinder, more sensible… Oh, you have done wonders for her. I have hope for her now. She don't mean wrong but no one before you has shown her how to go on properly. Look, she is making friends…"

"It is on the matter of her friends that I require your advice."

"Oh, I am sure that I could not help you on that score, I do not know who is right for her to know. I thought you seemed to be knowing just the kind of people her poor mama would have liked for her. You won't abandon her, will you?" The former matter was obviously preoccupying Mrs Drake and Petty realised that to get any sense out of her on the business of the Lockes would clearly not be possible at present.

She shook her head sadly. "Well, not for the present but I cannot stay for ever, you know."

"Why not?"

Petty was saved from answering her, by the entrance of Verity yawning loudly, and a peal on the front door. Mrs Drake bustled away to see who was calling and to get Verity some breakfast.

217

"What a delightful evening! Did you not think Mr Mordaunt most awfully handsome?" Verity remarked, buttering herself a large slice of toast. Petty nodded, inwardly groaning; she did not want Verity to fall prey to her notorious brother's charms; she saw more trouble ahead. She sighed. She wanted to run away again. It was all becoming too complicated. Drake came in. He coughed apologetically.

"Mrs Cornwall and Miss Mary to see you, Miss Verity, shall I show them into the saloon?"

"Oh no!" commanded Verity. "Show them in here, I am convinced they will not mind my continuing to eat."

The Cornwalls were accompanied by Harry Trevellyan. Verity squeaked her pleasure. "Oh, Mr Trevellyan you have returned! How perfectly delightful!"

She jumped up and ran to him in what Petty privately considered a most forward way; however, he seemed to find nothing amiss about Verity's welcome, and Petty herself was so grateful that he was so respectable and not Sir Godfrey or Cedric Scott-Waldor, found it not in herself to reprimand her.

"Come, Verity, finish your breakfast. How are you, Mrs Cornwall and Mary? May I offer you something? I must apologise for our tardiness."

"No! No, the fault is ours. We came to bid you walk with us this morning. The weather is so beautiful."

Petty was about to agree to that when there came another knock on the door and Drake was showing in Lord Milton, Aurelia and Dora.

"My goodness!" Petty, who was as secretly delighted to see Edward as Verity had been to see Harry, but who was more discreet, exclaimed, "The breakfast parlour cannot hold so many. Please let us adjourn to the saloon."

The younger members of the party desisted the pleasure of the company of their elders and Verity led Dora, Aurelia and

Harry into the morning room for a game of chequers, while Petty entertained His Lordship and Mrs Cornwall.

"My errand will take no time," Lord Milton explained. "I have merely come to suggest that our picnic in Richmond Park take place tomorrow as the weather promises to continue fair." He turned to Mrs Cornwall. "It will give me the greatest pleasure, ma'am, if you, Mary and Harry would join us." Mrs Cornwall started to demur but His Lordship insisted and the plans for the following day were quickly agreed.

"I must go now, Mrs Blakeston." Lord Milton clasped her hand to bid goodbye. "I look forward to seeing you tomorrow and I anticipate a great deal of enjoyment when you drive my team," he said provocatively, regarding her under slightly raised brows but with his face remaining quite straight.

Petty spluttered. "I too shall look forward to handling your greys," she challenged him laughingly. He bade farewell to Mrs Cornwall and, collecting Dora and Aurelia, left swiftly.

He was muddled. He found it hard to keep away from Portman Square, and yet he knew that the time must come very soon when he must release Petty from her obligation towards him. The thought of this caused him so much anguish that he kept, uncharacteristically, putting it off. I will deal with it after the party to Richmond, he decided as he drove home.

When they had departed, Petty and Mrs Cornwall summoned Verity, Harry and Mary to inform them of the projected treat; all three were delighted, Verity immediately planning what she should wear.

CHAPTER SEVENTEEN

Petty was awoken the next day by the early morning sun which poured through her window. She jumped out of bed and pulled back the flowered curtains. The morning mist hung in a light haze over the tops of the plane trees which lined the square. She opened the window and took a breath of the clean fresh air; it was going to be a beautiful day, she just knew that it was. The sky was a clear, deep blue; it was already warm, with the promise of excellent weather ahead.

Petty went to the wardrobe; she ran her hand over the muslin dresses so kindly provided by Mrs Lumley, trying to decide which to wear. The choice was difficult, for in truth, Mrs Lumley had ordered frocks of such taste and discernment that every one enhanced Petty. Eventually she chose a pale blue slip of a dress. She dressed quickly, brushing her curls into as fashionable a style as she could manage, not for the first time wishing that the simple room ran to a glass, so that she could see her reflection. Had she, in fact, possessed such an accessory she would have been pleased with the image that she presented. She whirled around. Her mood of excited anticipation had made her thin face look almost pretty; the dark-lashed eyes sparkled and a delicate flush coloured her usually sallow cheeks.

When she had finished she made her way through the dingy corridors to the breakfast parlour. The room was empty. The spotlessly laid table indicated that Verity was not yet down. Petty helped herself to a large cup of coffee and sat at the only part of the table that was touched by sunlight.

The room was very peaceful. She sat, her face in her hands, dwelling on the projected pleasures ahead. When Verity eventually did arrive it was obvious that she too had taken some time to dress. She was ravishingly attired in a flowered muslin half-dress with a delicate lace collar; her golden curls were gathered onto the top of her head on which sat a fetching straw hat decorated with tiny flowers. She helped herself to a generous repast and went to join Petty.

As they were finishing this, Drake arrived to inform them that several elegant equipages were drawn up outside Portman Square waiting to convey Lord Milton's party to Richmond. A chaise bearing His Lordship's crest accommodated the older members, Mrs Lumley accompanied by Cuthbert and Mrs Cornwall. The marquis had decided to ride. Captain Braybrooke who would, also, have much liked to ride but was too much the gentleman, drove his host's curricle with Dora and Mary. Harry, who came with a neat curricle driven by a rather solid pair of bays, chose to drive Verity and Aurelia. Petty, much to her joy, was taken aboard His Lordship's phaeton.

It was a perfect day, the sky a deep blue without a single cloud, warm but certainly not oppressively hot. Petty sat up high next to Edward and, as her brother before her, admired his driving. They did not speak much as he made his way through the crowded streets, but as they reached the fields of Chelsea and His Lordship was able to allow his greys to have their heads, he turned to Petty.

"How pretty you look today." Petty went pink with pleasure at the unexpected compliment. "Am I correct in assuming this elegant creation to be another of Mrs Lumley's gowns?"

Petty nodded and grinned. "You are quite correct." She unfurled her parasol and settled back happily.

His Lordship grinned back. "For someone who dresses in such an…" He stopped.

"Individual style!" Petty supplied helpfully with a stifled giggle.

"Exactly… individual style herself, she has the most exquisite taste where you and Dora are concerned."

"You should see her house, I have never seen so many frills! And yet it is most comfortable, and has such an admirable feeling."

"You forget," he murmured, "I have seen the house."

Petty blushed slightly; however, he did not continue with that uncomfortable subject. "How well you drive," she commented, recovering her composure. "I miss driving so much. My dear old horse, Jumper, I miss him too," she sighed. "I love the sensation of holding the reins, the feeling of control, the unleashing of all that power, the satisfaction when one negotiates a difficult corner."

He looked at her curiously, raising an eyebrow slightly. "But I thought that you… well… did not enjoy driving. Did you not tell me that you hated it?" He looked into her eyes, a laughing quizzical expression in his.

She looked at his from under her long dark lashes. "I lied," she said beguilingly.

Edward hooted with laughter. "And there I was thinking that I might persuade you to let me teach you."

Petty giggled again. "I have to confess that I am really quite competent. Shall I show you?" Edward was momentarily taken aback; he had assumed her to be joking; he let no one drive his greys, except occasionally, if necessity prevailed, Hardwick.

He was, however, far too much in love with Petty to have refused her anything and even if she had confessed that she had never driven before he might have handed over his ribbons to her, had she requested them of him.

He pulled up and with slight misgivings he handed her the reins. As soon as she moved off, he quickly realised that any fears he might have had were groundless. Petty had naturally light hands, drove fearlessly, controlling the greys with a professionalism that amazed him.

"You are wonderful," he told her, his eyes alight with genuine admiration.

"Thank you, my lord." She glanced fleetingly at him, her own shining with joy.

Richmond Park was soon reached, and due to the excellence of His Lordship's horses they had arrived well before the others. Petty stopped and Edward jumped down, leading the greys into the shade. Petty followed him, sitting on the verdant soft grass under some huge trees. "Are you sure that you do not want a rug? The ground is not too damp?" queried Edward, ever mindful of his love's comfort.

"No," Petty sighed happily. She ran her fingers over the green fronds. "I love to sit on the grass. It reminds me of Wakeham, of picnics with Anthony and Fonty and the littles, under the huge oak trees by the river. The smell of the damp trees and the moss. It makes me realise that I have hardly been out of a town since…" She stopped.

"Since you ran away from me. Do not be afraid to say it." He smiled at her. She flushed slightly, turning her face away from his.

"I have said that I am sorry!" she replied stiffly, embarrassed by her unacceptable conduct.

He, aware of her withdrawal, watched her; a man of consummate address he found himself floundering in his dealings with her. He wanted so much to make her happy. He felt her attraction for him, but as soon as he referred to their past she ran from him, as surely as if she had jumped to her feet and made off into the woods. He reached for her hand, but as he did so Harry arrived with Verity and Aurelia, the marquis riding alongside, and the moment was lost.

"I see that you have beaten us, Lord Milton," trilled Verity

 223

jumping down. "In truth, we have had a delightful ride but those horses of Harry's are certainly not of the fastest."

"And I have been forced to ride at a snail's pace next to you," Gideon retorted playfully.

"Indeed it was entirely your choice, Mr Mordaunt." Verity raised her chin and fluttered her eyelashes at him flirtatiously. Bother, Gidi, thought Petty.

Harry, who also observed Verity's interchange with His Lordship, merely exclaimed ruefully, "Hired nags I am afraid, sir. I cannot afford to bring my own team down from Huntingdon. These are inclined to consider that a slow trot is the best form of transport."

Aurelia giggled. "Oh, I can confirm that, Edward, I have rarely sat behind such a pair of dullards! Luckily it is the most beautiful ride and so much to look at that I did not mind. How pretty are the villages of Chelsea and Fulham, and the river meandering through the meadows, quite delightful. Do you not agree?" She turned to Petty, who nodded.

"Well, I would but I must confess that I did not have much time to observe the scenery."

"Why, did Edward drive you so fast?"

"No!" his brother demurred. "Mrs Blakeston drove herself. So fast!" He smiled.

Aurelia looked from one to the other, her eyes wide with astonishment. "Edward let you drive! He must be mad or in..." a quelling look from her brother stopped her, "in... in his dotage," she corrected quickly. "He has never been known to let anybody drive his greys. You must be flattered." She glanced curiously at Petty and Edward, but the former had turned from them to greet the older members of the party who had just driven up and her brother's expression was inscrutable.

"My, what a delightful spot," Mrs Lumley pronounced.

"Wait until you see inside the park, it is lovely," Edward replied, leading his horses from under the tree and handing Petty up.

The small cavalcade followed him into the park. Harry, who in spite of the sluggishness of his horses, had thoroughly enjoyed the sensation of driving two such beauties, was experiencing the pleasure of someone who sees Richmond Park for the time. A country boy at heart he was delighted by the spacious wild rides, by the beauty of the trees, by the numerous herds of deer.

In truth, apart from Lord Milton and the marquis, it was the first visit for all the party, but it was Harry who breathed deeply the country air and felt at home away from the city.

Verity was happy; Harry regarded her with frank admiration and she rather thought she had captured the heart of the handsome Mr Mordaunt. She was in her element as the captain, she also believed, was an ardent admirer. In this she was wrong; the captain had quickly got the measure of Verity and he realised that in order to make Petty's life easier he needed to fain adoration of her capricious charge.

Lord Milton led his party to a sheltered spot near the ponds where they were to picnic. He had chosen a shady spot near to the Pen ponds and had sent Hardwick and a footman on ahead with the food so that, when they arrived hot and tired and thirsty, they discovered a sumptuous spread laid out on the grass under some trees. His Lordship had thought of everything, and small folding chairs had been included for the three elder members; the younger ones were content to sit on rugs under the boughs. Petty flopped down on the grass beside Dora and the captain.

"How well you look, Mrs Blakeston," William commented as she helped herself to a large plate of the delicious victuals prepared by Edward's most excellent French chef.

"Thank you! It is in part due to the frocks so kindly given to me by Mrs Lumley." She grinned at Dora. The captain looked slightly perplexed and Petty wondered with a sense of fear whether Lord Milton had told him what had occurred; suddenly the confused look on his brow lifted, he smiled at Petty, but only said, "Immaculate taste, I congratulate her."

Petty half listened, her attention caught by the horribly forward behaviour of Verity, who was sitting with Gideon on one side and Harry on the other.

"Excuse me. I must just see how Verity is." She scrambled to her feet and crossed to her brother.

She stood in front of him and glared down into his eyes. "I would like a word with you, Mr Mordaunt!" she said fiercely.

Gideon returned her look laughingly. "Anything to oblige."

She grabbed hold of his arm and pulled him to his feet. "Over here," she hissed. If Verity was surprised at her governess's behaviour she did not show it, merely turning to Harry.

"Leave her alone, Gidi! Please," she pleaded.

He tickled her lazily under the chin. "Why, mouse? She is deliciously pretty and ripe for a gentle dalliance. Nothing serious, I promise."

"That is the problem… well, please leave… you see, she…" She wanted to explain about the Lockes and how important it was that Harry remained unchallenged, but she felt that her brother would not understand. She knew that he was not happy with, what he considered, her lowly position as Verity's governess, and she knew that if he thought she was mixing with the likes of Sir Godfrey she would be whisked away and back to Wakeham before she had a chance to justify herself. So she stopped, contenting herself with observing that Verity was very young and very volatile and would make Petty's life a misery if she did not get her own way with Gideon. He seemed to understand and crossed to take up her vacated place with Dora and the captain.

Petty heaved a sigh of relief and proceeded to join Mrs Lumley and Cuthbert. "La! How hot it is," said Mrs Lumley, fanning herself furiously. "But the food is delicious."

Petty smiled to herself; she knew that her former protectress was particularly fond of her meals. "Indeed!"

Mrs Lumley, who had taken in Petty's chat with her brother, her worried glances at Verity and her obvious happiness with

Lord Milton, determined to get to the bottom of everything. She patted the grass next to her.

"Come, sit down, my dear, and tell me, did you enjoy your drive here?"

"Oh yes! Above everything!" Petty stretched out contentedly, lazily watching Edward, her eyes unconsciously following him as he sat down with his sister and Mary. "Is it not a wonderful day? I do not know when I felt so happy." She transferred her eyes to the antics of the half-grown ducklings who were bobbing and chasing each other across the water.

"Indeed it is, although I must admit that I find the heat particularly oppressive, even in the shade." Petty took her eyes off the ducks and looked keenly at Mrs Lumley, whose cheeks were distinguished by two very large red spots and whose forehead was quite crimson.

"Are you feeling alright?" she enquired with concern.

"Yes! Yes! Do not worry yourself with me," responded Mrs Lumley, although she continued to fan herself vigorously. "When you are my size, my dear, you do not find the sun easy to deal with."

"Oh no! I do understand! Of course it is hard," Petty responded sympathetically, patting her hand.

"I shall be quite myself in a second. I am a little fatigued, that is all."

Petty surveyed the assembled company, who seemed to have disposed themselves agreeably. In some groups of people she had been with in the past she had noted a want of union, but although they had split into separate parties there was no sense of a want of willingness to mix.

She watched Aurelia and Mary laughing with Edward; she observed Harry and Verity in deep, quiet conversation; she knew that she should probably not encourage their closeness but he was such an unexceptional young man and perhaps encouragement of him would herald the demise of Matty and Jane, an outcome for which Petty desperately wished.

The captain, Dora and Mary were scrambling to their feet, obviously intent on exploring the walks surrounding the ponds on foot. She was idly watching them when Lord Milton appeared at her side.

"Would you do me the honour of walking with me?" he asked.

She nodded, her eyes smiling enchantingly at him. "Yes, I would very much like to explore the woods." He held out his hand, helping her to her feet.

"Will you be alright, Mrs Lumley?" Petty asked.

"You go along, I have Mrs Cornwall for company. I am perfectly fine."

Petty wanted to go with His Lordship so much that she suspended her usual perceptiveness and accepted Mrs Lumley's protestations without question. Although indeed, Mrs Lumley still looked alarmingly red, Petty merely smiled happily at her and, unfurling her parasol, prepared to follow Mary, Dora and the captain who had disappeared into the woods.

She took Edward's arm and without another thought accompanied him across the sunlit paths and into the shady enclaves of trees. The woods, which, in spite of the warmth of this day, were still damp from the rain, smelt of moss and rotting wood. It was not an unpleasant aroma, in fact Petty sniffed appreciatively, for it reminded her of the woods on her father's estates. The ground was covered with tiny white spheres. Petty poked one and laughed.

"It looks as if it is snowing, I have never seen so many mushrooms before!" she exclaimed, Edward knelt down beside her to examine the carpet of tiny fungi. She looked up at him; his face was very close to hers; his eyes regarded hers steadily. She felt a tremor run through her; she thought he was going to kiss her and she raised her head slightly in anticipation.

"Oh! Petty, Petty!" he sighed and turned from her. "I can no longer continue like this. I… We…" He stood up, pulling her sharply to her feet. "We must talk about our wedding! We must discuss what has happened and what you want for the future." His voice was flat and to Petty's ears it sounded cold. "I know you would prefer to continue as if nothing has occurred but you cannot prolong this absurdity anymore."

In his desire to control the urge to fling himself at her feet and declare himself, which he knew would only enhance her guilt, which he knew was very unfair on her, he made himself sound far harsher than he meant to. To Petty his tones were shocking; his words belied what she thought she saw in his face; she did not know how to answer him. She trembled with trepidation and said nothing; her negative response merely confirmed his worst fears: she did not care for him, she hated her marriage, he must let her go. The idea was sickening. He wanted to hit out at someone.

"Petty! Petty! Lord Milton! Come, come quickly!" Mrs Cornwall's normally calm voice was raised in terror.

"Dora! Dora! Lord Milton! Where are you? Please come."

Lord Milton whirled around, looked questioningly at Petty, and started back through the woods. She followed as swiftly as she could.

"Mrs Cornwall, I am here. What is the matter?" he called as she came panting up the path.

"Oh... Oh..." She could scarcely get the words out, so out of breath she was. "Oh... dear."

"Take a deep breath, Mrs Cornwall," suggested Petty, taking her arm and leading her towards the stump of a tree in a small clearing.

"Oh no! We must not sit down." By this time they had been joined by Dora, Mary and the captain. Mary's concern naturally was for her mama.

"Oh, Mama, are you well? You look quite exhausted."

"No, I am fine." Mrs Cornwall patted her daughter's hand. "But I am afraid that Mrs Lumley is not well. She has been quite overcome by the heat."

Dora turned quite pale, and started to tremble. The captain, with his usual presence of mind, caught her arm and sat her down on the convenient stump. "Mama! My dearest mama, I must go to her."

"Yes, yes," said William soothingly, "but recover your composure first."

"How bad is Mrs Lumley?" questioned Edward.

Mrs Cornwall, who by now had recovered her breath enough to make a sensible reply, said, "I do not think it is serious, Your Lordship. But I think we should return to town without delay."

"Naturally." He led the way and the others, in sombre fashion, followed him.

As soon as they got back, Dora rushed to her mother. She was on the ground where she had collapsed, fortuitously in the shade under an oak tree. Cuthbert was attending her with all the good sense engendered by many years' experience. Mrs Cornwall, before rushing off to find the others, had loosened her stays, and neither of them, sensibly, had attempted to move her. Cuthbert had folded up one of the rugs and placed it behind her head and was pleased to see that her alarming colour was now returning to normal.

"Mama! Mama!" Dora's agitated tones made the good lady raise her head. "Mama! Please! Oh! Someone help her."

"Shh, Dora," Petty, who with her own miseries uppermost, said rather more unkindly than was her usual mode. "You will not help by going off in that hysterical manner." She pushed the girl, who was now weeping quietly, in the direction of the patient captain. "Your mama will be fine in a minute."

She knelt down beside Mrs Lumley and felt her pulse which, although fast, was not racing, and her head, which was now quite cool. She looked around. Edward was next to her, his face full of concern.

"I think, if you agree, that we should get her back to Grafton Street as soon as we can." Petty nodded. He gestured to the servants and to Hardwick to bring the coach as close as possible. Together he, Gideon and Harry maneuvered the bulk of Mrs

Lumley onto the soft cushions of his travelling chaise. Dora, who by now had recovered her strength, vouched that she wished to travel with her mother.

"That seems a bonnie idea! I will undertake to go with Edward," volunteered Cuthbert. "Mrs Cornwall can give you a hand, lass, if you should need one." His eye caught Mrs Cornwall's sensible one and she nodded imperceptibly.

"Yes, Mr Philipson, and perhaps Aurelia can take Dora's place with my Mary?"

She looked to Edward, who nodded. "Yes, and Mrs Blakeston can accompany Verity and Harry."

Petty, who was quite aware of the ineligibility of Verity travelling with Harry, was nevertheless angry at his high-handedness and shot him a furious glance, which he had the good sense to ignore, as really there was no alternative.

As soon as they were all packed, they left, following the chaise which had departed as soon as Mrs Lumley was settled. Petty had as miserable a journey back to town as her outward journey had been happy.

She did not understand herself, she did not understand His Lordship. There were moments when she felt he loved her, but then his tones would turn harsh and forbidding and she thought she was merely castle-building. She, herself unloved as a child, found it far easier to believe that he did not love her than that he did. She wished she had never run away and yet she knew that she would never have lost her mousiness if she had not confronted the various situations that had overcome her since she had left Wakeham.

She sighed deeply, half listening to the flirtatious dalliance that composed conversation between Verity and young men. Another failure, Petty thought, determined to chastise herself further. I have totally failed to bring Verity to any senses of what is right and proper. She could not understand how Harry seemed to be enjoying the vacuous nature of Verity's stories, her trilling tones expounding her own concerns.

I suppose we are all cocooned in our own worlds, thought Petty, but really Verity is far worse than the rest of us. She seems to have no thought for anyone else at all.

The journey through the pretty villages which had delighted her so much this morning seemed endless. Harry's plodding nags appeared the worst type of horseflesh ever. Really the boy was so inconsiderate, why could he not have chosen a decent pair? Had he no idea of horseflesh at all? She knew she was unjust but she felt grudging, crabby, chagrined and very sad.

Why could she not be behind Edward's beautiful greys? Cuthbert could have chaperoned Verity. She knew she was unfair, but it seemed everyone was unfair to her. She knew this was not true either, but she just so much wanted to be somewhere else with someone else!

At last London was reached. She realised that Harry was conveying them direct to Portman Square back to the drab house, not to the light beauty of Grafton Street, which is where all the others had gone. She wanted to protest but realised that it would only make her sound as she felt, discontented! Soon they were outside the portals of number 38. Verity climbed down, issuing an invitation to Harry to accept refreshment. Although it was late afternoon, the sun was still shining and the square felt oppressive and hot to Petty; she climbed down crossly. Ungraciously refusing Harry's politely extended arm, she stomped into the house feeling restless and unhappy.

"Perhaps we should go and enquire how Mrs Lumley is?" suggested Harry.

"Oh yes! We should!" Petty brightened perceptibly.

"No! I am hot and stiff and tired of sitting in a carriage. I do not want to go out again. We will send a footman with a note," commanded Verity.

"I think it would be more polite if we went ourselves," said Petty desperately.

"Polite or not I am not going out again!" Verity pronounced

firmly. "Come, Harry, let us sit outside." She smiled beguilingly at him and swept him down the steps and out into the small garden at the back of the house, leaving Petty standing in the middle of the dingy hall feeling even more disgruntled. She was tempted to jump into a hackney and go to Grafton Street herself, but she realised that if she were to do this she would be quite rightly sacked by Sir Hugo for leaving Verity so patently unchaperoned, and she was not absolutely sure whether she wanted to be thrown out with nowhere to go, except Wakeham and disgrace. However, she was genuinely concerned about Mrs Lumley so she sat at a desk and wrote a short polite note to Edward, asking for news. When she had finished she summoned a footman and sent him to His Lordship.

Edward's journey back was as unsatisfactory as Petty's. He was so preoccupied that his grandfather could hardly get a civil answer out of him. Cuthbert wondered what had happened between Petty and his grandson that had given him that frozen saturnine look. He and Gertrude had had many comfortable proses on the subject of the romance between Petty and Edward. Gossip that would have horrified the two chief protagonists had they but known about it, but luckily they did not. They had both decided that all was going very well and that it would not be long before Petty occupied her rightful place in Grafton Street.

It was true that Gertrude had had some misgivings, which he had discounted. Women, in his experience, were often like that, filled with needless apprehensions. To him it was simple. Edward clearly adored Petty and she as clearly was not indifferent to him. What then had gone wrong? He longed to ask but he knew from the past that he could never break through that cold look. Edward had worn that look before when he was very unhappy as a seventeen-year-old. It had lasted for months after his mother's death, swiftly followed by his father's. It was Aurelia, so lovely, so special, who had restored the warmth to his countenance. But why now? What had gone wrong?

Edward, lost in his misery, was hardly aware of his grandfather. Now he knew he must go tomorrow to tell his beloved Petty that he would release her. He would not waste time. He would leave to visit his lawyer in Hitchin as soon as he had freed her. The thought caused a spasm of pain that Cuthbert watched cross his face. He could not entrap her any longer.

When they reached the house in Grafton Street, they found that the estimable Hardwick had followed orders and had got Mrs Lumley home with all possible speed, and she was now tucked up, attended by her excellent maid and Mrs Penn. Petty was not there and he felt an unreasonable disappointment. Why had she not bothered to come to see how Mrs Lumley did? Most inconsiderate. That it was unlike her he was too het up to think.

The rest of the party was gathered in the morning room. Mrs Cornwall and Mary were about to depart, and stayed merely to bid their adieus to him and to thank him for a most enjoyable day. Gideon was departing for an evening engagement with his latest flirt, and Aurelia with her usual calm was organising a footman to be sent to Sir Harley Wantage, Mrs Lumley's chosen doctor. Edward felt as though he were not quite there; he went through the motions of dealing but his mind was not on it.

About an hour after they had returned home, Petty's note was brought to him. He tore it open and read the few lines.

Your Lordship,

I am most concerned to have news on how Mrs Lumley does. Verity does not feel that she can come out again tonight, so I am forced to attend her and cannot therefore come personally to enquire of Mrs Lumley. Please would you be good enough to give us news of her?

Yours.

Edward stared down at the words. He did not know what he had expected but he was disappointed. For a moment his hopes had flared. Irrational, he knew, but a common enough fault in those who love someone. He sat down, scribbled a few lines about Mrs Lumley's return to health and included in his note the information that he intended to visit the next morning.

Chapter Eighteen

Petty received His Lordship's note with a combination of hope and trepidation. Lying in her narrow bed, unable to sleep, she tried to practice the lines of what she wanted to say to him the next day. They went something like this:

"Your Lordship. Edward. I know that I made a fool of you by running away, but I truly did not want to hurt you. I was just…" No, that would not do; she tried again. "Your Lordship. Edward. Please will you forgive me for what I did. Please can I now be your wife. For I want to beyond anything." No she would never be able to say those words, she just was not bold enough. Verity would have been able to, but she could not. She tried again.

"Your Lordship. Edward. I know that I was in the wrong but I would like to make amends. I would like to make our marriage work." No, that was not quite right. Eventually, as dawn was coming through the thin curtains, she drifted into sleep, waking sharply again at about eight o'clock.

She climbed out of bed. It was a good thing that she had no glass today, for she did not look her best. She had blue circles around her eyes which, for once, lacked their customary sparkle, her face looked sallow and her cheekbones seemed higher than ever.

She dressed carefully in the prettiest of her muslin day dresses and made to face whatever the day was to bring. The weather was not as it had been yesterday. Dark thundery clouds scudded across the grey sky. She shivered, returning for a shawl. She went down to the breakfast parlour, remembering the happiness of yesterday. Could it really only be yesterday? It seemed weeks ago. She poured a cup of coffee and went over the speeches she had prepared during the sleepless night. None of them seemed possible. In a panic, knowing that His Lordship would be there within the hour, she tried again, her efforts nearly bringing tears to her eyes. Oh, why could she not find the right words? Why was it so difficult?

Verity came in. She was dressed in buttercup yellow and was in very good humour. "I had the most glorious day yesterday." She thickly buttered a slice of toast. "What shall we do today?"

"I do not know. Lord Milton is coming to talk to me, and I had hoped that if she is better, we might visit Mrs Lumley."

"That sounds very dull. I would like to walk in the park." Petty's heart sank; surely the attentions of Harry and Gidi would be enough for Verity?

"Yes, I think a walk would do me very well." She stretched. "Petty, get me an egg and some more toast." Petty, who in normal circumstances would have remonstrated with such an imperious tone, got up and, without really thinking, got the egg and the toast.

"I do not think it is the weather for a walk, it looks as if it might rain," she pointed out, handing the plate to Verity.

"Nonsense. It is only a little cloudy but see," she looked out at the sky, "the sun is coming through."

This, unfortunately was true. The wind was blowing the clouds away and thin rays of sunlight were peeping through the stormy sky.

"Oh yes," Petty sighed. There was a peal at the door. Petty's knees turned to jelly. She sat very still and sipped her coffee. Drake appeared with Aurelia in tow.

"Lord Milton would like to see you, miss. I have put him in the saloon. Miss Milton would like some breakfast. I will just lay up another cover for her."

"Petty! Verity! I hope I do not intrude! As Edward was coming I thought I would bear him company." Petty watched her luminous magic light up the room, sadness engulfing her. She swallowed. "Oh, Aurelia, you know that you are always most welcome. Please, how is Mrs Lumley? I had thought to come to visit her this afternoon, if she is well enough."

"Oh, she is much recovered. I am sure that she would love to receive a visit from you. Edward has some business in Hitchin. He thought, perhaps, I could remain and return after nuncheon, so maybe we could all go back together?"

"That would be most agreeable. Would it not, Verity?" The girl grunted a reluctant acquiescence. "Now, I had better go and discover what Lord Milton wants. I will leave you here. Verity will entertain you," she said pointedly.

Verity's manners were not perfect but she quite liked Aurelia, although the girl's beauty and grace always made her feel slightly uneasy, so she nodded politely as Petty left the room.

Petty crossed the hall and mounted the staircase to the saloon. The hateful brown, dingy decorations reflected the darkness of her mood. Sir Hugo was very wealthy and it was a constant mystery to her why he did not spend some of his wealth improving his house. Her heart pounding she opened the doors to the saloon. Edward was standing with his back to them, his eyes, unseeing on the gardens of the square. He turned around. His face was very stiff and cold. She had seen him in all kinds of moods but never had she seen him looking so detached before.

"Good morning!" she vouchsafed somewhat blankly.

He merely nodded. "Please sit down, Petty. What I have to say to you will not take a minute."

She was irrationally reminded somehow of scolds that she had received in her childhood from her father. What had she done to make him look so black? She could think of no misdemeanor that could possibly occasion such a bleak manner.

She sat down. She did not know what to say. Her body trembled. Her heart fluttered. Lord Milton, in utter black despair, had no idea, of course, of how forbidding he looked. The truth was that he was trying not to cry himself. He held back every vestige of emotion, for he knew that if he gave way, he would fling himself onto the floor by her chair and bury his head in her lap. Without looking at her, he spoke.

"I understand how disagreeable our marriage is to you. I have known it from the first day that we were wed. I apologise for being instrumental in causing you such unhappiness. I have decided that the only honorable thing for me to do now, is to release you from all the ties that bind us. I have arranged for a divorce."

A strangled sound from Petty made him glance in her direction but only for a minute.

"I know that it must be as distasteful to you, as it is to anyone with any delicacy of feeling, but as no one knew of our marriage, I am hopeful that it can be executed with the minimum of scandal. When I leave here today, I shall visit my lawyer and he will institute the proceedings. That is all." He turned back to the window. Petty, so shocked, so devastated, found that she had no words at all. Her mouth was completely dry. It opened but no sounds came out. Nausea threatened to overcome her and she rushed out of the room. Lord Milton, his eyes unnaturally bright, watched her go.

"Goodbye, my love," he said quietly to himself, before picking up his hat and cane and striding out of the room and down the stairs.

He brushed Drake aside and strode into the street. Hardwick stood by the greys' heads. His Lordship jumped into his curricle and cracked the whip. "Let them go," he commanded, giving his groom hardly enough time to jump aboard, before the equipage swept around the corner of the square, making for the Great North Road. It was a moment before the old man could get his breath, but when he did he ventured cautiously, "Your Lordship… Miss Aurelia." His Lordship did not seem to hear. In truth, he had forgotten about his sister and only remembered when they were well on their way. He trusted Petty enough to make sure that she would be transferred back to Grafton Street without mishap.

Petty stumbled out of the room desirous only of making it to her bedroom, where she could enjoy her projected freedom with a torrent of tears. She could not believe what she had heard. Her stomach and heart seemed to be heaving in a most unwarranted way. Her legs felt as if they would not move, but she struggled towards the backstairs, and when she reached them she attempted to hurry up them as fast as the trembling in her limbs would allow. However, before she could reach the safety of her simple room, Mrs Drake, puffing as she climbed the steep stairs, caught up with her.

"Oh, Mrs Blakeston, the master wants you. Now, he says. In the library, he says." She took a deep breath. "Better go quick. He don't like to be kept waiting."

Petty, whose legs and body felt as though they did not belong to her, just turned as if sleepwalking and retraced her steps to the hall.

Outside the library door she tried to compose herself, but her brain would not work. All she knew was that she had lost him. Now she had lost him. He would divorce her, the scandal. Her parents would never forgive her; she could never go home now. She wanted to howl, to scream her pain out loud but no sounds came. She stood outside the door. She knocked.

"Come in."

Petty went in, her face ashen, her blue eyes round and staring. Sir Hugo noticed nothing. "At last. What took you so long?" he barked. Petty just looked at him. "Now, I have a job for you, it must be done at once." Petty looked astonished. "I want you to go to the House of Commons. I want you to go to the rooms of Hartley Stafford and collect some very important papers."

"Me?" stammered Petty.

"Yes. You. Who else? Are you an idiot, girl? I could hardly send a servant. I think, well, you appear to me to be fairly trustworthy, and I need someone I can trust. Now, you must go at once."

Petty forced her brain to come back to her. She swallowed hard. She remembered Aurelia, she remembered the plans laid for the visit to Mrs Lumley. She could never go to that house again. Tears sprang to her eyes. She wanted to scream and lie on the floor. She just managed to control herself.

"But, Sir Hugo, the girls. Aurelia Milton is here. I cannot just leave them."

"Oh, do not be so idiotic. They will be quite alright. I am here and Mrs Drake, what harm can they come to?" he went on dismissively.

"Can you not send a footman?"

"Stupid girl, I have just told you they are far too important to send a footman. No, you must go. I will order the coach. I was going to send you in a hackney but fear for the safety of the documents. I have decided they will be safer in my town coach. Here, take this letter of authority and go at once." He rang the bell, then he sanded down the few lines that he was writing, sealed the paper and handed it to her.

The contempt in his voice rendered her even more inarticulate than usual. She felt as though she were sleepwalking through a nightmare and at any moment she would wake up.

"I just… the girls…"

"Mrs Blakeston," his tone was such that you would use towards a impudent child, "please do not try my patience, I have told you that the girls are not babies. Ah, Drake. Mrs Blakeston is to collect some documents from the House for me. Please order the carriage immediately."

"Very good, sir."

"Miss Verity… Drake… Miss Milton… make sure… they st… stay here in the house with you," Petty stuttered. She seemed totally to have lost the power of speech.

"Mrs Blakeston! You will only be gone about two hours. What harm can they come to in two hours? Is that not so, Drake? Please try to be a little sensible."

In truth, she was gone for nearly five hours and it was approaching four o'clock before she returned. Petty had never visited the House of Commons before and in normal circumstances she would have been intrigued by her drive through the huge gates and into the very seat of government.

Petty's family had long been members of the Whig party. Fox had visited Wakeham many times and the duke had been a frequent visitor to Holland House. This leaning towards the Foxites meant that they approved reform in theory, although in practice they saw no merit in surrendering their power to a vociferous middle class and a bunch of nonconformists with Yorkshire accents.

The papers that Petty had been sent to collect were concerning this new band of reformers determined to instigate legal reform, fiscal reform and particularly to destroy the aristocratic monopoly of seats in Parliament.

She was intrinsically sympathetic to this cause, not from any experience of upbringing but from her own nature, and the discovery since she had left Wakeham of people such as Mrs Lumley and Cuthbert, but on this particular day she was too upset to even notice her surroundings.

She handed over the letter of authority given to her by Sir Hugo and was taken down endless corridors to Hartley Stafford's office. Then she was left sitting on a stone bench in a draughty corridor outside his door. Members came and went; young and

242

old clerks in black frock coats whisked past her carrying piles of leather-bound volumes. Petty sat and sat. She got colder and colder. She went over Lord Milton's words again and again. She wanted to cry but she felt as though even the tears were frozen. She heard Big Ben strike and strike but she really had no idea of how long she had sat there. Eventually Mr Stafford's secretary came out with a heavy black locked bag. He handed it over to her without a word. He turned to go.

"How do find my way out? Please?" Petty's strangled voice sounded strange to her ears.

He sighed crossly and without offering to carry the bag for her he hurried down corridor after corridor. Petty, her arms aching, her body stiff, tears in a lump in her throat, half ran after him. Eventually they reached the yard where Sir Hugo's coach waited for her and it was with great relief that she flopped back onto the tattered squabs.

She was surprised when she saw the clock and she realised that she had been waiting nearly three hours. Thank goodness this terrible day is nearly over, she thought as the coach bumped over the cobbles back to Portman Square. All she wanted was to go to bed. She could not remember when her limbs had ever been so tired. At last they reached number 38.

She climbed down. Drake was at the door awaiting her. "Where have you been, miss? The master is so angry! Why have you been so long?"

At that moment Sir Hugo appeared, clearly ready to depart. He was furious. "Mrs Blakeston! How dare you take so long! This was not a sightseeing pleasure trip, you know. You have been gone over four hours," he screamed. Tears ran down Petty's cheeks and splashed onto the bag. She tried to speak. The coachman, a kind man, felt moved to defend her.

"Aarh! Sir Hugo. Sure, we did not go anywhere. We's a'had ter wait for that bag!"

Slightly mollified, Sir Hugo seized the offending bag from

Petty's hands. Truly, he did not genuinely suspect her of going anywhere else, but the rage and frustration that had grown as he waited had to be vented on someone, and she with her inarticulate fear was as good a person to bully as anyone.

"Now, I must go!" He started to make for the carriage.

Petty swallowed hard, shook her head to try to bring her thoughts to some kind of order and asked, "Sir Hugo, please, will you be gone for long, as I must take Miss Milton home?" She stopped. "Where is Verity? Miss Aurelia?"

"Oh, they went to the park, miss." Drake continued to call her miss in spite of her supposed married status.

"The park! Alone! I thought I said they must stay here."

"I gave them permission. She is my daughter," Sir Hugo said icily.

"When did they go?" Petty demanded.

Drake considered a moment. "About half twelve, miss."

Suddenly Petty's own anger flared. She turned on Sir Hugo. "Half twelve? It is now four o'clock. I thought you said they would stay here. That they would come to no harm." Her fury quite took him by surprise.

"Do not be so absurd, Mrs Blakeston. You do not know that they have come to harm," he returned slightly shamefaced. "They have only gone to the park. They are perfectly sensible. Now you are back you can go and find them."

"I intend to. And sensible!" Petty stamped her foot. Her eyes blazed. "Your daughter, sensible! Sir Hugo, she has about as much sense as a dormouse! She has no idea of propriety at all. Have you forgotten how I found her?" By now she did not care if she did get dismissed, if only Aurelia was safe. Petty was filled with a sudden awful apprehension. But Aurelia was sensible. Sir Hugo had the grace to look slightly guilty.

"They'll be just fine, just you wait and see," he said to Petty's retreating back as she, her exhaustion forgotten, was hurrying down the steps and along the street.

As she raced along, her thoughts were in a jumble. She knew that Aurelia would not relish meeting the Lockes, and anyway she was too sensible to go anywhere with such a vulgar pair, but if Verity said that she, Petty, found them acceptable, what would Aurelia think then? Petty found that she did want Aurelia's good opinion. She did not want Edward's sister to think she associated with such people, but Edward... Oh, Edward! Now it did not matter. She was by now nothing to do with him. A divorce. Oh no! She grimaced with pain.

She was breathless but at the park gates she ran down the customary walk and could see no sign of Verity or Aurelia. The sky was clouding over. There was going to be another storm. It was hot and heavy. Petty increased her efforts. She ran, nearly distracted, through the small wood into the clearing where she had seen the man on horseback. She called and called, till her voice was hoarse, but no answer. She was boiling hot and utterly exhausted; her hair had escaped from its clips and was streaming all over her face. She pushed it behind her ears, her tears making white rivulets in the dusty streaks which covered her face. Eventually she realised that it was hopeless. They were not in the park and it would, in any case, be closing in a few moments. She retraced her steps to Portman Square. When she reached there, Drake came rushing to greet her.

"Miss Verity is home, miss. No need to get in a pother."

Petty's relief was enormous. They were here. Thank God. It was all for nothing. She ran up the steps.

"Where are they?" she demanded.

"In the morning room." The words were hardly out of his mouth, before Petty was flinging open the door. Verity was sitting at the oval writing table; she looked rather pale but her voice had a faint jaunty air.

"Hello! I gather you were worried but I am quite safe, you see."

"I told you to stay in." Petty closed the door behind her and collapsed into the large wing chair. She tucked her hair back into its cluster of curls.

Verity looked down. "But you were gone so long."

"Where is Aurelia?"

There was a momentary pause before Verity replied in an odd voice, "She went home."

Fear gripped Petty again. "How?" she demanded. "How?"

Verity did not answer. Petty jumped to her feet and took Verity by the shoulders. "How? Answer me!" Her tone was so fierce that Verity looked up at her in trepidation.

"In... In... a ... hackney carriage..." she stuttered. Petty, looking down into her eyes, knew that she was not telling the truth.

She shook her hard. "Tell me! Tell me the truth!"

"I... am..."

Petty hit her hard across the face. She had never felt such rage or such fear. Verity started to cry. "Tell me the truth, Verity." Her voice was low and menacing. Verity had never been so scared in her life.

"L... Let m... me go," she sobbed. Petty shook her harder. "I'll... I'll... I will tell you." Petty let her go and she sank back into the chair, rubbing her shoulders and weeping.

"Well? Where is Aurelia?" Fear made Petty's voice sharper than ever.

"She... She... She..."

"Yes... she what?"

"She was... was... taken... by..." She stopped.

"Taken!" Fear gripped Petty's stomach like a vice. "By whom?"

"B... B... By... M... M... Mr Mel...ville," Verity stammered.

"Mr Melville? You mean Bertram Melville?" Verity nodded. "Oh no! How?"

"Well, you see, we went to the park... and Matty and Jane were there and I... I talked to Matty while Jane escorted Aurelia." She gave a shuddering sob.

"What did you tell Matty about Aurelia?" Petty's tone was quiet but unmistakably firm.

"No… l… mean… well… I did not say anything," Verity finished lamely. Petty resisted her desire to hit the girl again; she knew she must remain calm and find out where Bertram had taken Aurelia.

"Verity! Come, tell the truth. I will not be cross but you must help me."

"Well, I did not mean any harm but I told Matty that Aurelia was a great heiress and that her brother was a lord, and that…"

"Oh! Verity, how could you be so silly!"

"You s… said you w… would not b… be cross," Verity wailed again. "How was I to know that they… well… h… he… would…"

"But I have warned you time and time again. You just would not listen," Petty returned irritably. "Now, go on, tell me what happened next."

Verity sniffed. "Then Matty said she did not feel well, and that she must return home for a rest. She did look alright though."

Petty sighed with exasperation; how could anyone be so devoid of brains? "Go on," she demanded.

"She went, and we continued our walk. We went all the way through those shady paths and to that little clearing; then Matty came back, she was very upset, she asked if I could come back towards the gate with her. She thought she had dropped her emerald brooch; it was a present from her papa. Of course, I offered to help, and I went back with her; the others were following, I thought. Suddenly, I heard a yell. I turned to rush back but Matty grabbed me. I broke from her and fled backwards. I saw Aurelia, she was being dragged by Mr Melville and Jane towards a coach…"

"Did you not try to stop them?"

"No… you see I was too scared… Remember he ran off with me…" she said defensively.

"Oh, I remember. I remember all too well. It is you who do not seem to have learnt from your experience. However, I begged you not to, you were determined to continue your friendship with those awful Lockes. You would not listen to me at all and now look what has occurred!" Petty replied furiously. Verity burst into floods of tears. Sobbing heavily, she got up to leave the room.

"I w… won't st… stay here to be insulted. It is not m… my f… f… fault."

"You will stay until I say you can go. It is your fault. You will not be advised by me. You behave with no propriety; one of these days you will find yourself in real trouble, you will have no reputation left. No man will marry you. You will be on the streets. That is if you are not in jail. Kidnapping is a very serious offence and you are an accomplice!" Petty finished triumphantly. She had been longing to give Verity a trimming for weeks; also if the girl was to help her, she needed to be very scared. The words had had the desired effect; she turned ashen.

"Now, we are going to visit these Lockes of yours and we will find out where Bertram has taken Aurelia so that I can rescue her."

"Rescue? You!"

"Yes, me! Who else?" Petty pulled herself out of the chair; every bone in her body ached.

She pushed Verity to the hall.

"Drake! Drake! Get me a hackney immediately."

CHAPTER NINETEEN

The hackney carriage made its way through the seedy streets of Paddington to the lodging occupied by the Misses Locke. Petty had never been in such an area before, and she was appalled as she looked out of the window at ragged children with no shoes, at women trudging wearily with three or four half-starved-looking children in tow. The cabman, an elderly individual with a prodigious lisp, was quick to give them his opinion of "young ladies what visited where they should not".

"Nobs like you, beggin' yer pardon, miss, shouldn'a be a wising 'ere. Yer mind yerselfs. That's as what Ned 'ere is telling yers."

"Thank you for your concern," Petty replied with her pleasantest smile. "Please be so good as to wait for us."

"That's I will. If yers 'as any bargy yers calls for Ned."

Petty smiled again. Her face did not feel as if it wanted to, but she recognised that if she were to need help, Ned could provide it, therefore, it was important to be pleasant.

Verity knocked on the door and waited. "They do not seem to be at home," she remarked with satisfaction.

"Bang again. I am sure they will come," said Petty with a confidence she did not feel. Eventually there was the sound of bolts being drawn back and as the door opened Petty observed with relief that Matty stood there. The girl's painted mouth fell open with a mixture of astonishment and dismay at the sight of a disheveled Petty and a nervous-looking Verity.

"Good evening, Matty! May we come in?"

Petty did not wait for an answer before pushing the reluctant Verity over the threshold and into the scruffy hall. "Lead on," she instructed with forced pleasantness. Matty glanced at her suspiciously and then evidently decided that she had better obey, as she reluctantly led the way upstairs to a small front parlour, which seemed to Petty's fastidious eye to be very grimy.

Jane was seated at a table sewing a violent orange piece of silk. She looked up as they entered; the flash of fear crossed her face was remarked by Petty.

"Well," Petty started, her voice glacial, "I am glad that I find you at home. I need some information from you." She glanced from one to the other. Matty, who had always rather despised Petty, suddenly wondered why she had become a great lady. Had she missed something? Petty looked every inch a duchess. She felt rather nervous.

"La! Mrs Blakeston, you know any small thing we can be of help to you," she simpered.

For her pains she received another icy look from Petty's fine eyes.

"Kidnapping, as I explained to Verity, is a very serious offence. Being an accessory to kidnapping is also, I am reliably informed, a transgression, the penalty of which is likely to be a long sojourn in prison." She surveyed her audience. "You are guilty on this account." She saw Jane glance at the door and then at Matty. "Do not even try, Miss Matty. You do not think that I come here without leaving exact details of what has happened with the constable. If anything happens to us you will be in jail before the evening is out." Matty sat down.

"Now, let us return to the matter in hand. Kidnapping a minor for the illicit purposes of selling her for money; my supposition as to what has transpired in this case, is, I think just."

She raised her voice slightly; it had started to attain depths of unpleasantness that Petty did not know she possessed. She was secretly quite pleased! Jane began to tremble. Matty thought she had underrated Mrs Blakeston most horribly. "It is a far more serious crime. I am not sure whether it carries the penalty of death, but it certainly is punishable by transportation."

Jane began to cry noisily. Verity thought she would collapse with anguish; Petty appeared so fearsome. Standing erect, her blue eyes were almost black and contained a most ugly expression. "You were allowed by me to get away with the procuring of Verity. I do not intend to repeat my leniency. Where has Mr Bertram Melville taken Miss Milton?"

"We do not know," Matty grovelled ingratiatingly.

Petty crossed and stood in front of her. She took hold of her shoulders in a vice-like grip. She shook her slightly. "I do not intend to be patient but I repeat once more. Where is Miss Milton?" Her voice, contemptuous, cracked across the room.

Matty took a deep breath. "I... I think Fr... France was his intention. B... B... But they will be there by now. W... W... Well, at Dover, to await the packet. He had no intention of stopping till he reached the Blue Hind. We did not mean any harm, Mrs Bl... Blakeston..." She stopped. Petty released her, rubbing the palms of her hands together as if to rid them of something distasteful. Raising her chin, she regarded the Lockes disdainfully.

"Then why did you continue?"

"Well... you... u... understand... our f... financial circumstances."

"Oh, so I am correct. You were to receive remuneration for passing over Verity and then Aurelia!"

Verity looked horrified. "Oh! No! How could you?" she breathed. "Matty, Jane! I thought you were my friends."

"Enough. Come, Verity. We have not a moment to waste." Petty pulled her shawl around her and swept out.

On reaching the street, she realised with some consternation that the promised storm was incipient; the sky was leaden, the wind was howling and it was spitting with rain.

"Come, we have no time to waste." She pushed Verity back into the hackney and gave the driver instructions.

It seemed to take a veritable age to reach Portman Square. When at last they got there, Petty got out and went to Ned. She smiled again.

"Another favour. Please, do you have any notion how I can hire a post-chaise and four? I need it to take me to D... out of London immediately!"

"Well, miss, my brother 'e's a postillion, like, at the Red 'art, like, I could ask 'im."

"Oh, would you? I would be much obliged," Petty said with relief, the first of the evening's problems over. "I need him as soon as possible."

"I'lls be back in a wink, miss."

"Oh, and Ned, I will want you to take that young lady to Grafton Street at the same time."

"Yes, miss." He departed to order Petty's coach, and Petty and Verity strode in.

"But where are you going?" asked Verity as soon as they were inside the hall.

"Why, as I told you. To rescue Aurelia."

"By yourself?" Verity asked, amazed.

"Well, who else is there to go? Lord Milton has gone to... Hitchin," she replied, a wave of misery sweeping over her. Was it really only this morning? She sighed, swallowed hard and continued, "Now, Verity, I want you to go and pack all that you will need for an overnight stay. You are going to Mrs Lumley."

Verity, who knew better than to argue with Petty in her present humour, went without her customary argument. Having dispatched the girl, Petty went with all speed to the morning room. Here she sat and wrote three letters. The first was comparatively easy; it was to Mrs Lumley and in it she explained briefly what had occurred and asked her to keep Verity. The second was a brief note to Sir Hugo, explaining where Verity could be found. The third was the most difficult and caused her much heartache; it was to Lord Milton.

My Lord,

I have been the cause of so much grief and now, fear, I have become, albeit unwittingly, the cause of even more. I do not quite know how to write the news I have just discovered.

After you left me this morning, I was suffering such distress. Believe me when I say that I never wanted to cause you pain, and indeed over the last few months have hoped that you would forgive me and that…

Here she stopped. She did not know whether it would be considered too forward to write her next sentence. In the end she decided that her life was so intolerable anyway, that what would it matter if she wrote as she felt. It was easier to put onto paper than to say it.

… we could make our marriage work.
Following your departure, I was summoned to Sir Hugo; he demanded that I go to collect some papers for him. I demurred, for I consider my responsibilities to Verity (and Aurelia) as paramount, but he was categorical in his demands.

I am afraid my wretched inability to express myself made me flounder as I tried to explain my reservations about the inadvisability in leaving the girls without my supervision. He dismissed my concerns, rendering me speechless, so reluctantly, I went.

My worries centred on Verity's undesirable friendship with some sisters called Locke. Indeed, my main reason for remaining with her over the past months has been to try to protect her from the machinations of these two, with the disastrous consequences of today.

As you know, I think, I met Verity when she was being abducted by one Mr Bertram Melville. I was fortunate enough to wrest her from this evil gentleman without damage. What I did not realise until tonight, was that having met the Lockes through Verity, Mr Melville then offered them remuneration if they helped procure a rich wife for him. Verity was, naturally, the first object, but having failed with her, it seems these wanton girls doubled their efforts, obviously seeing in Aurelia an opportunity to regain what they had lost.

I tried to persuade Verity to desist from seeing them but she refused. When I returned with his papers, I discovered that Sir Hugo had given them permission to visit the park against my express wishes. He did not know of the Lockes; I had tried to explain to him, but again he disdained to listen to my concerns. Another failure.

I rushed to the park but could find no trace of them. Eventually I gave up my search, returning to Portman Square where I discovered Verity.

She informed me that Aurelia had been kidnapped by Mr Melville. I have visited the Lockes, who confirm that this is the case. I have hired a coach and I am on the way to rescue her.

Please forgive me.
Petty

She reread the missive, hated what she had written and desperately wished to rewrite it. For it seemed rather cumbersome and stilted; however, she was realistic enough to know that she had not time for endless drafts, so she signed it, sealed it, and went quickly upstairs. Verity was in her bedroom; she was crying quietly and trying to pack a small carpet bag with her belongings. Petty went to help her.

"Stop weeping, Verity, this will serve no purpose. I have arranged for Ned to take you to Mrs Lumley's. Please ask her to pay the shot for I must preserve what precious reserves I have for the journey. I think I have enough from the money I took when I left... the money I had when I left my last post, to enable me to travel to rescue Aurelia. If, as I anticipate, I return tomorrow..." She paused, adding haltingly, "Has... Has your papa a gun?"

Verity's eyes opened wide with consternation. "A g... gun! Why do you need a gun?"

"l hope that I will not need a gun. It is merely a precaution." The girl stared at her open-mouthed. "Well, Verity?" said Petty in some vexation. "Has he a gun?"

"Y... Ye... Yes..." she replied nervously. "Bu... But can you use a gun?"

"Yes, of course I can use it. My papa, a notable shot, taught me," Petty answered. "So where is it?"

Verity looked at her with growing respect. "lt... It... is in the library," she volunteered guardedly.

"Good. Then when I have changed and packed we will go and collect it!"

"Oh!" said Verity, sitting down on her bed.

"Come on, Verity. This is no time to sit about. Finish your packing."

With these words Petty swept out. She hurried up to her own room where she changed her dirty, dusty dress for the simple brown one. It was not particularly becoming but she thought it more sensible to look as ordinary as possible. She, too, packed a small carpet bag. If she went without stopping, except to change horses, she expected to be back by the afternoon of the next day, but she thought she had better pack a few objects for contingencies. She decided that she had better take her thick cloak, for by now the wind was whistling through the windows and it was pouring with rain. When she had finished, she went cautiously downstairs, collecting Verity on the way.

Luckily, the hall was deserted. Warily they crept into the library. It was dark and gloomy. Petty had had the forethought to bring a candle and by its meagre light, Verity went to her father's big desk and tried to open the drawer on the right. She tugged at it. Consternation crossed her face.

"It's locked! Oh no! What shall we do now?"

"Where is the key?" Petty demanded.

Verity thought. "I do not know."

"You must know. Think!"

Verity thought. "I... think... um..." She stopped, then she went to the shelves that covered the side of the door and felt at the back. The key was there. Petty sighed with relief. She opened the drawer.

The gun was a very old pistol. Petty picked it up. "Just as I imagined, not a good one! Your papa never seems to purchase the best, but I suppose it will be better than nothing." She took the powder and shot and placed them in the pocket of her cape.

"Come, it is getting very late."

Her one remaining worry was the problem of getting past Mr and Mrs Drake, but as they emerged from the library, the hall was still deserted, so she and Verity could slip out, leaving the note for Sir Hugo on the hall table.

It was dark now and the streets were drenched with the deluge. Ned, sheltering under a large umbrella, was waiting at the corner of the street; next to him stood an identical man. Petty would have laughed if all abilities for amusement had not been suspended by the events of the day.

He waved at Petty. "'ere is me brofer Ted, 'e'll be a-driving yer, miss. Where was yers a'wantin to go?"

Ted doffed his cap to her. "Best get in, miss, y'll bes a'getting very wet," Ted said, his voice identical as well.

Petty looked at Verity. A wry smile twitched at the corner of her mouth. "Twins."

"That's as right! We's twins," hooted Ned. "Like as two peas. Now's wher's do you want me to take thisun young lady?" Petty quickly explained and told Ned that Mrs Lumley would pay him.

She gave Verity the notes for Mrs Lumley and Lord Milton, and pushed the girl into Ned's coach. Then she climbed into the post-chaise and directed Ted to drive to Dover as fast as possible, stopping only for new horses. He evinced no surprise at her request, merely remarking that the weather was much against them.

Petty lay back against the worn squabs, a prey to uncomfortable thoughts. Although her mind was racing, she was so tired that she found herself drifting off into a fitful sleep. The journey seemed interminable.

The winds were high and the rain slanted against the windows of the coach without stopping. It also became clear that the chaise was not very waterproof, an undesirable fact which Petty discovered quite early in the evening when drips of rain fell onto her shoulders. She tried to find a position where she did not get wet, but there were so many odd leaks that this was almost impossible.

In spite of all this, Petty dozed, awaking abruptly as the memory of Lord Milton's words obtruded into her brain. A divorce! Every feeling revolted. She shivered with repulsion, her whole body contorted with anguish, as she recollected what she had squandered so unthinkingly. "Why, oh why had she not stayed to become his wife? She could not now recall the repugnance she had felt towards him. That had all gone. She merely felt angry with herself for her stupidity.

The coach bumped on. Petty got colder and colder, stiffer and stiffer. Eventually they stopped to change horses and for something to eat. She thankfully descended from the coach.

"Now, missy, yers a'must have sem vitels," Ted pronounced, "whilss' I sees to them thers hosses." Petty's mouth twisted slightly. She went into the inn. The customary fat landlady bustled out to greet her, casting an eye over the damp Petty disparagingly.

"Yes?" she queried antagonistically. Petty sighed; it seemed that every time she encountered a landlady they were all of this mould!

"Please may I have a private parlour and some dinner?" she asked politely. The landlady tutted. She shook her head muttering loudly, "Unescorted females!"

Petty saw red; her fragile nerves snapped. She opened her eyes wide. "I know," she said, copying Verity's voice exactly, "but you see I am running away from my cruel parents-in-law. They beat me," she pronounced dramatically. "My husband beats me! I am attempting to return to the bosom of my family!"

The landlady looked perplexed. "Well..." she started doubtfully.

"Oh, please, you will not betray me!" Petty blinked her eyes as she had seen Verity do so often.

"Well, I do not know. Who are these people?"

Petty thought quickly. "Lord and Lady Hamel. My husband is The Hon. Frederic Hamel," she said, perjuring my Lady Hamel's eldest son. "He is of all men the most cruellest. You must help me." She paused; the landlady still looked doubtful. "You will know them, of course, they have a house in Charles Street and Hallbrook House in Gloucestershire; they have two daughters, Sophie and Emma."

The landlady scratched her head; the name Lady Hamel obviously meant something to her.

"Lady Hamel has a beak nose and crossed eyes," added Petty whimsically.

Suddenly the landlady smiled and nodded. Clearly she had been subject to one of my lady's dressing-downs. "Come this way, miss, I's amember that woman! Nasty tongue in 'er 'ead. That's as sure!"

She led the way to a small parlour where a welcome fire burnt. The landlady bustled off to bring some food. Petty took off her cloak, placing it in front of the fire to dry.

She stood at the window and looked at the dark windy night. Rain coursed down the panes relentlessly. Tears ran down Petty's cheeks. She made no move to stop them; they slid off her chin, landing on the front of her dress. She had not believed that it was possible to feel so desolate, so wretched, so entirely without hope. Petty had experienced despondency in her life at Wakeham, but nothing had prepared her for this level of misery. She had heard people speak of heartbreak, but she had never understood that it felt physically as if her heart had indeed broken, nay shattered into a million pieces that could never be mended.

The numbness of the morning had given way to a pain that pierced every part of her and from which she knew she would never recover. She did not know what to do. She wanted to die, not because she did not want to go on living, she did, but because it seemed the only way to make the pain disappear. The landlady came back. She brought a tray of food, which she set down on the table. She looked at Petty. "Come, my dear, try to eat. Build up your strength," she said, her voice far kinder than it had been. Petty sat at the table and tried to consume something, but the food seemed to get stuck in her gullet. She was glad when Ted came and summoned her to leave.

○○

Ned conveyed a nervous Verity to Grafton Street. She knocked apprehensively on the door. It was opened by Penn.

"Ah, miss! At last! We was wondering what had happened to you." He started then stopped as he realised that only Verity stood on the doorstep. "Where's Miss Aurelia?" he demanded sharply.

"P... Please take me to Mrs Lumley," Verity stuttered.

"What has happened? Where is Miss Aurelia?" The butler's worried voice did little to reassure Verity that her news would be greeted with equanimity. The enormity of what she had been party to swept over her and her voice wobbled.

"P... Please... Petty said... I must tell Mrs Lumley."

"I see. Who is this?" Penn indicated the scruffy Ned standing at the bottom of the steps stroking the old horse's nose.

"Petty told him to bring me to you. She said Mrs Lumley would pay him." Penn looked shocked. "She needs the money to pay his brother; he has taken her to find..." She burst into hysterical tears, unable to continue. Penn, who prided himself on his ability to deal more efficiently with any eventuality than any butler in London, thought a moment and then made a decision.

"You!" he called to Ned. "You better wait, we might need you. Go round to the stables. Leave your horses and then make your way to the kitchen. You will be well paid for your troubles," he continued, as Ned seemed to demur. In truth Ned was delighted to be, as he told his missus later, "haccepting the 'ospitality of a nobleman's house". So he did as he was bid.

Penn then led a weeping Verity to the library where Cuthbert, Mrs Lumley and Dora were waiting in some anxiety. He opened the door.

"Miss Verity," he announced. "It seems Mrs Blakeston has sent her to you."

Cuthbert quickly took in Verity's bedraggled state and her hysterical tears. "Thank you, Penn. That will be all. Come, Verity, sit down. What has happened?"

His calm tones had their effect on Verity. She gave a huge shuddering sob but allowed herself to be led to a chair by the fire. Mrs Lumley exchanged a worried look with Cuthbert. Something had occurred but what was it? However, it was Dora, pale with worry, who asked the question.

"Verity! Where is Aurelia?" The girl started to sob hysterically again. "Stop it!" Dora ordered. "Tell us what has happened? Stop it! Stop it!"

Amazingly, the girl's sobs seemed to slow down slightly. She pulled the two letters out of her reticule, and thrust the one addressed to Mrs Lumley at her. She took a breath and tried to speak; the words came in a confused rush.

"Me... My... I am... Petty gone to... My fault, all my fault. Oh, why did I not listen to Petty? She was right. If only I... if only..."

"But what has happened?" Dora demanded, her patience quite spent. "Tell us! You stupid girl! Tell us."

Suddenly Mrs Lumley, having read Petty's short note, intervened. "It would appear from this that Aurelia has been kidnapped."

"Kidnapped! What? How?" Cuthbert interrupted. He crossed to Verity and commanded, "Stop crying! Dora is right, you must tell us!"

"Petty says that she has been taken and that she has gone to rescue her. What does that mean?" Mrs Lumley asked. "You had better start at the beginning."

Verity took a shuddering breath. "I... You see... as you know, Petty found me when I had been kidnapped by Bertram Melville. She rescued me... and brought me back. Then Papa said she could be m... my chaperone. I had... I... These girls... I knew. I did not know that they had been implicated... been part of my kidnapping..." She paused then decided to make a clean breast of it. "I thought I liked the Lockes... Petty tried to tell me they were not proper friends for me. I did not listen." She hung her head. "I... thought I knew better. Today my father sent Petty to collect some documents for him. She did not want to go.

 261

He insisted. She told us to stay in and not to go to the park but I… we… went… The Lockes were there. Matty, the eldest, asked me about Aurelia, I told her she was a great heiress. Then she went back home and must have returned with M… Mr… M… Melville. They bundled Aurelia into a coach."

She ceased speaking. There was a horrified silence. Then Cuthbert spoke. "Do you know where they have taken her and where is Petty?"

"P… Petty hired a c… coach… She went to f… f… find her."

"Where has she gone?"

"I… do… not… know," Verity, too confused to be able to think, answered. "Oh, Ted took her."

"Ted?"

"Yes, he is Ned's brother!"

"Ned?" Cuthbert sounded perplexed.

"Yes, he brought me here. He drives a hackney! Oh no! Petty said to ask you to pay him as she needed all her money… Will you?"

"Of course. Where is he?"

"The butler… told him to… go…"

"Go?"

"N… No… go to the kitchen…"

"Good!" Cuthbert rang the bell. "Let us have him up here and see what he can tell us."

CHAPTER TWENTY

I t did not take Petty long to realise that it was essential that she reach Dover before Bertram had had the chance to convey Aurelia to France. She also discovered, somewhat to her alarm, just how expensive it was to travel post. Her funds being so strictly limited, she decided, after some thought, that it was imperative that such slim reserves as she possessed were spent on horses.

With this thought uppermost in her mind, she summoned Ted and instructed him to obtain the fastest teams possible, for as little money as he could. Ted looked her up and down, and for a moment she stood in dread that he would turn and leave her, afeared, perhaps, that he would not be remunerated. Such a thought had never crossed Ted's mind, he was merely concerned about the outcome of this trip to Dover. His own payment he had not even considered. He had taken a shine to Petty and would have defended her with his life. She had confided in him some part of her mission: that they were to collect Aurelia and return with her to London. This, however, did not serve to satisfy his curiosity for he knew there was more to the story and wished that she would depend upon him enough to tell him the truth, then he could protect her.

Ted nodded. "You leaves it to Ted, miss, I knows me hosses."

This proved to be no idle boast. The team he chose were

certainly not smooth-coated, prancing thoroughbreds. Indeed they were shaggy and slightly ill-kempt, but they were strong and possessed of considerable stamina. Ted took them in hand; he was also an excellent driver, gauging a corner to an inch and keeping his cattle well up. Somewhat surprisingly, Petty found herself much comforted by his presence! He was a very tall, very thin man with untidy wispy hair and a heavily lined face. He had bushy grey brows which jutted out over his twinkling brown eyes and when he smiled, she trusted him. This did not happen much, as most of the time he chewed a straw which projected from the corner of his mouth, and bounced up and down as he spoke.

The night seemed long. Petty lay huddled in one corner of the chilly coach wrapped in her damp cloak, with only her dismal thoughts for company. Finally, they reached the outskirts of Dover. By this time the rain had stopped, the dawn was breaking and the sky was streaked with pink. Petty stretched her cramped limbs and peered out through the dingy curtains. A young milkmaid, her pails on her shoulders, was meandering down the hill; she was clearly on her morning rounds to deliver her nutritious beverage to the sleeping folks of Dover. Ted slowed down; he enquired of her the direction of the Blue Hind. She had not heard of a 'Blue Hind' but offered directions to the Captain's Table or the Duck and Goose. Ted thanked her politely and drove on.

The next person they saw was an elderly vicar. He was clutching the lead of a huge shaggy dog, who was clearly taking his owner for a walk. It was such a funny sight that in ordinary circumstances it would have made Petty laugh heartily, but in her present condition did not even raise a smile. Ted drew up.

"'cuse me, Yer Honour, does you know a drinking house called the Blue Hind?" The vicar stopped. He regarded Ted steadily through rheumy, pale grey eyes.

"A drinking house?" In spite of his age, his speech was clear and sharp.

"Yees… Yer Worship… an alehouse… the Blue Hind?"

Petty popped her head through the window. "Oh, please can you help us?" she pleaded somewhat despairingly.

The vicar looked surprised as she appeared. "What would a lady like you be wanting with an out-of-the-way place like the Blue Hind?" he questioned. Ted shot her a fierce look. He shook his head at her. She withdrew dejectedly.

"Oh," remarked Ted in an offhand way, "if you do not know then I will have to find someone who does."

The reverend, however, had not lived in Dover for the past sixty-five years for nothing.

He looked Ted over, shrugged his bony shoulders, and proceeded to give succinct and excellent directions.

Petty considered the old vicar's reservations regarding the Blue Hind. Perhaps Bertram had chosen this inn so that he could not be readily discovered. She felt slightly uneasy and she began to wish that she had left more explicit information as to her whereabouts for Lord Milton. She shook herself and dismissed these misgivings firmly. She was confident of her ability to retrieve Aurelia from her captor and be on her way back to London in a wink.

During her sleepless hours on the coach she had worked on a strategy to use at the inn, so when the landlord came to greet her she had her story ready.

"Excuse me, sir. Do you have a lady and gentleman here by the name of…" She muttered the name Melville unintelligibly. She was not quite sure what name Bertram would have given. "A very beautiful lady, sir, dark hair, pale blue eyes, travelling with her brother, she is. I am her companion… I should have been here hours ago only a wheel came off the coach… I've got all their luggage…"

The landlord looked at her keenly but he had no reason to doubt her story. "Yes… I know, travelling to France on the eleven o'clock packet, Rooms 4 and 5. Up the stairs on the right."

"Thank you, sir… er… which room is the lady in? I would not want to disturb the gentleman. An evil temper 'e 'as when 'e's woke early."

"She was in 4, I think."

Petty hurried upstairs. She was congratulating herself on her strategy. Just time to whisk Aurelia out and back to London. She sighed with relief. She knocked quietly on the door of Room 4. There was no answer. She went in cautiously. The room was in darkness, the bed looked as if it had not been slept in. An icy dread gripped her. Without thinking what she did she went straight into Room 5.

Aurelia was sitting, fully dressed in the muslin dress that she had worn yesterday, bolt upright on a chair near the window. Bertram Melville sat in another chair. He was watching her, like a hawk watches its prey. As Petty opened the door he whipped around.

"What in damnation do you think you are doi…" he started, then his eyes lit on Petty. "You! Again!" he exclaimed.

Aurelia met her eyes; there was intense gratitude in them but wisely she said nothing.

"Yes, I am here. I have come to take Aurelia home," Petty announced. "You must realise that you cannot abduct young girls with impunity."

"And you must realise that you must not interfere." He moved so fast that Petty, unprepared, realised too late that he was between her and the door. He locked it and turned to her.

"Now, Miss Meddlesome! You are not going to outwit me this time!"

Petty was surprised. She had thought that if she turned up to claim Aurelia, he would let her go, as he had Verity. She was to find out how naive her belief had been.

"Come, Mr Melville, this is 1811, you cannot just run off with an unwilling girl."

"You are going to find out just how crass that remark is,"

he snarled. "I intend to marry Aurelia here, she is in any case compromised. She has spent the last night in my company. Her brother will be grateful that I should marry her," he continued unpleasantly.

"Ah ha! That is where you are wrong! She is not compromised, I am here," Petty returned bravely. It had still not occurred to her that her belief that it was only a matter of time before he released Aurelia, and they would be on their way back to London, could be incorrect.

"Now, please unlock the door and let us proceed."

He laughed. A very disagreeable laugh. "We are going to France, Miss Meddlesome, and you shall accompany us."

Petty spluttered with rage. "I will NOT!" she declared.

She met Aurelia's eyes. The girl mouthed, "Take care!" but her warning was too late. Bertram leapt across to Petty. He grabbed her arms, pinioning them behind her back. He took a length of twine and bound her arms.

"You will not get away with this. I found you! Lord Milton will find you."

Too late she realised that, in her complacency that she would just be able to bring Aurelia back, she had not told anyone where they would be. Her heart sank. Bertram accurately gauged her thoughts.

"You did not leave word where you were going, did you? You are a ridiculous girl."

Privately, Petty agreed with him. There was still Ted, but even he knew only too little of what was going on. Petty opened her mouth to scream. Bertram put his hand over her mouth. "Viper," he said as she bit him. He pushed her onto the bed, and still with one hand over her mouth he poured a concoction into a small glass. He is going to kill me, thought Petty. He held her nose in a vice-like grip, and forced the liquid down her throat. Petty had no choice but to swallow. Within minutes she found her legs floating away from her; she slipped into unconsciousness.

It was nearly two o'clock before Lord Milton returned home. As he turned the corner into Grafton Street he was amazed to see a blaze of lights from his house reflected in the puddles that covered the ground. He stopped his horses; leaping down, he threw the reins at the sleepy groom, then with rain slashing his grim face he strode up his front steps. Penn opened the door.

"Oh, Your Lordship… Thank goodness… you…"

"What is it, Penn?" His Lordship said sharply; it was unlike his imperturbable butler to worry unduly about anything.

"I… think that Mr Philipson had better explain…"

"Cuthbert still up?" Edward was now concerned himself, his first thought being that something had happened to Petty. "Where is he?"

"He and Mrs Lumley are in the library. My lord…"

Before Penn had finished speaking, Edward was across the hall and flinging open the book room door. Despite his dejected spirits the sight that met his eyes made his mouth twitch and his dark eyes twinkle responsively. Mrs Lumley was dozing on the sofa, her copious figure swathed in an outrageous dressing wrap. Her huge bonnet had fallen askew across one eye and her brightly coloured mouth had flopped open. Cuthbert presented no less an elegant sight! He was leaning on the wings of a chair near the fire, snoring loudly. Edward paused, for a moment appreciating the scene, before closing the door behind him with a deliberate bang. Both of the sleeping parties jumped. Cuthbert jerked awake, shook his head, and puffed wildly. Mrs Lumley's head shot upward; she opened her eyes, staring at him and blinking as those who are awoken precipitously do. She made to straighten her bonnet, and having managed to set it at a more satisfactory angle, she took a breath, looked at Cuthbert for support, and started to speak.

However, His Lordship, who had not been dozing in front of a large fire, spoke first. "What is it?" he demanded. "What has occurred that would keep you two from the comfort of your beds at this hour of night?"

They exchanged looks in the manner of naughty schoolchildren caught stealing sweets.

"It is... well, something truly..."

"It's Aurelia." Cuthbert and Mrs Lumley spoke in unison.

"Aurelia!" Lord Milton spoke sharply. "What has happened to Aurelia?"

It took Cuthbert another second to shake the sleep from his brain before he could explain in measured tones, "It appears that Aurelia has been kidnapped by an unpleasant party by the name of Bertram Melville..."

"Kidnapped! What do you mean? By whom?" Lord Milton frowned, trying to remember why that name was so familiar.

"Bertram Melville, apparently he is the man who kidnapped Verity."

"Melville, Melville, I know that name... but it is not from Verity, but come, tell me quickly, how did he manage to abduct Aurelia?"

"From what I can discover from Verity, it appears that after you left her at Portman Square, they went to the park unaccompanied and met these friends of Verity's who seemed to be... in the pay of Melville." Cuthbert, who by this time was thoroughly awake, started to tell what he knew.

"Unaccompanied! Has Petty gone mad?" Edward's fury at the girl who, inadvertently, as he would have admitted if he had been less overwrought, was the cause of so much of his misery. "How can she have been so irresponsible?"

"No! No!" said Mrs Lumley soothingly. "It is not Petty's fault."

"Not her fault! Of course it is her fault. How could she do this to me on top of everything else?" Mrs Lumley exchanged a quick look with Cuthbert. "Everything else?" she questioned.

"Yes… Oh, not now." His Lordship harshly dismissed her gentle enquiry. "Now I must find Aurelia. Where has this Melville taken her?"

"We do not know. All the information that we can obtain from Verity is that Petty has gone after her."

"Gone after her? Has the girl quite taken leave of her senses? Has she not meddled enough?" It was a good thing that Petty, already termed Miss Meddlesome by Bertram Melville, did not hear this pronouncement.

"I think that she was trying to help," said Mrs Lumley defensively.

"Help! How can such an action help? Why did she not leave it to me?" His anxiety for Aurelia was combined with a fear that something might happen to Petty. This worry and anger became intermixed. He struck out at the person he loved best. Mrs Lumley understood his dread, but Cuthbert, a far more straightforward man, felt moved to defend Petty.

"Edward!" he replied, shocked. "She was only trying to help."

"I suppose she has left you exact detail on where I can find them?" Edward started, hardly hearing his grandfather's words. The two looked slightly shamefaced.

"Well, Edward, we did not see Petty. She sent Verity to us. You were not here so we sent round for Lord Slaughan, but it seems he has gone to Wakeham. We were unsure of what we could do until you returned. Oh, Petty left you a letter."

"Well! Why the deuce did you not say so before?" He stopped; a slight blush touched his cheeks. "Beg pardon, ma'am. It's been a hell of a day." Mrs Lumley smiled broadly at him, her wise eyes taking in his tight lips, the bleak lost expression in his dark eyes.

"I see that, my lord. Come, sit down, take some refreshment and let us consider how you can get Petty back." Her words were calm and deliberate.

"Back? I cannot get Petty back, I have lost her for ever…" His Lordship, his voice tight with emotion turned from them, walking to the window hardly aware of his words. Cuthbert started to speak. Mrs Lumley caught his eye; she put a finger to her lips and shook her head. Then she went on, "I do not believe you have lost her, Edward! She cares so much for you…"

He wheeled round, his voice harsh, not hearing her words. "You do not understand. I have today arranged with Mr Collect to divorce her."

"Divorce? No! No! You cannot." The amazement and wrath were mixed in his grandfather's voice. "No, my boy, in this you have gone too far. I forbid it!"

"You forbid it? You have no say in the matter. I tell you, I have today arranged the divorce. It will go through." His grandson faced him, his dark eyes blazing. "Do not interfere."

The unruffled tones of Mrs Lumley's voice broke in on their rage. "But, Edward, why do you want to divorce Petty?" She hesitated for a moment and then decided the matter had reached such a moment as to warrant her intervention. "Why do you want to give her up when it clearly pains you both so much?"

Edward's face contorted. He was a man of infinite control but the distress he was suffering was of such a level that even he was unable to hide his emotions. One fist went to his mouth, the other gripped the edge of the chair. He did not answer Mrs Lumley, but she did not give up. Her voice gentle, she continued, "Edward, you know how much Petty loves you and you, I believe, are not wholly indifferent to her."

"Indifferent? No, ma'am, I am not indifferent but do you not see, I cannot trap her." His voice choked with feeling. He twisted away so that she could not see his face.

"Trap her?" She sounded surprised. "Believe me as one who knows, she does not feel trapped."

"Why did she run away?"

"That was then." She faced him; her grey eyes looking solidly into his, she repeated, "Petty loves you greatly. I can guarantee she is as miserable as you are by your…"

"L… Loves me?" he swallowed. "No, I do not think you are correct."

"I am sure that I am correct," came the firm reply.

"Why then did she insist on staying with Verity? She would not leave them?"

"Oh, the letter!" She crossed and picked it up off the desk. "I must confess it bothered me not a little. I mean it was as obvious as the nose on my face that she was besotted by you… could not take her eyes off you."

Edward swallowed again; his own eyes lightened as he thought of the look in Petty's.

"But now I understand the silly girl was trying to protect Verity from these appalling girls, the ones who have assisted in the abduction of Aurelia. See, read her letter." She held it out to him. He tore it open and quickly perused its contents. He smiled.

"Silly mouse. Why did she not tell me? This father of Verity's, wait until I speak to him!"

"Yes, quite!" Mrs Lumley replied. "But that must wait, I think."

Cuthbert strode across to his grandson. He put one arm on his shoulder. "Apologies… my boy…"

Edward gripped his arm. "No! It is I who should apologise. Now, I think I have work in hand." He rang the bell. "I shall leave immediately."

"Stop, Edward!" Cuthbert interrupted. "We do not know where Melville took Aurelia."

"We must know… Did not you say that Petty followed them?"

"Yes, she found out but she left no word."

"Where is Verity? We must visit these Lockes and find out what they know."

"The girl is upstairs asleep."

"Then wake her. There is no time to waste."

"But, Edward, it is nearly three o'clock…" Cuthbert started but he wasted his words.

Edward ordered the footman, who answered his summons, to wake Verity and bring her down here, and to tell Hardwick to have his travelling chaise prepared and his valet to pack clothes for three days.

Then he walked to the window. He felt almost deliriously happy; Mrs Lumley's words bathed his battered soul in warmth. Petty loved him, he could see, he understood it now. Then suddenly an icy fear gripped him; suppose something had happened to her and Aurelia. He must leave! Where was Verity? At that moment the sleepy girl arrived. She looked very young and wan; the many tears she had shed the previous night had made her usually beautiful eyes puffy and her smooth face was blotchy. She looked terrified when she saw Lord Milton.

"Well, Verity!" His Lordship's tone was not conciliatory. "Where have these undesirable friends of yours taken my sister?"

"P… Please… th… they have not taken her… it… it… is B… Bertram."

"Alright, but where has he taken her? And where has Petty gone?"

"I do not know." Tears slid down Verity's face. Lord Milton took her shoulders and shook her none too gently.

"Come, I do not believe you! Where did Petty go?"

"I… All I know is that they… she… he… took Aurelia to F… F… France."

"France! France! What do you mean? Where in France?"

"I do not know," Verity went on unhappily.

"How did Petty know? Was it from the Lockes?" he demanded. Verity nodded miserably. "Get dressed, we are going to visit these Lockes."

"What, now?" Verity spoke with horror.

"Yes! Now!"

"But, Edward, will it not wait until the morning?" Cuthbert enquired.

"It will not. By tomorrow he will have carried them across the Channel. Quick, girl, get dressed." He pushed Verity roughly out of the room, then he sent for Penn and commanded him to wake a servant girl to accompany them to the Lockes'.

Chapter Twenty-One

Petty awoke to a world that was swaying and tossing. Her head ached unbearably and she knew she was going to be sick. She raised herself gingerly onto one elbow to search for a suitable receptacle. Her head swam. As she moved she was suddenly aware of a cool hand on her brow, whilst the other held out an inviting basin; Petty thought she had never felt so ill. She flopped back on the hard bed and groaned.

"That's better." Aurelia's calm tones filtered through the recesses of her brain. "You will be right as a trivet in a moment."

Petty tried to work out where she could be. Wherever it was, it was moving in a most uncomfortable fashion. Her stomach lurched again. Slowly she remembered Dover, the Blue Hind, Bertram, the awful overconfident way she had bungled everything. She gave an angry sob.

"Shh… rest." Aurelia placed a cold towel on her head. It was most soothing. Petty closed her eyes.

The next time she awoke she was more herself. Her head still pounded but her brain was clearer. She realised that they were on a ship, obviously crossing the Channel. She looked around for Aurelia. The girl was sitting sewing quietly in the corner.

"Aurelia," she whispered. "What happened?"

At the sound of her voice the girl stood up and, folding her sewing, crossed to her. She glanced towards the door, then putting a finger on her mouth she crossed and sat on the bed beside Petty and whispered, "Bertram drugged you. You must be more careful of him."

"Clearly!" Petty replied ruefully, passing her hand across her aching brow. "I thought it would be so easy. I thought I could just walk in and take you back to London as I did with Verity. Oh, I am so foolish." Angry tears sprang into her eyes.

"Shh." Aurelia patted her hand. "I think you underestimated Mr Melville. I am also not without blame. You told us not to go to the park but Verity was so insistent. I should not have given in to her. I know how idiotic she can be but I just did not think... I just had no idea that such characters as the Lockes existed."

"Appalling, aren't they?" Petty's mouth twisted slightly. "I should not have left you. I... I..." She looked at Aurelia. "I am not very good with... with people who shout and who... who... are so dismissive. I am stupidly timid. I tried to question Sir Hugo. I tried to say that I must remain with you but he would not listen and I could not speak. The words deserted me, all my good intentions went to no avail," she gave another sob, "and now look at the mess I have got us into!"

"Shh..." Aurelia repeated, then she smiled. "I am glad that you have come. I must admit I was very scared. I do not like Mr Melville." She stopped and looked at Petty. "If I may suggest, I think we should treat him with the utmost prudence."

Petty rubbed her head regretfully. "I agree, I was very foolish." She sighed. Even more than you understand, she thought to herself. How could she have been so stupid as not to have left details of her whereabouts for Lord Milton? Now he would never find them, they would be forever marooned... but where? For the first time she looked around the room. "Where are we going, Aurelia?"

"France, we are on the packet."

"What! Oh no!" Her worst fears realised. "No one will find us now!" She shuddered.

"Edward?"

Petty turned her head. How could she have been so remiss? Why had she not left word with Edward? Her idiotic complacency! Reluctantly she conceded to herself that part of her determination to recover his sister without help was her desire to demonstrate her capabilities to Edward. Edward! Oh, Edward! She would never see him again. From the corner of her eyes silent tears slid down her face. She felt extremely sorry for herself. Aurelia, in her quiet way, watched her.

"Edward will find us, I am sure," she replied comfortingly. "He will get us away from that awful Mr Melville."

Petty looked back at her. Gently she shook her head. She did not quite know what to say. She hesitated to admit her folly in failing to inform Aurelia's brother of her intentions, and she did not want to scare the girl unnecessarily.

"Bertram Melville is perfectly intolerable, is he not?" she remarked instead. "The whole family is dreadful."

"So you do know them?" Aurelia asked curiously.

Petty groaned. "Oh yes, I know them." She paused a second, while she decided whether to tell Aurelia everything. She knew that Cuthbert knew who she was but she was unsure if Aurelia had been told of her brother's unfortunate marriage. In spite of her impending divorce from Lord Milton and his obvious desire to have nothing more to do with her, she discovered that she was hesitant to do anything which might antagonise him. So she deliberated before she spoke.

"I know… well… my family knows the Melvilles. Sir Stanley, who is Bertram Melville's father, was an arch enemy of my grandfather's. He is an out-and-out blackguard, a scoundrel of the first order. I had never encountered Mr Melville myself. He is of course considerably older than I am, but… as I think you know, I first met him with Verity…" She hesitated; her eyes searched Aurelia's face. She was not positive that the girl knew how she had met Verity or Bertram's part in it.

Aurelia met her eyes calmly. She said in her direct way, "I

have not been told what happened and if you think that it would be indiscreet for me to know, please do not think you must divulge the information."

"No. On balance I think that if we are to get out of this hole, you must know the truth. I was run... I was at an inn in Tonbridge... and as I was going down to dine I heard crying. A girl rushed out of the door opposite. It was Verity, but of course I did not know that then. She was sobbing wildly! She was followed by a man. He was dark and rather evil looking; I must admit I was scared. However, for the first time in my life I managed to stand up to someone. I told him to desist in his evil intentions and to leave Verity alone and he did. I comforted Verity, who was, as you can imagine, nearly hysterical. Aurelia giggled. "And... I... took her back to her papa."

Aurelia regarded her sagely. "You were her companion and from what Dora divulged, hers beforehand, but I do not think you are naturally a governess."

As she spoke there were sounds of someone outside the door. Aurelia jumped. She looked around. "I think you should pretend to still be asleep!" she whispered quickly.

Gideon obeyed the summons from his father to return to Wakeham somewhat reluctantly. He was enjoying his sojourn in London. He had commenced a flirtation with a capital girl and he was most disinclined to leave her at such a delicate point in their connection. He was not at all sure that she would succumb to his wiles but he had taken bets on the conclusion with Lord Arnley and was hopeful of a successful and lucrative outcome. It was not, therefore, with pleasure that he received the peremptory order from the duke. Having to depart now would constitute almost certain loss and he was most loath to lose his bet and the pleasure of a liaison with Miss Harriet Petersome!

Gideon had been introduced to the agreeable Miss Petersome by his cousin, The Hon. Hector Edgerton; the hopeful eldest son of the Mordaunts' popular Aunt Amelia, Lady Edgerton, was a lively young man, who slightly to his parents' dismay showed signs of resembling his grandfather! However, these indications were misleading, indeed he did have a penchant for gaming and pretty women and horses, it was true, but underneath his flamboyant exterior there lurked a kind and conscientious soul. He was Gideon's younger by two years and at twenty-three much of his behaviour was still of the nursery.

Harriet was a bewitching young woman with black hair, dark eyes and a vivacious temperament. She was quick-witted and possessed of a smile that bowled over all those privileged enough to receive it. She seemed ready enough to indulge Slaughan's amour to its zenith, although in truth she was more circumspect than might at first sight appear and was determined not to be sold short of what she regarded as her rights. If Harriet had a fault, it was that she had been indulged in every way possible and bordered on the spoilt.

She was just seventeen, the only daughter of the fashionable Sir Harley Petersome, doctor to the ton, and his determined lady wife. Her papa may have attended patients in the drawing rooms of the ton but this did not mean that they were invited everywhere; however, her parents, and more particularly her mama, Lady Petersome, had pretensions in that direction and she was not averse to encouraging Lord Slaughan's suit. Harriet was also, to add to her manifold attractions, a considerable heiress, and as such was much feted by gazetted fortune hunters, playing one beau off against another with a light-hearted shrewdness that had given her the nickname of 'The Scorcher'; but Gideon was different. She was fast developing a tendre for the dashing marquis, a fact that made her watchful mama heedful of a necessity to guide her headstrong daughter carefully.

His father's message was brought to him as he was preparing to ride in Hyde Park at the fashionable hour of five o'clock. Gideon read it quickly, cursed under his breath and then, instead, drove to Wimpole Street where Sir Harley lived. He was shown into the morning room. Lady Petersome and Harriet were alone when he was announced.

"My lord! How delightful." Lady Petersome rose and greeted His Lordship most cordially. "Harriet, my love, here is Lord Slaughan come to pay his respects to us." She held out her hand to him. He kissed it politely.

"We were planning a drive in the park." Her Ladyship could hardly keep the triumph out of her voice. "I do hope, my lord, that you will be able to drive with us." As she contemplated the glory of driving with the marquis in her carriage, a slow smile crept over her face. "Such a perfect day for a drive, do you not think?"

"A ride had been my intention." Her Ladyship glowed with exultation. "Although I am afraid that you will find driving oppressively hot, Your Ladyship," Gideon replied.

"Oh, we do not mind the heat do we, my dear?" She nodded ingratiatingly at Harriet, who rose and crossed to Gideon, her hands outstretched.

"How perfectly sweet you are to pay us a visit." She smiled coquettishly, her dark eyes laughing. "I declare you look so handsome in your riding attire. You are proposing to ride in the park, are you not? Oh, may I please accompany you? It would be so much more fun than sitting in a boring carriage." She smiled enchantingly again. "It will take me only a moment to change."

Gideon caught her hands in his. "Oh, Miss Petersome, I have sisters and a fashionable mama, I know that what you claim is surely an impossibility!"

"Oh, my lord, you do not know my sweet Harriet! She is as unlike your other damsels as is possible to imagine; she will, I promise, keep you waiting only a moment."

"Alas, would that I could ride with you, most perfect of creatures." Gideon kissed the tiny hand that reposed so enchantingly in his. "Alas, I cannot. I have come to wish you farewell. I have to go out of town on urgent business and must leave instantly, I cannot delay." Harriet's face puckered, she pulled her hand away.

"How unfair," she remarked, crossly shaking her head.

"Oh, my love," her mama remarked pointedly. She did not want her wayward daughter to exhibit her true colours at this juncture. "I am sure that Lord Slaughan has good reason for his departure. Have you not, my lord?"

Gideon, well used to the spoilt wiles of pretty girls, picked up the beauty's chin and pinched it gently. "Harriet! Most lovely of girls. Do you think that I wish to leave you?" he pleaded longingly. "Indeed, I do not. But I have this moment received a summons from my father. I am afraid it cannot be ignored."

"I should think not," Lady Petersome, all smiles, responded.

Harriet peeped up at the handsome visage of the marquis. "Of course, I perfectly understand you must visit your mama. Will you be gone for long?"

"I do hope that the dear duke and duchess and your sweet sisters are all well?" enquired Lady Petersome.

Gideon looked slightly surprised at her presumption but rejoindered courteously, "Quite well, I thank you, ma'am, but I am afraid I have no time to waste. Goodbye, Harriet." He kissed her hands again, bade farewell to her mama and left swiftly.

"Bother! Just as you were getting on so well with him… I hope…" She stopped.

Harriet stamped her foot. "How can he go and leave me now!" She started to cry. "Just when I wanted to show him off to everyone!"

"It is all very strange," the lady mused. "I hope that he is not being removed from town because of his friendship with you… I should have been a great deal happier if he had declared himself… We shall have to wait patiently and see what occurs."

In reality they could not have been further from the truth. Although, it must be admitted, that Her Grace would have promptly removed her heir from the cloying hands of one such as Lady Petersome, had she known about her and her daughter, but fortunately she did not! Having bidden adieu to Harriet, Gideon left for Wakeham without delay. He had only been gone a few hours when the servant dispatched by Cuthbert reached his lodging in Bruton Street. The evening was hot and humid. Gideon made good speed on the journey. He was keen to push on, for the sky was clouding over and the heavy stillness foretold a storm; however, it had not broken when he reached Wakeham; the house itself was bathed in the last of the sun's rays with the grey, lowering clouds billowing out behind it.

Lord Milton banged peremptorily on the door of the house in Westborn Street. Eventually the sound of the bolts being drawn back was heard by a relieved Verity, who was beginning to believe that the Lockes had decamped. Matty opened the door. She was dressed in a grubby robe. Her coarse face was free of the paint that generally covered it and her hair was in curling papers. She looked quite vulgar. Verity could not understand how she could have thought these tasteless girls were at all the thing! Matty looked at her wide-eyed with astonishment.

"This is Lord Milton," Verity mumbled. Matty started to close the door but Edward was too quick for her; he stuck his foot in the door.

"Not so fast, Miss Locke. I need some information from you and I intend to obtain it. Now, we can either stand here in the street or we can come in. Which shall it be?" His face was as stern as Verity had ever seen. The dark eyes more hostile than she could have dreamed possible. She quivered slightly, drawing her cloak around her. Matty lowered her eyes. Silently she led the way upstairs. The room in which they had been with Petty earlier seemed even seedier to Verity's eyes. How could she have wanted to be friends with such people? She must have been mad, and when she thought of what could have happened, she shivered again.

Matty took a plate of half-eaten food off a soiled sofa and gestured that they sit down. She did not look at Verity and for once the girl was glad of that. Edward turned up his nose fastidiously. "No, thank you! We will not remain here long. Now, where has Mr Melville taken my sister?"

Matty glanced at him nervously. "I told that Mrs Blakeston, stuck up piece," she answered sulkily.

"How dare you speak of her in those tones?" He moved towards her menacingly. She backed away.

"To France… well, Dover first… the Blue Hind," she returned quickly, deciding that the sooner she got rid of these threatening visitors the better.

"That is better. Now, Miss Locke, may I suggest that you leave London as soon as you can? If I find that you are still here when I return, you will find yourselves answering the magistrate."

On these words he turned heel and was gone. Matty stared dourly after him. She knew the game was up, there was no mistaking his words. He meant what he said! She sighed and returned to her bed for what remained of the night. There was much she would have to do on the morrow.

Lord Milton made all speed back to Grafton Street where he intended to drop Verity, pick up Hardwick and his travelling chaise. His plans were somewhat thwarted, however, because as he entered his hall, Cuthbert and Mrs Lumley appeared from the book room. They regarded him enquiringly but, before he could answer their questions, Hardwick appeared with a thin wispy man in tow.

"Wants to have a word with you, he does," Hardwick imparted fiercely.

"That's as right, Yer Lordship, a'beggin' Yers 'onour's pardon."

"Not now, Hardwick. I must be gone."

"That's it, d'ussum yers a'know where yers a'going? If yers is a'going after that young'un, yers a must go to Dover to the Blue Hind!" he finished triumphantly.

Enraged, Edward turned abruptly on Hardwick. "Why did no one tell me he was here?" he demanded. "I have wasted two hours."

"Beg pardon, my lord, but I did not know… it was Mr Philipson what told him to wait… he was in the kitchen."

Inwardly Edward fumed but he knew that it was not Hardwick's fault, but why had his grandfather omitted to tell him about the groom? Hiding his irritation, he turned to the man.

"Please tell me how you come to be involved, what do you know?"

"Me name's Ned, I took Miss…" he waved at Verity, "and the lady, the grand one, to that disgusting Place in Paddington, no place for ladies in my opinion."

"Yes! Yes, no doubt but what happened next?"

"Yes! Beg pardon… the other lady says as she wants a coach… to go out of town… well, me brofer – he's Ted, I'm Ned, he was a postillion and I didn't think it right for her to travel without some protection. So I brot 'im round and 'e took her hoff and she told me to bring her," he nodded at Verity again, "to your house and he… tolds me as to wait so I dus!"

"Now, as I see it, your brother…"

"Yes, my lord, me twin brofer… like as two peas, we is…"

"Your brother is with Mrs Blakeston?" Ted nodded vigorously. Lord Milton felt some kind of relief. Instinctively he found himself trusting Ted and imagined he would trust his brother, "and they have gone to Dover?" Ted nodded again.

"Then I must leave immediately."

"Beg pardon, my lord, but I think I should haccompany you."

Hardwick's face was a study in horror as Ted uttered these words. "My lord!" he protested. "I will accompany Lord Milton."

"No! Hardwick, he is right, you have been driving all day and night and I think you should stay here and take care of Mr

Philipson and Mrs Lumley. Grandfather, I want you to visit Sir Hugo tomorrow… today… I imagine that you will know what to say to him." He nodded briskly to his family, swept down the steps and into the chaise which awaited him.

It was starting to rain as Gideon arrived at the ornate gates which led to Wakeham; he still had two miles of drive to cover and the rain was fast becoming a deluge. He cursed slightly, turning up the collar of his drab caped greatcoat and pulling his curly beaver hat over his eyes. Still the rain poured down in torrents over his face, and he was heartily glad when he finally reached the great front entrance of the house. He did not, in fact, go in by the flanked door but made his way around the back to the stables, giving his horse to a groom with instructions to rub him down carefully. He, then, entered through the gun room door. He shook his wet clothes, handing his coat and hat to a convenient footman. At that moment Croft appeared.

"My lord! My lord! How wet you are, why did you not ring?" he scolded.

"I thought I would get under cover as soon as possible. Not hanging around waiting for you to cover the corridors," Gideon teased.

"Now, my lord, is that fair?" Croft admonished. "I will go and inform Their Graces that you are here."

"Thank you, but I think I had better change out of these wet clothes before I see them." It was a good half hour before he joined his parents in the library. The duchess was seated next to an excellent fire; she wore her customary expression of woe and was attended by the ubiquitous Holtby. The duke was standing at the window peering out in the dark at the sodden home park with unseeing eyes.

At Gideon's entrance Her Grace looked up and exclaimed, "Oh! Gidi! Gidi! Thank goodness you have come."

His Grace gave a curt dismissive nod to Holtby, who somewhat reluctantly left the room, contenting herself with the thought that whatever the duke was going to impart to Gideon would be told to her, as she sympathised with her mistress's uncaring treatment. The duke waited only for the door to close behind her before he swung around onto Gideon.

"What is this?" he demanded, his eyes blazing, waving a letter in Gideon's face. His son thought quickly. Surely Lady Petersome would never be so foolish as to write to his father with importunate demands.

"This..." the duke continued answering his own question, "... is a letter from Lord Milton! In which he tells me he is intending to divorce Perpetua."

Whatever Gideon had been expecting, it had certainly not been that. He stood dumbfounded, staring at his father.

"Di... vorce?" he eventually managed. "Divorce? No! Not possible, why, he adores her."

"So you had led me to believe."

"Now, what has that troublesome daughter of mine done to bring this kind of disgrace on the family?" The duchess spoke in a fragile voice which, however weak, did not hide her underlying malice. "Ingrate! Unnatural wretch! Most insensible of children!" Her beautiful eyes brimmed with tears. "She was always ungrateful for all that was done for her, but now..." She flopped back onto the chaise fanning herself.

"Let me take a look at that." Gideon unceremoniously snatched the letter from his father's hand and perused its contents. It was brief and to the point. It had been written immediately Edward returned from the picnic and dispatched that evening. Gideon stared at the words.

My Lord Duke,

It is with the utmost regret that I feel myself charged to write to you on this matter. I feel that it is now impossible for Perpetua and me to remain married. I have not yet informed her of my intention to seek a divorce, but I must let her go, I must free her from what is clearly a distasteful alliance. I will visit my solicitor in Hitchin to arrange it. Please understand that I do not wish for any return of the settlements. I am glad that I can repair some of the damage to an illustrious family.

I remain, your dutiful son.

"Why? Why, Gideon? Can you make me understand?" The duke sounded so despondent, so unlike himself. He sat in his favourite chair, his face in his hands, and when he spoke it was without any of his usual brusque authority. "It has not been easy. Your grandfather... you understand... Oh, I know that you do... I thought that I was achieving the best for us all. It was important that Petty married. The match was not such a bad one, was it?" He looked at Gideon almost pleadingly.

"No! No, Papa, far from it. This is what I do not comprehend. Edward adores Petty and she is most definitely not indifferent to him. When he is in the room she sparkles. She is almost beautiful. I must admit I did not recognise her at first." He paused, staring at the letter. "Oh... just a moment I think perhaps I do understand, the key is in his words. 'I must let her go...' Because he loves her, he thinks he must free her."

"I have never heard such idiocy," Her Grace started.

"No! I think Gideon might be right," His Grace replied thoughtfully. "But we must prevent this; it will be a catastrophe!"

Chapter Twenty-Two

Bertram marched into the cabin. He peered at Petty, lying motionless, pretending to be asleep.

"I had thought she would have woken by now. Perhaps I gave her more than I thought." He turned on Aurelia, his dark eyes narrowing as he surveyed her trim figure.

"You at least appear sensible. I hope you are now reconciled to our marriage." Then, his thin mouth twisting in an unpleasant leer, he advanced upon her. Aurelia remained very still and erect in front of him, her beautiful eyes defiant, a look of contempt on her face. Petty, peeping through her eyelashes, watched in horror as Bertram proceeded to grab the girl's wrist, dragging her to her feet. He pulled her towards him and Petty thought that he meant to kiss her. She was about to spring to her feet to defend Aurelia, when the girl spoke in her measured way.

"Mr Melville, please desist. You would not wish that I consider you not a gentleman, would you?" He grunted and wrenched himself from her. He glanced at Petty's recumbent form and went out.

Aurelia exhaled. "Thank goodness."

Petty jumped up. "You were wonderful! How did you manage to stay so calm? So unafraid?"

"Oh, I am scared but it would never do to let him see it. Now sit down and finish your story."

Petty looked her in the eyes, took a deep breath and plunged in. "I… I… I… am…" She lowered her eyes. "Oh, I do not know how to say this."

"In love with my brother," Aurelia supplied helpfully; Petty's eyes flew open. A red blush suffused her face. Her hand went instinctively to her flaming cheeks. She turned away.

"Oh, I am sorry I did not wish to discompose you."

"Do you think everyone knows?" Petty said so miserably that Aurelia laughed.

"I am afraid so but please take comfort; his feelings for you are as transparent as yours for him."

Petty whirled back to face her. "His feelings for me? But he hates me, he does not care for me a bit. If not, why he is going to divorce me?"

Now it was Aurelia's turn to be dumbfounded. "Divorce you! What on earth do you mean?"

Petty went crimson. She swallowed hard; the dreadful day, Lord Milton's face, their hopeless predicament was too much for her. The unwelcome tears coursed down her cheeks. She slumped back onto the bed and broke down. She cried and cried, therapeutic tears. Aurelia sat beside her. She patted her hand but said nothing. Eventually the tears stopped. Petty sniffed hard, Aurelia handed her a handkerchief.

"Better?" Petty nodded. "Please, now, tell me what you meant?"

Petty sat up. She covered her eyes with her hand and in a flat voice she told her sister the truth. "I was… am married to Lord Milton. I… my family, was in dire financial straits… It suited your brother to marry me… My father is… a… duke…" Aurelia looked amazed but wisely she said nothing. "The eighth Duke of Staplefield. Lord Milton settled a great deal of money on my family in exchange for my hand… I told you, I am hopeless with people. I am not at all brave… I tried to tell my father that I did not want to m… marry Lord Milton." She raised her puffy eyes and smiled apologetically at Aurelia. "You see, I had not even met him before then."

Aurelia looked shocked. "I do not blame you," she felt moved to exclaim.

"They would not listen to me… they never do… I could not make them understand I did not want to marry him… then," she said sadly. She sighed again. "I do not see how I could have been so stupid." She screwed her face up in an attempt to halt the flow of tears which started so uncontrollably. "I agreed to do as they demanded, I was horribly selfish. I did not bother to think how it could affect him… After the wedding I ran away… I went to Bath."

"Alone?"

"Yes. It was scary." Petty gave a watery smile. "I applied to be a governess… There was a hateful woman called Mrs Friday. She would have sent me away but for Mrs Lumley, who employed me to be Dora's companion. I had a lovely time in Bath. I was happier there than at any time…" she disclosed wistfully. "Then one day we went to a party and Edward was there and he shouted at me. Said he would return me to Wakeham, to my papa and worse… to my mama! Oh, I am sorry, Aurelia. I did not mean to speak ill of your brother."

"No, Edward can be ill-tempered if he has a mind to," she responded understandingly, "but go on, what happened next?"

"I ran away again… I caught the first available stage and found myself at an inn in Tonbridge, which is where I met Verity, as I told you, escaping from Bertram… I took her back to her papa, Sir Hugo, and he gave me this job. Then we went to the party given by Mrs Cornwall and there was Edward again. I was horrified, but this time he was… different." She sighed dejectedly.

"And you fell in love with him and he with you. No, do not look abashed. It is clear to all those who love you both, but what we could not understand was why you wanted to stay with Verity. That is until now; now I see why you felt you must protect her."

Petty sat, her arms clasped around her knees. She seemed in a kind of daze, hardly listening to what Aurelia said. Could it be true? Could Edward love her? At times it had appeared to her that this was indeed the case, but he had been so cold, so distant, when he had told her about the divorce. She coloured again and with difficulty asked falteringly awkwardly, "If… If… what… you say is true… then why did he tell me he was going to d… divorce… me?" She gave an involuntary shudder, the prospect too dreadful to contemplate.

"I confess I do not know… When I first met you I must admit I did not think that you were the girl for Edward, his taste has always run to…" She stopped, embarrassed.

Petty laughed. "Beauties with lots of dash!"

"I am sorry, I did not mean that," Aurelia said frankly. "Now that I know you I realise that you are just the wife for him!"

"He clearly does not think so!" Petty responded, misery clouding her face again.

"I do not agree… I know my brother very well…" Before she had time to deliberate further, the ship gave a tilt, listing over quite substantially. Petty gulped. Aurelia peered out of the porthole; the coast of France was just visible through the early morning mist. "I can see land," she stated. "I think we had better stop this conversation and make a plan."

Petty nodded; she had recovered her composure and the enticing information that Edward loved her had had the most beneficial effect on her spirits, making her even more determined to get away from Bertram. "I think it would be best if I continued to pretend to be asleep. That way he will not think he has two of us to contend with."

Aurelia nodded. "I wonder where he will take us?" As she spoke there came the sound of a key being turned in the lock. Petty lay down quickly, her back to the door, for she suspected that her colour was improved and she did not want Bertram to see her face.

Bertram pushed open the door; a quick glance around the room, then he moved across to Petty's recumbent form and ungently poked it. It was all she could do not to jump.

"Huh. Now what shall do with her?" He glared at Aurelia. "I… I suppose we had better take her with us." The half smile Aurelia gave him was strained, but he who could never be termed a perceptive man did not notice.

She nodded. "l think that would be wise…"

"We will dock in half an hour. Collect your things. Oh!" he gave a raucous laugh. "You have nothing, of course." He laughed again; her possessionless state seemed to amuse him greatly. "We will buy you whatever you need in Calais. That is, if you have any money." He guffawed at this piece of wit and left, slamming the door behind him.

"I hate him!" Aurelia proclaimed vehemently at the closed door. "He is the most detestable of men."

"I agree." Petty sat up again. "Have you any money? I only have a few guineas left. I took all that I had but had to use most of it on horses. I did not think I would need any more… I should have borrowed from Verity…"

"If she would have lent you any."

Petty grinned. "Unlikely… she really is the most niggardly person. However, you will be pleased to know that she was most contrite about you. I think she has finally decided to have nothing more to do with those dreadful Lockes."

"Not before time and not before we have landed in this awful predicament, thanks to her."

Petty smiled. "We will get away, I know we will."

The boat had ceased to plunge and was slowing down; they seemed to be docking. Petty wrapped herself in her cloak and lay on the bed. A minute later the key turned in the lock. Bertram had returned. He gestured to Aurelia to follow him, then he picked Petty up roughly and threw her over his shoulder.

 292

As they disembarked onto the quay in Calais, the breeze smelt fresh and sweet. Petty took deep breaths of this reviving air, making sure as she did so that she hardly moved. This could be regarded as quite a feat but she was used to staying perfectly still, as the duchess considered that wriggly children were utterly abhorrent and all her children had spent hours sitting, hardly being allowed to move a muscle. Bertram, slightly breathless due to the burden of Petty, marched up to an elderly carrier who was standing beside an ancient horse and carriage and demanded in English: "Now, my man, I want you to take us to an out-of-the-way inn." He pulled open the door of the carriage and dumped Petty unceremoniously on the seat.

"Comment?" The elderly Frenchman had no time for Mr Melville. The outpouring that followed this gentleman's overbearing act in assuming that odd females could be deposited on the seats of his vehicle made Petty, who had excellent French, giggle quietly to herself.

"What is the man saying?" Bertram declared angrily. Petty heard Aurelia's measured tones.

"Perhaps I can help, I speak French."

Bertram nodded gruffly. "Get on with it then."

"Where do you want to go?" Aurelia enquired.

His nondescript answer made it obvious that beyond his immediate design to get them both to France, Bertram had laid no more plans. He blustered and then said that he wanted to go to a quiet inn for the next night. Aurelia explained this to the carrier.

Jean grunted. His sister ran a small inn. Would they like to go there?

Aurelia agreed, explaining to Bertram, in a friendlier voice than Petty would have used, what was happening. The carrier clambered into his seat and the elderly horse proceeded cautiously forward. Petty, who had been wedged onto the seat in a most uncomfortable position, found her arms going numb.

Edward drove his horses as they had never been driven before. He had an imperative desire to reach Dover as fast as possible. He said not a word to Ned on the way, his face uncompromisingly hard, his eyes like gimlets focused on the road ahead. Ned watched him dispassionately. Edward did not notice, so wrapped was he in his own thoughts. These thoughts were a mixture of worry, combined with an intense feeling of excitement. Petty did love him! He was now sure of it; he smiled to himself. Silly mouse! Well, she would not get away from him this time... but where were they? Would he be in time? What had happened to Aurelia? He was glad that Petty was with her, it would at least preserve the proprieties.

Impatiently, he pushed his horses even faster. He must get there. Although haste was pressing, his horses were tiring. He must change them. He must stop at the next village. When this was reached, he drove up to the small inn, the White Swan, which stood on the edge of the village pond and which, fortuitously, was the one recently visited by Petty.

While Ned hurried into the stable, grandly announcing my Lord Milton's arrival and demanding instant furtherance of his equine needs, his master strode into the inn, where he was met by the landlady, who bustled out to greet her noble visitor. "A private parlour and breakfast," he commanded.

"Very good, my lord," the landlady responded, much in awe of this grim-looking member of the aristocracy, who ordered her about so fiercely. "Immediately, my lord. If you would be so good as to follow me." She led the way to the room so recently vacated by Petty. Edward stripped of his caped driving coat and gloves and stood by the fire. She made to go.

"A moment." She paused at the door. His tones were hard, disagreeable. "Have you seen a young girl by herself?" His eyes narrowed. "She would have passed through here sometime last night."

She realised in a moment that this uncompromising stranger was after that poor young girl. She must not betray her. Unfortunately, the momentary hesitation before she answered him, and the confused panic in her face, gave her away.

"No! No, my lord, no one, no one at all… I have not seen any young girls…"

"Are you quite sure? Come, I see from your face that you are not telling me the truth."

"No! No! No! No one came last night."

Edward was confounded. He was sure that this woman knew more than she was telling him but why should this woman deny Petty? He felt a shiver of fear, his voice became even harder.

"Tell me the truth, woman. This is a matter of life and death."

The landlady was by now thoroughly scared; she looked about her for help but none was forthcoming. Lord Milton crossed to her and stared at her menacingly.

"Yes, yes?" he snapped.

"She… well, I do not want to betray her… such a little thing."

Betray her? Edward was perplexed. "Betray her! What do your mean?" his tone altogether more conciliatory. "Come, I mean her no harm. Quite the contrary, I want to help her."

The landlady, completely flummoxed, gazed at him suspiciously. "You will not take her back?" she ventured.

"Take her back? To whom?"

"To that husband of hers… that man who is so cruel to her…"

A quiver of pain crossed his face. Mrs Lumley was wrong. Petty did not care for him. He drew in his breath, his mouth twisting, closing his eyes with hurt. The landlady regarded him steadily. He appeared to her motherly eyes as suddenly vulnerable. She nodded her head sagely, but continued.

"That Mr Hamel... what is the son of that beak-faced woman... complains, she does... always saying my sheets ain't aired, I ask you, what a charge... I keeps a good house, I does..."

Edward was now totally bewildered. "Hamel? Mr Hamel's wife? I do not think we mean the same girl."

"Maybes not, my lord. A little thin thing... beautiful blue eyes, she had... I did not want to take her in first... but when she explained, as to how she had been married to that Mr Hamel and him so cruel. Well, I ask you, I could not refuse."

A gleam of amusement sprang into Edward's eyes; relief swept over him. His inventive love; now he understood what had occurred.

"Oh yes," he added. "I do not want to return her to Mr Hamel, a dreadful family. I am her br..." he thought that might be too risky, "... her cousin," he amended. "I want to return her to the bosom of her loving family."

"Not very loving to marry her to a monster like that," the landlady commented.

"Indeed, we were quite wrong." Edward's amusement gave way to foolishness. He hung his head contritely. "We have, I venture to think, learnt our lesson. But now my breakfast! It is necessary that I catch up with her post haste."

She bobbed a curtsey and bustled away to fulfill his culinary demands.

They left the inn soon after they had eaten and the new horses had been put to. These, as Ned was quick to point out, were "the best they had, me lord, but as scavegy a pair as I've seen in a long day, regular touched in the wind, they is."

"So I can see," Edward replied grimly, his natural impatience aggravated by the dullness of the horses he was forced to drive. "We must stop again as soon as we can."

The next coaching inn did not appear promising. It was a small white square building set well back from the road and almost entirely surrounded by fields. Edward spoke in despair. "This is hopeless, they will have nothing here."

They were, luckily, proved wrong. The house, although small, was run by a host who prided himself on his cattle and the team he supplied were most superior animals. "Regular goers!" observed the wiry henchman.

With these animals harnessed, they made excellent progress, arriving in Dover by mid- afternoon. They enquired for the Blue Hind and were luckier than Petty for they were directed to this hostelry with all speed.

As they drew up outside it, Edward found his stomach knotted with trepidation. This state was as unlike his natural unflappability as was possible to imagine. He jumped agitatedly down, throwing the reins to Ned, and hurried into the inn. The landlord who bestirred himself to greet him was having a somewhat unusual few days. He ran a very ordinary house. He had his regular taproom customers, but as he was very much off the beaten track, the quality certainly did not honour his establishment with their needs, and suddenly in two days he had been visited by undoubted members of the upper echelons of society. Bertram Melville may have been a villain but it was clear that he was a well-bred rogue, his wife was most definitely a lady, and now, hot on the heels of this couple, came a lord. Mr Chard was most perplexed. However, he was not one to turn a blind eye to the largesse that generally accompanied the arrival of the gentry, and he scraped a bow and proffered his help.

"Have you had a gentleman by the name of Bertram Melville staying here with a young girl, very beautiful, dark, pale blue eyes and perhaps accompanied by a small girl with brown hair?"

"Well, my lord, I…"

Edward threw some coins onto the counter. "I need to know where they have gone."

The landlord became immediately more loquacious. "Why, yes, my lord, the gentleman and his lady wife… and her maid…"

Edward gasped, but maintained his equilibrium. "Maid?" he queried.

"Yes! The mousy girl came after the other two, said her coach had broke down with the luggage. Not too well, she weren't, had to be carried aboard the packet." Edward felt his heart miss a beat; he was deeply agitated now; he frowned. What had happened to his Petty? Why had she been prostrate?

"Carried?" he asked.

"Yes, thought she might have been a goner." The landlord laughed heartily at his joke. "Expect it was the daffy though!" He roared at his humour.

Edward, stern-faced, did not share his merriment. "Yes," he went on crossly. "When did the packet depart?"

"This morning 'bout eleven. Won't be another till the morrow. Beg pardon, me lord, I did not mean that she was one over, it was jest me funning," he guffawed again.

"Be quiet," Edward commanded. "I do not share your humour. A private parlour and rooms for the night."

Mr Chard bowed. He nodded. "At once, my lord, at once."

He led the way down the narrow corridor and opened the door on the only private parlour that the inn possessed. This was a drab, unprepossessing room that smelt fusty and although not exactly dirty could hardly be described as sparkling clean. A thin layer of dust lay on the table and, to Edward's fastidious eye, small balls of dust were clinging to the corners of the floor. He turned up his nose disparagingly, tempted to remove immediately to the Swan's Neck, an excellent hostelry which overlooked the harbour and which had enjoyed his custom in the past. Whilst he waited to embark to France, however, his Petty and Aurelia had most certainly been in this place and there may be more to be found out.

He threw his coat over a chair and paced the room, his natural impatience chafing at the unavoidable delay. It was not naturally part of his disposition to defer action because a duty was irksome, and he longed to get on with catching up with Bertram Melville. He found he had a strong urge to get his fingers around that gentleman's neck and to slowly squeeze the life out of him.

At that moment came a knock at the door. Mr Chard looked at him enquiringly. "Permit me," he murmured. Edward nodded. The landlord opened the door to admit Ted and Ned. At the sight of them Edward's brows shot up and amusement played around his mouth. They were extraordinarily alike. In both, the wispy grey hair stuck up off the top of their heads at an identical angle; they were thin and their bones projected in exactly the same way.

"This 'ere is me brofer, me twin brofer!" vouchsafed Ned somewhat unnecessarily.

"So I see," responded Edward, his brown eyes laughing.

"This 'ere is My Lord Milton!"

The heavy emphasis on the Lord Milton made Edward laugh out loud. He felt suddenly better, Ted had come with Petty, maybe he had encouraging news? He put out his hand to Ted.

"I gather I have to thank you," Ted raised a craggy brow, "for taking care of my... Mrs Blakeston."

"Seems as though you should be a'strangling me, as thanking me. Fine ways I did me job. Taken hoff she was by as nasty a piece of nob as I've seen this long day... I should have gones after them. I should but she told me to wait for her. By the time I realised the error, it was too late. He a'spirited her away hoff on that boat and the beauty with her."

"Never mind, we must see what we can do to rescue them. I think I must take one of you with me and one must stay here and wait for our return."

Chapter Twenty-Three

P etty lay as inert as she could in the corner of the shabby coach as it bumped over the uneven dirt tracks that passed for roads in this out-of-the-way part of Northern France. She knew that she just had to move, she could not stay still any longer! Her left arm had no feeling in it and she thought the pain in her left hip would make her scream if she did not change her position. When she knew she could bear it no longer, she wriggled; the alleviation of discomfort as she eased her leg forward was intense. She took a deep breath, rubbed the back of her hand over her eyes and appeared to wake up. As she looked up she met Aurelia's startled eyes.

"Where am I?" she murmured, blinking at the unaccustomed light.

"Oh, so you've chosen to honour us with your company at last," Bertram pronounced nastily.

Petty resisted a strong desire to give him a piece of her mind. It would not do to antagonise him further. Then she smiled to herself. How she had changed; in her former life she would have died rather than confront a man of Melville's stamp, yet here she was contemplating it with equanimity. Indeed, relishing the idea of raking him down! Whatever happened in the future, she realised how much she had altered and how much for the better. I could take on Mama now, she thought to herself.

"Why are you grinning like that?" Bertram demanded. Petty smiled docilely at him.

"I was just so glad that the…" She stopped in time. She had been going to say that she was pleased the boat had docked. "The… sun is shining…" she finished.

Indeed, after the weather of the previous days, today was lovely. Tiny clouds scudded across an otherwise blue sky and the sun was warm. Petty pulled herself up to peer out of the window. They were passing through peaceful French countryside, the old horse plodding slowly but firmly on. Petty looked to see if she could find any landmarks but there were none that she could return to. Bertram regarded her suspiciously. He did not trust her, docile or not, and he was unsure of what to do with her. He presumed that, when he had married Aurelia, she would need some kind of maid, but he was not sure that he wanted Petty as part of his establishment. He could just leave her, he supposed, somewhere in a French village. He wondered if she spoke the language.

"Do you speak French?" he asked.

Petty thought quickly. "No," she lied.

She regarded him thoughtfully, remembering their first meeting. She pondered on the fact of how strange it was that a man such as Bertram, whose face was well aspected, could become so repellent and one who may, on first acquaintance, appear quite ugly, but who, with increased intimacy, could become so likeable. Bertram was a personable man; of that there was no doubt, but he was loathsome. She shivered.

"Cold, Mrs Blakeston? I thought you were admiring the sun."

"Perhaps I…" Petty searched for words.

"Perhaps the ship made her unwell?" Aurelia supplied helpfully.

"Yes!" Petty nodded vigorously "The ship… were we on a ship? Where are we now?"

"France! That is why I asked you if you could speak French. I thought that as you were an unwelcome addition to our party perhaps I could leave you in a village here."

Petty's eyes flew to Aurelia's in horror; she swallowed. "Oh no! Please..." Petty stuttered, utterly dismayed, not only for herself but for Aurelia. If Bertram abandoned her, then Aurelia would be utterly compromised! It seemed they were entirely under his domination, in his power.

However, at that moment, when there seemed little hope of retrieving their situation, fate intervened. Suddenly, there came a loud splintering sound and the ancient carriage lurched forward; it had run over a particularly deep rut and the front wheel had quite split off its shank. Petty clutched onto Aurelia as the coach spun sideways, landing in a ditch on its side.

Petty clambered out. She was bruised but unhurt. Aurelia, however, seemed to have sustained a rather severe blow to the head, and was lying dazed at the side of the path. Petty ran across to her. She was conscious but moaning slightly; a little blood oozed from a nasty cut on the side of her head.

"Quick!" Petty said. "We must get help." She turned to the coachman and, forgetting herself, demanded in fluent French to know where the nearest inn could be found. The coachman, sensing that perhaps he was going to be blamed for the accident, offered to be off to find help from his sister. Petty accepted his offer but told him firmly that he had better return, warning him steadfastly that she would set the police after him if he ran off.

"You were deceiving me. You do speak French," Bertram remarked sullenly.

"Oh, do be quiet! This is not time for that," Petty snapped at him. "Come and help me move Aurelia to a shadier spot."

Together they lifted the girl and placed her under the trees by the wayside. She had revived a little by now, and Petty was glad to see her colour returning. She mopped up the gash on her face as best she could with Bertram's handkerchief.

"Good. Now that she seems recovered we can continue our journey," he asserted.

"Out of the question!" Petty replied firmly. "We must find somewhere to stay and remain for the night. Aurelia must not be moved. You do not want to increase her distress, do you?" she demanded accusingly.

Bertram shook his head. He walked a little way away from the two girls, enabling Petty to whisper to Aurelia.

"Go on pretending to be unwell, then at least we can stop and he would hardly dare to leave me in a village when you are ill and need nursing."

A gleam of appreciation brightened Aurelia's eyes; she grinned weakly at Petty. Then groaned loudly and lay back on the grass. Petty called to Bertram; she widened her eyes as if in fear. "I do not think she is very well, I do hope that Jean hurries back with help." She peered down the road, which was empty. Bertram shrugged his shoulders and sighed.

"Alright. I will go and see what I can find," he said.

"Thank you!" Petty smiled charmingly.

With bad grace Bertram made to set off down the hot dusty road, but he had hardly gone a few yards when he saw a smart gig trotting towards them; it was driven by a young man, who pulled up beside them.

"I am Pierre, the nephew of Jean. He sent me to help you," he offered in French.

"Merci," responded Petty.

"What is he saying?" Flustered by his inability to comprehend the language, Bertram grew more belligerent, his face glowering. "What is the idiot saying?"

"Just that he is Jean's nephew and that he is here to help us," Petty replied soothingly.

She turned to the young man. "Please, is there an auberge where we could rest?"

"Yes, but it is not at all the kind of establishment for girls of your quality," he replied waveringly.

"Oh, that is not important," Petty answered. "We just need somewhere for my sister."

He nodded doubtfully. "If you please to come, the auberge is run by my parents. My mama will make you most welcome. Please, we will put your sister in the gig and you and the gentleman can walk."

Petty agreed readily, her only concern being that should Lord Milton choose to come after them, he would never find them in an obscure French inn. Most important, however, at the moment was to get Aurelia into bed. The girl was looking rather grey again and causing Petty some alarm. Pierre helped Petty lift her into the gig, and they set off. Judging by its pristine condition and that of Pierre's clothes, Petty was hopeful that the inn would prove to be as clean.

She was right. The auberge was a warm red building with green shutters. A few fat chickens clucked their way around the front of the porch scratching for grain. A field to the right of the house was filled with apple trees, heavy with fruit, that clearly promised well for a bumper harvest later in the year. A plump madame came bustling out of the door. She clucked, as one of the chickens, when she saw Aurelia, who was so white now that Petty was really scared. However, this redoubtable female swept her up in a trice and whisked her up to a spotless, shady bedroom on the first floor. Petty accompanied her upstairs and had the satisfaction of seeing her safely installed in a huge bed filled with fluffy thick quilts, cased in pure white linen covers. Madame asked after their luggage. Petty, who by now had become most inventive, explained that all their things had been left by mistake in Dover and that they had not had time to purchase new ones in Calais. Madame promised to find them essentials and then kindly dismissed Petty, who was very reluctant to leave, not because she did not trust Madame Fournier, she could see that her nursing would be everything that was admirable, but because going downstairs meant another encounter with Bertram.

Sense told her that it would be expedient to be polite to him but the idea was abhorrent to her. Commonplace words stuck in her throat; all she wanted to do was to berate him! She went down to the parlour that Madame had indicated would be for their use. It was a pleasant, half-wood-panelled room, which smelt of polish and sweet flowers; the scent, Petty discovered, was wafting from a huge vase which stood in the centre of the shining table. On the sideboard which faced the window reposed a tray stacked with refreshments. Petty observed with satisfaction, that Bertram was nowhere to be seen. Discovering that she was starving, she helped herself to a large plate of ham and bread and butter. She sat down at the table and poured herself a glass of creamy milk, which she drank slowly while pondering their predicament.

The accident had, she realised, given them a breathing space. Whilst Aurelia was ill, Bertram could not move them, but the problem was what to do once she was better and he wanted to leave. She deliberated on the possibility of asking Madame to come to their aid but decided that if she were unwilling, they would be in a worse position than they had been before. Just as she was contemplating their future, there was a sound outside. Instinctively her head swivelled towards the door.

After Lord Milton had left to drive to Dover, Cuthbert and Mrs Lumley retired to bed. Neither of them slept a wink, and at nine o'clock Mrs Lumley rang the bell to summon her maid to bring her her morning chocolate. She sat in bed, supping the comforting beverage and going over the previous days' happenings to herself. Now she understood why Petty had stayed with Verity, now she understood why she had not wanted to come back to them. She was glad that she had told Edward of Petty's feelings for him; it would have been the silliest of things if he had divorced her. A gentle knock on the door and Dora's head appeared around the frame.

"Good morning, Mama! May I come in?"

"Of course, Dora." Mrs Lumley nodded vigorously and then found herself obliged to adjust her elegant night cap. Dora trotted across the room, she kissed her mama on the cheek and then sat on the bed.

"Verity is not up yet," she pronounced. Then she turned to her mama questioningly. "What happened?"

Mrs Lumley patted her hand. "In truth I am not at all surprised," she answered ruefully. "Such a to-do we had last night…"

Dora's eyes widened. "Why?"

Her mama raised her eyes to heaven. "Verity was pulled out of bed at three o'clock this morning"

"Three o'clock?" Dora looked astonished.

"Yes! His Lordship bundled her and Amy into a coach, and bore her off to those Locke creatures. Came back about two hours later, then off he set for Dover. I declare it was six before he left or at least before I put my head to pillow."

"Has he gone after Petty?"

"Yes, who went after Aurelia and Mr Melville."

"Do you think he will rescue them? How exciting it is. Wait until I tell Cecily. It is like a story in a book."

"You will not be telling Cecily or anyone, my girl," responded her dearest mama sharply. "What I tell you must remain entre nous."

"Entre nous, Mama. Of course, I will not say anything to anyone if you do not wish it. But I long to hear from Aurelia what happened when she returns."

"Being kidnapped is not an adventure, Dora. It is not fun, I expect she will be very scared."

"Oh no! Not Aurelia and not Petty. They are very brave."

Mrs Lumley sighed. Sometimes Dora could be very silly, but then the young were, and she was only nineteen. She yawned; she was exhausted but she was conscious that sleep would elude her until she knew that Aurelia and Petty were safe. She wondered what time Edward would reach Dover. Would it be too late? She did hope they had not been taken to France. "Ring for Peters, my love. I will get up." Dora hastened to obey her mama.

When Mrs Lumley was attired in a round dress of orchid yellow with an overdress of salmon pink and her usual original headgear, she went down. Cuthbert, too, had been unable to sleep. He was in the morning room idly turning over the pages of a book. He greeted Mrs Lumley warmly.

"I fear this is going to be a long day," he pronounced.

"When do you expect to hear from Edward?"

"Not until late tonight at the earliest, maybe tomorrow morning. I must say, I entertain not very charitable feelings towards that Verity. How could she be so stupid as to expose my little Aurelia to such danger?"

"Even less charity, I must say, I feel to that Sir Hugo. Why do you not go and pay your visit to him? That will be an outlet for your spleen!"

He laughed. "Quite right! Would you like to accompany me?"

"Nothing I would like more than to give him a piece of my mind, but I do not think we should take Verity there and I do not want to leave my Dora with her alone."

She was to get her wish without endangering her daughter for as she spoke, there was a peal on the bell. As Cuthbert was about to deny that they were in to morning callers, Sir Hugo strode into the room followed by a flustered Penn.

"I apologise, Mr Philipson, but he insisted…" He looked appealingly at Mrs Lumley. "He would come up…"

"That is alright, Penn. We were on our way to visit Sir Hugo; his presence here will merely prevent an unnecessary journey."

"Where is my daughter?" Sir Hugo demanded.

"Good morning, Sir Hugo, won't you sit down." Mrs Lumley ignored his rudeness and gestured that he sit on the sofa. Cuthbert turned from him, disgusted by his boorishness.

"Your daughter is, I imagine, still asleep. Lord Milton was forced to get her up last night to take her to those dreadful friends of hers, the Lockes, so that they could divulge where Mr Melville had taken Aurelia and Mrs Blakeston." Her words were deliberately provoking.

"What do you mean forced her up? How dare he! If Mr Melville took the girls somewhere that is a matter for him not for my daughter. Will you please summon her this instant. I desire to remove her from your undesirable influence with all haste."

Cuthbert turned around. Mrs Lumley could have cheered when she saw the look on his face. Now we are in for fireworks, she thought delightedly to herself.

"Our undesirable influence," Cuthbert repeated slowly. "Our undesirable influence." He walked across the room, his eyes blazing and faced Sir Hugo. "We have been very long suffering with you up until now, Sir Hugo. I think our patience and tolerance derives from the fact that we all feel very sorry for Verity. I know that Mrs Blakeston felt an immense sense of responsibility for her safety, a responsibility that it was a pity you did not share."

Sir Hugo looked apoplectic. "Me! How dare you... I will..."

Cuthbert cut short his fury. "Be quiet and listen to me. Through your idiocy my granddaughter is in grave danger. Through your inability to care for your child, for your inadequate support of Mrs Blakeston, she too is now exposed to danger."

Sir Hugo started to protest that he had always supported Petty but Cuthbert silenced him. "You did not! She came to you and tried to tell you about these entirely unsuitable Lockes that

Verity had taken up with, mostly because the poor girl was not put in the way to meet suitable friends, and you dismissed her. Yesterday when she tried to stay with her charges, you sent her on an errand that should have been done by a footman. You countermanded her orders where the girls were concerned, allowing them to go to the park unsupervised, which resulted in Aurelia being kidnapped by the same man who had abducted Verity and who you had encouraged to come to your house!"

Sir Hugo had the grace to look slightly shamefaced. "Kidnapped? Has Aurelia been kidnapped?" Cuthbert his pent-up spleen vented, nodded.

"I apologise," Sir Hugo said stiffly. "I left the house as soon as Mrs Blakeston returned with my documents. I knew none of this. I was merely told that Verity was staying here, and that Mrs Blakeston had departed suddenly."

"Did you think Petty had let you down?" Mrs Lumley entered the fray fiercely. "Deplorable man! After she stayed on and in miserable circumstances; treated like a servant just to care for your spoilt daughter. Simply to make sure that she came to no harm. When all the time she could have been here, with those that love her."

Sir Hugo, his ire spent, sat down sadly. "I see that I have been in the wrong... When Verity's mama died I was not ready to care for a child. I know that my work comes first with me." He turned to Cuthbert. "It is of the utmost importance for the future of the working man in this country. I admit I had no time for Verity. After the episode with Melville, I should have done something for her..." He paused, thinking.

Cuthbert sighed. "It is not easy. I have had to bring up Aurelia. I understand."

"Thank you! Now, please tell me where has Melville taken Aurelia?"

"We think to Dover. At least, that is what the Lockes told first Petty and then my grandson, last night. Petty hired a coach and went after them and Edward left as soon as he could. We think he must be in Dover soon but we do not anticipate hearing from them for several hours. If only he has not taken them to France…"

Mrs Lumley's worried face bobbed around under the outrageous headgear. "France, the Channel, not what I holds with… I never did like being over all that sea in a tiny boat."

Cuthbert smiled grimly. "Let us hope that they are still in Dover…"

Sir Hugo stayed only to see Verity, who begged to be allowed to remain in Grafton Street, then he made his apologies and left. The occupants of this said mansion sat down for nuncheon with heavy hearts and a long slow wait ahead of them. The afternoon was enlivened by a visit from Lord Slaughan, who had stayed the night at Wakeham, leaving very early the next morning to return to London.

It had not been a very pleasant evening. The atmosphere between Their Graces was not agreeable, and Lord Slaughan was only too glad to get away. The prospect of the delectable Harriet loomed ahead, once he had done his duty and visited Lord Milton in Grafton Street. It was a lovely day and he enjoyed his ride to London, although he was extremely hot by the time he reached the city. He made for his lodging, so that he could wash away the dust of the road before presenting himself to Edward. He was not quite sure how to approach the question of the divorce. It was obviously quite ineligible and must be stopped. He was pondering the question as his valet shaved him. Eventually, attired in a new coat of superfine cloth which had just been delivered by Weston, his cravat tied in the latest waterfall, he arrived in Grafton Street.

He asked for Lord Milton and was told by Penn that he had gone from town, but that Mr Philipson and Mrs Lumley were in the saloon and would see him.

"My business is with Lord Milton," Gideon pronounced firmly. Harriet's dainty face swam in his sights.

Penn coughed deprecatingly. "I think you... um... should pa... see Mr Philipson."

Gideon looked perplexed but found that the old butler was quietly manoeuvring him up the stairs. He was shown into the saloon. Cuthbert rose to his feet. He wrung His Lordship's hand warmly.

"Lord Slaughan! Thank goodness!"

Gideon glanced from him to Mrs Lumley's worried face. "What is it?"

"Sit down, my boy," invited Cuthbert. "Bad news, I am afraid. Aurelia has been kidnapped."

"What!" Gideon exclaimed in astonishment.

"Yes... by one Bertram Melville."

"What? Bertram Melville... I hope he is nowhere near my sister..."

"Um... we... I am afraid Petty has gone after them."

"What? Petty and that scoundrel... Where have they gone?" He jumped up. "There is no time to waste. Is that why you sent for me? I am off after them..."

"Hold your horses..." replied Mrs Lumley. "Edward has gone after them and I rather think that he will be at Dover now... We are all hoping that Melville has not taken them to France..."

"What! France? No! Why did he...? How did he manage to get Aurelia? He is the most out-and-out blackguard, you know. Our family have quarrelled with their family most prodigiously. Of all the men in the world... Is he punishing us?" He paced the room in agitation.

"Please sit down, my lord. I will try to explain. Firstly, he does not know that Petty has anything to do with your family. He knows her only as Mrs Blakeston. Secondly, he abducted Aurelia for her wealth; apparently he wishes a rich wife and sees no need to woo one in a conventional manner." Cuthbert's voice was bitter.

"That is like them. All the same, those Melvilles. No morals." He paused, furiously taking a breath. "Bertram's father killed my grandfather, you know!"

Mrs Lumley's eyes opened in amazement. "Y... Your gr... grandfather!"

"Yes, the seventh duke. Mind you, he was no angel. The reason we are in queer street now, correction, we were, till Edward obligingly married Petty, was because of his licentiousness."

Cuthbert suddenly remembered; his face became stern. "Ah! Lord Slaughan. Divorce... is what I will not hold with... you may inform your papa."

"Oh, you and my papa will be in complete agreement. He will not countenance divorce either. He sent for me to tell Edward that." Gideon crossed to the windows, his face puzzled. "But I do not understand, Edward adores Perpetua."

"Oh, I think I have sorted the silly pair out now... idiotic nobility. I think you will find all talk of divorce disappears when they return," Mrs Lumley commented.

"If they return." Cuthbert sounded worried again. "Why have we not heard from Edward?" He paced the room...

"I must go after them. I cannot just sit here and wait." Gideon's energy and worry needed an outlet. As he hurried towards the doors, Cuthbert moved in front of him.

"No, no! I believe it is best left to Edward. We do not want anyone to know that Lady Perpetua and Mrs Blakeston are one and the same person... and with due respect, my lord, if you go careering after them, you may expose her."

Reluctantly Gideon recognised the efficacy in this sagacious observation. "Then shall I wait here? With you?" he asked enthusiastically. Mrs Lumley, on whom His Lordship's restless spirit was not exercising too beneficial an effect, suggested calmly, "Perhaps, my lord, you should go and visit... a friend... then you could come back later. We will send for you if we have any news."

Chapter Twenty-Four

The door knob turned. Petty gave a small stifled gasp. She felt her heart pounding inside her chest. She took a deep breath and swallowed hard. She was determined she would not appear afraid. It was, as she expected, Bertram. He looked her over unpleasantly but said nothing; he was followed by a rotund man who was speaking French volubly. Petty regarded him questioningly.

"Surgeon," Bertram muttered, scowling churlishly.

"Oh, I am so pleased to see you," Petty greeted the man in her immaculate French. "Please come to my sister immediately."

Bertram scowled. "Why can you not speak in English?"

Petty smiled at him patronisingly. "Because he has no English, he only speaks French. Now, if you will forgive me, I will take him to Aurelia with all haste."

Grudgingly, he moved from in front of the door and Petty beckoned to the doctor to follow her. When they were outside she gave a sigh of relief. Not only was the doctor now here to see Aurelia, but his presence had avoided all disagreeable conversation! Or perhaps, she ruefully decided, postponed it. She led the way up to the bedroom. Aurelia, who was lying in the huge bed dozing, opened her eyes when Petty entered. Petty was glad to see she had lost her grey colour. Madame Fournier was seated quietly in a corner. She was shelling a vast pot of peas, which she deposited on the floor as she saw the doctor.

"Louis! Tiens, we have here the English girl who is hurt…"

The French surgeon hugged her and kissed her on both cheeks; they were clearly on excellent terms. In spite of his propensity to talk continually, he appeared most capable, reassuring Petty that Aurelia had suffered no long-term damage but that she must rest. He then issued instructions as to the dressing of the gash and departed, telling them that he would return if they were in the slightest worried. Madame, having chased Petty out of the room, turned her attention back to her charge. Petty would have far preferred not to have gone. She would have liked to remain with Aurelia, but recognising the superiority of Madame's nursing and the indubitable fact that she would be in the way, she was forced, most reluctantly, to descend to the parlour. Bertram looked up as she came in.

"Well, how is she?"

"He says it is essential that she rests," Petty replied.

"For how long? I do not want to waste time, I want to get away from here… and you as fast as possible," he replied nastily. Petty felt her temper rising, but she pushed down the hot retort that sprang to her lips, and merely answered as pleasantly as she could.

"Perhaps you had better ask the doctor. Although I do not imagine that he will know the answer to that problem today."

Then she picked up the only book which the inn possessed, and sat in the window enclosure, until the pink-cheeked maid came to lay the covers for dinner. In fact she read not a word, which was a good thing as the book was on 'propagation of apples'! Her mind was racing; she had to find a way to escape. She wondered how far they were from a village. Tomorrow, she determined, she would make it her business to explore the locality. Unless she could hire a conveyance and hide it at the inn, she could see no easy way to get away from Bertram. If they could not abscond, then she would have to defend their virtue in another way. She thought about the pistol secreted in the pocket of her cloak, and then carefully hidden under her bed. Shooting Bertram was not a particularly attractive prospect; not only was she not naturally bloodthirsty, but, although she was a good shot, and perfectly capable of merely incapacitating him without rendering him any long-term damage, she did not like to use a gun she had never tried before. If, however, they could not break free there may not be another alternative; so rather apprehensively she decided that after dinner she would retire to her room to inspect the gun. She was sure that anything that belonged to Sir Hugo would be proved to be inferior, and, on examining the pistol, her worst expectations were realised. She was, however, not entirely without optimism. His Grace had instructed his children well. Not only were they fine shots but they had also been taught to load and clean a gun. Having ascertained that the weapon worked, she hid it again as carefully as she could, and lay down on the narrow, hard bed.

It was sweltering under the eves and sleep would not come. The auberge was very small, and Petty thought that she had probably been given Pierre's sister's room. This bed was far more uncomfortable than the one in Portman Square, and it made her room at Wakeham seem positively luxurious. She was tired of all this. She wished she was with Aurelia, but Madame made it clear that that was to be her privilege.

Petty tossed and turned, eventually falling into a fitful sleep. As soon as it was light, she decided she could stand the heat no longer, so she got up and went out.

The sun was coming up over the hill as she came out into the farmyard. The dawn light sharpened the images of the shadowless house and barns and the trees heavy with fruit. She climbed up a small bank behind the house and perched herself on it, relishing the feel of the damp, dewy grass. She took deep breaths of fresh, cool air and looked about her. From her position, there was only one building visible. It was a small cottage about a mile away. In the distance she could hear faint sounds of cows on the way to be milked. A small goat came trotting up to her; he was quite tame and nuzzled her as she sat.

It was very peaceful. She thought of Edward and wished and wished that he were here with her. She knew he would appreciate the still beauty of the morning. Eventually, there were more sounds. Very faintly she could hear a church bell ringing and the barking of a dog. Then the herd of cows, lumbering across the fields, their udders swollen with milk, came into her view, a small boy and the dog leisurely driving them. They turned into the lower fields. The little goat lay down beside her. He put his head on her lap; she laughed at him.

Suddenly she heard her name being called. Bertram was standing in front of the inn; he was seeking her. She sighed; the idyll was over. Regretfully, she pulled herself to her feet, brushed the strands of grass from her dress, and prepared to face the enemy. Bertram was sitting at the breakfast table when she entered the parlour. He put down his teacup and stood up on seeing her. Petty, who had decided that she must at all costs be agreeable, greeted him.

"Oh, please, do sit down, Mr Melville. I have been walking around, it is a glorious day. I watched the cows coming to be milked." She sat at the table and helped herself to a piece of freshly baked bread.

His reply was friendlier than she had heard before. "Good morning, Mrs Blakeston, I trust you slept well?"

"Not very, it was so hot."

"May I pour you some tea? How is Miss Milton today?"

"Thank you. I do not know, I did not care to wake her but I will visit her as soon as I have breakfasted."

"I hope that she will prove ready to leave soon."

Petty's eyes flew to his face, but he was pouring a cup of tea which he passed to her without further comment.

Aurelia was sitting up in bed partaking of a substantial plate of ham and bread and butter. She was clearly much recovered. "Good morning," she said brightly. "I am perfectly fine."

"Oh dear!" said Petty.

Aurelia grinned. "Well, I had imagined that you might have been pleased but I see I am wrong, you would prefer that I was lying on my death bed," she teased.

Petty giggled. "No! You know I did not mean that but as soon as you are well, Bertram will want to move you on, leaving me here, I expect, and we must not let that happen."

"Indeed, we must not! I think you had better tell him I am still not at all well."

"Yes, because he has not a word of French, so he will not be able to ask Madame or Pierre how you really are." They grinned at each other conspiratorially.

Then Petty sighed. "This will do for today but we will have to find a better solution, as he will not believe that you are ill for ever. I will have to see what I can discover today."

"Mon dieu! The little thin one." Madame entered; she clasped Petty's hand. "She is better? N'est-ce pas?" she beamed.

Petty grinned. Madame might help them but she had no real confidence in the good lady's ability to dupe one of Bertram's deviousness and she was most reluctant to take any chances. No, the answer to their predicament lay in her hands. Madame smiled broadly at her, then in no uncertain terms shooed her away. As Petty left, she was asking Aurelia what she would like to eat as she was sending Jean into Calais to buy her delicacies. Petty made her way down to Bertram to report that Aurelia remained very ill.

The skipper of the packet carrying His Lordship was extremely proud. The journey had been made in record time. Admittedly the sea was calm with a fair wind, but still Captain Wills was delighted with his record. His old friend and rival, Captain Darn, had never managed a time even close to the one which Tom Wills had established, even with the advantage of a smooth wind and little swell. The captain was therefore a trifle miffed when a gentleman claiming to be a lord arrived on the bridge and enquired, "When will we reach Calais?"

"Beg pardon, me lord, if that you be, but this is a very record crossing. No one done it in less time," Captain Wills replied indignantly. "It's clear that hif you was a lord... you would know what a splendid sevis you is a'gettin', and no complaints," he added severely.

Edward's ready sense of humour overcame his impatience. His eyes danced but he said with a straight face, "I stand corrected. I appreciate the speed of the journey but I merely wanted to know how much longer we would be."

"Not any much about it." The captain looked at him sagely. He took in the understated elegance of the cut of His Lordship's coat and the shine on his hessians; maybe he was a member of the aristocracy.

"Yous a'right impatient to be on the other side. Escaping the creditors, are you?"

Edward gave a crack of laughter and shook his head. "No..." he thought a moment, maybe the man could help, "... but I am searching for my sisters, they crossed on yesterday's packet... Were you the captain on that?"

"No, that was Captain Darn. He'd be on his way back, going to Dover now. Not as fast as us." He looked Edward up and down. "Have you lost your sisters?"

"Not exactly," Edward answered firmly. He wanted no more discussion. "Thank you, Captain." He turned and went down to Ted.

As soon as they docked, Edward considered that their first task must be to find somewhere that hired horses. He knew Calais well but he did not want to waste a minute.

 318

"I think it will be faster if you ride," he told Ted, adding, "Do you speak any French?"

The surprising Ted nodded. "I was in the army quartered in France… me and Ned was invalided out. Me Frenchie lingo ain't grand, bit I can make meself understood."

"Yes," Edward cut him short, "you take the hotels in the upper part of the town, and I will take the port. We'd better get started."

"Better 'ave a time and place to meet, me lord, nothing like searching each one over each place, hopeless."

"Indeed," agreed Edward, amused. "Let us meet at Dessein's in… say, two hours?"

Ted nodded, mounted his nag and, spurring the creature on, made for the main part of the town.

The quay was busy. There were sailors unloading cargo from several boats, including the packet from which they had descended. A rough burly individual in a dirty and tatty uniform appeared to be in charge. He was shouting vociferously at the disorderly crew. Edward went up to him.

"Excuse me, I am seeking three people who travelled on the packet from Dover yesterday."

The man regarded him with a sneer. "Of course, I would know where everybody who came off every boat went, wouldn't I?" he responded sarcastically.

Edward's eyes were hard. "If you let me finish, I would have asked you if there was anyone who might have known anything about these three persons. I would pay well for information." The man ran a grubby hand over his face; he peered at Edward avariciously. Edward took out a bag of coins and rattled them suggestively. He addressed the sailors. "You will find me very generous to anyone who can bring me word to Dessein's of two girls, one dark and very beautiful, the other small, thin with brown hair and very blue eyes. They were accompanied by a dark, swarthy gentleman, they journeyed yesterday. Have any of you seen them?"

The men shook their heads. They would have liked to help. English milords who stayed at Monsieur Quillac's hotel were usually forthcoming with ample remuneration! They were triste that they had not seen anyone answering the description Edward gave them. Finding they had nothing to offer him, Edward then made his way to the busiest of coaching inns. The ostler, who would also have been pleased to have something of use to impart to such a generous gentleman, had reluctantly to admit that he had not been party to hiring a vehicle to a group that contained a girl of Aurelia's description.

Edward tried various other persons who, for one reason or another, had business around the port, but no one had any intelligence for him. Two hours being nearly up, he made his way to Dessein's hoping that perhaps Ted had had better fortune.

Madame Quillac welcomed him warmly at the hotel named after her grandfather. He bespoke rooms for himself and Ted, who had returned a few minutes ahead of him. Ted had faithfully visited all the moderate hotels, and the only clue he had was that an Englishman had hired a coach and four this morning to convey himself to Paris. The innkeeper who divulged this had seen no ladies with him but Ted thought it could possibly have been Bertram.

Edward considered what they should do; he was tempted to try to follow the man who had taken the Paris road. After some thought, he decided that he would do this, and that Ted must go back to the taverns on the quay to drink with the sailors; one of them must surely know something.

Jean drove the gig into Calais slowly; he was glad to get away from the auberge. The occupancy of these English was proving hard work for one with no natural inclination for travail, and he was looking forward to an evening spent with his cronies. As he entered the town he had to pull over sharply to allow a coach travelling fast in the opposite direction to proceed. The coach passed within a whisker of his wheels. Jean turned and watched in admiration; the driver was most accomplished. He was a tall dark man who handled his rather indifferent team like a master. Jean shook his head with approval; he liked to see a man who could drive to an inch.

Lord Milton did not enjoy driving unresponsive cattle. As he swept from the town he nearly collided with a gig that was coming in, driven by an ancient Frenchman. He waved a thank you to the man who moved out of his path, while keeping his team up to their bits.

Having at last performed the many errands given to him by Madame Fournier, Jean made his way to his favourite tavern, the Chien Mechant. He pushed open the door, bumping into a tall wispy-haired man who was just leaving.

"Bonsoir." Jean nodded to the man, who replied politely with a definite English accent.

Ted had been in every tavern along the front and had drawn a blank everywhere. He was now feeling much the worse for an evening spent drinking with French sailors and he had decided that the Chien Mechant would be his last call. He would now return to the unaccustomed luxury of Dessein's to await Edward, whom he hoped had had a better chance. He had laid out a lot of Lord Milton's blunt to mine hosts, promising them more if they had news for him.

He left the bar and walked unsteadily back through the warm night air. The task of finding Aurelia and Petty was proving harder than he or His Lordship had anticipated. He reached the hotel and went to the private parlour hired by Edward. He sat by the open window and wondered where Petty was. In his short acquaintance with her he had grown surprisingly attached to her and he was much interested in her welfare. Aurelia he did not know, but he esteemed Lord Milton, and any sister of his was now Ted's concern. He was determined to await His Lordship, but the combined effects of travel and his evening activities made his eyes heavy. Inevitably, unable to keep them open anymore, the grey head drooped onto his chest.

It was thus, that several hours later Lord Milton found him. He, too, had had an unproductive night. He had eventually caught up with the Englishman, who turned out to be a magistrate from the West Country travelling to Paris to see his married daughter. He was somewhat astonished to see Edward, who apologised profusely and turned back to Calais. He was tired and angry and dispirited. He had every intention of tracking down Bertram Melville, if it took the rest of his life, and when he found him it was going to be very pleasurable to call him out and kill him. He missed Petty. The missing was like a physical pain. He shuddered. Seeing Ted made him smile slightly but his humour was deserting him. Ted jerked awake as he came in.

"Any news, my lord?"

Edward shook his head. He threw down his caped coat and collapsed into a chair. "How about you, any luck?"

"No, my lord, no one has seen them. I went into all them taverns. I left money, told them there would be more if anyone had any information."

"Good. I think if we are to start early tomorrow, we had better go to bed now." Wearily he stood up.

"Good night, Ted."

"Good night, my lord. Don't you worry, we'll find them."

Jean came into the taproom. "Good evening, Jean! Where have you been?" Baptiste the barman and his especial friend wrung his hand warmly.

"Baptiste, my good friend! It has been work, work! My sister, Madame Fournier, she is a hard taskmaster. I am glad I am not wed. To be nagged by a sister and a wife is no life for anyone! I tell you, my friend, I have carried trays! I have killed chickens! I have waited on tables! I tell you I am only here now because I had errands. It was, get this, go to the shops, bring me special food, all for these English girls." But Baptiste had turned to greet Yves and did not hear the last words.

He was used to Jean complaining; it went on so much that he hardly heard it these days. Jean sat down and downed his first jug of ale. He felt better. He did not see why his brother-in-law, Leon, should not perform these duties. Just because the man was clerk to the priest, he thought he was too grand for such menial tasks. In truth, Leon, who was an admirable man, did not consider anything above him but he was a weak man who found physical tasks hard. The evening was well advanced when Baptiste came and sat with his friend.

"So, mon ami, you are busy? No?"

Jean nodded. "Indeed, indeed! You know my sister... these English girls... she has..."

Baptiste pricked up his ears. "English?" he said indifferently. It would not do to let Jean know about the English milord who had money to spend for information. Oh no! These perks must be Baptiste's privilege.

"Yes, she has... these English... pah... their gig went into a ditch... one of the girls was injured... now I have to fetch and carry like a dog! "

"Where were they going, these English?"

"I don't know... there is a man with them... he is a cur... not a sou have I received for all my work..."

Ah! So he was right. This must be the party that the lord searched for. Baptiste saw gold before his eyes. He changed the subject. By the time Jean left to drive home, it was too late for Baptiste to report his information to milord at Dessein's; the morning would have to do.

The next day, as soon as he could escape from his duties, he made his way up to the hotel.

Madame Quillac regarded him sourly. "Yes?" Her question was not friendly.

"I wish to speak to the English milord. I have news for him…"

"What could you possibly know that would be of interest to him? Be off with you, Baptiste… you are half befuddled and it is only eleven o'clock…"

"No, must see him… come, Madame Quillac," he wheedled.

"No! No!" She shooed him out of the spotless foyer of her hotel.

Baptiste was not quite sure what to do next. He thought he might wait to see if the milord left the hotel. He sat down at the bar opposite, where he could watch the doors to the hotel, and prepared to wait. After an hour Baptiste decided that he could wait no longer so he left and returned to work.

Lord Milton scoured the town. Suddenly, his heart leapt; a thin girl with mousy hair was walking into the patisserie. She resembled Petty exactly. Could it be her? He raced across the road. As he reached the shop and peered in the window, he saw how mistaken he had been. It was not Petty at all; she was not like her in any particular.

He had arranged to meet Ted at noon. As he reached Dessein's, unbeknownst, he passed Baptiste shuffling along. Neither of them had seen the other before; they passed each other without comment.

Edward went on into the hotel. Madame bustled out. His face was hard, his eyes bleak. "Did you have a successful morning, my lord?" In reply, Edward shook his head. "Never mind I expect you will find what you want very soon."

Edward, his face austere, turned away from her. "I very much hope so," he replied desolately. He started to move across the foyer to the parlour.

Madame Quillac, whose nature it was to be inquisitive, stopped him by enquiring, "Perhaps I can help you, monsieur?"

"It is not likely."

"For what do you search?"

"For my sisters. They were… taken… brought here by a man who wishes to marry one of them… I do not wish it."

"And does mademoiselle like to marry this man…?"

"Oh no! Not at all."

"Tiens! Mais non… it is essential that you find them… no?"

"Essential… we have tried everywhere but to no avail. Someone must know something… Surely, Madame, in this age, people cannot just disappear."

Madame Quillac went rather red. "Tiens! I think that I have been wrong… One man… Baptiste, very greedy… very stupid, he came this morning… he says he had information for you… but I sent him away. You do not want to mix with the like of Baptiste."

"Why did you not tell me this sooner? Who are you to judge what I need to know?" Edward said angrily. "It may be just what we need. Where is this Baptiste to be found?"

"Many apologies, my lord. Baptiste, he works at the Chien Merchant. My son will show you." Within minutes the boy arrived; he led Edward through the winding streets to the tavern.

CHAPTER TWENTY-FÍVE

Petty left Madame bathing Aurelia and went back downstairs. The day stretched ahead. In truth, she was totally unused to inactivity and she found herself considerably irked by having no tasks to perform. It was also unbearably hot and she possessed only one dress, which was certainly unsuitable for this weather. In her precipitate rush from Portman Square, she had not even brought her book with her, and this was proving an increasing loss to Petty, who was such a bookworm that she felt insecure when not accompanied by a tome! She had hunted and hunted all over the auberge for something to read. Her French was excellent and anything would have done, but there was nothing except the book on apples and even Petty was not that deprived.

Next she wandered outside, and found herself drifting around the garden aimlessly. She plonked herself down in the shade, but even under the trees, there was no respite for her from the heat. She searched the horizon for signs of habitation, but the only house she could see was the small white cottage on the far hill. She sighed. Eventually, unable to bear it any longer, she went to search for Madame; she found her in the kitchen.

"Madame, have you any dress I could borrow? I am so hot in this and it is so dirty."

Madame Fournier threw up her hands. "Tiens, mademoiselle!

I have only dresses for Marie and a lady such as you could not wear a dress for a maid."

"I do not mind. As long as it is not so heavy and close."

Madame ran her eyes over Petty's red face and the dark grogram dress. "Mais oui... I see..." she assented.

A half an hour later, Petty, feeling much more the thing, made her way out of the inn to explore. She was attired in a pink checked gingham open gown with puffed sleeves and an unfashionably low waist. A small white fischu around the neck crossed the bodice and tucked into the waistband. On her head, to protect her from the effects of the sun, she wore a white mop cap. She half giggled to herself. What a thing it was to be a French peasant! She wished her mama could see her. That the duchess would be aghast, she never doubted, but it would be truly wonderful just to see her face.

She had enquired of Madame of the nearest village, and been told that it was Pihen-les-Guines, but that good lady had pointed out firmly it was far too far for a lady such as she to walk to. "But I am not a lady, I am a milkmaid!" Petty had replied, twirling around in her new outfit. Actually, the dress suited her better than many of the heavy dark dresses chosen by her mama. Dismissing Madame's misgivings about the distance to Pihen with a wave of her hand, she was used to long walks, she started out, only too aware that with the rapid recovery that Aurelia was making it was only a matter of time before Bertram insisted that they proceed. It was necessary that she find out as much as possible about their surroundings.

Following Madame's instructions, she turned left through the orchard, making her way across the fields. The golden corn smelt wonderful. It reminded her of Wakeham. Thinking of her home had a lowering effect on her spirits; would she ever see it again? She did not believe that Lord Milton would make no push to discover where they were, but how was he to find them? In any case, once he tracked them down, it would probably be too late. It was, after all, only two days since Aurelia had been kidnapped, although it seemed to her an age. He may still be in... wherever it was he was going to arrange her divorce. In spite of the sun, Petty shivered. Oh, Edward! Edward! If only she had... but it was no good regretting the past. She walked on quickly, passing no one on the road except for a small boy carrying a large sack and leading a donkey. She found herself in Pihen in less than an hour.

It was most disappointing. Hardly a village, just a tiny gaggle of cottages encircling a small church. No shops and clearly nowhere where she could hire a gig or truck. There was no one in the tiny square and all the houses were shuttered for a midday siesta; no help for her here. She wondered how far away was the next village. She sighed; there was no one to ask and she could not embark on a search for another habitation whilst having no idea which way to go. She sighed again, and prepared to retrace her steps. She was unsure of what she had expected, but perhaps a village such as were found around Wakeham, but this, she realised ruefully, was rural France, even less a part of the nineteenth century than rural Gloucestershire.

She trudged back along the dusty roads, more slowly. The sun beat down on her head and was really most uncomfortable. She was glad when she saw the auberge ahead of her. By now it was late afternoon, time was running out and she was no nearer a solution to their problems. She washed her face in cool water and realised she was starving, having eaten nothing since her slice of bread at breakfast, many hours earlier. She proceeded to the parlour. As she approached the loaded sideboard she was relieved to see that both the chicken and ham had been attacked. Bertram had obviously helped himself to food and was now nowhere to be seen. Having partaken of an excellent meal she felt much better. She went quickly to see how Aurelia did, and apart from a blackening eye, found her so much recovered that she was out of bed sitting in a chair and chafing at her enforced confinement. She greeted Petty warmly.

"Where have you been? I am getting blue-devilled being immured in this room. May I not come downstairs? Please?"

Petty shook her head. "I fear not. I think if Bertram saw you so well he…" She got no further for Aurelia gave a peal of laughter.

"What are you wearing? You look as if you have come to make the bed and clean the grate."

Petty looked down at the gingham dress and giggled. "I borrowed it; it is rather too large." She demonstrated by pulling out the waist a good six inches. "It may not be elegant but it has the benefit of being cool." She grinned at Aurelia. "I took off my shoes and stockings and wandered barefoot through the grass." She closed her eyes. "It was delightful." She twirled around, the skirt of the dress standing out from her slim frame. "How horrified my mama would be if she could see me," she chuckled. Then struck by a sober thought, she replied, "I have been to the nearest village, Pihen… I hoped that we might find a vehicle to escape in but it is tiny, there is nothing there at all."

"Can we not run away at night?" demanded Aurelia. "I am not at all scared, it would be the most thrilling adventure."

"I think not," responded the practical Petty. "Where would we run to? It is miles to anywhere… and how do you propose to find your way in the dark?"

"By moonlight! It is so light tonight we could go anywhere."

This was actually true. Although the night was black and still, the sky was clear and the full moon shed its bright light over everything.

"Yes, but remember if we can see, then so can Bertram," was Petty's sensible answer.

"Can we ask Madame to guard us?"

"I had thought of that but suppose she lets it slip to Bertram somehow. I know he has no French but he is not at all stupid and he watches like a hawk. I am not confident that she may not, inadvertently, betray us, and then he may try to drug and abduct you again." She looked worried.

"He is not interested in me… he wants to compromise you so that… Oh… there must be a way?"

The evening proving no cooler, they pondered their problem, sitting by the open window. Petty, her head cupped in her hands, gazed at the night sky, spattered with its hundreds of stars. The tiny sparkles of light seemed so close it was almost as if she could stretch out a hand and touch them. The sweet smell from the flowers that twined their course around the house wafted into the window. It would have been perfect if only Edward had been there and Bertram had not.

She went over and over their dilemma, but by the time she left Aurelia for the night, she was no nearer a conclusion. Of Bertram there was no sign; Petty was not sure whether to be relieved or worried. It was clear to them both that by tomorrow they could stall him no longer; they were going to have to confront him.

Petty spent another sleepless night. Her room was oppressive. The next morning she again rose with the dawn, dressing in the pink gingham. She crept downstairs, letting herself out into the fresh morning air. Before leaving her room she pulled her cloak from under the bed and took out the pistol. She loaded it carefully. The other advantage that the maid's dress possessed, apart from its lightness, was the large side pockets stitched under the waist. Petty tried to decide whether to place the pistol in the pocket now or later, eventually concluding that after breakfast would be early enough.

She crossed the farmyard and climbed up to her favourite place on the little hill. She sat there for about an hour watching the sky change as the sun came up. She was resigned to the certainty that she was going to have to shoot Bertram, although her plan was merely to disable him slightly, a scratch to make it impossible to carry them off. Her knowledge of the law being imprecise, she had no idea of the penalties that she might sustain for shooting him, even if the injury received was minor, and she imagined that they might be severe. She was gloomy indeed about her future. A life spent in jail seemed bleak.

Eventually, as she was stiff and hungry, she went back into the inn for breakfast.

Bertram was in the parlour.

"Good morning, you are up early!"

"It was so hot," said Petty non-committedly.

"I gather that Miss Milton is completely recovered, so we will be able to continue our journey."

Petty felt herself go cold. "Indeed, I have not seen her yet, so I cannot comment."

"Oh, it is true, I know that you would prefer her to continue to be ill." Petty coloured. "I am not entirely without brains, you know," he went on unpleasantly. "We will leave as soon as we have breakfasted. You will not come with us." Petty said nothing, her mind was working fast. She must delay their departure for as long as she could. "I shall go and hire a conveyance as soon as I can. Tell Aurelia to pack." And with that parting shot he left the room.

Good, thought Petty. It must take some time to find something suitable to travel in. She swallowed her tea and ran up to Aurelia, who was fully dressed.

"How did Bertram discover that you were not ill anymore?" Petty wondered.

"It was my fault," Aurelia confessed. "I went down the corridor and out for some fresh air. I saw him as I returned."

"Bother! Well, it cannot be helped, he would have found out today anyway. I just hope that it takes him a long time to find a conveyance."

In fact it was nearly two o'clock by the time Bertram returned. He was hot and flustered. He had had to walk miles to hire a coach and pair and they were certainly no goers. Petty and

Aurelia were outside under the apple trees when they saw the extremely ancient coach coming over the hill. They exchanged glances; Petty got up.

"Go back to your room, Aurelia," she commanded. Aurelia made to answer but something in Petty's serious face made her go without demur.

Petty went into the parlour. She pulled out the pistol and checked it thoroughly, then she returned it to her pocket. She took up her position in a chair on the right of the fireplace. After some thought she had decided that from that point, she could aim at Bertram in any place in the room. Her heart was beating furiously and her knees shook.

She heard him come in; he called to Madame but luckily she was in the kitchen. "Hello!" Petty called. "Mr Melville?"

He came into the room. Petty's mouth felt quite dry and although her lips would hardly move she smiled woodenly at Bertram and remarked docilely, "Mr Melville, please can I have a word with you?" He looked hot and cross but her pleasant tone lulled him into a sense of security. She obviously knew that he had won; there was nothing that she or Aurelia could do to his supremacy.

He went to the sideboard next to her and poured himself a long glass of lemonade. "Yes? You have two minutes while I drink this."

"Thank you," Petty replied submissively. She gestured to the chair that faced her on the other side of the fireplace. "Please, will you not sit down?"

Bertram was tired; he was only too glad to sit for a moment before starting on the next stage of his journey. He had decided to take Aurelia to the outskirts of Paris, where he would find a small inn. Once there he could write to Lord Milton for permission to marry her.

Petty waited until he was easily settled in the chair. Nervously she put her hand in her pocket. She felt the shank of the pistol, her hand closed comfortingly around the handle. Her stomach felt as if it had disappeared. She swallowed hard. She was ready.

"Mr Melville, please do not continue with this. You cannot really want to marry a reluctant bride."

His head shot up in surprise; whatever he had expected it was not this. "I do not care," he said, his mouth twisting into an ugly curl. "It is a matter of complete indifference to me. As soon as I marry and get my hand on her fortune, I care nothing for Miss Milton, except," he thought a moment, "that she is very beautiful…"

Petty felt her temper rising. He was the most unprincipled villain that she had ever encountered.

She would show him, for Aurelia and for her grandfather. "I ask you again. Please let us go…"

He gave an offensive laugh. "No! Under no circumstances." He stood up.

"Then I shall be forced to kill you," said Petty bravely. She whipped out the gun and pointed it at him. He stopped, looked at her and went slightly white. "Now come, Mrs Blakeston, I am persuaded you do not know how to use that thing, give it to me before you hurt yourself."

"You will be surprised how well I know how to use 'this thing'… my papa made sure that all his children know how to shoot."

"Unnatural man," rasped Bertram. "Now, give the gun to me."

"No, I mean to kill you!" Petty lied, enjoying the swift look of fear that contorted his face at her words.

"Give me the gun…" He started towards her. "You are bluffing girls do not know how to load pistols."

"That is where you are sadly mistaken," replied Petty softly. "One more step and I shoot."

He sniggered. "Bluffing!" He moved quickly towards her. She aimed and pulled the trigger. There was an enormous retort and Bertram was catapulted backwards onto the floor clutching his shoulder. Petty watched, satisfied; just as she had planned, enough to incapacitate the beast.

"Well shot," came a drawling voice from the doorway. Petty turned and saw Lord Milton standing there at the door smiling at her. Without hesitation she flew across the room, landing in his arms. He caught her to him, holding her tightly. Then, releasing her slightly, he held her away from him regarding her steadily, amusement in his eyes.

"Yes... was there something?"

Petty giggled. She raised her beautiful eyes to him; the expression in his made her body tremble. He reached behind her and removed the pistol from the hand clasped firmly around his neck and slipped it into the pocket of his greatcoat. He bent his lips to hers, his touch sending a quiver deep down inside her. Very gently, he ran his lips along hers reducing her to jelly, then he tightened his hold, his lips becoming more demanding.

"Mon dieu! What is this?" Madame Fournier, swiftly followed by Aurelia, Ted and Pierre, burst into the room. Edward released Petty regretfully.

"My wife!" he said to Madame. Petty met his eyes, hers brimming with relief and laughter.

"Edward! Edward!" Aurelia threw herself into her brother's arms. "Thank goodness you have come."

"My sister," Edward felt moved to explain to Madame. At that moment came a groan from the floor.

"Oh, Bertram." Petty's hand went to her mouth guiltily. "I had forgotten about him."

"You do not seem to have killed him, thank goodness," Edward remarked.

"Of course I have not killed him," Petty replied indignantly.

She crossed to inspect Bertram. "I only told him I meant to kill him to scare him. I am an excellent shot, although I am afraid the pistol shot a little to the left, so he has more damage than I anticipated. It is often the case when using a gun that one has not used before." Ted and Edward burst out laughing. "I had expected that anything owned by Sir Hugo would not shoot true."

Edward was by now doubled up with laughter. "I thought you had no accomplishments," he managed through gales, "but I see I married a most resourceful girl." He picked up her hand and kissed it, his eyes never leaving hers.

"Mon dieu." Madame was by now at Bertram's side. She pushed Edward aside. "Excuse me, Monsieur Blakeston."

Edward looked up in astonishment. Then Aurelia started to giggle too. "Oh, Edward..." she spluttered between gales of laughter, Madame obviously rather shocked by their mirth with an injured man lying on the floor.

"Tut... tut... Come, Pierre."

"Pardon, madame," said Edward suddenly serious. "He tried to fire on Madame here," he held Petty's hand in a firm clasp, "but she managed to turn the gun onto him. He is an out-and-out scoundrel, a blackguard of the first degree." As this was said in Edward's excellent French, Bertram did not understand what was being said; however, he understood that they were paying him some attention. He groaned again.

"The damage is superficial, nevertheless, we cannot leave him to bleed all over your floor. So perhaps, madame, you would be so good as to dress the wound. Is there a surgeon to remove the ball?" Madame, on whom his measured words had their effect, was galvanised into action. With much tutting of disapproval, she sent Pierre for water and bandages and Jean for the doctor. Once he was bound up, she and Pierre helped him to his bedchamber to await medical assistance.

"Oh, dearest Edward, I am so pleased you came. It is such a relief," pronounced Aurelia.

"It is a great relief to me to find you both comparatively unharmed," responded Edward, his eyes never leaving Petty's face, "although I am curious to discover how you got that black eye."

"Oh, Edward, it was awful. The coach went over and Aurelia was knocked quite out."

"And, may I say, dearest brother, that I am glad you have come to your senses about Petty, she really is the most admirable wife for you," teased his sister.

Edward picked up Petty's hand. He lifted it to his mouth. "I came to my senses about my beloved bride ages ago," he said, his eyes never leaving her face. "But I did not wish her to be a reluctant wife!"

Petty giggled, she touched his cheek. "And I for so long have realised the foolishness of running away from you…" she started.

"What, incidentally, are you wearing?' Edward suddenly demanded, his eyes alight with amusement. "It hardly seems appropriate for a member of the aristocracy…" He picked up a corner of the pink gingham. "If this is what you intend to wear in your role as my wife perhaps I better reconsider my position!" Petty and Aurelia choked.

"Madame lent it to me… I was so hot… I only had one dress… When Bertram drugged me and took me onto the boat all my luggage was left in Dover…"

"Serves you right for running off so independently to rescue my sister…" he teased. "Not that I am not glad that you were with her… a most excellent chaperone. Now, for the future, I intend to take a house in Paris; we shall depart as soon as possible. I shall send a notice to the Morning Post announcing our marriage and that we have gone abroad for our honeymoon. By the time we return, anyone who might have heard of Mrs Blakeston will have forgotten her. I shall send for Mrs Lumley and Cuthbert to come to take charge you, my dearest sister. You and Dora will enjoy the sights of Paris, I suspect."

Aurelia nodded enthusiastically. "Oh yes! I would like it above everything," she exclaimed.

At that moment Madame returned. "Monsieur the villain, he is comfortable." She turned to Edward. "You will stay here tonight, monsieur? I think mademoiselle," she pointed at Aurelia who was beginning to look rather pale, "should be back in bed."

Edward glanced quickly at his sister. "l agree. I will send Ted back to Calais." He beckoned to the old man. "You will return to Dessein's tonight in the curricle. Tomorrow you will bring the best sprung travelling chaise to convey my sister to the hotel. Tell Madame Quillac to prepare rooms." He threw a bag of coins to Ted and waved dismissal.

He turned to the landlady. "Now, Madame Fournier, can you put us all up tonight?" He smiled his most charming smile at this good lady, pulling out another bag and depositing a pile of Louis on the table which he indicated she take. "Thank you for all you have done for my sister and my wife." Petty blushed slightly; her eyes met his, which twinkled at her appreciatively.

Madame, not averse to that smile, nodded vigorously. She was thoroughly enjoying herself. "Mais oui! Oui! Monsieur Blakeston! Pas de problem." She grinned broadly, sliding the coins into her copious pocket and whisking Aurelia out of the room.

Edward smiled at Petty, a look which made her heart beat and her mind race with pleasure. "At last, my love, I get you alone." He clasped both her hands in his, gazing down upon her with a look that made her delirious with happiness.

"Will you marry me?" he asked.

Petty giggled. "But we are married…"

"l know but when I first asked you I did not care, and then when I knew I loved you and you seemed so set on staying with Verity, I had to assume that you did not want…"

"I stayed with Verity because I felt it my duty to protect her from those awful Lockes," Petty interrupted.

"They were dreadful, weren't they? Although I suspect that if I had not been quite so worried and angry I might have found them quite diverting."

"Oh, did you see them?"

"Yes. I dragged poor Verity out of her bed and around to the Lockes' in the middle of the night because you, my love, in your supreme confidence, had not told anyone where you were going."

"Confidence! Stupidity, rather! I came to regret my over-assurance on that boat, I can tell you. I thought you would never find us."

"Not much faith in me," murmured His Lordship.

Petty kissed his cheek. "Speaking of Verity, it would be a kindness if she came to Paris, too, if she could be sensible. She is not all bad, just terribly spoilt and unloved."

"Yes, you are kind..." he agreed. "Now I see why you would not leave her... I thought you did not want to be with me... I had to let you go, you see." His voice was suddenly serious. "I loved you too much by then to force you to be with me."

"Is that why you wanted to divorce me? I was so miserable."

"Oh, my darling, I never wanted to make you unhappy." He pulled her back into his arms and kissed her resolutely.

Before retiring for the night, Lord Milton paid a visit to Melville, as unpleasant an interview as that man would ever have to endure. Bertram was lying propped up against the pillows. He was pale but not badly hurt; he regarded Lord Milton sullenly.

Edward's eyes were as hard as agates. He wasted no time on civilities.

"I have a few words to say to you, Melville. I will not comment on your despicable behaviour to my sister and to Miss Croisthwaite. Sufficient to say that if I ever find you on English soil again, you will find yourself in jail for the rest of your life. May I suggest that you travel abroad, somewhere a long way off, and never return."

"That is all very well but how I am to get there, I have not a guinea," Melville replied sourly.

"I had anticipated that. I will leave a ticket to India for you to collect at the office in Calais. No, please, do not thank me for my generosity," he remarked sardonically. "The outlay is worth it never to see your face again!"

While Edward dealt with Melville, Petty went to bid Aurelia goodnight. She was tucked into the bed, and bouncing with anticipation.

"Oh, dearest Petty, is it not exciting! Everything is to be wonderful! We shall go to Paris! I am sure that I will like it above everything." She wriggled down in her bed like an naughty child. "And you and Edward... Oh, how I shall enjoy having you as a sister."

Petty kissed her. "It has worked out so well! I cannot quite believe it. Goodnight, Aurelia."

Petty made her way to her room under the eves. She climbed into the borrowed nightdress and lay on the narrow bed and thought of Edward. She could feel the strength of his arms around her. She missed him. Suddenly she sat up in bed, smiled and slipped out. The inn was very quiet. She made her way down the corridor to Madame Fournier's room which she had vacated for her generous guest.

Without knocking she went in, closing the door quietly behind her. He was seated, wearing a shirt and his breeches, at the table writing a letter. He looked up as he heard the door close. Surprise and delight leapt in his eyes as he saw her. He started to stand up but she ran across to him and sat at his feet, her head on his knee.

"I missed you," she said boldly, peeping at him from under her dark lashes.

He stroked her curls gently. "Are you sure?" She raised her eyes to his and nodded tremulously.

He stood up, pulling her gently to her feet. She slid into his open arms.

 Matador

For exclusive discounts on Matador titles,
sign up to our occasional newsletter at
troubador.co.uk/bookshop